PRINCE *Of the* TOWER

AIMEE CLINTON

First edition

ISBN: 978-1-7391432-3-7

Author's Note

For my readers who live beyond the shores of my little kingdom, please be aware that this, and all my other books, are written in British English. Therefore, you will find an abundance of U, L and S in the most unexpected of places.

While the advice writing world is to please the masses by adopting American English, I just *can't*. I was the kid who studied for her spelling tests like her life depended on it, so even if I tried, the Brit in me would still slip through the net, and then nobody would be happy. This is the hill I've chosen, so please, just let me die on it.

Content Warning

This book contains graphic injury detail (including but not limited to serious burns), mention of suicide, infertility (historical) and child loss (historical).

Pronunciation Guide

- Idris - Id (like lid) -ris
- Anwir - An-waa
- Maelgwyn - Mihl-gwihn
- Taryn - Tair-in
- Celyn - Kehl-in
- Tir o Gwanwyn - Ti-r oh Gwae nwin (The Spring Court)
- Tir o Haf - Ti-r oh Hav (The Summer Court)
- Tir o Hydref - Ti-r oh Hu-drev (The Autumn Court)
- Tir o Gaeaf - Ti-r oh Guy-av (The Winter Court)
- Ymyl Cefnfor - Um-il Kevn-vor (The Witch Kingdom)
- Rhodd Anfarwol - hR-or-th An-var-wol

For Rachel, who never stopped believing in Fairy Land,
and Lorna, who helped me close the rifts

1

Go Camping, They Said...

If there was one thing I hated on this stupid planet, it was spiders. Actually, as of last night, I hated two things; spiders and camping. As luck would have it, those two seemed to go hand in hand.

Squinting, I peered into the shadowy depths of the cave, nerves jangling in anticipation of a many-legged, hairy monstrosity crawling out of the depths of hell. Nothing stirred, but that was no guarantee. Where spiders were concerned, it was always wise to play it safe.

As for camping, it had seemed a good idea at the time; a fun way to spend a weekend with friends, relaxing and drinking away the stresses of the last few weeks of university. And, best of all, cheap. I'd spent the last five years counting pennies as I slogged my way through veterinary school, but now, it was finally over. Graduation loomed, and then I'd be able to get a real job, earn real money, and take a *real* holiday. Until then, roughing it in a field was the best I could do, and with every passing hour, I regretted that decision more and more.

After a horrendous night of flapping canvas and freezing damp, followed by a brutally early start and several hours of hiking, my darkest fears were realised. The so-called Fairy Glen, the apparent highlight of our trip, was nothing more than a stagnant pond and a few dark, smelly caves. Judging by the stench of piss radiating from one damp side cavern, the glen was also home to a local tramp.

I toyed with my necklace, rubbing the pad of my thumb over the sharp point of the golden initial. A sideways A for Aliza. A character from my favourite show had worn one just like it, and for the first time in my life, I'd been glad of the unique spelling of my name when Mum and Dad had bought me the very same necklace for my twenty-first birthday. I wore it every day. Not only was it pretty and unusual, but it gave me something to fiddle with when I was nervous, like now.

"I bet you wish you were still in the tent, moisturising all that leg," my best friend Abby drawled from where she perched on a large rock, glancing at my tanned legs which were barely covered by my scandalously skimpy denim shorts.

She knew me well enough to know I'd actually rather drain a dog's anal glands without gloves than go into that cave. I knew *her* well enough to know she felt the same, even if she had chosen a different discipline and would never suffer the stench of a dog's bottom. She would suffer the stench of the cave though. If I had to go in, I wouldn't go alone.

Missing the point entirely, Isobel said, "She had to make sure she looked gorgeous for the fairy prince. The legend says that he'll marry the woman who wakes him."

My smile became fixed. If Abby was my favourite of our group of friends, Isobel was the one I barely tolerated. She was okay most of the time; a bit over-enthusiastic, a bit weird, maybe, but okay. Even if she did believe in things the rest of the population gave up around the age of seven. This weekend, she was a firm believer in fairies, which was why I'd been roped into going on this hike, to visit some magical glen.

She'd spent the weekend talking non-stop about some fairy prince trapped under a sleeping curse, and *that* was why I could only bare my teeth at her.

"Since when have I ever done anything to impress a man, prince or not?" Never. That was the answer, unless you counted my dad, and I knew he'd be far from pleased if he could see the tiny shorts I was wearing.

I had no hope of impressing anyone today. Not even imaginary men. Not even with my long legs displayed in all their glory.

Abby hauled herself to her feet, groaning. "I reckon you'll meet a nice man in your new practice, and then you'll change your tune."

"No chance," I said with confidence, tossing my ponytail over my shoulder in a whirl of colour. Most men didn't like my hair, bleached and dyed to an ombre rainbow of pastel shades. I happened to like my hair better than I liked the idea of a serious relationship. "I've got better things to think about, like my next holiday, which will absolutely *not* be in a field in the middle of nowhere."

"You mean you're not enjoying getting blisters and sweating your tits off?" Abby whispered slyly, so only I could hear.

My answering grimace told her all she needed to know, and she gave a wicked chuckle. She always laughed like a villain, which was ironic, because she was five foot nothing and the least scary person I knew. She looked as though a strong breeze might blow her away. I always felt like a hulking beast next to her, a full foot taller, and far from delicate, but when we'd met on our first day in high school, we'd clicked immediately, and been best friends ever since. If it hadn't been for her, I might have loaded myself up into my battered old car and driven home at two this morning, rather than spend another minute in the wild. I'd been seriously tempted, but Abby and I were sharing a blow-up bed, and she'd have been terrified on her own. Besides, her regular jokes and dry comments through the long hours of survival had made it worthwhile. Almost.

Isobel had already disappeared into the largest cave, staring around in awe as she faded into the dark. Abby and I hovered at the mouth of the cave. Her expression was a picture of disgust and apprehension; I guessed it was a mirror to my own face.

"Are we going in, or not?" she muttered in an uncharacteristically small voice. My friend was usually loud, the life of the party. Maybe she shared my concerns about the whole thing crashing down on our heads and burying us alive, second only to my fear of getting a spider in my hair.

"We don't have to if you don't want to," I said optimistically, as though I needed talking out of it.

What I could see of the cave floor was basically one giant puddle, and the air radiating from within was stale and stinking. At least this one didn't smell of piss, only mould and damp. I lifted my eyes to the cave roof. There wasn't much to see, dark as it was, but I was willing to bet my life there were spiders up there. The overall effect was unappealing. Had we really walked all this way to see this? I glanced at my watch. It was way past lunchtime, and the falafel wrap in my backpack was calling my name. My stomach grumbled. The sooner we went in, the sooner we'd be back in the sunshine, sprawled on the grass, stuffing our faces.

I heaved a sigh. "Come on, let's get it over with. If we don't go in, we'll never hear the end of it."

I had no doubt that Isobel would set up camp in the cave, refusing to come out until each of us had been suitably awed and expressed our burning desire to wed the fairy prince. The longer we waited outside, the longer we dragged out our own suffering.

Abby went first, the brave little soul. I followed her wine-red ponytail, grimacing as the soles of my boots sank into what I hoped, with every atom of my being, was only water. Before the summer was out, I'd be dealing with all manner of bodily fluids, but that didn't mean I wanted to wade through human piss while I was on my holidays.

Our sloshing footsteps echoed around the cave walls, but other than that, neither of us made a sound as we followed the narrowing walls deeper into the cave. My eyes remained fixed firmly on Abby. The last thing I wanted to see was a spider creeping down the wall or dangling from a thread. My skin prickled at the thought, warning me to back out into the sunshine before I was assaulted by a hideous beast, but Isobel wasn't far ahead.

I could do this.

No doubt alerted by our wet footsteps, she called, "Isn't it amazing? It makes you wonder, doesn't it? How many people have been here before us, looking for the doorway in the legend?"

"I don't know," Abby replied doubtfully. "I was thinking more along the lines of what must have inspired the story in the first place. I mean, this place doesn't exactly scream fairyland. I can't imagine fairies living here."

"They didn't live here," Isobel explained. "This is just the gateway. They live on the other side."

"Personally," I cut in, raising my voice enough to carry as we closed the remaining distance, "I can't imagine fairies living anywhere. You know, because they don't exist?"

A beam of light whipped in my direction, scorching my retinas.

"Oh! Sorry, Aliza," Isobel chuckled. "You scared me."

She lowered her torch, leaving me blind and blinking. The urge to snatch it from her hands, throw it to the ground and stamp on it repeatedly was almost overwhelming. God, I needed sleep. And food. I usually had enough patience to tolerate her, but today, I was struggling. I took a few deep breaths of air fragranced with stagnant water, and forced a smile onto my face, just in case anyone was watching.

"Found anything interesting?" I asked, already knowing the answer.

Isobel proved me wrong, though. Apparently, she'd seen all kinds of mystical crap. I should have known better. I let her words wash over me and retrieved my own torch from my bag. It was darker than expected inside this god-forsaken hole, and the last thing I needed was to slip and have to walk back to the site covered in cave slime. The campsite showers were simply not up to such tasks. I'd even avoided washing my hair, instead dousing my pride and joy in dry shampoo and tying the pastel lengths into a ponytail.

Isobel was still waffling on about nonsense when I flicked my torch to life, directing the beam carefully at the floor. I didn't want to see what lurked above my head. Ignorance was bliss. Sadly, there was no ignoring Isobel's outfit. My torch illuminated scuffed boots, similar to my own, but clearly well used, whereas mine were fresh out of the box, an extravagance I couldn't really afford. That wasn't the worst of it. She wore khaki green waterproof trousers, if that was the right word for such shapeless sacks of cloth, and a bobbled, zip-up fleece in the most hideous shade of orange I'd ever seen. She looked like someone who enjoyed this sort of outdoorsy stuff. A crazy person, which was exactly what she was. There was no other explanation for this horrendous trip, which had been her bright idea. Apparently, she came from a family of avid campers. I was no human doctor, but I didn't think there was a cure for that.

Unable to stand another moment of such a crime against fashion, I set off deeper into the cave, leaving Isobel and her orange fleece behind. I picked my way between the puddles, avoiding a particularly nasty patch of uneven rock. The dark stone stretched ahead of me, beyond my little sphere of light. With every step, I was convinced the back wall of the caves would emerge from the shadows, but it never did. How big was this place? And was it my imagination, or was the ground beginning to slant down? The last thing I wanted was to end up lost in some underground cavern. In fact, I didn't want any of this. I wanted to be back outside, with the breeze stirring my ponytail and the mild sunshine warming my skin. What better accessory for my graduation gown than a good tan? My belly flipped in apprehension and excitement at the thought. I was going to be a *vet*. Even after five years of study, I still couldn't quite believe it. I couldn't wait for Mum and Dad to see me graduate. As an only child, the responsibility of making them proud fell squarely on my shoulders. It had seemed like a burden at times, one I wasn't strong or clever enough to carry, but now, I was glad that I would have all the glory. It would be worth all the work and stress to see their faces on the day, if nothing else.

Maybe it was some strange desire to be the first to find the end of this god-forsaken warren, or maybe I wasn't as clever as I thought I was, but I didn't turn back. My wet footsteps echoed off the cave walls as I took step after step after step. The voices of my friends grew fainter, an indiscernible murmur. The air grew cold. I shivered in the chill, and as I did, my torch flickered.

Weird. It was borrowed from my dad, and he'd ensured it was in full working order before I'd left, dithering and fussing over every tent peg and battery pack.

The beam sputtered again. I gave it a whack against my palm, and light flared bright again. Maybe a battery was loose.

I continued my walk of madness. The walls pressed in closer, the cave growing narrower the deeper in I went. I'd have to give up soon. I had no desire to become wedged and have to be cut free by the fire brigade. Most of the firefighters I'd seen were getting on in years and balding. They never lived up to the fantasy, and frankly, it just wasn't worth the humiliation or horror.

My skin prickled again, and I paused to sweep my hand over my itching neck. I would *not* think about spiders.

My torch gave out, plunging me into pitch darkness.

"Shit," I hissed, slapping it again. Nothing happened, not even a flicker of light. Not even a spark.

I whacked it harder, my sense of panic building rapidly. How was I supposed to find my way out if I couldn't even see my own body? If I shouted for the others, would I cause the ceiling to collapse on top of me?

Whack, whack, whack. My palm began to sting. My heart began to race. What was I thinking? Why had I ventured so far in, alone? I didn't even want to be here. I had to get out. My eyes stretched wide in an attempt to drink in any scrap of light, but the darkness was complete, pressing against my eyeballs. My breath grew louder, my chest rising and falling in a rapid dance.

My first blind step was faltering, unsteady. Spiders be damned. They were the least of my concerns. I stretched my hand out, reaching for the walls I couldn't see. My fingers found nothing. That was a good thing, or so I told myself. The passage was narrow and I'd turned around, so as long as I didn't hit a wall, I had to be going in the right direction.

My lungs sucked in shallow, noisy breaths. My muscles tensed up, telling me to run. I fought against all of it, determined to keep my head. If I gave in to fear, I'd break my ankle, and then I'd be stuck in here for hours. That couldn't happen. I couldn't be trapped here in the dark with unseen spiders inching closer.

I concentrated on my feet, on placing one in front of the other, carefully navigating the hidden, uneven rock. A puddle seeped into my boot, soaking my sock, but I didn't care. I'd walk home barefoot if that was what it took. The sound of rushing water echoed on the cave walls, and it occurred to me that I couldn't hear anything but that and my own breathing. No voices, muffled or otherwise. Not even Isobel's droning. I fell still, my already straining eyes beginning to sting. A warm wet tear spilled down my cheek.

"Abby?" I called, as loudly as I dared. My voice shook and squeaked. "Isobel?"

There was no answer. My knees began to quake.

"Hello?" A hysterical note worked itself into my voice. "Abby? Where are you?"

Nothing. Only silence, and my rasping breath, growing more desperate with every passing second.

Fuck it all.

I stumbled into a run, my boots slipping on wet stone. Rock thudded against my shoulder, sending me careening off course. My feet fought to steady me, scrambling and sliding, but all at once, they whipped out from under me. A yelp burst from my throat as my bottom collided with cold, unforgiving rock, but I didn't stop there. The ground swept downwards, a slick, sharp slide into blind darkness. Stone skinned the backs of my bare legs and cracked against my elbows as my arms flailed, searching for purchase. My screams echoed back to me, as though a hundred idiots were falling into the same pit. Somehow, I flipped onto my belly, accelerating rapidly, feet first. My nails cracked and tore as I scrambled for a hold. Something sliced my chin, clacking my teeth together hard enough to vibrate through my skull.

The unyielding rock beneath me disappeared as suddenly as it had crashed into me, and with the roar of running water filling my ears, I was in freefall. There was nothing but rushing air on all sides. I flailed in the empty air, but even then, I knew it was hopeless. Any moment now I would splatter on the rocks.

I didn't want to die in these horrible caves. I didn't want to die at all.

With my ears full of my own deafening screams, I plunged into icy water. It engulfed me, rushing down my throat, swallowing me whole in its awful, crushing dark.

2

Fairies Can't Hurt You, They're Not Real

Gold.

Glowing. Dancing lights.

So pretty.

Why was it moving like that?

I blinked, and the golden, glimmering light turned into sun-stained ripples of crystal-clear water, lapping against my pounding head.

I blinked again, and a wide, shallow pool swam into view, edged by lush, grassy banks and dense trees. The sun hung low in the cloudless sky, beaming through the leaves and branches of the trees, dappling the shaded ground. Judging by the rich quality of the light, it was golden hour, daylight's last act before easing into the finale of sunset.

Where was I? What had happened?

An involuntary groan rumbled in my throat as I struggled into a sitting position, sending cold water sloshing around me. It was impossible to say which part of my body hurt the most, but my head was a strong contender. I pressed my shivering hand to my skull but flinched away at the stinging the touch invoked. I blinked in dull surprise at my tattered hands. My palms were cut and sliced, with thin flaps of skin dangling from the wounds in places. As for my nails... my stomach churned threateningly at the sight of the cracks, the blood. I looked away hurriedly, but now I'd seen, the pain intensified tenfold. My whole body began to tremble.

Oh, right. I was cold.

My senses seemed to be coming back, at least, even if they were delayed. A bone-rattling shudder drove me to my feet with another splash. Something heavy dragged at my shoulders, almost unbalancing me, and water streamed freely from the drenched backpack. My aching legs trembled under my weight like I was a newborn lamb. Blood streaked down my shins and calves, wafting away in the gentle ebb of the river. Countless tiny cuts and grazes were smattered over my shins and thighs, but the majority of the blood came from my skinned knee, which throbbed horribly the moment I noticed it. What on earth had happened to me?

Limping and shivering, I waded to the bank and clambered onto the dense bed of grass. I only managed a few steps before my legs gave an almighty wobble, and I sank back down onto my bottom amongst the cool, green blades, panting at my pathetic efforts.

Where am I?

With a slightly clearer head, I took in my surroundings again. At my back, a serene woodland was filled with the musical chirps of unseen birds. Large mushrooms sprouted on the tree trunks, and colourful wildflowers perfumed the air with their sweet fragrance. Before me, my shallow pool stretched into a wide river. The water rushed past at a pace that had me shivering again. I was lucky to have made it into the pool, otherwise I would undoubtedly have drowned. On the far side of the river, more trees loomed, and beyond them, snowcapped mountains rose stark against a clear sky. Everything was too bright, too colourful. I gingerly lifted a hand to the back of my head, and sure enough, my stinging fingers probed at an impressive bump beneath my sodden hair.

No wonder I couldn't remember how I'd ended up here.

I eased the backpack from my shoulders, dumping it beside me in the thick bed of grass.

"Think, Aliza," I whispered to myself, cajoling my waterlogged brain into action.

I'd been camping, I remembered that much. Abby had been there. I remembered her red hair. But then what? There was a dark, blank space between there and here. Maybe my campsite was nearby? Maybe Abby was?

"Abby?" I called, my voice raw in my throat.

Tiny birds burst into the air from the nearby trees, their startled shrieks piercing the air, but otherwise, there was no response. What was I missing?

I screwed my eyes shut, blocking out the light that bore into my aching eyeballs. A torch. A beam of light. Stinging eyes.

The cave! We'd gone for a hike. We'd explored the caves. I'd been separated.

My relieved laugh was quickly strangled as I opened my eyes and swept them over my surroundings. Where was the cave? There was no sign of rocky protrusions this side of the river, and the trees on the far side obscured my view. Not that I fancied my chances of making it across the rushing torrent anyway. Screwing my face up, I tried to bully my brain into remembering the mention of such a huge river in the vicinity of our camp. I certainly hadn't glimpsed one during our morning hike, and I didn't remember passing this pretty little woodland either. My stomach dropped as the mountains snagged my gaze. I didn't remember those at all, and I was fairly certain I would have noticed such a hulking, great mountain range. Come to think of it, I didn't even think there were any mountains that big in England. How far had the river swept me?

Panic prickled over my skin. How was anyone going to find me? I checked my watch, only to find the second hand resolutely unmoving. Great. Wincing and hissing, I fumbled with my backpack, and after an infuriatingly long time, I managed to unzip it and tip the contents over the grass. There was my phone, thank God. I snatched it up, ignoring the fresh sting of my fingers, but the screen stayed dark. Despair clogged my throat, making it difficult to draw a breath. I had no clue where I was, no way to contact anyone and no idea what to do next.

If you get lost, stay where you are. Don't wander off. I'll come to you.

Mum's wise words sounded in my ear, as though she was right beside me. As a kid, I'd been terrified of getting lost in the shops. It had never happened, but would Mum's advice be the same now? This was no supermarket. Should I stay put, waiting for my rescue party to find me? I stared over my shoulder at the woods once more. They looked serene, pretty enough that I'd have snapped a picture if my phone had been working, but if I went into those trees, I'd probably never find my way out. And I'd be harder to find. Maybe they'd send a helicopter out, and if they did, I had every intention of being seen. Mum was right. I'd be better off staying on the riverbank.

My stomach gave a loud, overlong rumble and another sense awakened. Starvation. How many hours had passed since breakfast? The packed lunch I'd been looking forward to had seen better days. The cardboard packaging of my wrap was pulpy and misshapen. In fact, everything was drenched. I rifled through my possessions, hoping to find something useful, or edible. The bottle of water I'd saved for the walk back to camp was dented in places, but still in one piece, and though the wrapper of my cereal bar was faded and wet, it was still sealed. As I had no idea how long my rescuers would take to reach me, I allowed myself only a single sip of water, but I scarfed the cereal bar down in a few bites. If I was lucky, it'd help with the trembling of my limbs. If I wasn't lucky, it'd at least see me through until my water-logged wrap dried out. I'd never normally consider eating such a battered, soggy thing, but until I was found and wrapped in a thermal blanket, I wasn't going to pass it up. My chances of successfully foraging food that wouldn't kill me the moment it passed my lips were almost non-existent, and I needed to eat *something*.

When I'd finished my pathetic meal, I tried my phone again. Still nothing. Sighing, I turned my attention to the sky. I had no clue what time it was, but the sun was sinking lower and lower. Soon, it'd disappear behind the mountains. Did a night out in the open await me? Would anyone even look for me after dark, or would the search be called off until morning? I shivered again. My sodden clothes clung to my chilled skin. There wouldn't be time to dry them before nightfall, especially the denim shorts. Memories of how cold I'd been the previous night assaulted me. I'd been freezing even with pyjamas and a sleeping bag. How on earth was I supposed to survive the night in wet shorts and a hoodie? Tears sprang to my eyes. This couldn't be real, could it? I was just a normal girl, with a normal life. I couldn't be lost. I couldn't be in *danger*. Those were the sort of things that happened to girls on the news, not me. Hiking accidents happened to adrenaline junkies who tried climbing mountains during a storm, not girls who went for a walk in the country with their friends.

Sniffing, I wiped my tears on my forearms, carefully avoiding my grazes. Though they stung, they were superficial, and the river had cleaned them as thoroughly as anything could out in the wild. With any luck, I'd avoid infection, though I grimaced at the thought of what microscopic nasties lurked on the cave floor. Still, it was nothing a course of antibiotics wouldn't fix, and I had bigger things to worry about right now than an infection that was still days away.

Crying was pointless. Sitting around would do no good at all. I tugged my sodden boots and socks off, flexing my poor wrinkled toes, before easing to my feet, giving my legs time to adjust to my weight. My knee stung like a bitch, but I clenched my teeth and rode the wave of pain until it eased a little. I limped to the nearest tree. Its lowest branches were within reach if I stretched my arms above my head. Wincing at the aches of my body, I struggled out of my hoody and draped it over the branch, then proceeded to unbutton my shorts and peel them from my hips, before hanging them beside the top. I had enough sense to know that wearing them would rob me of whatever body heat I managed to produce, and I needed all the help I could get. With any luck, they'd be dry by morning. Assuming I didn't freeze to death overnight.

I was contemplating removing my shirt when something caught my eye in the shade cast by the trees. A flicker of colour. Light. I frowned, staring between the trunks. Nothing in particular stood out. Maybe I'd glimpsed a ray of fading sunlight catching the petal of a wildflower. I glanced at the sky. Dark indigo gave way to gorgeous streaks of candy floss pink and burning orange, blazing over the dark silhouette of the mountain range. My breath caught in my throat. I'd seen plenty of stunning sunsets, but this topped them all. I'd never seen colours like that before. If only my phone was working, though, photos never did the sky justice, but with a good filter...

What was I thinking? This wasn't the time to be worrying about aesthetic. I had real problems. Like keeping warm. I looked around, hoping to find some sticks. I'd never lit a fire before in my life, apart from the gas fire in the living room back home, and I wasn't even sure I knew how, but it was either that or freeze. I'd stick near the riverbank, and gather up whatever I could find. Nothing else could possibly go wrong. I gave a humourless bark of laughter, and from the shade of the woods, something laughed back.

My entire body froze, primed to run, as my ears strained. I had to have imagined the tiny, high-pitched chirp of amusement. I was alone. My mind was playing tricks on me, no doubt thanks to the enormous bump on the back of my head. Even so, my gaze roved between the trunks.

Colour caught my eye again, and I did a double take.

There, on a small shrub. A faint, winking blue light. Was it some sort of insect? I'd never come across one that glowed blue before, but then, I didn't pretend to be an expert on creepy crawlies. Intrigued, I edged closer. Another light popped into life; a yellowy-green glow nestled between the leaves. Faint chittering sounds drifted to my ears as I grew close, and heedless of my injured knee, I crouched low, peering amongst the branches.

A fairy stared back at me.

I laughed again, this time more of a howl than a bark. How absolutely typical. Of all the hallucinations I could have chosen, it had to be a fucking *fairy*. I was going to kill Isobel when I got out of this mess. But beneath the delirious irony of it all, a tiny part of me remembered to be concerned. I definitely shouldn't be hallucinating. That was bad. Maybe I wasn't in the woods at all. Maybe this whole scene was some beautiful coping mechanism dreamt up by my brain to shield me from the fact that I was actually lying broken and alone at the bottom of an underground ravine.

My laughter stopped abruptly.

The blue fairy cocked her head at me. The gesture reminded me so much of a dog that a smile found its way to my lips. I leaned closer. My imaginary friend was no bigger than a common caterpillar, but apart from the blue glow and the shimmering, iridescent wings, she looked like a perfectly formed, if tiny, human. And she was clearly as interested in me as I was in her. She strolled along the thin branch with all the grace of a catwalk model, and then, with a hum of sparkling wings, rose into the air, hovering at the end of my nose. Even though I knew she boded ill for my sanity, I couldn't help but smile. The fairy smiled back.

More lights winked into life, a swarm of rainbow orbs. They rose into the air, flitting and diving around my head. I didn't know where to look first. I held out my hand, and the blue fairy perched on a patch of intact skin on my outstretched finger. She weighed nothing at all, which made sense, as she didn't really exist. Would I remember this after I'd been rescued and treated? Part of me hoped so. This entire camping trip had been awful. Meeting fairies didn't exactly make the experience worthwhile, but it didn't make it worse either. Blue took flight again, joining her friends as they continued to whirl around me. I couldn't say how long I watched them, entranced, but I eventually noticed that their lights shone brighter, because night was falling in earnest.

No sooner had I noticed, than the buzzing of tiny wings grew frantic. A fairy shot at me, seizing a tiny handful of my ponytail, and tugged. She was immediately joined by several of her companions, all dragging ineffectively at my hair. It didn't hurt, but it was quite rude.

"Oi!" I flapped a hand at them. "Stop it!"

They ignored my protests, their little voices rising into shrill shrieks. Annoyed, I gave my head a shake, dislodging a few fairies from the ends of my hair, but my small victory seemed to rile them. More and more swooped down, enough that I began to feel a slight tugging sensation at the roots of my hair.

Enough was enough. I'd changed my mind. They *were* making my holiday worse. Lurching to my feet, I tossed my head and slapped the air. I made contact with a tiny body, which sailed through the air and burst into a shower of red sparks as it collided with a tree trunk. My heart lurched, but the fairy only fluttered angrily, and shot straight up into the canopy of leaves above, where her light was promptly extinguished. The others followed, their lights sputtering out, leaving me in semi-darkness, the attack over as quickly as it had begun.

Weird. The absolute weirdest thing to happen to anyone, ever. I didn't know I'd had it in me to dream up such madness. I touched my fingers to the bump at the back of my head again. Was it really that bad? With one last glance up into the dark branches, I wandered back to the riverbank.

Faint silver light painted every edge and plane before me. The thick grass rippled slightly, the moonlight moving with it, making it look like a gently shifting sea. I found my backpack and began to stow away my useless possessions. Everything was still wet, but I couldn't stop a bubble of hope from rising in my chest as I tested my phone.

Nothing.

With a resigned sigh, I slid it into a side pocket of my bag. Maybe it would dry out. Apart from desperately needing to make a call, I wanted my photos. I should have backed them up. I'd meant to do it, but it was one of those things that I was always going to do later. When I had time. Well, time had run out at last.

Shivering in my knickers and t-shirt, I wrapped my arms around myself in a pathetic attempt to chase away the chill. What I'd give for an annoying, rustling tent and a restrictive sleeping bag. When this was over, I would never, ever complain about my life, ever again. Nothing could be as bad as this.

I stared out over the river, watching the silver ribbon slide by. The search would definitely have been called off for the night. I was on my own, cold and hungry and sore *everywhere*, and there wasn't a thing I could do about it. Shoulders sagging, I poked a bare toe at the grass, hoping to unearth a stick. Finding firewood in the dark seemed a sure way to meet a spider.

Slowly, a sense of unease crept over me, making my goosebumps stand out further. The skin on the back of my neck prickled. Something or someone was watching me.

Hesitantly, afraid of what I might hallucinate next, I looked over my shoulder. The scene was as peaceful as ever, completely devoid of manic fairies. For a long moment, I stared into the dense shadow of the trees, but nothing stirred. My battered brain didn't invent any monstrous shapes from the silhouettes, as it had done when I was a little girl, alone in my dark bedroom. Everything was still and tranquil. Even the singing birds had fallen silent, settling down for the night.

Comforted that I wasn't alone, even if my only companions were sleeping birds, I turned back to the river. I'd have to find a place to rest for the night. Somewhere offering even the slightest hint of shelter. Maybe a little hollow between the tree roots, or—

Movement caught my eye.

A shadow flitted along the riverbank, furling and unravelling like ribbons of smoke. A shadow in the vague shape of a person. A person with glowing, white eyes.

3

Weirdos Grow On Trees, Apparently

Time stopped. It was as simple as that. The world had stopped turning, clocks had stopped ticking, and even my heart had stopped beating. I knew that wasn't possible, but I was quickly learning that, here in wherever the hell I was, the lines between possible and impossible were less blurred, more completely erased. I could do nothing but stare, open-mouthed and frozen, suspended in time, as a flitting, humanoid shadow drifted along the riverbank.

Another hallucination. That was all it was. Nothing to be overly concerned about at this stage. Perfectly unsurprising for a person who'd taken a crack to the skull. As long as I was found in the morning, treated for apparent injury, and given a strong dose of antibiotics, I had absolutely nothing at all to worry about. But... it was creepy. More sinister by far than the swarm of fairies. So creepy that the tiny hairs all over my body rose in silent protest, and my muscles went rigid, primed to run. I *wanted* to run. Every instinct in my body screamed at me to do so. But it was stupid. It wasn't real. Whatever that thing was, it simply didn't exist.

Despite its clear lack of justification for being anywhere at all, the shadow continued to waft closer, oblivious to my presence. For now. My body screamed at me to do something about the *for now* part before it was too late, but I only stood stock still, clutching my backpack, which dripped steadily onto the grass.

A hideous, unearthly howl rent the peaceful night, echoing between trees and mountain tops. I jumped, barely managing to stifle my scream. At the same moment, the shadow snapped its smoky, billowing head towards the trees, emitting a bone-chilling hiss as it did so.

Fuck this.

Real or not, I was done with this shit. Wolves were long extinct in the United Kingdom, but I wasn't about to take any more chances. Being eaten alive was not on my bucket list. Dragging my backpack haphazardly onto my shoulders, I hurtled to the fairy tree and began to climb.

Or, at least, I began to try.

The great outdoors wasn't really my thing, and I hadn't attempted to climb anything but the stairs since primary school. As it turned out, I wasn't very good at it. I scrambled clumsily against the trunk, rough bark skinning my already battered shins as I fought to reach the lowest branch. For once in my life, I was exceptionally glad of my height as, wedging the toe of my boot into a knot in the trunk, my outstretched fingers closed around a branch. If I'd been as petite and dainty as the friends I'd always envied, I wouldn't have stood a chance. Arms quivering, I braced my legs against the trunk and hauled myself up, slumping gracelessly over the broad tree limb. God, I was out of shape. I really did need to join a gym once this was all over. But I was up, even if I was panting like a winded pug. The ground looked a lot further away than I'd anticipated. Clinging to the trunk, I forced myself to climb a little higher, refusing to so much as consider the possibility of a spider living amongst the twigs and leaves. Faced with the prospect of becoming supper for a wolf and… whatever the hell that shadow was, I'd just have to pretend that spiders didn't exist. Maybe they didn't. This was my hallucination, after all.

Once I'd climbed high enough that the lower boughs hid me from view, I straddled the widest branch I could find, letting my legs dangle, and leaned back against the trunk. Bark bit into my bare thighs and almost naked arse, but my eyes drifted shut with exhaustion. This was the worst day of my life, ever. Worse even than the New Year's night out that had resulted in standing in the freezing rain for three hours, waiting for a taxi, without a coat. I shivered, tonight's damp clothes and ample bare skin making the memory all the more vivid.

"Enchantée, ma belle."

I really did scream then.

My eyes snapped open as my hand slapped to my mouth, muffling my cry.

The owner of the velvet smooth, amused voice looked right back from his vantage point in the nearest tree, where he balanced atop a branch with unnatural ease. Smooth, pale skin stretched tight over too-prominent cheekbones. His eyes looked over-large in his malnourished face.

His eyes.

Once again, I could do nothing but stare. It was too dark to guess at the shade of those pale orbs, but even so, they seemed to gleam. To burn through the night.

The man smiled, smooth and self-assured, revealing too many teeth, then he pressed a long, thin finger to his lips. My eyes snagged on the talon-like fingernail, painted in a layer of chipped, black polish.

Gross.

But yeah, I knew. Be quiet. That was what I'd been doing before he showed up and nearly made me fall off my perch.

He pointed down between the leaves, and, like a fool, I looked. The shadowy figure seeped silently around the trunk of my tree, a darker shade of night to its surroundings, its dark tendrils wrapping around the bark I'd so recently clung to. Was it looking for me? What might have happened if I'd been a little slower?

Nothing, I wanted to scream at myself. *Nothing would have happened, because it wasn't real.*

Even so, my stomach flipped at the thought.

After a few tense minutes, the shadow seemed to grow bored and drifted away, fading into the woods.

My attention snapped back to the man opposite. He was already watching me with his strange, bright eyes and faint smile. Of all the things to happen today, he was somehow the most unnerving. A proud, defiant part of me wanted to be unafraid, but I liked to think I wasn't a fool, not all the time, at least. I was lost, injured and vulnerable, not to mention half naked, and he was a man. Men could be the worst predators of all.

I managed to lift my chin as I asked, "And you are?"

His leather jacket creaked as he leaned forward slightly, his nostrils flaring delicately as he sniffed the air. Okay, that wasn't weird at all. Definitely not serial killerish. My mind ran through the contents of my backpack again. Unless I wanted to squirt suncream in his eyes, I had nothing that could be used as a weapon. If only I hadn't dropped my torch. It wasn't much, but clubbing him over the head with it would have improved my situation slightly.

My injured fingers throbbed, and I realised I gripped the branch as though my life depended on it.

"Never mind me, who are you, and how did you get here?" His intense gaze skewered me to the trunk. I pressed myself back, the contents of my bag digging into my spine.

The further back I leaned, the closer he seemed to get. Without seeing him move, he was suddenly further along the branch, closer to me. The tree limb didn't so much as sag under his weight. A tumble of dark, shoulder length waves fell over one eye, and he swept them back with a careless toss of his head. The fine chains around his neck whispered at the movement. There was absolutely no way I was giving him my name, never mind admitting to being lost.

"Nice boots," I said instead, my voice surprisingly steady.

He grinned, not taking his eyes off me to glance at the army boots he wore, laces hung loose at his ankles. "Merci. Tell me your name."

"I asked first."

He sighed, a sad sound, no hint of frustration. "My name is of no consequence. Yours, however..." His too pale tongue darted over his full mouth, snagging on a lip ring. "I have a feeling we shall all know your name soon enough. Won't you give me the honour of hearing it first?"

Fucking weirdo. "No."

"Jacques."

I blinked. "What?"

"My name. Jacques."

"Oh. And what do you want, Jacques?"

He grinned, hissing out the word, "Nothing." God, he had too many teeth. Like a shark. Goosebumps coated my arms again. "Only to help you."

Yeah, right.

He moved, slowly and with all the grace of a panther, taking a careful step along the branch, which, once again, didn't so much as shiver. "Are you lost, belle fille?"

Obviously.

I longed to scour the woodland for any hint of a late-night rescue party, come to save me before I ended up chopped into pieces and scattered all over the forest, but I couldn't look away from his eyes. They glittered like stars. So pretty, but terrifying. I gulped, and he stilled, dipping into a crouch, his claw-like hands dangling over his knees.

"I smell your fear, but I mean you no harm."

Whatever. Out of all the things I'd experienced so far, that statement was the most difficult to believe.

"You're wise to be wary," he went on in that low, amused voice. "I will give you some friendly advice. Stay in the tree until sunup. That thing we just saw is the least of your concerns."

Yep. I'd gathered as much.

"What was it?" A shiver of doubt slipped into my voice. It was a hallucination, wasn't it? It had to be.

"An agent of Maelgwyn. They are called shades. It will be gone come sunrise."

Right, of course. How silly of me. I didn't know or care what a Maelgwyn was, but this bright-eyed stranger thought I should stay in the tree, and I couldn't find a compelling counter argument, not after what I'd witnessed so far.

"What howled?" I asked, unsure his next answer would offer the slightest insight.

He shrugged, bored. "It has no name in your world, but the ground is unsafe by night. When the sun rises, climb down, and head south."

Was that where he kept his freezer full of body parts? "What's south?"

He waved an airy hand, encompassing the entire mess that was me. "Assistance."

I squared my shoulders as best I could, all things considered. "I don't need help."

A lie. A pathetic, transparent lie.

Jacques smiled, raising an eyebrow, and I was seized by the overwhelming urge to plant my heel squarely in his pretty little runway-chic face. His grin widened as though he'd read my thoughts. Creep.

His expression turned solemn as he studied me. Something flickered in his magnificent eyes. Longing? Hunger? Pity?

He shrugged out of his jacket and tossed it at me. I caught it on reflex, my mouth falling open in surprise.

"We have waited a long time for you, ma belle," he whisper-hissed. "Be careful."

I took a breath to respond, but with a shiver of movement, the branch was empty. A delicate thud sounded on the ground below, and I looked down in time to catch Jacques' eye as he straightened. Sliding his hand into the pockets of his pants, he nodded, and strolled away through the trees.

I stared at the darkness he'd melted into, reeling. Had that even happened, or was it another consequence of the blow to my head? The last thing I needed when I was finally rescued was a padded cell. Or maybe that was exactly what I *did* need, if recent events were anything to go by. Was the jacket I clutched to my chest even real? Gingerly, conscious of the drop, I bent my throbbing knees to my chest and wrapped the jacket around myself, wincing as my ruined nails snagged. Tears sprang to my eyes.

I wanted to go *home*.

It was a while before I noticed that Jacques' leather jacket, fresh from his body, was as cold as the grave.

4

Mum Warned Me About Talking To Strangers

Birds were singing at the top of their tiny little lungs when I startled awake with a snort. Pale, golden sunlight filtered through the leafy canopy overhead, painting a mottled pattern over the black leather draped over my chest.

Great. It hadn't been a horrible, weird nightmare after all.

Exhaustion lay heavy on me. I'd clearly managed to doze, somehow, but it hadn't been a restful sleep. If anything, I felt worse than I had yesterday. Despite the jacket, I was cold, stiff and aching. My ruined fingertips pulsed.

Groaning, I pushed away from the trunk, my back clicking and popping, and peered at the ground. It was a long way down but gone were the shadows of the previous evening. Everything glowed, gilded by the dawn light. A red squirrel scampered across the lush grass below, disappearing into a clump of bluebells. I could deal with squirrels.

Wincing at the sting of my fingers, I unhooked my backpack and eased my stiff arms into the jacket. It was warm now, after a night wrapped around my body. I didn't let myself think too long about Jacques and his complete lack of body heat.

Another rifle through my backpack confirmed that nothing of value had mysteriously appeared overnight. My phone was, unsurprisingly, still dead. Dismally, I slipped it into the pocket of the jacket, took a long swig of water from my bottle, and zipped away my useless belongings. I let my backpack fall, landing on the grass below with a wet splat. Nothing with fangs and claws appeared to shred it to pieces. A reassuring start.

My stomach growled, and I needed the toilet desperately.

Sighing and wincing, I twisted, swinging my leg over the branch, and began my awkward descent. Lowering myself from the bottom-most branch proved to be my most challenging task so far. It wasn't that I was scared of heights, but breaking an ankle was pretty low on my to do list. I eyed the drop, empty belly flipping, and, with one leg hooked over the branch, eased myself down, my throbbing hands protesting at the bite of the bark. Letting my leg slide free, I swung, my body colliding with the trunk. The air huffed from my lungs and my fingers slipped. I couldn't help my cry as I thudded to the floor in an ungainly heap.

For a moment, I could do nothing but stare up at the leaves, taking stock of my body. It still hurt everywhere, but nothing seemed to be broken, at least. At this point, I'd take any good news I could find. I staggered to my feet, scooping up my backpack, and looked around.

There was the river, gleaming in the early morning light, and beyond it, mountains. Behind me, the woods spanned as far as the eye could see. Birds continued to trill, unconcerned by my fall. Leaves whispered on a faint breeze. There was no other sound. It was too quiet, without the distant rumble of traffic, the familiar hum of city life. There was nothing to hint at my location, no clue to guide me towards home.

My stomach growled again.

There was nothing else for it. With mounting despair at how far I'd sunk, I dug the soggy wrap out of my backpack. The wrapper was still intact, at least. I sighed. Never had I imagined becoming the type of person forced to eat food barely fit for human consumption, but with my rescuers taking their sweet time, I had few options available. And worse, I had a horrible feeling that I wouldn't find even a public toilet nestled amongst the trees.

Grimacing at the indignity of it all, I was left with no option but to peel off my still damp underwear, and squat behind a tree like a dog while keeping a wary eye out for Jacques, or any other approaching weirdos. It would be just my luck to be found in such an unfortunate situation.

Nobody came.

The woods stayed as still and quiet as ever, and by the time I'd managed to shimmy back into my still-damp shorts, I knew I couldn't stay put. It was pretty clear that nobody was coming for me. If there was a search at all, it was happening far away from... wherever this was, and it was a miracle I'd survived one night. Another might finish me off.

Reluctant as I was to follow the advice of a creepy, cold man, I had nothing else to go off. I squinted up at the sky. The sun rose in the east. Or was it west? Somewhere in the depths of my mind, I knew the answer, but my brain refused to work. Maybe it was the blow to the head, or panic, or hypothermia. Whatever it was, I apparently had candy floss for brains. East. It was definitely east.

To Hell with it.

I set off along the riverbank. I'd been carried downstream, which meant I'd find my way back if I went upstream. With any luck, the caves were just around the bend. For God's sake, I was going to *kill* Isobel when I got home.

As the hours dragged past, as I walked on weak, weary legs, the sun rose higher, and the temperature rose with it.

Before long I was forced to tie the jacket around my waist, and drink half of my water, but sweat still coated my brow. I lathered on some sunscreen, thankful that Abby had insisted we pack it. I had enough to contend with without sunburn as well. At least my clothes and backpack were drying quickly in the heat. Small victories...

I clung to the shade of the trees, keeping the river in my sights, and a watchful eye on the sun, now blazing overhead. It must have been hours since I'd left my tree, and still there was no hint of civilisation. No sound. Only the rustling of what I desperately hoped were more squirrels in the shade of the wood, and the song of the birds. It would have been nice, had I not been nursing a growing sense of panic.

In the city it was rare to hear anything over the traffic, except maybe the cooing of pigeons. Only in my parents lovingly tended garden could I listen to the trill of songbirds, and even then, it was usually drowned by the thumping, irritating music blasting from the neighbour's garden. A bit of sunshine, and the middle aged, balding man next door was out, proudly subjecting the street to his questionable music tastes. Dad would have loved it here. He had a bird spotting book, and he always kept his feeder well stocked. Maybe, once I'd been found and figured out where on earth I'd been, I would bring him here for the day. Despite everything, I could appreciate how pretty it was. Jacques had said it was safe by day, hadn't he? He wouldn't lie to me, would he?

I laughed aloud at my delusional hope, but stifled the sound. What if he *had* lied? What if shadow men and nameless howling creatures prowled nearby, unperturbed by the sunshine? Would my laugh attract them? My steps faltered as I peered into the trees, the heat fading from my skin.

Sun beamed through the branches in glowing, golden columns, illuminating the undergrowth. Nothing monstrous appeared to me. Neither did any fairies. Maybe Jacques had told the truth, or maybe I was getting better, and my hallucinations were fading? The leather jacket tied around my waist told me otherwise.

Shivering, I abandoned the shade of the trees and clung to the riverbank. I'd take sunburn over becoming something's dinner any day.

The dense grass soothed my bare, blistered feet, and once or twice, I spotted enormous fish basking in the shallows of the river. Yeah, Dad would like it here. I couldn't bring myself to feel the same way.

The hours dragged by, and my hopelessness increased with every painful step. There was no end to it, to the green landscape, or the river, which had gradually picked up speed until it became a violent, churning torrent. Though I didn't want to admit it, I doubted very much I'd ever been this far upstream during my unconscious river cruise. I would definitely have drowned. Despair stung my eyes, and hunger made my head swim. Before long, I'd be forced to forage. Dad had always warned me about the old apple tree in the garden back home; eating the fruit before it was ready could give me the sort of tummy upset that would make my ordeal even worse than it already was, but that was the extent of my survival knowledge. Where would I begin? Certainly not with the mushrooms that were as likely to poison me as sustain me.

When my wobbly legs could carry me no further, I dropped down onto the grassy bank, and let my tears fall at last. Sobs wracked my body.

Was I going to die out here, lost and alone? Would I ever see my parents again? If only I could speak to them or send them a message. Anything. I'd tell them I was alive, that I loved them. They would know how to fix this.

I was well and truly alone.

Rubbing my eyes on the back of my arm, I hugged my legs. My shins and elbows had bloomed with purple bruises and my shredded hands made my empty stomach churn. Every time I looked at them, their throbbing increased in intensity. If they did get infected, if I wasn't found... Sniffing, I averted my eyes. I refused to die of broken fingernails.

Blackberries!

Fat, juicy blackberries, hung from a nearby bramble. My stomach roared its desperate encouragement. Unable to bring myself to stand again so soon, I shuffled closer, plucked a few berries and stuffed them greedily into my mouth.

The tart juices flooded my tongue, and, seized by a ravenous frenzy, I continued to strip the bramble. When I'd been a little girl, Nana had grown a blackberry bush at the end of her garden. Whenever I'd visited in the summer, we would spend a happy hour harvesting the ripe fruit, and an afternoon baking crumbles or pies. What wouldn't I do for

Nana's crumble drowned in custard right now? I couldn't think of a single thing.

When I'd eaten so many berries that my limbs began to feel a little steadier, when my fingers and no doubt my lips were stained purple, I struggled to my aching feet. It was then I noticed the little trail leading from the bush and weaving away through the trees. It wasn't a proper path, just sparse, flattened grass, as though someone regularly walked this way. Hope flared in my chest.

Heedless of the blisters, courtesy of my stupid boots, I hurried along the path, peering through the trees for signs of life. When I rounded a corner and glimpsed a gorgeous little cottage nestled in a clearing, I almost sobbed with relief. I was saved. I would be home in time for dinner.

Grinning broadly, I hurried to the white picket fence, almost hidden beneath a cloud of blue hydrangeas. A small but well-kept garden lay beyond, beds in full bloom, fat bumblebees and enormous butterflies tumbling over flowers of all shapes and colours. The cottage itself was of rough-hewn grey stone, with a low wooden door, painted pink, nestled in the thick walls. A bed of herbs grew below the window, all labelled with painted stones. The roof was neatly thatched, like something from a postcard.

Smiling, I pushed open the gate. Its hinges creaked. An old lady lived here, I decided. Someone like Nana, short and plump with a homemade cardigan and a halo of white hair. I just knew I was about to be plied with more cookies than I could eat. I hurried up the uneven path and knocked on the door, practically bouncing up and down in anticipation.

It was not an old lady who answered.

A wary, unlined eye of moss green peered through a crack in the door, widening as it beheld me, bruised and dishevelled, on the doorstep. The pastel pink door opened wider.

A breathtakingly beautiful young woman stood before me, shock written all over her stunning face. Like most women, she was shorter than me, the top of her head barely skimming my shoulder. A cascade of thick, slightly unkempt blonde hair fell to her narrow waist. Her feet were bare beneath the hem of her dress, the same shade of green as her eyes, which swept me up and down. They lingered on my cut knee and my hair. I didn't even want to imagine what sort of state *that* was in.

"Sorry," I said in a rush. "I wondered if I could use your phone? Mine's broken, and I got separated from my friends. I'll only be a minute."

The woman blinked, pulling the door open wider. She glanced left and right, scanning the trees with those wide eyes.

"Come in," she said. "Quickly."

I stepped gratefully over the threshold, staring around eagerly. The door snapped shut behind me, and my shoulders sagged with relief. It was good to be indoors again, surrounded by homely comforts. I cast an admiring gaze around the interior of the cottage. It wasn't exactly what I'd expected of the pretty young owner. I couldn't spot a television, or even a microwave in the open plan living room and kitchen. Everything looked old, but well kept.

Movement sounded behind me.

"Who else knows you are here, human?"

5

It's Giving Hansel & Gretel

It took a minute for the weird word choice to register in my brain. I frowned at the fussy lace cloth covering a little round table nearby.

"What do you mean *human*?" I turned to find the woman watching me intently, hands braced on her hips.

"That is what you are, is it not?"

No, I was a Norwegian Forest Cat. Honestly, why couldn't I find a normal person? "Well, I mean, yeah, obviously. Aren't we all?"

My host gave me a small, sly smile. "No."

She bustled past me, leaving a faint trace of rose scent in the air as she wove between the cluttered furniture, stopping before a shelf on the far wall. Crystals of all shapes, sizes and colours were displayed there, along with bunches of dried herbs and a few potted plants. She began to rummage through the contents of the shelf.

"When did you arrive?" She tossed the question over her shoulder, not bothering to look back.

"Yesterday, but, listen, I only need to use your phone, then I'll be on my way—"

"Have you spoken with anyone else since your arrival?" The woman stalked to the table, placing down a matte black rock, before squeezing between a low coffee table piled with battered old books, and a faded, overstuffed couch. She knelt on the rug before an empty grate, her back to me, and busied herself with something I couldn't see. Within seconds, flames crackled to life. "Tea?"

Something wasn't right. I wrapped my arms around myself and edged silently towards the firmly closed door, one silent step at a time. "No, thanks. I just need to use the phone."

"You look as though you could use a drink," the woman said, eyeing me again, a hint of disapproval on her perfect face.

"Honestly, I'm fine." I glimpsed a large, metal teapot suspended over the fire. Who made tea like that? Why didn't she have a kettle? Did she even have electricity?

Frowning, I scanned the cottage again. Although it was crammed, there were no lamps, or plug sockets, or, come to think of it, not even a light fitting hanging from the low beamed ceiling. It did not look like a house with good Wi-Fi speed. I took another sideways step towards the door.

"I wouldn't do that if I were you," the woman said in a bored voice as she clambered onto a stool, opening a cupboard that I could have reached without so much as craning my neck. She began pulling jars and tins out, placing them on the counter. A moment later, faster than I would have believed possible, she carried a tray piled with thick slices of crusty bread, jars of jam and a slab of butter to the table. "Here. Eat."

I eyed the food, my aching stomach growling. So, the cottage belonged to an eccentric loner. Did it mean I should refuse a half decent meal? No. No, it did not. I was starving. Sliding into a spindly chair, praying it would hold my weight, I began to spread butter, keeping one watchful eye on my host, who had returned to the fireside.

China clinked, and by the time I'd smothered my bread in a thick layer of jam and taken an enormous bite, the woman settled opposite, placing two dainty cups and saucers on the table. The delicate little vessel was a far cry from the oversized mugs I used to caffeinate myself at home, but I was gasping for a sip. My water rations hadn't gone far. I eyed my meal. What if it was poisoned? Everybody knew not to accept food and drink from strangers. My stomach growled, louder this time. Maybe I was being overly cautious, after all, what were the chances that this tiny little woman in the middle of nowhere would have something sinister mixed in her jam? If I didn't eat something substantial soon, there'd be no need of poison to finish me off. To Hell with it. I took a sip of my tea, groaning as I did.

"My name is Sage," the woman offered, watching me intently.

"Aliza, with an A," I grunted through another mouthful of food, wondering if it was wise to share such details. But, I reasoned, this was a woman as alone in the woods as I was, and barely half my height. If she tried to murder me, I was pretty sure I could put up a decent fight. "Do you live here alone?"

"For the most part, yes. I grew up with many sisters, so I enjoy the peace. I return home when I am needed."

I didn't have any siblings. My parents had struggled enough to conceive me, resorting to IVF in the end. They'd made the decision to stop at one and count their blessings, to avoid any further heartache. I couldn't pretend to understand their desperation for a child, but I knew the disappearance of one, even a fully grown one, would be torture to any parent. I *had* to get home.

"Do you think I could use the phone now? My parents will be crawling the walls."

Perfectly arched, pale eyebrows rumpled into a frown. "How would they do that?"

"It's just a figure of speech," I sighed. It was one thing to enjoy the solitude, but I couldn't understand why Sage wanted to be so secluded, so out of touch with the world. "It means they're worried."

"They are concerned about your quest?"

I laughed into my tea, splashing it over my nose. "I guess you could say that, yeah. I need to let them know I'm safe."

Sage smiled again, a tiny flicker at the corners of her mouth, as though she was unused to such showy gestures as smiles. "I am sorry to say, there is no way to contact the human world."

There she was again with the human thing. What harm would it do to play along? Maybe it would make her more sympathetic towards me if I went along with her delusions. Maybe we could send out a carrier pigeon or something. Isobel would love her.

"If you're not human, what are you?"

"Me? I am a witch."

Okay. Definitely crazy, but at least that explained the crystals. I forced myself to smile. "Nice. Can you, like, do magic and stuff?"

"Of course."

"Are you going to do something with that?" I poked the dull black rock. It seemed to absorb all the light. There were no shadows or reflections interrupting its smooth surface, only flat, empty blackness. Like a void.

"That is a warp crystal. It will open a portal back to my ancestral home, but I thought it wise to talk first."

"Oh, yeah, okay." I took another gloriously sweet bite of my bread and wracked my brain for a polite way out of this situation. My new witch friend seemed harmless enough, but I had no time to waste, and if she wouldn't help me, I'd have to thank her for her hospitality and move along.

Sage lifted her cup, taking a tiny sip. "Have you encountered anyone else since you arrived in our world?"

Why with the weird interest in my speaking to other people? Was I going to be held hostage as the new super-best-friend-forever? Was speaking to other people a crime?

"I met a man last night," I admitted. If anyone would accept my stories of hallucinations, it was the crazy lady opposite me. Besides, it wouldn't hurt to let her know that, if she did lock me in her cellar, someone nearby had seen me. Would remember me. The police would come sniffing... eventually.

Sage frowned, her green eyes burning. "What sort of a man?"

What sort of a question was *that*? "I don't know, just a man type, I guess." I certainly wasn't about to reveal that I wasn't convinced he was, well, *human*. Not with his cold body and strange eyes.

"Of what did he speak?"

"Not much. He was a bit weird, to be honest. He wanted to know my name." I gave Sage a '*crazy, right?*' look, but the self-proclaimed witch was far from amused. "Said that it wasn't safe at night. Oh, and to go south."

"That is all?"

"Pretty much, yeah."

"He did not... do anything?"

"Just gave me his jacket." I plucked at the sleeve, fastened around my belly. Sage glared at the leather as though it had deeply offended her ancestors.

"Very well," she muttered. "If you came south, and arrived yesterday, I assume you came through the mountain rift?"

I stared blankly. "I don't know. I'm not sure if I came south. I followed the river."

"Where were you before you arrived?"

"In a cave. I slipped and fell, and woke up on a riverbank, just a few hours from here."

Something flickered over her pretty face. "You slipped? Do you mean to tell me you did not come here purposely?"

I laughed again. My full stomach had improved my mood to no end. "Definitely not."

"Then you do not know why you are here?"

"I'm here because I need to use the phone." Not that I had any hope of finding one in this museum of a cottage.

"No, girl." Sage shook her head. "That is not why you are here at all. It was no mere chance that saw you take a tumble in those caves. You are supposed to be here. You have come to break the curse. You are here to save us all."

Crazy. Absolutely batshit crazy. Perfect. Exactly what I needed. *Not*.

My bland smile had become quite fixed. I was definitely going to end up bubbling in a cauldron full of stew before the day was out. Typical. It served me right for going camping.

"Erm," I croaked, clearing my tight throat. "Curse? I don't know anything about a curse. I just really need to get home—"

Sage sighed heavily, placing down her teacup, and settling back in her chair. "I can see you do not believe a word I am saying. Do humans really forget so quickly?"

Unnerved as I was, I was rapidly losing patience with this bullshit. I didn't have time to sit around talking about curses and witches. My parents were looking for me. They'd be beside themselves. I wanted to go home, now, or better yet, yesterday.

"Look," I said, injecting a steely tone into my voice. One of my workplace voices. I had a few. Most were varying ratios of gentleness and coaxing, but sometimes, a vet needed to be firm. "I don't know anything about curses, or magic, or portals. I just want to go home."

Sage giggled, a surprisingly high, girlish sound that didn't suit her at all. "I have met many humans, Aliza with an A, all eager and determined, all desperate for their chance at the prize. I admit, it has been a long while since I saw the last one. We had begun to believe the rifts had sealed on your end, or the humans had learnt to stay away. I never dreamt that, in only a few generations, you would have forgotten us. Forgotten what has been promised."

"Look, I'm sorry but—"

"Enough!" Sage slapped her hand on the table. "It is clear you are ignorant. Allow me to prove who *I* am, and then, perhaps, you will be inclined to hear the rest."

The witch got to her feet and snatched down a brown cloak from a peg by the door, swinging it around her shoulders as she wiggled her feet into black ballet pumps. Then she pressed her palm flat against the door, closed her eyes, and began to mutter. At first, nothing happened, but then the house gave a low groan, like an old ship at sea, and all at once, the lock on the door clanked and shutters slammed over the windows, bolts sliding across of their own accord, plunging the cottage into semi-darkness. Gasping, I skidded my chair back against the wall. The fact that I was well and truly trapped paled in the face of *magic.*

Sage's shadowy silhouette approached, causing me to shrink back against the unforgiving wood of my chair. She snatched the crystal up from the table.

"Get up," she demanded. "We will only have a moment."

"For what?" I squeaked, rising on trembling legs. So much for being firm.

The witch, the real, actual witch, ignored me. In the dimness, I watched as she held out her hand, the black rock lying on the flat of her palm. Sage began to mutter again, her words in no language I'd ever heard. Then, she moved her hand, pulling it back to her side, but the crystal stayed where it was, suspended in mid-air.

Not real. Not fucking real.

What little light was left in the room began to bend, as though sucked into the dark pit of the crystal. I gave another shuddering gasp and pressed myself flat against the wall, as though that would help me.

The black rock began to expand rapidly, the light twisting around it, as though it was some great whirlpool of darkness, hung in the middle of the quaint little cottage. When it was large enough to swallow a person hole, Sage turned to me.

"Quickly."

My fingertips pressed against the wall, as though I could cling to it like a gecko. "I—I don't know what—"

"It is a portal. Jump."

My mouth hung open as I shook my head. "I don't think—"

A small but surprisingly strong hand closed around my wrist, tugging me away from the wall. Sage shoved my spine, pushing me headlong into the vortex. Darkness engulfed me for the second time in twenty-four hours. I screamed, or, at least, I tried to. My throat burnt, and yet, no sound came out. I drifted, floating, the darkness and silence pressing in on all sides, obliterating all else. If Sage was with me, I couldn't see even a hint of her.

And then, quite suddenly, light and noise came rushing back.

I sprawled face down on a smooth stone floor. Not the ornate rug in the cottage. Gone was the crackle of flames, the distant twitter of birds. Instead, voices sounded all around me, exclaiming in shock.

I lifted my head.

An enormous, cavernous chamber of stone greeted me. Huge, arched windows took up one wall, beyond which gulls soared in a clear sky. Several women wearing frilly, ruffled dresses stood nearby, staring down at me.

Feet clad in black ballet pumps appeared beside my head, and I looked up to find Sage primly patting dust from her cloak. She winked at me, then turned to the assembled women.

"Sisters! I come with a gift."

6

Blink Twice If You Need Help

"Is that... a human?"

"It is, indeed. Aliza with an A, she calls herself. She appeared at my doorstep not a half hour ago."

I scrambled to my feet, sliding behind Sage, who barely came up to my collarbone, as the women drifted closer, shock replaced by eager curiosity. Sage might call them sisters, but they did not look related. They were all as short as her, but the resemblance ended there. One had hair of burning orange with skin coated in freckles. Another had tightly wound, black curls and rich dark skin. None had Sage's blonde hair.

"Aliza with an A," the redhead said, testing the name on her tongue as she drifted closer. "I don't know, it's a strange name".

"I like it," said another with upswept, chestnut eyes. "It is quite pretty."

Clearly, they were all fucking insane. Where was I? Definitely not in the wood. What on earth was going on now? I glanced around, my eyes landing on a large door at the far side of the room.

Noted.

I had a way out if things got hairy, but there was no telling what fresh horrors awaited on the other side of that door. Gulping, I turned my attention back to the women. They couldn't suspect I was primed to flee. I willed my breathing to slow.

The redhead gave Sage a swift look. The blonde witch only sighed and said, "She knows nothing. I tried to explain, but she did not believe a word of it, not even that I am a witch."

"So you warped the poor thing here to prove a point?" The brown-skinned woman grasped my upper arms in her warm hands. "Poor girl. You look *horrible*."

"She was like that when I found her," Sage muttered.

Woah. Okay. I didn't need a mirror to know I wasn't looking my best, but was there any need? They'd look a little worse for wear too if they'd been through the things I'd endured.

"You did not think to tidy her up?"

"I told you, she did not believe me. Besides, she told me she spoke with a man. I needed her here quickly."

Several gasps sounded in unison and my muscles tensed in answer.

"A man?" The hands grasping my arms tightened. "What was he?"

"She does not know. I believe she thinks us all human."

"This man," the brown-skinned witch pressed, peering up at me with rich, dark eyes, lined at the outer corners. "What shape were his ears?"

Half an hour ago, I might have thought it a weird question, but now, the words just rolled over me as though the witch had asked the time. "Erm, just ear shaped, I think. Like mine. I didn't really notice."

The witch visibly relaxed, though shot a pointed look at a nearby companion. "Fetch Granny." She turned back to me. "My name is Hyacinth, and this is Nairsgarth Castle, house of the Western Witches. You will be perfectly safe and comfortable here."

"Actually." I cleared my throat, attempting to inject my voice with a little authority. "I was saying to Sage, I really need to get home to—to the human world." It felt ridiculous even saying it, but nothing had been normal since I went into those stupid caves. "I can't stay here."

Hyacinth gave me a pitying look. "Have your kind truly become so unlearned?"

Reluctantly, I shook my head, glancing again to the window. Glittering ocean spanned to the horizon, revealing no hint of my location. How the tables had turned. I was supposed to be the one people came to for answers. I was supposed to figure things out and set them right. To reassure other people. There were few mysteries that could not be solved with a culture dish or a scalpel.

Not here, apparently. Here, I was *unlearned*. Here, I didn't have the faintest clue of where to look for answers. I certainly wasn't going to get them from this gang of weirdos with their cryptic superstitions and evasions.

"I tried to explain, but she would not listen," Sage insisted.

"Oh, I wonder why," I spat, my temper and embarrassment getting the better of me. I was beyond exhausted, and nothing made any sense. This was all bullshit. What had I done to deserve this?

"I understand your desire to return to your world," Hyacinth said hurriedly. She took my hand in her own, clucking at the state of my fingers. "But, dear girl, there is much you do not know. Our world, beyond the wards of Nairsgarth, is a dreadfully dangerous place for a human. You cannot wander alone. It's a blessing you made it to Sister Sage in one piece. Why don't you rest a while, let us tidy you up, and then we will talk more, and see what we can do to help."

The idea was not appealing. Despite the bone-aching tiredness, I didn't want to waste time resting. I could rest when I got home, safe in my own bed, with Mum fussing and making all my favourite foods. Her coddling could be intense at times, but my chosen career wasn't always cute puppies and kittens. Sometimes it was hard. On days like that, I was grateful for Mum and her fussing. I'd lap it up when this was over. Tears sprang to my eyes again, but I blinked them away. I had long since learnt to hold my emotions at bay. It was a necessity, really, in my line of work. I had to be the strong, steady one, while others dissolved into grief. I'd been present through countless goodbyes. I could handle this.

"My parents are looking for me," I sniffed. "I have to go."

Sage appeared at Hyacinth's elbow. "You will never make it back to the human world if you charge ahead without a plan. Would your parents prefer to have you delivered safely if a little late, or not at all?"

Hyacinth shifted, her face the image of sympathy, but she didn't argue my cause. "Come. Let us get you settled. Granny will want to see you, and those fingers look sore. Let us tidy you up."

With no other immediate option open to me, I nodded. I *was* sore. My nails were throbbing. Probably infected. There wasn't a single part of me that didn't hurt. Hyacinth smiled encouragingly, leading me across the chamber, past the silently watching women. Witches, I assumed. I thought of Sage's portal and shivered; if they could do that, there was no telling what terrible powers they might have. Did they turn people into frogs? Would *I* become a frog? The thought should have sent me running down the corridors, screaming for help, but I couldn't find any resistance left in me. Was this the shock equivalent of grief's acceptance stage? I didn't believe any of it, but so far, not believing had gotten me nowhere. I was past caring, as long as the *witches* helped me get home.

"We will get you some proper clothes," Hyacinth said, misreading my shudder. "Though you are a little tall."

I gave a weak smile. If they thought I was wearing too-short clothes, they could think again. As a tall woman, there was little worse than a hem that missed its mark. I would make do with my shorts and T-shirt a while longer, even if they were filthy. My life was shaping up to be bad enough without the addition of awkwardly fitting clothes. Besides, I'd be home soon. I *had* to be. I'd have no need of their ugly garments.

I meekly followed Hyacinth through the door I'd spotted earlier, out into a wide corridor that looked like something from a fairy tale castle with its vaulted ceilings, tiled floors and candles burning in brackets. Sage stalked along at my other side, her short strides quick. We passed a cluster of women, gathered around a window, who all did double takes when they saw me, and followed my progress with wide eyes.

"Did you see that?" one hissed.

"Was that a *human*?"

I blocked out their words. I had no idea what time it was, but it had already been a long day. Longer even than yesterday. The last thing I wanted or needed was to be gawked at like some endangered animal at the zoo. I felt freakish enough, towering head and shoulders over my escorts, without the human obsession.

Hyacinth led us out through some open doors, into a balmy courtyard. Shaded walkways spanned the edges, but the middle was full of neat lawns and beds of plants and flowers. Benches were spaced along paths of gravel. The scent of the nearby ocean mingled with the delicate perfume of flowers.

"This is a communal area," Hyacinth said with a bright smile. "Feel free to come here if you ever need a little air. It is open night and day."

I didn't like the way she spoke, as though I'd be staying long enough to make use of the facilities, but it was pointless to argue. Nobody seemed to care that I didn't want to be here. If I was going to find my way home, I would just have to cooperate, at least until I figured out my own plan. We skirted the garden, drawing yet more whispers from the women enjoying the sunshine. Some were young, others old. I spotted a white-haired old lady leaning on a cane. There were no men. No children.

Back into the chilled shade of the building we went, up stone staircases and down long passages, while I looked about with mounting interest. Though the passages were busy, I saw only women.

"Don't you have any wizards here?" I asked.

Hyacinth shot me a questioning look, but it was Sage who answered. "There are no males within these halls. Witches are all born female."

I frowned. "How do you... have kids?"

Sage smirked. "When a man and a woman love one another—"

"Don't tease," Hyacinth snapped. "The poor girl knows nothing."

"I know plenty," I insisted, blushing. "I obviously know *how* babies are made, but what I meant was, you need men for that. Unless witches can reproduce asexually."

"What?"

Ha. Finally. I knew something they didn't. The little spark of triumph glowed all the brighter in such a dark nest of emotion. "Reproduce without a partner."

Sage laughed. "No, we are not like that. We require a male. Unfortunately, we do not have any. No witches have been born in many years."

"But if you're all born female—"

"Humans," Sage said simply. "Human males, brought through the rift. But you are the first of your kind to come here in a long, long time."

"You *bring* human men through the rift? As studs? Do they have a choice?"

Sage gave me a wry smirk. "There were plenty of volunteers, believe me. They were well kept and enjoyed their duties. We were once able to be selective, choosing only the finest specimens to enhance our lines, but now, I fear compromises would be made should a male become available."

That was one way of putting it.

"Anyway, here we are." Hyacinth pushed open a large door, revealing a sunlit bedroom beyond. "Your quarters. They are comfortably equipped."

I stepped cautiously into the room. Comfortably equipped was an understatement. It was just like a dream. A large four-poster bed stood on a dais opposite the door, draped in heavy cream curtains embroidered with pink blossoms. An elaborate wardrobe and matching table stood to my right, with a dressing table further along the wall, just past a closed door. A low table and a selection of chairs clustered around a large fireplace, and a desk was tucked under one window. The room was almost as big as my entire house.

"Wow," I said, despite myself.

"I will see to the fire." Sage crossed the room.

This time, I watched her closely. The witch stacked logs in the grate, but she didn't use matches or a lighter or whatever tools they might have used in the old days. Instead, she merely whispered something and clicked her fingers. A flame sparked to life in the logs, catching quickly. I gulped.

"You will be given a guide to settle you in and help you find your way about," Hyacinth explained as she pulled open the wardrobe, frowning at its contents. "The neophytes once tended to our needs and such when they were not in lessons. They have all long since graduated into fully fledged witches, and so we share menial duties amongst us all. That does mean we try to maintain our quarters ourselves, to make the work a little easier. I'm afraid that will apply to you, too."

"Okay," I said blandly, as though I intended on having an extended stay.

I drifted to the windows and peered out. The drop was dizzying, made so much worse by the sheer cliff that plunged down to the churning water, far below. There would be no escape through the window. It didn't matter. I'd just have to find another way.

Scraping and tinkling drifted from behind me, along with the rustle of fabrics.

"Aliza, come. Sit." Sage commanded me like a dog. I wrestled my frown into submission before turning to find the witch gesturing to a chair before the fire. "Let me see your wounds."

Passing Hyacinth, now laying numerous dresses out on the bed, I sank into the chair. I almost moaned with relief as I settled into the plush cushions, letting my head loll back. I hadn't realised just how much I needed a soft seat after a night of bark biting my arse. The armchair was absolute bliss. Sage knelt before me, eyeing my scabbing knee with distaste.

"This will need cleaning. It will sting."

A sideboard to the right of the fireplace stood open, revealing more bowls and jars within. On its surface a wooden chopping board lay cluttered with diced greenery and a large, gleaming knife. Not a drop of saline to be seen. The witch laid a selection of bowls on the hearth, along with a pestle and mortar.

"A poultice," Sage explained, following my gaze. "But that comes afterwards."

"Go ahead." I fluttered my fingers to my knee. I was too exhausted to care about anything, even wound hygiene. My eyelids dragged irresistibly down.

The witch fished a cloth from a bowl of liquid and pressed it to the cut, which immediately exploded with pain. I winced, sucking a breath through my clenched teeth, all thoughts of sleep abandoned, but Sage paid no heed as she proceeded to dab gently.

"You can't just heal it with your magic?" If magic had to be real, then couldn't it at least have the decency to patch me up?

The witch smiled wryly. "No. Witch magic does not work like that. The world has already given us all we need to heal ourselves. It is a simple matter of knowing how to use it. Witches can do a little of this and that, but if you want raw healing magic, it is the elves you need."

Elves. Of course. How silly of me. My brain presented me with an image of a sea of tiny people in stripy tights and Santa hats. I swallowed a giggle. If the elves were as good at healing as Sage claimed, maybe I would take a few home and set them to work in my practice. First, I had to figure out a way out of this mess.

Sage laid down her cloth and turned her attention to the thick, green paste she had ground in the pestle. She smeared a layer over the smarting wound, and immediately, a cool, tingling sensation spread over the damaged skin, driving away the sting.

"How does that feel?"

"A bit better," I admitted reluctantly. "Thanks."

"You look tired." The witch shot a wry glance up at me.

Nearby, Hyacinth tutted. "You will soon learn that Sister Sage is lacking in tact. What she means to say is that you have had quite an ordeal. You should rest, maybe take a nap."

A nap. God, I wanted to relent, but Mum and Dad were undoubtedly beside themselves. The enormous bed *did* look inviting though.

As though Hyacinth sensed my argument, she continued, "My sisters and I will put our heads together while you sleep, and by this evening we will have a plan."

An hour of sleep wouldn't hurt. Perching in a tree like some ridiculous bird hadn't been the most refreshing way to spend the night. Besides, if this world was as dangerous as everyone said it was, a plan wouldn't go amiss.

I mulled it over as Sage finished smothering my cuts in paste. Not even the smallest of grazes was left untouched, right down to the blisters on my feet. When she'd finished, she bandaged my hands and knee. I examined her precise work, finding no cause for complaint as she packed away her things.

"We'll leave you to get some rest," Hyacinth offered, her voice soothing and soft.

"Don't get the bandages wet," Sage all but barked, "and don't pick at them."

If I hadn't been exhausted, I might have rolled my eyes. What next? Would she whip out a cone of shame and collar me with it?

"I've left some clothes on the bench," Hyacinth called as the witches retreated through the door. It clicked behind them.

I half expected to hear a key turn in the lock, but apparently, I wasn't exactly a prisoner, and the door was left unbarred.

With a monumental effort, I rose from the warm embrace of the armchair and aimed for the bed. One hour. Just one hour.

7

So, Apparently I'm The Chosen One

When I opened my eyes, the room was dark. Damn. So much for an hour.

Lying flat on my back on my obscenely comfortable bed, my bandaged hands and knees tingling gently, I mulled over everything that had happened. Though I no longer felt the urge to drop dead from exhaustion, the softness of my pillow and the warmth of the blanket held me captive. Just five more minutes, *then* I'd get up and escape the castle.

A tentative knock sounded at the door. I sat up, peering through the gloom.

"Yeah?"

The door cracked open, and for a minute, I thought it was Hyacinth's head that popped into the room, beaming at me, but then I saw that the woman was younger, her skin a lighter shade of brown.

"Hello, I hope you weren't sleeping?"

"No. Can I help you?"

The woman bounded into the room, clasping her hands before her. She was clad in the same fussy cut of dress as the other witches, though she had opted for a cheery shade of purple. "I can't believe I'm looking at a real, live *human*! I never thought I'd see the day. My name's Pansy, by the way."

"Aliza." I was in no mood to humour the human obsession, not unless it involved delivering me back to my own world.

"Are you feeling rested? Only, Granny is ready to receive you. I've been sent to escort you." She spoke as though the news would thrill me, but I didn't care one bit for a meeting with Granny, whoever the hell she was. Maybe this was it though, the plan to get me home.

Sighing, I slid off the bed, laying my bare feet on the cold tiles. Though Sage had applied a salve to the blisters, the thought of stuffing my feet back into those awful boots was too much. I hadn't bothered to change into the too-short dress Hyacinth had laid out. The pink gown lay discarded over the upholstered bench at the end of my bed. It was clearly supposed to skim the calves, but on me I'd be lucky if it covered my knees. Granny would just have to see me as I was. At least the lingering dampness of my shorts had been driven away by a few hours traipsing through the wilds. I plucked up Jacques' jacket, donning it as I padded to Pansy. The evening air carried a chill, but the sleeves were delightfully long, falling over my hands, hiding my bandages from view. I was grateful for the unlikely gift, and felt almost fondly towards the mysterious Jacques. I'd been convinced he was a murderer, but now, he seemed the least of my concerns.

"Lead the way."

If Pansy had any thoughts of my bare legs and feet, she kept them to herself as she hurried along beside me. The witch was short, though her dark, spiralling curls, piled on top of her head in buns resembling mouse ears, gave the illusion of height.

"I should warn you," Pansy said as we walked the corridors, "Granny can be a bit prickly, but don't be intimidated."

"Who exactly is she? I've heard three people call her Granny now." And all of them were as different from the other as could be. I was no geneticist, but I wouldn't have pinned such a collection as blood relatives.

"She's not a real granny, not to most of us anyway. But that's just what we call her, because she's the High Priestess, and—" she dropped her voice to a whisper "—she is really *old*."

Based on the conversations I'd had so far, I didn't want to contemplate what old meant. If magic was real, it would surely be used to preserve life. Maybe there was a plant growing in Sage's cottage garden that, when brewed at a full moon, produced the elixir of life. I blew a derisive huff out of my nose. What a lot of nonsense. This was shaping up to be a terrible concussion.

"How long do witches live?" I asked, giving in to my curiosity. If my damaged brain had concocted all of this, I was tempted to see how far it went before it unravelled completely. It was quite impressive, in a terrifying sort of way.

"It varies according to our power, but we all live a lot longer than humans. I'm the youngest witch here, I'm only two hundred and sixty-eight."

God. *Only* two hundred and sixty-eight. She didn't look a day over eighteen. I gave my thigh a sharp pinch with two lightly bandaged fingers. It stung, so I supposed I wasn't dreaming. Isobel would kill to trade places with me, and I would certainly have no complaints. Still, I'd be home soon. All I had to do was convince this infamous High Priestess to escort me back to the caves. I'd simply present the facts and explain, in no uncertain terms, that I needed to get home immediately. Easy.

My new certainty stuttered as we came to a halt before a firmly closed door. A pair of silent, grim-faced women, no, *witches*, flanked it, but one nodded, eyeing me eagerly, and the door swung open of its own accord.

"Good luck," Pansy whispered.

"What? You're not coming with me?" I didn't know why it mattered. I'd barely exchanged a word with the woman, but the thought of facing the infamous Granny alone turned my legs to jelly.

"I'm not important enough to listen to this conversation," Pansy hissed, "but don't worry! Just remember, you're the human! You hold all the power."

Was that cryptic nonsense supposed to calm me? I tried to swallow, but my throat was swollen and numb. My heart thudded against my ribs, but then I remembered that none of this actually concerned me. I was drifting through a dream, that was all. Sooner or later, I'd either wake up or die, and none of this would be a problem anymore. Soothed slightly, I squared my shoulders and donned my workplace persona, all calm authority and unhurried serenity, and strolled in as though it was my very own room in the surgery I would soon be working at.

My outward show of confidence and ease was exactly that. Outward. A group of witches waited at the far end of a large hall, all standing with stiff backs and raised noses as they judged my approach. Was it magic that made me feel like the smallest person in the room despite being the tallest by a foot, or was it only because I was at a distinct disadvantage, surrounded by extremely strange strangers, and far from my natural element?

My legs wobbled like jelly as they carried me across the vast, empty space. My numb feet passed over something dark. I dropped my eyes to the floor, where a large shape was depicted on the tiles. I stilled, my lips parting as I stared at my saviour.

A *map*.

So, it couldn't fit in my pocket, but if I memorised it now, it would at least give me some vague sense of my surroundings, which was better than nothing. This was exactly what I needed. A way to point myself in the direction of home.

Enormous slabs of gleaming green crystal, maybe emerald, had been shaped and smoothed into tiles, showing a sprawling island. The map was edged in glittering gold grout which gave way to the dull, sand-coloured slabs making up the rest of the floor. I took a cautious step further. Yet more gold depicted mountains and rivers, and even what looked like border lines, weaving over the polished green surface.

I scanned the shape of the landmass. It wasn't England, that much was certain. It wasn't anywhere I'd ever noticed on an atlas, but I was no longer surprised by the unfamiliarity. I scanned the map for the rivers and mountains that had been the backdrop to my arrival, but there were too many to narrow down my location. And besides, as far as I could tell, I was miles away from where I'd started, thanks to Sage and her spooky crystal.

A small cough drew my attention back to the gaggle of witches, all watching me expectantly. Sage and Hyacinth were among them, as well as the one with chestnut eyes whose name I hadn't learnt. She'd said *my* name was 'quite pretty'. In the centre of the cluster, an enormous, throne-like armchair loomed, and perched atop its dated, floral upholstery was a little old lady.

Granny.

The High Priestess was as wrinkled as a Shar Pei, with white-streaked iron-grey hair arranged in a smart updo. One gnarled hand clutched the ornate handle of a walking stick, which she braced herself against, leaning forward to peer at me with watery, pale eyes. Her gaze travelled down to my bare feet, and back up again, her already lined face wrinkling further with disapproval. She blinked several times as she beheld my hair, then shifted with the awkwardness of great age, waving a frail hand at the group of witches clustered at her side.

"Sage, dear," she said in a reedy but elegant voice, "come here."

The blonde witch hastened to the old woman's side at once. Granny peered up at her.

"Whatever is the matter with her hair?"

As easily as that, my nerves gave way to bristling indignation. My hair was always a topic of conversation with new people, and though I didn't usually mind, the older generation laboured under the illusion that their opinions were facts to be freely shared. If I had a pound for every time a pensioner had explained how impractical my colours were, I'd have enough to... well, maybe not retire, but treat myself to a fancy meal at least.

Sage opened her mouth, but I answered for her. "It needs a wash and a brush, but I assume you're referring to the colour. My name is Aliza, by the way. Not that you asked."

Granny jolted, her mouth falling open in apparent shock that I'd dared to address her directly.

"We have never encountered a human with hair like yours before," Sage interjected, but there was no hint of an apology in her voice, just cold, blunt facts. "The colour is... disconcerting."

"It's dye," I sighed, my fighting spirit sapping away on that long breath. My shoulders sagged. What I'd give to be back in that enormous bed. No, back in *my* bed, at home, with a steaming cup of hot chocolate, mounds of whipped cream, and a heap of vegan marshmallows. "My natural colour is dark blonde."

"And do all humans indulge in this newfangled *dye*?" Granny asked, speaking to me directly for the first time.

"A lot, yeah. Most have natural looking colours, but some of us prefer this." I gestured wearily to my hair. Maybe my argument would have been easier to accept if my hair had been anything close to its usual magnificence. As it was, they were probably wondering why anyone would choose to look like a dog had mauled a stuffed unicorn and left it on top of their head.

"Mother above," Granny muttered, in a tone much like I'd say *good God*. "Whatever will Prince Anwir make of her?"

Prince? Nobody had mentioned meeting any princes. This conversation wasn't going at all the way I wanted. Was I going home, or not? I glanced over my shoulder at the beautiful map. My fingers twitched toward my pocket and the useless phone within. Even if I hadn't needed to remember every river and valley, I would have liked to take a picture. It was a pretty thing, and if the tiles were really emerald, worth more than everything I owned.

Sage took a few brisk steps closer to me, her footsteps drawing my attention back. "Aliza, you mentioned returning to the human world."

I was pretty sure I'd done more than mention it, but whatever. Finally, we could get on with the matter at hand. "I did."

"Unfortunately, that will not be possible."

"*What*?" Had I misheard? Was I being *kidnapped*? Were they going to chop me up and bake me into a pie? I stumbled back a step, putting distance between me and the little witch. She made no move to stop me. Could I make it to the door, and if I did, could I find my way out of the castle before the witches caught up to me? They only had little legs, but I was injured and, to be brutally honest, horribly unfit. "I have to."

"The gateways linking Neath to the human world have been sealed on our side for centuries. Nobody can leave, not even you. That is, unless the curse is broken."

"What curse?" Not this nonsense again? Curses weren't real, but then again, neither were witches or fairies, and definitely not swirling portals of gaping darkness. I probed the tender lump at the back of my head, half-hoping the pain would wake me from my fever dream. The prod was sharp enough to make me wince, but the witches didn't fade into nothing as I'd hoped.

"To understand it, you must understand our world." Hyacinth approached slowly, her body language unthreatening, as though I was a cornered dog, primed to snap. She laid a light hand on my arm, steering me around to the tiled map. I shrugged out of her grasp, but followed on numb feet, my mind whirring. "The island you see depicted here is known as Neath. It is split into courts, all ruled over by one monarch. We are here, in Nairsgarth Castle–" she toed the south-eastern coastline "–which is located in the court of Ymyl Cefn-for. The fae king or queen, ruler of all Neath, resides in Tir o Haf."

She gestured to the western coast. "Several centuries ago, the true king died, a bloody coup followed, disrupting the succession. The throne *should* have passed to his eldest son."

"Should have?" I asked. None of this mattered to me. It had all happened hundreds of years before I was born, and besides, I wasn't even a part of this world, never mind this ancient drama. Even so, I hung on every word, storing away every scrap of information like a hamster stuffing its pouches. Somewhere amongst this rubbish there had to be a clue. A seemingly innocuous detail that would get me home, with or without the witches' help. "Are the princes dead, then?"

"No, child. The throne is imbued with primordial magic, ensuring it cannot be seized with violence."

"There are no rules in place to prevent trickery, though," Sage groused, as though whatever irked her was all Hyacinth's doing.

"Indeed," Hyacinth agreed, her voice oozing disapproval. "The late king's brother, Maelgwyn, is a powerful warlock. He worked for his brother for the majority of his reign, but Maelgwyn was ever dissatisfied with his own abilities. With the king's resources and blessing, he was able to push the boundaries and discover new, ever more... *unnatural* powers. All in the name of service to the crown. When the king died, Maelgwyn used these powers to trick the throne."

"Tricked the–what? How can a throne be tricked?" Was she implying that a chair was sentient?

Before I had time to contemplate such an impossible claim further, Hyacinth continued her irrelevant tale. "He placed a curse of eternal sleep on his nephews. As they were physically unharmed, but subdued, the throne assumed them dead and passed to Maelgwyn."

"Sucks to be them," I muttered. "But what's this got to do with me?" More importantly, how did it affect my going home?

Hyacinth turned a sympathetic smile on me. "There are gateways between our world and yours. That is how you arrived here. There was a time when humans and witches alike travelled freely between Neath and Earth, though your kind were not always receptive to ours. The Fae would even pay the occasional visit to Earth, though their magic is greatly weakened there. The gateways are called rifts, and they are scattered throughout the courts. After speaking with Sister Sage, we have determined that you arrived through the Blood Gate."

"I did?" I scanned the map, searching for the name etched in gold. If I'd come that way, why couldn't I depart that way too? I feigned curious innocence as I asked, "Where's the Blood Gate?"

Nobody answered. Maybe I wasn't as subtle as I liked to believe.

"An incredibly reckless choice," Sage offered, as though I'd had any say in the matter. I suppressed a scowl, channelling my glare at the map. There were no words. Nothing to mark the Blood Gate, at least nothing I understood.

Hyacinth patted my arm. "Savage beasts roam those mountains. Let us just say you are exceptionally lucky that Sister Sage found a living woman, rather than a corpse."

Maybe making a bid for The Blood Gate wasn't such a good idea, or maybe... maybe I wasn't as good a liar as I believed. Maybe the witches knew exactly what I planned to do and were trying to put me off. To frighten me.

Either way, that rift had brought me here, which meant it could take me home. I'd managed to get here well enough without anything eating me, there was no reason I couldn't do it again.

Hyacinth continued her history lesson. "As powerful as Maelgwyn is, even he cannot cast a curse without a caveat. Everything must exist in balance. Just as you were wounded, nature provided the ingredients for Sister Sage to heal you. It is the same for all things, even magic. A curse cannot exist without a way to break it. It is said that only a human can wake the princes."

The hairs on my arms rose to attention as a cold sense of foreboding settled over me. I was starting to see where this was going, and I didn't like it one bit. I glanced at the door again. Somehow, it looked further away than ever.

Sage appeared at my elbow, glaring at the map as though it had been Maelgwyn's accomplice. "I'm certain he thought himself both clever and amusing, choosing the most incompetent species in the realm. To make an already unlikely achievement all but impossible, Maelgwyn sealed the rifts. The human world is toxic to fae, weakening their powers greatly, and so your side of the gateways remain open, though I believe they go some way to repelling your kind. We, however, are trapped here. As are any hapless humans who stumble into Neath. Believe me, there have been many."

A bubble of hope swelled in my chest. "Well, can't one of them break the curse? Where are they?"

"Dead," Sage said with all the emotion of a weatherwoman announcing yet more rain. My little bubble popped, skewered by her answer. "In the early days after the casting of the curse, Maelgwyn sent out beasts. Great monsters of his own creation. They hunted down and killed every human. None survived. For many a decade, humans continued to come to Neath, keen to break the curse and earn the reward, but they all failed. As time went on, fewer arrived until, eventually, they stopped." She lifted her moss-green eyes to mine. "You are the first in over two and a half centuries."

Bad. This was very bad. The worst.

"And certainly, the first to arrive completely unarmed with at least a vague idea of why they were here." Sage spoke with a tone of distinct disapproval, as though I was somehow at fault.

I blinked, straightening my spine at the audacity. "None of this is *why* I'm here! I'm here because I took a wrong turn in a cave, that's all."

Sage levelled a cool glare at me. "So you say, girl, but why do you think you took the wrong turn? You are *meant* to be here."

Sweat pricked between my shoulder blades. Nope. Absolutely not. I was *meant* to be at home, eating snacks and watching TV from under the safety of a fuzzy blanket. Breaking curses was for main characters in the shows I liked to watch, not for *me*. I was a boring, ordinary woman with a boring, ordinary life. I wouldn't have it any other way.

"Don't be stupid. What about all those other humans? The ones who died? Were they meant to be here too? Meant to die? I'm sorry, but there's absolutely no way I'm getting myself killed trying to save some princes I've never even met."

Their fate was definitely unfortunate, but there were worse things happening in the world. Not that I was cut out for dealing with those either, but still. Besides, for all anyone knew, they might be enjoying their nap. It would be rude to wake them.

Sage narrowed her eyes in assessment. "They were here because they chose to be. I knew many of them myself. The last one, Georgina, came of her own free will. She wanted to break the curse. Fate had no part in it. This is different."

"It's different because, unlike them, I'm going home."

"You cannot."

"I can."

"Mother above," Sage muttered, rolling her eyes. "I am not about to repeat myself, girl."

"Aliza," I snarled. "I have a name."

"Yes, and I have a job to do. The curse must be broken, and like it or not, you will be the one to do it."

"Why do you even care? You're not a - a fae." Truth be told, I wasn't even sure what a fae was. The term rang a distant bell in the dusty corners of my memory, maybe from some fairytale my grandparents had read to me, but I couldn't conjure an image of what, exactly, I was supposed to die to save. "What does it matter to you?"

"It matters to all the people of Neath, not only me." The witch turned her attention back to the map, but Hyacinth stepped closer, offering me a gentle smile.

"As you know, without human men, witches face extinction, but that is not the worst of it." She heaved a sigh, her smile fading into an expression of sorrow. "Maelgwyn has not been content these past centuries. He has the throne he coveted, he has his unnatural power, but it has not been enough to sate him into peace. In the years following his rise, Tir all but one fae kingdom fell to him. Since then, he has waged constant war against Tir o Gaeaf, the last court to stand between Maelgwyn and witch territory. If Gaeaf falls, we fall. There will be no free lands left in Neath, no free people."

"Do his people suffer?" I asked, my voice soft, though I wasn't sure I wanted to know the answer. It would only make turning my back on them harder. Ignorance was bliss, and yet, I asked anyway.

"Yes. Many have tried to flee."

"Tried?"

"They died for their efforts. The immortals died when they crossed over Maelgwyn's borders. Those that remain are enslaved or... used. The king is, for want of a better word, a scholar. He is hungry for knowledge. Knowledge he gains from the suffering of his people."

An image of a dissection floated across my mind, unbidden and unwelcome, particularly as the humanoid subject, who resembled Pansy, was still breathing.

"Not only his people," Sage grumbled. "His agents often prey on the free fae of Tir o Gaeaf. They come by night, moving through the shadows and spiriting children from their beds, never to be seen again."

Despite my determination to remain unmoved, I shuddered. It was the stuff of nightmares. Every child's irrational fear come true. The more I learnt of this world, the less inclined I was to stay. A place where the monsters under the bed were real was no place for... well, anyone, but least of all me.

"Witches have long been allies to the fae. They are our neighbours. Our friends. That is what it has to do with us. That is why you must break the curse."

I shook my head, setting my bedraggled ponytail swaying. "I'm sorry, but you can't expect me to die for your friends."

"I expect no such thing. I expect you to live. Forever in fact."

It took a long moment for Sage's words to drudge into my brain. My brows knotted into a frown. "What?"

The witch smirked. "Why do you think your predecessors came willingly? There is a reward for breaking the curse, girl. You will become a queen. You will live forever."

8

As Pretty As A Picture

Nothing lived forever. I didn't need my degree to know that much. It was nothing more than some elaborate lie designed to trick and tempt me into going along with their crazed plan. They had to think I was stupid.

I risked a surreptitious sideways glance at my companion.

Pansy walked half a step ahead of me. Though she maintained her silence, anticipation poured from her in waves. She was obviously dying to assault me with a barrage of questions, and if I spoke, it would open the flood gates.

I pressed my lips together. Too much scattered and tangled information weighed down my brain. I needed time to think, to process it myself before I could even consider answering somebody else's questions. Curses, magic, immortality...

Pansy claimed to be centuries old, yet she could have passed as fresh out of school. She'd said Granny was old, and the High Priestess certainly looked it. Forever clearly wasn't in her future. Was it only the fae who could claim immortality? Or maybe their curse breaking stooges.

It was all a load of shit. It had to be a lie, or a hallucination, or *something*. But if it was real...

What would it be like to live forever? To not have time stalking every step, waiting for its chance to claim me? The things I could do. Would it be possible to learn all there was to know about *everything*? To master every art, every science? There was so much I half-fancied doing, but would never have the time for, so many things that didn't make the cut when it came to planning my years. Places I would never go, information I would never learn, things I would never experience. What if I could do it all?

My heart rate sped up at the possibilities, but it was just a fantasy, and one with a dark side at that. What good was a head full of facts when it came hand in hand with a heart full of lost love? I might be able to win gold on the ice with my perfect triple axels while simultaneously becoming an elite violinist and winning a Nobel prize for my scientific studies, but I would outlive everyone I'd ever known. My life would fizzle into emptiness, and I'd be left alone in the bleak vastness of eternity.

I shivered. The corridors had grown gloomy and chilled while I'd been lectured in Granny's chamber, and my legs pricked with goosebumps. The cold of the stone floors seeped into my bare feet, making me think longingly of all the fluffy socks in the bottom drawer in my bedroom, back in the real world. The few narrow windows we passed revealed glimpses of shadowy landscapes, too dark to make out any details. I'd have to wait until morning to compare my surroundings to my memory of the emerald map. Mum and Dad would have to spend another night fearing the worst. My guts curled in shame. They didn't deserve the hell they were going through. If only I'd been smarter. If only I'd never gone on that stupid camping trip.

A flame flickered to life in a nearby sconce, completely by itself. My feet fell still, muscles tense, as one by one, more flames sputtered into existence, filling the corridor with dancing, orange light.

"It's alright," Pansy said, turning to see where I'd got to. "It's just a spell."

The magical version of streetlights, I supposed, coming to life at dusk. I rolled my shoulders, peeling my gaze from the nearest sconce. "I can't make myself believe any of this is real."

Pansy gave an understanding nod. "It can't be easy. Is it true there's no magic at all in your world?"

"Yeah." I gulped. What had the witches said? That fae magic was weaker on my side? Weaker, but not non-existent. Were all the old wives tales and superstitions founded in a shred of truth? Had magical creatures once walked among us?

"Bizarre. I couldn't live without magic."

"Pansy?"

The witch turned her round, chocolate button eyes on me.

"What exactly is a fae?"

"You don't know?" I'd been accused of a lot of ignorance since my arrival at Sage's door, but Pansy's words didn't carry any judgement, only fizzing excitement. "Mother above, no wonder you're quiet. Come with me."

She seized my hand and tugged me down the now glowing corridor.

"Where are we going?"

"You'll see."

Down a flight of stairs and into another hall we went. The scent of something delicious cooking hung in the air, and witches milled around, talking amongst themselves. One did a double take as Pansy and I passed. Silence spread from her like a wave, blanketing the entire hall. My pace slowed as I glanced around. Every set of eyes was trained on me. My ears heated at the attention, at the mouths hung open in surprise, at the expressions of blatant awe.

"Ignore it," Pansy hissed at my side tugging me along. "It's been a long time since they've seen a human. Some of them never have."

My face was burning by the time we emerged into another corridor. My chilled feet sank into a long plush rug carpeting the length of the passage, and the tension in my muscles eased in response.

"This is the gallery," Pansy announced. "There are paintings of all our most exceptional witches, dating back thousands of years."

What did this have to do with anything? I thought longingly of the cloud-like bed waiting in my suite, of the solitude that would allow me to form a plan. The witches had thoroughly rejected my arguments for going home, insisting that I had to wake the princes and marry the eldest brother. Become an immortal queen of the fae. Their reward was almost as off putting as the task they'd set me. I had no desire to marry a stranger, however rich and magical. I would have to form my own escape plan, and the sooner I began, the better.

Pansy dragged me along the corridor, pausing to admire the witches gazing haughtily down at us.

"There's Granny," Pansy said in a hushed whisper, as though the old bat was hanging from the rafters, listening to every word we said. "When she was young."

I studied the painting, wondering how such a bright eyed, round cheeked beauty had withered into such an intolerable heap of crêpe.

"And there's an empty space here. That's for Sage."

"Sage? Why?"

"Well, it's not confirmed, but everyone says she'll take over as High Priestess when Granny… dies." Pansy swallowed audibly.

I could just picture Sage in Granny's chair, passing judgement over all the world.

"But look at this one, this is what I really wanted to show you." Pansy seized my hand and led me further down the corridor, past several paintings. "There."

I followed her pointing finger.

Two young, handsome faces stared down at me. Identical twins, and the only men I'd seen in the gallery. Both had matching shocks of dark, floppy hair, and piercing pale green eyes. Both faces looked as though they'd been carved by angels, but my attention snagged on the silver circlet perched atop one dark head. A crown.

"Are these—"

"The fae princes." Pansy gave me a sly smile. "Handsome, aren't they?"

Damn her, but they were. Handsome was an understatement. They were… breathtaking. If this was an accurate representation of the fae, it was no wonder droves of women had gone to their deaths for their chance to marry one. They were almost human in appearance, but their ethereal beauty and pointed ears marked them as *other*. Had such creatures once walked in my world, enchanting unsuspecting humans?

"That's Anwir." Pansy indicated to the crowned man. "He's the rightful king."

My promised reward. Anwir smiled down at me from under his crown, his grin slightly lopsided, but all the more alluring for it. His eyes were bright with what I imagined was mischief. He looked the sort to have a sharp tongue and an even sharper sense of humour. Trouble, in other words. I shifted my gaze to the younger one.

"What's his name?"

"Idris."

Idris, in contrast to his brother, looked sullen. His head was angled in a way that had him staring from under a frown, but he was beautiful all the same. My eyes slid back to the spellbinding elder prince.

"Wow," I breathed, all the confession I was going to make. "They don't make men like that where I come from." They didn't make *anyone* like that where I came from, not even princes.

"Males," Pansy corrected. "Fae prefer to be known as male, or female. Man and woman are human terms."

With a face like that, I'd call him anything he asked me to.

He possessed an other-worldly beauty, like some higher being. I wouldn't have been surprised if the princes sprouted feathered wings and stripped to loincloths. A blush crept up my neck. What would I look like on the arm of *Anwir*? Like a pig fresh from a sty, no doubt. I'd never lacked confidence, content with my looks, but next to such perfection... No human stood a chance, especially not me. Every little flaw would be magnified to a hideous deformity.

It was a good thing I had absolutely no intentions of marrying anybody, least of all a fae runway model. An angel, or perhaps a demon if that smile was anything to go by. A heartbreakingly beautiful demon. I tore my gaze from the painting.

"I'm a bit tired."

Pansy looked crestfallen. "Oh. Of course, follow me."

I followed the witch back through the castle, my thoughts of escape warring with mysterious, pale eyes and lop-sided grins.

Back in the solitude of my fairytale room, Pansy lit the candles before disappearing through a door. The hiss of running water drifted through the gap, and when the witch reappeared a few minutes later, she came in a cloud of fragrant steam.

"Is it alright if I check your wounds before I go?"

I blinked, flexing my fingers. Apart from the slightly annoying bulk of the bandages, I'd almost forgotten my cuts and bruises. No pain, not even the slightest sting or ache, answered the movement. And my knee... when I bent it experimentally... nothing. Just a normal knee, stiff only due to the dressing.

Dumbfounded, I sank into the nearest chair, stretching out my leg. The witch knelt, tiny, warm hands brushing my skin as she unravelled the bandage. It fell away, and she procured a cloth from inside her apron pocket, gently wiping away the thick green paste Sage had made.

Smooth, pink skin was all that lay beneath. No grazes, no bruising, just skin.

"Impossible..." I muttered under my breath, straightening my leg.

I could see where the cut had been; the skin was definitely new, soft and pink like a newborn's, but otherwise, it was perfect.

Pansy glanced up at me. "Do you not have anything like this in the human world?"

No, we certainly did not. I shook my head, my mind reeled. The things I could do with that paste. Would it work on surgery wounds? Take away the need for the cone of shame? And humans. The hospitals would go mad to get their hands on this stuff.

"Your hands?"

I shoved both hands at Pansy, keen to see what miracles had been worked on my ruined nails. The bandages couldn't unravel fast enough, but lo and behold, within minutes, I was admiring my perfectly uninjured hands, complete with neat, strong nails.

"What's in that stuff?" I breathed.

Pansy laughed, rising to her feet. "It's Sage's own recipe, but it's all natural. Your bath should have run by now. You'll find everything you need laid out. Get some rest."

Pansy headed out into the corridor, half closing the door but continuing to talk through the gap. "I'll see you in the morning."

"See you later." I wasn't exactly sure how my foggy, battered brain managed to string the words together when it was so full of that painted map, magical healing creams, and handsome princes with crooked smiles.

No sooner had the door clicked shut than I darted for the desk tucked under a tall window, tripping over my feet in my hurry. Dragging open the drawers, I laughed in relief at the sight of crisp sheets of paper laid within. I snatched up the black quill and unscrewed the ink pot. I couldn't pretend I'd ever used such outdated writing implements before, but I'd seen enough movies to have some idea. Dipping the quill, I began to draw.

When I was finished, I leaned back in my chair and admired my work. I was no artist, and geography wasn't my strong suit, but my map was a passable copy of the emerald one. I'd drawn as many landmarks as I could remember, but the western portion was sparse due to my inattentiveness. It didn't matter though; it was The Blood Gate I needed. I stared and stared at the little black blotch that would lead me home.

When I finally padded to the bathroom, intent on washing away the grime of my ordeal and the new splotches of ink staining my miraculously healed fingers, I was once more stunned into silence. It wasn't a bath, not like the ones at home. It wasn't white, or porcelain, or even really a tub. An enormous half-boulder of palest pink crystal glinted by the light of countless candles scattered around the chamber, its edges raw and unpolished. Curls of steam rose from the carved hollow, large and deep enough to comfortably hold two people. Tentative feet carried me closer, and I peered inside. Milky water, dotted with rose petals, swirled gently inside the smooth centre of the crystal. I dragged my fingers through the hot, silky water, as an alluring scent drifted to my nose. Jasmine, I guessed, or something like it. On the thick sides of the bath, a stack of fluffy towels and an assortment of glass bottles waited. I didn't need telling twice. Stripping off my filthy garments, I sank beneath the waters.

The heat dragged a gasp from me as I stretched my legs. It was a luxury I hadn't experienced for many years. I'd grown too tall for the little bathtub back home at approximately ten years old, and since then, I'd been forced to fold my long legs into increasingly uncomfortable angles, never able to fully submerge myself. Eventually, I'd given up altogether and settled for showers.

Taking a deep breath, I sank beneath the surface. Hot water hugged every inch of my body, and my hair wafted around my head, as light as air, drifting like seaweed. It would have made the perfect photograph; a pastel rainbow wafting in a tub of pink crystal.

It was heaven. No bath I'd ever had could compare. Even my pulse, beating steadily under my skin, had slowed. Dramatically, actually. I scowled, counting. The faint throbs came dangerously slowly. I surged upward, setting water sloshing against the crystal and spilling onto the tiles with a slap. My fingers went straight to my wrist. The last thing I needed now was to finally succumb to the death I'd narrowly avoided, not when I was hatching a plan of escape.

A few seconds of counting confirmed that my pulse was normal, if slightly elevated. Certainly not the sluggish funeral beat of impending oblivion I thought I'd felt...

As the disturbed water stilled, the lazy thrum returned, a faint rhythm humming over my submerged skin. Not my pulse at all. My eyes grew wide, and I held my breath, my attention narrowing to the sensation. If not me, what was it? Could it be... magic?

Only this morning, I would have rolled my eyes at the notion, but with my miraculously healed skin glaring up at me, with the memory of Sage's portal, and fairies, and creepy, wispy shadow men fresh in my mind, I wasn't nearly as dismissive as I should have been. Was it some sort of potion mixed into the water, making it hum, or even the magic of the crystal tub? I couldn't pretend I'd paid much attention to the crystal craze that had swept my world, seeing vending machines full of pretty rocks spring up in the unlikeliest of places. Was it normal for crystals to have their own pulse? If I hadn't been frozen in wary disbelief, I might have laughed at myself for thinking such nonsense, but...

Magic was real. Witches were real. Curses were real. Was it that far-fetched to believe that crystals had powers?

Whatever it was, the minutes ticked by, and the odd sensation did nothing to harm me. In fact, the tension in my muscles dissolved into the water. Who cared about magic and crystals when heat seeped into my bones, easing the knots and aches away?

Unable to resist the lure of a full body soak, I sank back, resting my head against the smooth innards of the crystal. Water lapped at my jaw. God, I needed this. I drifted for a while, my relaxation so complete that barely a thought crossed my mind, but eventually, the bottles Pansy had left beckoned, each one filled with thick, pearly liquids. More of Sage's recipes? The bottles gave little away, though I found one with the consistency of shampoo, and rubbed it into my hair, breathing deep the luxurious floral scent.

At last, clean and obscenely relaxed, I left the magic tub, dried myself and wrapped my hair, before donning a silk robe trimmed with lace and heading back to the main room. It seemed a shame to put my dirty clothes back on when I smelt like an expensive bouquet.

To my surprise, I found a dinner tray and a neat little pile of clothes laid on my pristinely made bed. Had Pansy returned while I floated in a bath fit for a queen?

My stomach grumbled loudly.

"I know, I know," I muttered, massaging the deep ache in my belly. "Give me a minute."

The clothes laid on the bed were not my own, but I lifted the soft fabric, and the folds tumbled away to reveal a nightdress of palest lilac. Where had it come from? It certainly smelled new. I glanced at my grimy shorts, then stripped off my robe and donned the dress. It fit perfectly, hugging my curves as though it had been made for me alone, the skirt skimming my hips and falling elegantly to my calves.

I turned my attention to my dinner. A cloche covered plate, cutlery and steaming pot of tea awaited me on a tray, along with a dainty cup and saucer. I thought sadly of my enormous mugs back home. Nothing was right in this world. Still, tea was tea, and I was in dire need of it after the day I'd had. I lifted the cloche, freeing a plume of fragrant steam. My heart sank at the sight awaiting me.

Steak.

A beautifully cooked one, to be fair, but steak nonetheless. I'd been a vegetarian since the age of seven, roughly around the time I'd made the connection between the chicken on my plate and my feathery little friends at the farm Mum took me to visit. Maybe I should have mentioned something to the witches, but it had slipped my mind amongst all the saving the world stuff.

Thank God for side dishes. A hearty stack of new potatoes and a mound of green beans and roasted tomatoes would ease the ache in my belly. When had I last eaten a real meal? Had it been the barbeque at the campsite, the night before we visited the caves? Sage's jam and bread didn't count, and those blackberries definitely didn't.

I ate my dinner right there on the end of my bed, wolfing it down without pausing to taste it. By the time my plate was clear of vegetables, my stomach was warm and heavy, as were my eyelids. I transferred my tray to the coffee table in the sitting area of my room and began the seemingly endless task of blowing out the candles. No doubt the witches could have extinguished them with a snap of their fingers. When only the one on my nightstand remained, I crawled into bed. The cool, crisp sheets against my freshly bathed skin dragged a soft sigh from me as I nestled into the pillows. With one last puff of breath, I was plunged into darkness.

The nostalgic scent of candle smoke drifted up my nose, reminding me of birthday cake and happier, easier times. My birthday was still two months away. I had plenty of time. I'd find a way to escape Neath and get home with weeks to spare. Maybe I'd have a party. Twenty-five wasn't an important milestone, but I wasn't going to miss a single opportunity to spend time with the people I loved. I would take nothing for granted.

My eyes drifted closed, the knots in my muscles easing as I envisioned the celebration. I'd have an enormous cake. Maybe even party hats, for old times' sake. Metallic cones topped with coiling ribbons and pom poms. I'd wear a crown...

My crown was much heavier than I expected. It made my neck ache with the strain of holding my head aloft. The weight lifted, easing from my scalp, and I breathed a sigh of relief, rolling my head from side to side. A heavy clink sounded nearby, but before I had time to look for my expensive headwear, a set of large hands closed around my trapezius muscles, kneading and rolling the tension away with body melting pressure.

I moaned into the mattress. Had I been lying down the whole time? Naked?

Those clever hands swept down my slick spine in heavy, lazy strokes, unhindered by any hint of fabric. Whose hands were they anyway? I didn't care, actually, as long as they kept working their magic. When they reached my waist, they veered off course, dragging over the tickly spots below my ribs. I squirmed, flinching away. I hated being tickled.

Teeth clamped between my shoulder and my neck. Sharp teeth, threatening pain, like cat claws primed to pierce flesh. With a gasp, I fell still. Something loomed over me, hovering over my back. What? *Who*? Warm breath fanned over my skin, pinned between the clamp of vicious jaws, but then the pinch disappeared, replaced by a hot, wet tongue, lapping away any hint of pain. The contrast of sensations had my eyes rolling back in my skull, and I stopped caring about anything at all.

A hand slid around my throat, large enough to cover my entire neck as it arched my head back with gentle force. The teeth returned, nibbling at the lobe of my ear. My skin burst to life in an explosion of tingles that robbed me of my breath. Every inch of my body thrummed in response to those teeth, to every nip, to the tiny licks and kisses that interspersed them. In my peripheral vision I glimpsed skin as pale as moonlight and hair black as the night, topped with a silver circlet. I knew him after all. I'd seen him smiling down at me with his lop-sided grin. I was supposed to be his. Why had I ever resisted the idea?

The hand around my neck tightened slightly, not enough to hurt, but enough to claim.

I didn't need to be claimed. I wasn't going anywhere.

9

There Goes My Escape Plan

An enormous crash shattered my devilish visions of fae princes. With a ragged gasp I lurched upright. Darkness pressed against me, obliterating my senses, and hiding the world. Rapid footsteps thudded toward me, bringing a glaring light that scorched my retinas.

"Isobel!" I snapped, screwing my eyes shut and shying away from the beam. "Turn off the torch!"

Instead of unyielding rock, something soft and warm shifted beneath me. A mattress. I wasn't in the cave at all, and Isobel wasn't waving her torch around without a care in the world for my vision. My thundering heart sank to the pit of my stomach as glimpses of the past day came back to me.

"Aliza, you have to get up."

Light glared against my closed eyelids. "What?"

"Come on, quick. We have to hide."

Hide? Why? What? Glimpses of my dream came back to me. A hand around my neck. Sharp teeth. The prince. Had he come for us? Were we hiding from him? No, that couldn't be right. He was cursed, and I was supposed to save *him*.

I peeped through a crack in my eyelids. Pansy's eyes stared back at me, ringed with white and brimming with fear. Her clammy hand closed around mine and she hauled me unceremoniously from the bed.

"Can't see," I muttered, stumbling over the duvet that had been dragged with me.

Pansy didn't put out the light or offer an explanation. Instead, she tightened her grip on my hand and led me in a blind rush across the room. My bare feet scuffed the stone floor and tripped on rugs before finally slapping against the smooth cold of tiles. The faint scent of jasmine drifted up my nose. The bathroom.

"Pansy, what's going on?" I dared to open my eyes wider. The light, though still bright, no longer threatened the permanent loss of my vision.

The sky outside the bare window was still fully black, and the glass reflected my dishevelled self and Pansy's terror-stricken face with the clarity of a mirror.

"Get into the bath."

"What?"

"Now, Aliza!"

I hadn't imagined Pansy, sweet little thing that she was, to be capable of shouting. I lurched into action, hopping obediently into the empty crystal basin without another thought of protest. At once, the witch began circling the tub in short, hurried steps, muttering incoherently all the while. Her light came from an ornate lantern, swinging from one hand. The other hand sprinkled powder of some sort in a circular trail. I held my torrent of questions at bay and stayed silent apart from my thundering heart and shallow breaths. Was this normal witch behaviour? Some fun sleepover ritual? It had to be. They'd promised that Nairsgarth castle was safe. Any moment now,

Pansy would smile and explain it all. Maybe it was an initiation into the coven.

No matter what explanations my sleep logged brain offered up, I couldn't quell my unease, not when Pansy's face told me everything I needed to know.

This, whatever it was, was bad.

I shivered, wrapping my arms around myself and thinking longingly of the duvet left in a heap beside my bed. I didn't dare ask if I could retrieve it, or even just my robe.

Pansy finished her muttering and vaulted into the tub. At last, her eyes lifted to mine. I didn't bother to repeat my questions.

"The castle is under attack," she whispered. "Maelgwyn has sent his shades."

"Shades?" I parroted, a chill skating down my spine. The same shades I'd narrowly avoided on my first night in Neath? The ones Jacques had warned me of? I glanced to the dark corners of the cavernous bathroom, where Pansy's light failed to penetrate the shadows. Nothing stirred, thank God. Not yet, anyway.

The witch nodded. "Creatures of shadow. They travel by darkness. They're immune to wards and weapons. We have no way to fight them off."

Okay, so this was *really* bad.

"All we can do is wait for it to end and pray."

Well, I wouldn't be doing the latter, no matter how dire the situation. Then again, if witches and fairies were real, why not gods? I glanced around again. The bathroom was empty but for us. "Where are the other witches?"

"Hiding, with any luck." Pansy sank down, crossing her legs. The lantern rattled as she placed it on the bottom of the tub with quaking hands. My heart forgot to beat as the flame guttered, plunging low, but it recovered, bathing the room in light.

I sat opposite Pansy, trying not to envy the knitted dressing gown she wore over her nightdress, or the slippers on her feet. The cold, smooth crystal nipped at the bare skin of my legs and seeped through the thin fabric of my nightdress, chilling my backside.

"My mother woke me," Pansy continued in hushed tones. "This is her lantern. It's not enough to stop them on its own, but combined with the protection circle, it should repel them."

Should. The word did nothing to comfort me. "What happens if it's not enough?"

The witch's plump lips thinned, and she held my gaze for a long moment before answering. "The shades come at night and take people from their beds. Usually fae, but sometimes witches. They never come back. Nobody really knows what happens to them, but knowing Maelgwyn..."

She didn't need to finish her sentence. The other witches had mentioned children being taken from their beds to be *used* by Maelgwyn. I'd only discovered the sorcerer's existence a few hours ago, but I'd heard enough that my imagination ran rampant with ideas of what 'used' might mean, each worse than the last. I shivered, opening my mouth to ask another question, but my words dried up on my tongue.

The darkness at the edges of the room swelled and grew, spreading across the floor like fingers of smoke. Pansy gave a tiny, squeaking gasp and huddled in on herself, eyes screwed shut. I did no such thing. Paralysed by fear, I stared open-mouthed as the shadow rose into the air, the hairs on my arms rising with it as it shifted into a vaguely human form. Glowing, white eyes sparked to life, and though they were devoid of pupils, the shudder in my soul told me the shade looked straight back at me.

I couldn't move. Couldn't breathe. All I could do was stare into those glaring, white eyes.

Maybe it was because I was huddled at the bottom of a bath, or maybe it was because I had a vague idea of what the creature was capable of, but it seemed much larger than the one I'd spotted on the riverbank. It towered over us, a shifting shape of dense darkness.

Worst of all, it wasn't alone. Identical, wispy figures rose from the floor all around us, their impossible forms wafting like smoke. They drifted to the tub, pressing close, shoulder to gently whirling shoulder. Were they smoke or shadow? How could they exist? Why were they here?

Many blank eyes drank in the sight of us. They clamoured closer, crowding my end of the tub, their shadows merging. Were they after *me*?

God, no. This was the last thing I needed. Pansy's protection circle seemed incredibly feeble as the wall of shades grew denser, blocking everything beyond the tub. A ring of darkness, with only a sprinkle of powder and a skittering flame preventing them from snatching me away.

What would become of me if the murderous, human-hating king got his hands on me?

The nearest shade grew denser, its shadows bordering on solid form. What was, unmistakably, a claw like hand lifted, reaching for me.

With a shuddering gasp, I leaned away, only to remember my assailant's fellows on my far side.

Shit. This was it. This was how I died. Somehow, I couldn't tear my horrified eyes away as death itself reached for me.

The shade's hand sizzled as its fingers crossed the circle, and the beast snatched it back, letting out a hideous hiss.

Fervent relief surged through my terror. It worked. Pansy's magic worked.

The witch began muttering again, rocking back and forth. Whatever she said only seemed to aggravate the monsters. The tendrils drifting from them snapped and jerked, like flames caught in the wind. Another drawn-out hiss sent a shiver streaking down my spine.

The shades grew agitated, their coiling and furling movements becoming sharper, as though a brisk wind tugged at them. They faded back a step, circling the tub. Were they searching for a way through Pansy's protection circle? Was the light not strong enough to drive them away?

I glanced again at the dark window. No hint of dawn offered to save us from whatever fate the shades had in store. Hours of night lay ahead. Shuffling closer to Pansy and the lantern, I reached for the witch's hands. She clamped her small yet surprisingly strong fingers around mine and squeezed.

Please, I begged a god I didn't believe in. *Please make them go away. Don't let us die.*

If there was an old man in the sky looking down on us, I had no right to ask him for anything. I didn't believe a word of any religion. I scoffed at it. I believed in science. As far as I knew, witches were the natural enemy of the church, but there I was, clinging to Pansy and praying for our survival while monsters swarmed around a giant magic crystal. The pope would burn me at the stake for this.

My pulse thudding in my ears was my only indication of time passing us by. A drumbeat, leading us to morning, to the safety of sunshine. I focused on the sound, letting it ground me with its insistent reminder that I was still alive, somehow. At times, I could have sworn an echoing beat answered from the crystal pressed against my skin.

The shades made no further attempts to reach me as time slithered by. I tried to resist the urge, when my eyes slid sideways. My heart swelled with hope. Most of the monsters had vanished, faded back to wherever they'd come from. Only three remained. One lingered nearby, maintaining its vigil, but the other two meandered closer to the dark edges of the bathroom. Even as I watched, one faded out of existence as though it had never been. Maybe it hadn't. Maybe this was all one drawn-out, hellish nightmare.

No. Even I couldn't convince myself of that anymore.

I squeezed Pansy's hands again, as real as my own. As much as I didn't want to accept it, this was my life now. No amount of wishing or pretending or even praying would get me out of it. Only action. I had to get home. I couldn't survive another night like this one. I wanted my normal life back, where the only things keeping me from sleep were assessment jitters or handsome men. Plan or not, I was leaving. When the sun rose, I'd take my map and knife, and I'd make for the Blood Gate, which I would find open. The witches had to have lied about them being sealed. I would *not* live like this. I would find my way home.

With a faint hiss of frustration, the nearest shade jerked away, its shadows whipping. It sank into the depths of darkness clinging to the corners and disappeared. On the far side of the bathroom, its companion followed suit.

"Pansy," I croaked through my tight throat. "They've gone."

My unlikely friend snapped her head up, staring around as though she doubted my words. "Thank the Mother," she breathed, her hushed voice dripping with relief. "I thought they would be the end of us."

I eased into a new position, stretching my stiff, trembling limbs. "Does this happen often?"

Pansy shook her head. "Not here. Never in my lifetime."

Should I be relieved or concerned that the first attack on Nairsgarth had happened the very same day I'd arrived at the castle? Could it be a coincidence that the loony human-hating king would send his minions to the bathroom of the only human to set foot in these lands in centuries? I shivered again.

"Let's hope it doesn't happen for another few hundred years. Are they gone? For real? Can we get up?"

"I'm not sure." Pansy glanced over her shoulder. "What if they come back? Maybe we should just stay here until morning."

I was far from brave, but the thought of sitting in a cold, empty rock until daybreak was almost as terrifying as the shades. Sleeping in a tree had been bad enough. "No, I saw them leave, and besides, we have the lantern. Come on. Let's find the others."

If the shades did return, I'd rather have the protection of the entire coven over one relatively young witch.

Pansy opened her mouth as though she wanted to argue but instead, she peered around the innocently empty bathroom before rising to her feet, clutching the lantern. "Alright, but stay close to me. Don't stray into the shadows."

Trying hard not to imagine what it would be like to have the dark edges of the corridors swell around me and whisk me off to a grizzly, unknown fate, I clambered awkwardly from the tub, leaving the protection of Pansy's circle behind. Nothing rushed out to grab me.

The witch spoke in those strange words she'd used earlier, no language I'd ever heard, and followed me.

"What powder did you use for the spell?" I asked as we crept back to the bedroom, shoulder to shoulder.

"Salt from the Emrallt Sea. It's the best you can get, very powerful, but any will do in a pinch."

Would I ever recover from this ordeal, or would Pansy's information prove useful to me? Would I go back home, only to become paranoid and afraid of my own shadow? What would Mum think when she found circles of table salt all over the house and crystals on every surface?

Mercifully, my dark room was completely devoid of creepy shadow men. I tugged Pansy to my bedside, sliding my freezing feet into my slippers and donning my robe, glancing over my shoulder all the while.

"Emrallt? Is that the one I can see from my window?" Why was I asking when I didn't care in the slightest? To ease my frazzled nerves, or distract Pansy from hers?

"Yes. That's why the coven originally settled here, thousands of years ago. The area makes our magic more powerful."

"That's handy." I only half-heard the reply leaving my lips. My galloping heart drowned out everything else with its incessant drum roll.

Our slippers scuffed as we shuffled out into the corridor. To my relief, candles gleamed in all the sconces, and Pansy and I huddled our way through their skittish light. We lapsed into silence, but somehow ended up clasping hands again as we crept along the deserted corridors. With every corner, every gloomy alcove, my muscles clenched, braced for an attack from an otherworldly being, but all was quiet and still. Unnervingly so.

Pansy led the way down to the bottom levels of the castle, and narrower, tunnel-like corridors.

"My room is down here," she whispered. "It's not much. We're supposed to get better quarters as we progress, and younger witches take up the basic rooms. But there are no younger witches, not any-more."

The plain doors lining the corridor were all firmly closed, most with light beaming under the gaps. Hopefully that meant the inhabitants were safe.

"This is m–oh..."

A little way ahead, a door stood open. Pansy stumbled to a halt, holding her lantern aloft. The light washed over the otherwise dark room, revealing the carnage within. Covers were torn off the bed, baring a slashed mattress, its feathery guts spilling over the sheets. Colourful cushions littered the floor, and a chest of drawers lay on its side, its contents pooled around it like the blood of a fallen soldier.

"Pansy!"

I almost leapt clean out of my slippers at the shriek echoing along the corridor. I snapped my head around to find Hyacinth barrelling toward us, eyes wild. The witches collided, forcing me to concede a step, but I lingered closer than I might usually have done. Though I'd seen no hint of a shade on our journey here, I wasn't sure I'd ever leave the little patch of lantern light ever again.

"Mother." The lantern's glow dipped as Pansy hugged the older woman, clinging to her as though her life depended on it. "You're alright."

Hyacinth stepped back, gripping Pansy by the shoulders and examining her. "I came by your room and saw I've been worried half to death–I thought I told you to hide!"

"I did! I hid with Aliza."

Hyacinth threw a glance at me. I returned it with a shifty smile and a small wave.

"She was alone, Mother. She's new here, and she had no idea what to expect or do. Nobody but me thought to go to her. The shades were in her room! We've only just found her, and we could have lost her on the first night! You said it yourself, she's our only–"

"Alright, dear, it's alright," Hyacinth interrupted her daughter's increasingly hysterical tirade. "You're safe, and so is Aliza, that's all that matters. I just had a fright when I saw the state of your room. I thought..."

She thought Pansy had been taken. My eyes slid back to the trashed room. Hyacinth's fears could have easily been the truth. Pansy could have been, even now, enduring some God-awful fate, never to be seen again. My guts twisted at the thought. I barely knew the witch, but I liked her. She was cheerful and sweet, and she'd risked her own safety to protect me. What if she hadn't bothered? Would those monsters have crept from my bathroom to find me sleeping, unaware and unprotected? Would I have woken to find them towering over me, surrounding my bed, or would I have died in my sleep without ever having the chance to make it home?

My shudder had nothing to do with the chilly night air.

"What of the others?" Pansy asked, drawing my attention from the slashed mattress. "Is everyone safe?"

Hyacinth's brown skin paled slightly, her brow puckering. "I'm afraid not. Three were taken."

Pansy pressed a hand to her mouth, stifling a shuddering gasp. "Who?"

"Rosemary, Lavender and Daisy."

I wracked my brain, but the names meant nothing to me. Whoever the victims were, they hadn't been present at my curse induction. That didn't mean they weren't real women though. Real women who could very well be as gutted as Pansy's mattress. The knot in my stomach tightened.

"How do we save them?" My voice came out small and hoarse, but the knowledge that three witches were suffering steadied me, strangely. It made things clearer. Helping them was the only thing to be done, but how?

Hyacinth's gaze softened as she turned it on me, her lips pressing together in a sympathetic smile. "We don't. They are beyond our reach now."

I didn't mean to laugh, but the scornful scoff burst from my lips anyway. "That's it then? We just give up?"

The idea was ludicrous. There was almost always something to be done. Some course of action to at least *try*, however bleak the outlook.

"It is not a matter of giving up, Aliza–"

"Has anyone ever tried to get people back from the shades? They can't just disappear. There has to be something we can do."

"Oh, there is," Hyacinth agreed earnestly. "But it will not make a difference to those we have lost tonight. It will, however, save countless innocent lives in future."

My argument dried up in the face of what was coming next. The answer. The experimental solution, untried and undesirable, but the last hope. Like a rabbit in the headlights, I waited for the blow to fall.

"Prince Anwir is the only known wielder of lightning magic, which, incidentally, is the one brand of weapon effective against the shades. Only he can kill them. The curse must be broken, Aliza. There is no other way."

My tongue stuck to the roof of my mouth, damming whatever excuses might otherwise find their way out.

The two witches watched me, as though waiting for an answer to what hadn't sounded like a question.

Along the corridor, doors creaked open and wary faces peeped out. Innocent faces. Any of them might have been lost tonight, might still be lost in the future. It could have been Pansy. It shouldn't have been possible for shadow to slash fabric, but the evidence was undeniable. What if Pansy had been in her bed tonight? Would something other than feathers have been spilt? This was bigger than me. Bigger than my parents. How could I turn my back on an entire *world*?

"Okay." I nodded stiffly. "Okay, let's break this curse."

10

The Witch Is A Bitch

I didn't sleep again that night. Nobody did. The coven was a hive of activity, preparing for my noble quest. Dawn's golden light was creeping across my room, making the rekindled candles useless when Pansy appeared, bearing a woven basket propped on her hip.

"Clothes," she announced, depositing the basket on my bed. "For the expedition."

This was it then. It was really happening. Reluctantly, I uncurled myself from the armchair by the fire and crossed to the bed. I hadn't fancied putting my feet on the floor where a lurking shade might grab them, but now the sun had risen, I had one less thing to fear.

Yeah right. I was heading out into a world ruled by a human hating king, where monsters would stalk my every step, intent on my blood. I was supposed to break a curse that had claimed the lives of countless other people. There was every reason to be afraid. Terrified. To change my mind and make a run for the rift.

But shades were real. Magic was real. As unbelievable as any of it was, I could no longer deny that the witches had told the truth, which meant the rifts were sealed. Even if I made it to the Blood Gate alive, I would only find the way barred. What choice did I have? Had there ever been a choice at all?

Even if the rifts had been wide open, could I really leave Neath to its fate? Leave its people to suffer? The tick of the clock on the mantlepiece, barely noticeable yesterday, had boomed like a gong through the hours following the attack, rattling around my head. Three witches gone, as easily as that. Were they dead yet, or did the king have a worse fate in store for them? Vet school had taught me that death wasn't always the worst case scenario. Some things were not meant to be endured. Did every passing second bring a new wave of suffering upon those three witches? I had a chance to put a stop to this. How could I turn away?

On the other hand, every hour that passed meant my parents' torment grew. Had they given up hope yet? I couldn't see it. Even if I never found my way back, which I *would*, they wouldn't give up. Even if I were here until well beyond middle age, Dad would still print missing person posters with my twenty-four-year-old face plastered across them, begging for information from anyone who would listen. Mum would keep my room clean, never changing anything, ready for my return at a moment's notice. Did they worry that I was rotting in a dark cave somewhere, or worse, did they think I'd been snatched, spirited away to meet a grisly end in some weirdo's cellar? My stomach knotted, writhing like maggots at the thought of what they must be enduring at this very moment. At least with the witches it was abstract. With Mum and Dad, it was all too easy to picture every harrowing moment.

"Are you alright?"

I blinked rapidly, clearing away the scenes unfolding in my mind. Pansy stared up at me, her doe eyes ringed in shadows. It robbed her of some of her youthful looks, or maybe that was the horror we had endured together.

"Just tired," I lied, forcing a small smile. "What are you wearing?"

For the first time, I noticed her outfit. Gone was the quaint dress of yesterday, the old-fashioned nightgown of last night. Instead, she wore a collarless shirt and trousers in muted shades of green and brown, the colours merging and weaving in a sort of organic wave. Witch camouflage. Chunky soled brown boots came up to her knee, a far cry from the dainty pumps she'd favoured the day before.

Her smile was slightly more enthusiastic than the one I'd managed. "Do you like it? It's my quest outfit. I managed to talk Mother into letting me come along. I played on the whole 'history in the making' and 'I'll be safer with you' thing."

My heart tried to sink and leap at the same time, resulting in a strange flopping sensation in my chest. I didn't know who else was coming along, but I had a vague idea of the dangers awaiting my team, and I didn't believe for a minute that Pansy would be safe anywhere near me, even if her mother was there. At the same time, a friendly face, a...*friend*, could be exactly what I needed to get me through whatever lay ahead.

"It looks great." Great wasn't an accurate description, but I could see how the patterns and colours would provide protection. It wasn't entirely dissimilar to zebra stripes. Not that it would hide me. My colourful hair would be a beacon, and for the first time in the years since I'd picked up the bleach, I felt a twinge of regret. My natural dark blonde, boring as it was, would have been less noticeable in a landscape of grass and trees. "Hyacinth is your mother, right?"

I already knew the answer after witnessing their reunion, but I needed a distraction. Something to take my mind off my looming, impossible task.

Pansy rolled her eyes. "Yes. Do not tell me how much I look like her, it's all I ever hear."

My laugh was brittle but genuine. "It could be worse. Everyone tells me I look like my dad."

Too late, I realised that Pansy's own dad was probably long dead. He had been human, after all. But if I'd offended or upset her, she didn't let it show. I risked probing further. "Witches breed with humans, yeah?"

"That's right." The witch looked... proud. Impressed that I'd bothered to listen, maybe. She laughed. "It's been problematic in recent years. The coven is half the size it once was, and shrinking. Every winter takes more of the old ones, and the last one was particularly bad. Mother says that we won't be strong enough to defend our borders if it goes on much longer. Maybe that's why the shades attacked. Maelgwyn must know we're weakening. When the curse was first cast, the witches and fae of Tir o Gaeaf combined our powers to create wards protecting both kingdoms. They don't work against shades, but they keep Maelgwyn out. They need constant renewal. Without new witches, the wards will eventually fall."

So much for the distraction. "What about fae? You can't breed with them?" They looked human enough, in a god-like sort of way. A memory of my dream rushed to the forefront of my mind. Fangs clamped onto my shoulder, a hand around my neck. My ears heated and I shifted my feet.

Pansy sighed. "There were attempts, long ago. The babies were stillborn, every single one of them. Some were malformed. It's believed that our magics clash in a way that can't support life."

Interesting, if terrible. There had to be some tangible link between magic and genetics. It would make a fascinating study. With time and proper resources, maybe a treatment of sorts could be found. A way to counter whatever was going wrong. Maybe humans wouldn't be needed at all, though, in my experience of men, they would be more than happy to be used in such a way.

"Anyway, you'd better get dressed. Sage has us on a tight schedule." Pansy pushed the basket into my arms. She crossed the room and pulled out a tall, woven screen set near my dressing table. "I won't look."

As I draped my nightdress and robe over the top of the screen and picked up the trousers, I couldn't decide whether the fizzing in my belly was excitement or terror. These were the things I would wear to break the curse. My hero uniform. Except, I was no hero. I was just Aliza, an ordinary woman with a boring, safe life. I had a much better chance of joining the ranks of dead would-be heroes than I did of succeeding.

Guilt tightened its grip on my guts. What if I failed? It wouldn't exactly come as a surprise, but if I was the first human in centuries to cross the rift, how long would it be before another came along? How many people would suffer and die in that time? I pressed my lips together and dressed in silence. The garments, identical to Pansy's, fit perfectly and were as soft as butter. Several items remained in the basket, a blanket, a belt and some gloves. The day was shaping up to be mild, so gloves would prove useless, and I had no intention of lugging a blanket around. I left them in the basket. When I emerged from my hiding place, I couldn't help but grin as I lifted my arms to show off my outfit.

"Ooh, it looks wonderful!" Pansy said, ushering me to the mirror.

My smile faded. Not only did my hair clash horribly with the greens and browns, but my skin carried a ghostly pallor. Tiredness or dread? Whatever it was, I looked halfway to the grave already. I didn't believe in signs, but then again, I didn't believe in magic either, yet here I was.

Pansy disappeared behind the screen, leaving me to scowl at my reflection. When she emerged a moment later, she was armed with the basket. Despite my reluctance to carry it, I kept my mouth shut as she draped the blanket over my shoulder and slid in front of me, adjusting the folds and tweaking the fabric. She fastened the belt around my waist, holding the blanket in place around my shoulders, but leaving my arms free.

"There," she said. "It will keep you warm, and you can lift it over your head if it rains, and at night you can unfasten it and use it as an extra blanket. And look, gloves too."

I pulled them on obligingly. The cuffs came halfway up my bare forearms and, despite being entirely impractical, they were sort of cute. I twisted, admiring my reflection from different angles. Even I had to admit, it looked pretty good, like a costume from a movie. I could just picture myself traipsing through the woods on my epic quest. All I needed was a bow and arrow and a wolf trotting at my side.

"I love it," I said truthfully. It was better than Isobel's hideous trekking outfit, that was certain. The thought of her orange fleece brought a smile to my lips. One day soon, I'd see her again, and I would never complain about her annoying tendencies again, not unless she tried to make me go hunting for fairies. *That* would be stamped out at once.

"I'd better go and finish getting myself ready. We're leaving soon. I'll come and collect you when it's time. Bye for now!" Pansy gave an enthusiastic wave as she disappeared through the door.

I couldn't summon any of her excitement. The clock continued to tick. Somewhere, witches were dying. Were my remaining moments numbered too?

When the witches summoned me for our departure, I slipped my phone into the deep pocket on the thigh of my new trousers. I didn't know why I bothered; it hadn't shown even the faintest glimmer of life since I'd crawled out of the river, but it felt wrong to leave it behind. I knew Mum and Dad, maybe even my friends, would still be trying to call me, hoping that, this time, it would connect, and I'd answer. I held absolutely no hope of the damn thing waking up, but it was a link to home. To the people who loved me. They were just on the other side of that stubbornly dark screen.

The castle was busier than it had been yesterday. I passed several groups of witches on my way downstairs, each armed with crates stuffed full of candles. They all paused to watch me pass. Some even wished me good fortune. I offered only thin-lipped smiles in response. It would take more than a few well-intentioned words of encouragement to get me through my coming ordeal. Had I been an idiot to sign myself up for this quest? Had I signed my own death certificate?

A group of nine witches dressed in identical uniforms to my own waited in the entrance hall. Most, I didn't recognise, but Sage was among them, her blonde mane woven into a thick braid, and sure enough, Pansy beamed at me from her mother's side as I descended the stairs.

"There you are." Sage spoke with a tone suggesting she'd been kept waiting for forty minutes. She strode to meet me at the bottom of the stairs, pulling a belt from around her waist. "These are for you."

Without waiting for my consent, she strapped the belt around me, over the wrap. A pair of daggers hung at each of my hips. I extracted one from its sheath. The evil-looking blade was as black as night, though the handle, predictably, sported a large crystal in a sickly shade of green. One edge of the blade was serrated, bringing to mind images of the internal damage they would inflict if used.

"A matching pair," Sage explained, "and very old. A relic of the first fae queen, in fact. Do try not to lose them."

Lose them? I didn't even know how to use them. I knew how to handle a scalpel, but I had a niggling suspicion that hand to hand combat with twin daggers might prove slightly different. Still, heading into monster infested territory was slightly less daunting now that I was armed. With great care, I slid the blade back into place and followed Sage to the waiting group.

"You already know Sisters Hyacinth and Pansy. This is Hazel, Aspen, Clover, Laurel, Daffodil and Meadow."

The last witch was short, even by witch standards, with dark angular eyes that crinkled as she smiled at me.

I returned the gesture but didn't have the chance to speak before Sage continued. "We head for Tir o Haf. Make no mistake, the journey will be dangerous, and discretion will be vital. It is likely Maelgwyn's shades have informed him of the presence of a human here in Nairsgarth. He is likely to focus his attention on the castle, in which case, luck may be on our side if we remain undetected. Our aim is to arrive unnoticed, retrieve the princes, and leave as quickly as possible." She approached a heap of hiking packs piled near the bannister and shouldered one. "I have my warp crystal to return us to Nairsgarth, though the princes may prefer to teleport us to Tir o Gaeaf, which would be safer in any case. Once they wake, we concede to them, but until then, Granny has placed me in charge."

Nobody voiced any reservations about Sage's appointment as group leader, so I swallowed my own complaints. The witch was efficient. Maybe that was exactly what we needed. Instead, I asked, "What about the castle? Will the shades come back?"

"Yes. Our wards have been reinforced to protect against Maelgwyn himself, and we are increasing light within the castle to guard against shades. There will be no dark corners in Nairsgarth come nightfall."

That was something, at least. The remaining witches would be safe enough, but despite Sage's plan of discretion, I couldn't find the same relief for me and my party. The sooner I broke the curse, the sooner we'd be safe. "How do you know where the princes are?"

"I don't."

My blood plummeted to my legs, leaving me cold and light-headed. "What? So, we're just going to Tir of Haf on the off chance? Shall we knock on the palace doors and ask for directions?"

Moss green eyes narrowed in my direction. "Do not mistake me for an idle-brained idiot, girl. What do you think I've been doing these past centuries?"

Stealing candy from children? Pulling wings off butterflies? Practising her not-so-resting bitch face in the mirror?

"I have been studying past attempts to break the curse, looking at what went wrong, searching for patterns and discrepancies, themes and clues. I have travelled the courts testing my theories as far as I was able without a human to–"

"Sacrifice?" I suggested.

"*Aid* me. Several decades ago, I discovered an area of Tir o Haf that bears an unusual energy. Some strange power is woven into the air. Unnatural creatures dwell there, beasts that should not exist. I believe that is where we will find the princes, though I could only progress so far without *you*."

Despite what Hyacinth had told me, I couldn't quell the hope that the lost witches would be saved if I actually broke this God-damned curse. Maybe there was still time. Still a chance.

"Okay, that sounds promising," I admitted. "Are we leaving after breakfast?"

Sage gave me a rare, sly smile, but Pansy darted to a console table, retrieving a cloth covered parcel from a stack of its fellows and handing it to me with a beaming smile. It was warm and soft.

"I assume you are able to eat and walk at the same time?" Sage asked. "This will not keep until after breakfast. Sisters, come."

Talk broke out at once as the party divided into what I assumed were friend groups. While the witches retrieved the packs, I unwrapped my parcel. The suffocating stench of charred bacon escaped the folds, and my heart sank. Inside was a fluffy flatbread wrapped around bacon, eggs and some sort of salad.

"I don't suppose there's any without meat?" I called over the clamour of activity and conversation.

Sage stiffened, and though she had her back to me, I had no problem picturing the disapproval on her face. After a moment of rigid stillness, she whipped around. "Mother above! What's wrong with the bacon?"

"Nothing, only... I'm a vegetarian. I don't eat any meat."

The witch shucked off her pack and rummaged inside one of its many compartments. She straightened, proffering a shiny, red apple. "Here."

Hyacinth laid a placating hand on her arm. "Sister Sage... Aliza needs her strength. We can afford a small delay, and I'm certain the kitchens won't mind making her a new breakfast. Besides, we will have to adjust our supplies if our human can't eat meat."

"Can't, or won't?" Sage muttered, rolling her eyes.

"Won't," I answered, my voice flat and cold. "Very definitely *won't*."

The witches needed me. I was essential to their mission, and if Sage wanted my help, she would have to play by at least some of my rules. I wouldn't stoop to ending lives just to make *her* life easier. Neither would I accept judgement from someone lacking the slightest shred of compassion.

"Inform the kitchens," Sage barked at nobody in particular.

One of the witches rushed away at her words, leaving the rest of us milling around with nothing to do but await our doom.

11

Fine, I Guess I'll Save The World

The twenty or so minutes we waited for our new supplies, including an egg and cheese wrap, may as well have been half a day judging by Sage's dark glares and scowls, but finally, we were ready. Armed with my useless phone and weapons I had no clue how to use, I followed the witches as we trooped out of the double doors and into the sunshine.

Since my arrival, I'd only seen the castle from the inside. I stared over my shoulder with more than a little awe as we crossed the grounds. Behind me, an imposing structure of yellow stone, blackened in places by age, rose into the sky. It was no fairytale palace. It was a squat, medieval-looking castle, with battlements and not enough windows, exactly what anyone would expect. Apart from me, apparently.

Maybe it was because everything else in this world was straight out of a children's book, but I'd expected impossibly tall twisting turrets, topped by flags blowing in the wind. Even so, it was still a castle. Who did I think I was? Me, Aliza, sleeping in a *castle,* and having the audacity to find it ugly? The grounds were nice though, a broad sweep of tall grass and seemingly unkempt but beautiful flowers. In the distance, a clump of trees stood dark against the blue sky, and ahead of us, a tall wall kept the monsters at bay. Most of them, anyway.

Beyond the thick castle gates, the view was dominated by rolling moors, stretching as far as the eye could see. Only a distant, dark smudge on the horizon hinted at a break in scenery. A cobbled road aimed in that general direction, and Sage set off along it at a brisk march. Her short legs covered the ground surprisingly quickly, and I soon grew warm beneath my wrap, despite the gusting, salty wind buffeting and tugging at my hair. I'd opted for a fishtail side braid, and before long, the strands around my face were blown loose, stirring and whipping in all directions. It was going to be a long and annoying walk.

"Sage. Sage!" I jogged to our leader's side, only to receive a withering glance. "Can't we use your crystal to get there?"

The witch cocked an eyebrow. "Obviously not, or we would not be walking. It is a warp crystal, which means it has been charged at a particular location. It will open a portal back to that location from anywhere in the world, but it cannot be used to travel elsewhere. My crystal returns to Nairsgarth."

"Oh." I lapsed into silence and fell back into line. It had been worth a try. Walking it was, then.

My shins were aching by the time the moors gave way to fields of crops. The dark smudge on the horizon turned out to be a village of stone cottages with thatched roofs, not dissimilar to Sage's cute little home, and my heart lifted at the sight. I'd kill for a coffee, and maybe a cake, never mind the chance to take the weight from my feet for half an hour. It was exactly the sort of countryside village that would sport a tiny teashop bedecked in pastel bunting and selling freshly baked scones.

But Sage led us around the outskirts of the settlement without as much as a breather. Beyond the village were yet more fields of crops, and then a swathe of woodland sporting gnarly, dark trees. A grim, ancient wood, no doubt full of lurking monsters. It wasn't all bad though. Cheery birdsong filled my ears. Everything was very green, with moss and ferns blanketing every surface, including the trunks and branches, and everywhere I looked, colourful fairies winked and glowed. They avoided the sparse sunbeams that managed to break through the dense canopy overhead, instead clinging to the shade of the tree trunks, drifting like fireflies, and clustering around the enormous red mushrooms with white spots that dared to break the dense mossy carpet.

Much to my own disbelief, I began to think fondly of Isobel and her endless enthusiasm. She would have bounced on the balls of her feet and reeled off a story about the unicorns who lived in the forest, or some other such lovely nonsense. She should have been the one to cross the rift, not me. She knew about legends and myths. She'd have appreciated it all a lot more than I did, and probably made a better curse breaker too.

Not that I was lacking enthusiastic companions. What Sage lacked in charisma, Pansy made up for. The witch marched along at my side, talking until she was breathless, and then talking some more. She took it upon herself to point out interesting plants and list their uses in magic. A plant tour may have been incredibly boring in the human world, but I found myself hanging on every word. Such incredible fauna would demand a fortune back home. Pharma would go *insane* to get their hands on this stuff. My head filled with fantasies of selling those magical plants to the highest bidder. I'd be able to buy a house.

Two houses. One for me, one for my parents, and they'd both be a lot nicer than the cramped three-bedroom house we currently lived in. I'd upgrade my car, maybe even open my own practise and go on several exotic holidays a year. If the rifts opened, maybe I would do exactly that. Just because I didn't want to become some simpering queen didn't mean I could never come back to this weird and, dare I say, wonderful world. Did it?

Pansy only fell quiet when, after walking until my legs had long since turned to jelly and my head swam with hunger, Sage announced it was time for a rest, and lunch made a long overdue appearance.

I flopped down on a moss-covered log and scarfed down my cheese and salad sandwich faster than any dog could have managed it. It barely made a dent in my hunger. What I'd give for a packet of crisps to chase it down with, or a big bar of chocolate, but all I had was the measly apple Sage had given me. I eyed it with longing before returning it to my pack. I'd learnt what it was to be lost and hungry, and I had no intentions of revisiting the experience.

Pansy was quieter after filling her stomach, and when we set off through the shaded woods once more, we walked in companionable silence, which turned to exhausted silence before too long. There was a path of sorts through the trees, but it was a narrow and uneven dirt track. My legs wobbled with every step, and I stumbled on more than one twisting root. Mercifully, my hiking boots had been broken in by my last trek, leaving me free of blisters, but that didn't stop my feet from throbbing.

When, at last, Sage declared it was time to stop and make camp, I could have wept with relief.

We'd come upon a little glade, and the golden light before dusk shone between the trees in glowing pillars. I threw myself to the ground in the nearest sunbeam, turning my face to the light and heaving a sigh of relief. I was slightly sweaty beneath my artfully draped blanket, but I soaked the sun into my bones, letting it ease the aches of my poor, tired body. I wasn't cut out for all this activity. Adventures weren't all they'd cracked up to be.

"Are we almost at Tir o Haf?" I asked nobody in particular. By my calculations, we'd soon come upon a mountain range that would, if I chose to follow it, lead me away from Tir o Haf, toward the southern coast and, eventually, the Blood Gate. My route home. At least, it would have been if I hadn't gotten myself roped into saving the world.

Mum and Dad were that way, but they would have to wait.

I received a chorus of chuckles in response to my question.

"Tir o Haf is the westernmost kingdom on this island," Hyacinth reminded me gently, though she still smirked at my expense. "It's a long journey. Luckily for us, we're not walking all that way."

"We're not?" I perked up at that. I knew Tir o Haf's location on my map, but I had no idea of scale. After all the walking we'd done that day, I thought it was perfectly reasonable to be close. Wherever we were, my aching legs felt as though I'd been given a curse of my own, doomed to trudge to the ends of the earth on my poor tired feet. Was it only two days ago that I'd embarked on a light, morning trek with my friends? We'd planned to be back in time for dinner. Our cool boxes had been stuffed with food for the barbeque, and a few cocktails in cans. What had become of the halloumi skewers I'd been looking forward to?

"Mother above, no. Such a journey would take weeks. Maybe even months. No child, we're heading to Tir o Gaeaf first."

I wracked my brain. If I remembered rightly, and I almost always did, then Tir o Gaeaf was the last fae kingdom standing between King Maelgwyn and the witches.

"I thought the princes were somewhere in Haf?"

Hyacinth smiled encouragingly. "We believe they are, but Tir o Gaeaf is our ally, and they can get us to where we need to be quickly and without detection."

Well, that sounded promising, even if the thought of meeting fae had my pulse quickening. I didn't know much about them, I didn't even understand what exactly they were, but they expected *me* to save them. To be their promised queen. Me, a human without magic, sent to save an entire race of powerfully magical beings who couldn't save themselves.

I stewed over such thoughts as we set up camp. One of the witches, Clover, was set to cooking our evening meal, while the rest of us pitched our little tents. They were a far cry from the spacious one I'd left back in the human world. To think, I'd scorned such a palace of canvas. I stared glumly at my dismal two-man tent. It looked like little more than a bedsheet draped over a few sticks, with barely enough room for Pansy and me to squash our sleeping rolls inside. The rolls themselves were similar to sleeping bags, only without the insulation. Just a thin layer of padding to lie on, and a blanket to fold over our shivering bodies. The mild weather would soon give way to the chill of night, and as far as I could see, we were ill-prepared. Maybe I'd need my gloves after all. It was going to be a long night. God, I hoped we'd be in Tir o Gaeaf tomorrow, even if it did mean meeting a few fae.

Supper turned out to be stew and thickly sliced bread. I wasn't sure if it was only because I was so ravenous that I thought I might faint, but it was delicious. It hadn't escaped my notice that the witches prepared me a small, separate pot filled with beans, while theirs bubbled with whatever meat they'd packed for the journey. Their act of compassion warmed me, even though Sage cast regular dark glares at my separate pot. No sooner had I handed my bowl to the poor soul ordered to wash up in a nearby stream than our leader got to her feet.

"Bedtime." Her eyes fixed on me as she spoke, as though daring me to argue. As if I would. I was dead on my feet. "Hyacinth and I will take the first watch. Meadow, Hazel, you'll take second. Everybody else, get some rest. We have another long day tomorrow, and I don't intend to be delayed again."

Ah, that was why she was glaring at me. Well, if she expected me to break this curse, she'd have to learn to tolerate me and my delays.

I crawled into my tent with Pansy close behind me. There was barely room to unfasten my belt without elbowing my companion in the ribs, but I managed it, unwrapping the blanket from my shoulders. When my boots came off, tossed carelessly at the bottom of my bed roll, I groaned with relief and flopped down onto my paper-thin bed, pulling my blankets up to my chin.

"I hope you're not too tired for these." Pansy grinned as she rummaged in her pack, pulling out a little paper bag. She handed me a fat, gooey cookie. "I convinced the kitchen to sneak me these. I thought we'd deserve a few treats."

Sleepiness forgotten, I sat up, accepting the cookie. "Ooh, thanks. I'm never too tired for dessert."

I took a bite, letting my eyes roll shut as sweetness flooded my tongue.

"Cherry and chocolate." Pansy answered my unasked question before tucking into her own cookie. "And there's more for tomorrow."

I could face another day like this one if I knew I had a treat waiting for me at the end of it.

"Has Sage always been such a bitch?" I asked at length, keeping my voice low.

Pansy snorted, her eyes darting around as though she expected the witch to burst into the tent. "Yes. Don't ever repeat this, but I think that's why Granny likes her so much."

"She'll be the perfect replacement for the old cow."

We descended into giggles, fuelled by sugar and exhaustion, until a harsh bark rang through the tent.

"Quiet!"

We fell silent, not daring to meet each other's eyes. If I so much as glanced in her direction, I'd burst into laughter again. I pressed my lips together and laid back down, closing my eyes.

Before long, Pansy's slow breathing filled the tent, and the last light of dusk faded into darkness, but tired as I was, I couldn't sleep. Even though we'd chosen a relatively smooth patch of land to pitch our tent, I felt every lump in the ground, digging into my back. The air chilled as darkness swelled, seeping through my blankets and clothes, down to my skin, and strange noises filled the night. I told myself it was only woodland creatures, coming out in search of food, but I now knew exactly what creatures lurked in these strange lands. The thought of two tired witches standing guard was not enough to soothe me.

Inevitably, as the hours crawled past, I became aware of the need to relieve myself. I ignored it for as long as possible, unwilling to leave my blankets, but eventually, I decided that if I wanted any sleep at all, I'd have to take action.

Stiff and shivering, I crawled to the bottom of the tent, wrapped my blanket around my shoulders and pulled on my boots, before easing out into the night.

Our fire still burnt, and combined with moonlight, the glade was lit well enough to see by. Would it be enough to keep Maelgwyn's shades at bay? I clambered to my feet.

At the edge of the camp, I found Meadow keeping guard. The shift had changed already. I'd lain awake longer than I thought. Ignoring the small stab of panic at how I'd survive another hike on zero sleep, I told the witch where I was going, showing her my dagger to prove I didn't need an escort, and left the glade.

I didn't travel far. I knew what lurked in the dark places of this world, and I had no intention of becoming anything's dinner. Just out of sight of the camp, but well within earshot should I feel the need to scream, I saw to my business. God, what had I become? Back home, I wouldn't even use a public bathroom, never mind *this* indignity. Now I was peeing in the woods on a regular basis.

With a sigh, I straightened and adjusted my clothes, peering over my shoulder for any hint of stalking monsters. If I was going to die, it was not going to be like this.

All was peaceful. No hulking beasts of flickering shadows waited amongst the trees. I looked at the branches overhead, just to be certain. Nothing. Nothing but stars winking between the gently swaying leaves.

The stars were beautiful here, even more so than back home. And there were so many. Was it the same universe I looked up at from the human world, or was everything different here?

Not that it made much difference. What was I planning to do? Find the North Star and follow it home like some pirate captain? I wouldn't know where to begin.

I sighed but didn't lower my gaze from the heavens. Who was I kidding? I was barely brave enough to go for a wee on my own, never mind run away. Besides, who would help the witches, if not me? Not to mention the small matter of the Blood Gate being infested with... something, some horribly dangerous creature.

"The stars make our own problems fade into insignificance, do they not?"

I yelped, spinning, to find Jacques the creep leaning against the trees I'd just inspected, his arms folded and eyes gleaming.

"We meet again, mademoiselle."

Oh, for crying out loud. This was the last thing I needed. I glanced in the direction of the camp, my hand tightening around my dagger, hidden beneath the drape of my blanket. Jacques stood between me and the camp. Could I dodge him if need be?

"Where did you come from?" I'd scanned these woods in every direction, not seconds ago. Why hadn't I seen him? A thought occurred to me. "Wait. Are you a *fae*?"

Jacques' chuckle slaked down my spine, leaving a trail of ice in its wake. "Mon Dieu, no!"

Well, that was something, I supposed, but it didn't slip my notice that he hadn't offered any explanation as to what he actually was. I'd seen enough of this world by now to know he wasn't human. Not with those pale eyes, bright as starlight, and the silent way he moved.

As though proving my point, he pushed away from the tree, straightening. The foliage beneath his boots didn't so much as rustle. My grip on my dagger tightened. I didn't want to hurt him, or anyone, but if I had to...

"You need not fear me, belle fille. I told you last time we met, I mean you no harm."

"Well, excuse me for being cautious," I hissed, irritation strangling my fear. "I'm trapped in a world where *everything* wants to kill me."

"Not everything." The way his eyes roved over me contradicted his words. I'd encountered enough men to recognise lust, but this was something different. It was the way I might look at a cheese board, shortly before devouring it.

A thought popped into my head. Not a very nice thought, either. I'd seen and enjoyed plenty of cringy teen dramas in my time. I knew about beautiful creatures who lurked in the night and looked at humans the way Jacques was looking at me. Like a meal.

"Are you... a vampire?" The words came out strangled by my too tight throat.

Please say no. Please, please, please.

The vehement denial I prayed for didn't come. Jacques' eyes lifted to mine, and his lips pulled back in a smile, revealing all those white teeth. No fangs, thank God, but that meant nothing. "Very clever, ma belle. Or should I call you Aliza?"

My already chilled skin erupted with goosebumps. "What did you call me?"

"Aliza. It is your name, is it not?" He nodded at the golden letter A hung between my collar bones.

I lifted a hand, shielding the necklace from his amused gaze, but what was the point if he already knew the truth? I may as well give up the act. What difference did a name make? I glanced to the camp once more. I'd been gone an awfully long time, hadn't I? Why had nobody come looking for me? Had Jacques the vampire slaughtered them all, saving me for last? His human dessert.

"How do you know my name?" As I spoke, I looked back to Jacques, only he wasn't where I'd left him. He was right in front of me.

My scream never made it out of my lungs. Fear clamped around my throat, squeezing tight, blocking all sound and breath. I wanted to run, I wanted to sink my cursed dagger into his undead heart, but my body did nothing. My legs locked, refusing to respond to the frantic orders of my brain.

Icy fingertips touched my cheek, and I sucked in a sharp breath. Jacques' strange eyes flickered over my face, lingering on my throat. His nostrils flared, and he swallowed. I could almost see him salivating, but when his lips parted, it wasn't in attack. "I listen, and I learn. You would be wise to do the same here, where plenty of things want you dead. But I see you listened when I told you to head south, and now you're with the witches, on your way to save us all."

It was an effort to master myself enough to breathe, never mind find the guts to tell him I hadn't followed his advice, but the river. "Vampires—vampires need saving too?"

"Of course, ma chéri." His breath was cool and clean on my face, no different to a night breeze. "Will you be the one to do it?"

No, I wanted to scream. Why did everyone want me to save them? How had the fate of this entire magical world landed on my shoulders? And did I even *want* to save vampires? Were they monsters of traditional tales, or the angsty heroes of recent times? Jacques had made no move to hurt me, but every instinct in my body roared at me to flee. If only I could feel my legs.

"Have you been following me?" I croaked instead, but I already knew the answer. How else could he have learnt my name? Was he herding me? An unseen, undead sheepdog, driving me to break this curse? Or did he live in these woods? Hunt in these woods?

He smiled again, and my attention fixed on his teeth. I watched them as he spoke. "It would not be gentlemanly to leave a lady to brave these lands alone."

Fuck. Just when I thought things couldn't get any worse, I acquired a human eating stalker.

"I'm not alone," I whispered. "I have the witches."

"And you have me. Be brave, Aliza."

Cold but soft lips pressed against my forehead, and I squeezed my eyes closed. This was it. I was going to die, and I clearly wasn't going to do a damn thing to prevent it.

The lips disappeared, though their chill lingered on my skin.

I waited for the blow to fall, my chest rising and falling with every panted breath, but nothing happened. I squinted from one eye, then opened the other.

The woods were still and empty.

Jacques was gone.

12

Wait, This Isn't A Trashy Vampire Movie, Is It?

"Tell me more about this world."

The sun had risen, melting the chill from my bones. Breakfast had been eaten, and the camp packed away. The witches and I traipsed once more through the woods. Though my eyes ached with the intensity with which I stared between the trees, I saw no sign of Jacques. Then again, it was daylight. Would the sun scorch him into a little pile of ashes? Or would he sparkle like a diamond? My laugh died in my throat.

Pansy, walking at my side, lifted her brown eyes to me. "What do you want to know?"

"Tell me about the people who live here. I know about witches and fae, and obviously, humans used to live here too. Is there anything else? I—I've seen the fairies."

Only a few days ago, I would sooner have died than admit to such a thing, but maybe those old fairytales and folk stories were more than just pretty little lies. Maybe modern humans had forgotten the truth they'd once known.

"Oh, I adore fairies." Pansy beamed. "They can be quite shy, but they're so pretty, aren't they? I love the colours. They come into the castle grounds from time to time, but mostly they keep to themselves.

Children would try to catch them in nets and keep them in jars, and that's enough to put anyone off visiting."

Indeed.

"The fae are actually a closer relative of the fairies than they are of elves, though you wouldn't know it to look at them."

It was the second time I'd heard elves mentioned. Sage had said they had healing magic.

"What are elves?" I couldn't decide whether I was picturing Santa's elves or Lord Elrond.

Pansy met my eyes in the mirror. Was it my imagination, or did she look a little fearful? "They're woodland creatures. They keep to themselves. Most people never see one, and nobody knows much about their ways, but I learnt a bit about them in my lessons. They look a lot like the fae, only they have hair that changes colour with the seasons, like the leaves, for camouflage. They'd probably love your hair. They're supposedly very good at healing magics, and there are stories of desperate people venturing into the forest to seek out the elves. Most never return, according to the tales."

"That explains the camouflage, I can see why I'd want to hide from them." Were there elves in *these* woods? I smoothed my hands over my colourful hair. Would it make them more or less inclined to murder me if we came across them? "What about the fae? Tell me about them."

"Oh, that's easier. They're very... human, apart from the ears, and the magic. There are a few things you should know, though. Most importantly, they love bargains and bonds, but they're also mischievous. Never make a bargain with one. They're almost always worded in a way that will hide their true meaning. They'll trick you into something awful. That's actually how the curse came about. Their first queen,

Claudia, created a deal with her children. None of her descendants are able to harm a blood relative, which meant Maelgwyn had to get creative."

"I can see why we're so keen to save them," I drawled, rolling my eyes. It was just my luck to get roped into a mission to rescue a pair of would-be murderous tricksters.

"Unfortunately, they're the most powerfully magical of all the people in Neath, which puts them in charge, and some are worse than others. Putting a slightly less awful fae on the throne benefits us all. The good news is, they love hospitality. They'll almost never harm a guest who has been invited to dine."

I stored that little tidbit away for later. As I was heading to a fae kingdom, I was keen to learn more about them, but not now. There was only one creature on my mind today.

"Is there anything else?"

Vampires, I wanted to say. *Tell me about the vampires.*

"Nymphs. Another shy species. They guard nature. You'd only really see one if you were causing harm, and by then it'd be too late. Same with the vampires. With them, it's always too late."

Finally.

"Vampires?" I tried to sound only mildly interested, and not at all as though a vampire had kissed me in the woods a few hours ago.

Pansy shuddered. "Horrible things. They're not really even alive. They hunt by night. Humans used to be their prey of choice," she gave me a serious nod, "but these days they'll go for anything. Witches, animals, even fae if they find a weak one. When the curse was cast, we hoped the silver lining might be that the vampires starved. But of course, they're already dead, so we had no such luck, and they adapted. They're much weaker than they once were, though. That's something."

I thought of the way Jacques had looked at me, as though he'd wanted to bleed me dry, right then and there. It was true that he was thin. The bones in his face were all too sharp. Was he starving? Was he waiting for me to break the curse before he ate me? Was he lurking overhead, listening to every word?

It all made sense. The curse had closed the rifts, and no rifts meant no humans. No decent food. Except the strong, magical sort that could fight back. My heart sank. When the rifts opened, would my world be flooded with magical creatures? Isobel would be pleased to know her fairytales were real, at least at first. Would she be as giddy when our world became as much of a shit show as this one?

"We have stories of all these things back in the human world," I mused at length. "Do you think they came from the humans who used to come here?"

"Most likely. All of these creatures used to visit the human world too. The elves rarely bothered, of course, and the fairies and fae never lingered. It's said they grow weaker the longer they spend there. But witches used to go back and forth all the time. I've never been," Pansy finished sadly.

I offered her a smile. "I'll take you. When all this is over, you can come and visit, and I'll show you around."

Did I actually want to break the curse and open the rifts if it meant unleashing bloodsuckers into my world? Could I put my friends and family in danger, just so I could see them again? My parents would be in bits without me, but if they were given a choice, would they want me back if I brought a plague of vampires with me? Maybe it would be better for the princes to stay sleeping, and me to stay lost. Only, if I announced that I had no intention of breaking the curse, the witches would drop me. They'd done so much for me, but only because they knew what I could do for them. I was under no illusions. I'd be trapped, alone and friendless, in a world where I had no place. No home. Nothing to my name. If that was my future, I'd be better off dead.

"Mother above, would you really?" Pansy fizzed with excitement at my side, distracting me from my bleak choices. "Please don't say you're lying, or my heart might break. I've *always* wanted to see the human world!"

I smiled. "You might be disappointed, but yeah, of course, I'll take you."

"Can I have hair like yours when I come?"

I blinked in surprise. "You want colourful hair?" I pursed my lips as I eyed her dark coils. There was no hope of bleaching it light enough to reach a pastel shade, not if she still wanted hair on her head, but a darker shade could work.

"Purple," she said at once, as though she'd been thinking about it for a lot longer than our chat warranted. "It suits me best, *and* it's my favourite colour. Can I have purple hair?"

My lips curved into a smile. She'd clearly put thought into this. "Yeah, why not? I'll do it for you."

Pansy slipped into a fast-paced monologue of all the reasons she wanted to visit my world, and all the things she was going to do while she was there. I smiled blandly, agreeing now and again, but my thoughts were far away. Everything rested on my breaking the curse. On me being the human to survive what my countless predecessors had not. All these hopes, all these dreams. They settled on my shoulders, heavier than they should have been. The witches and I worked for a brighter future.

From where I was standing, it looked horribly bleak.

As the day went on, the shadows lengthened, and the pleasant morning warmth began to fade. The sun was still shining when I was forced to adjust my wrap, tucking it snugly into my belt to ward off the chill.

Sage, noticing my fussing, said, "We're approaching Tir o Gaeaf. It is a land of snow and ice."

Ice? But we were in the midst of summer. Not that anyone would believe it, judging by the growing cold.

"This might seem like a stupid question, but is it cold there?"

Sage's lips twitched. Was that a *smile*?

"I have been to the human world, girl. I remember your seasons well. One after another, on an endless rotation. Things are different here." *No shit.* "Tir o Gaeaf is blanketed in permanent snow."

"Because of the curse?" I whispered.

It was the last kingdom standing against King Maelgwyn, and we all knew how he liked to deal with his problems. Kidnap and torture and death.

"No. It's just the way of it. Each kingdom has its own climate. Gaeaf is a land of everlasting winter."

Sure enough, the further we walked, the colder it became, until I was forced to pull my wrap over my head and retrieve my gloves from my pack. The trees we passed had fewer leaves, and then none at all, just arthritic, dark limbs tangling overhead. Even the fairies dwindled, and the few that remained glowed in shades of blue and green. My breath grew white, puffing out before me like dragon smoke. As the light failed, glittering frost coated the ground, crunching underfoot as the woodland turned to firs and evergreens. I began to think longingly of my favourite coat, stuffed in my crowded wardrobe back home, but the cold couldn't stop me from staring around in wonder. It seemed that no matter how long I spent in this world, no matter how much magic and danger I encountered, there would always be a new surprise waiting just around the corner. I didn't bother to question how we'd gone from midsummer to winter in just a few short hours, but when the first patches of snow appeared between the trees, I did wonder how much further we had to go.

When the trees grew sparse, with wider glimpses of the darkening sky above them, I spotted the edge of the forest. A snow-covered hill sloped away from us, leading into a wide, white valley encircled by low mountains. We paused at the treeline, and I took a moment to catch my breath and admire the ethereal beauty of Tir o Gaeaf.

In the valley basin sat a great frozen lake. It was a dull, flat shade of iron grey at that moment, but my heart swelled against my ribs at the sight of it. Beyond the lake, hundreds of glowing lights twinkled, and past those, a breathtaking structure rose, pale and ghostly, against the dark mountains. A palace. Not an ugly little castle like Nairsgarth, but a proper fairytale castle, with all the spires and towers and spikes I could have asked for. Unless I was much mistaken, it was made of *ice*.

"Aliza," Sage said at my shoulder. "Welcome to Tir o Gaeaf."

Something whistled past my head, close enough to ruffle my hair, and a thud sounded at my back.

I spun in time to see a shower of snow falling from the fir tree behind me, set loose by the arrow protruding from the trunk.

Panicked voices rose around me, but Sage held up a gloved hand, her voice rising over the din. "Quiet! Stay calm. It was only a warning."

"A warning?" I snapped, my near-death experience getting the better of my temper. "It almost killed me!"

"Exactly." Sage levelled a flat glare at me. "If it had been fired in earnest, there would be no almost about it."

My mouth fell open, but a hand closed around my upper arm, gripping tight enough to hurt. Pansy stood at my side, the brown of her skin giving way to a greenish pallor. I followed her terrified gaze.

Two men approached, their eyes and loaded bows trained on us as they stomped up the snowy hill.

"Border guards," Sage muttered, before raising both her hands into the air and stepping forward. "Friends. We come from Ymyl Cefnfor on the business of the High Priestess of Nairsgarth. We mean no harm."

"Then drop your weapons. All of them," barked one of the men.

They were both unnervingly handsome, tall and broad, though as they were wrapped in leather and fur, it was impossible to guess how much of their bulk was owed to muscle. *Not* that I was interested in that. Not beyond sizing up my newest enemy, anyway.

Sage unbuckled the short sword she carried at her hip, tossing it into the snow several feet ahead of her. The other witches hesitated before following her lead. I fumbled with my own daggers, wondering how wise this course of action was, but my numb fingers made slow work, and one of the guards fixed his attention on me.

Maybe it was something to do with all the snow and ice, but his irises were almost painfully blue.

Damn me to hell, but I couldn't hold that beautiful gaze. I lowered my eyes hurriedly and dropped my daggers at my feet. Snow crunched, and leather boots came into view, too big to belong to any witch. I lifted my eyes. A leather breastplate, and a fancy buckle holding a fur capped cloak. I swallowed down my unease, almost choking on it, and looked up.

Even with the fae guard standing slightly further down the slope, he was taller than me. My lips parted in surprise. It was a rare thing to meet anyone, even a man, who forced me to look up. And fuck me, he was gorgeous. Rugged but pretty, his eyes threatening to skewer my soul if only he met my own, but he was, predictably, looking at my hair. My fishtail plait fell over my left shoulder, and a few strands of candy floss pink had come loose around my face.

"What are you?" the guard asked, and God damn him, I wanted to fall to my knees there and then. There was certainly nobody like this on the hookup apps back home.

"This is Aliza with an A," Sage answered his question with a note of smug victory in her voice. "A human."

Human was a magic word around these parts, it seemed, capable of melting away the hostility of even the sexiest of fae. As it happened, it wasn't me who fell to my knees at all. At Sage's words, both guards had dropped to kneel in the snow at my feet, leaving me blushing furiously and trying not to imagine the things they might do while they were down there.

Before long, I was escorted down the hill at the head of my group, a guard at each side, and the witches hurrying along behind us, struggling to keep up on their little legs. A girl could get used to such power, but I checked my pace. They might all be using me for their own gain, but without the witches, I wouldn't have made it this far. My new fae friends slowed their steps to match mine, and I fought a silent battle with my smirk.

When we reached the bottom of the hill, we came to a road of packed snow. There, the guards halted, and we all waited in a huddle, dithering. I tried stamping my feet to keep warm, but it was hopeless. The wrap the witches had given me was no match for the climate of Gaeaf. Hopefully, our stay would be short, and we'd arrive in Tir o Haf before long. Never mind that my life would be in danger from the second I set foot in the king's territory, at least I'd die warm.

A faint jingle interrupted my thoughts, and I squinted through the haze of frosty air. Something was whizzing along the road in our direction. The guards showed no sign of worry, however, so I contented myself with watching the shape grow closer until...

I gasped, clapping my gloves to my mouth in delight.

It was a sleigh, pulled by a team of tiny, hairy ponies with bells attached to their harnesses. Beside me, Pansy let out a stifled squeal.

The sleigh whooshed to a halt before us in a wave of snow, and a guard offered his hand to help me aboard. I was quite sure I could manage it alone, but I wasn't going to let a small matter like that ruin my fun. I smiled, accepting his offer, and clambered onto the fur-covered bench of the sleigh. Sage took a seat next to me, along with a guard, and three witches squashed themselves into the row behind.

"Another will be along shortly," the guard told the remaining witches, who all sported matching grim faces. I couldn't blame them, not as I arranged a thick, knitted blanket over my lap.

"Put your hood up," Sage hissed in my ear as the sleigh began to move. "We don't want to draw unnecessary attention, even here."

I obeyed gladly. The rush of cold air as we sped past the lake made my ears feel like they might fall off, but I couldn't resist peering around the edge of the fabric and admiring the thick layer of opaque ice. As we neared the city, I huddled in, tugging the fabric lower to hide my hair, but still I caught glimpses of grand townhouses, their frosted railings hung with icicles, and their marble pillars carved with intricate designs that I couldn't quite catch. I spotted a tall, beautiful woman–*female*–who looked fresh from the runway, wrapped in fur, walking along with a little white fox trotting at her heels. She glanced at the sleigh as it passed, and I quickly lowered my head and kept it there for the remainder of our ride.

By the time the sleigh slowed to a stop, I was frozen solid and shivering violently. My hopes of warming up were quickly dashed when I lifted my eyes and saw that we'd arrived at an enormous set of double doors, made of the same dark ice as the lake. My gaze wandered, falling upon walls of glowing blue, towering high overhead. The same strange light shone through facets and windows, throwing a ghostly tinge over everything and everyone.

Beautiful. There was no doubt about it, the castle was breathtaking beyond belief, but how practical could it be? I'd have much preferred the squat, ugly walls of Nairsgarth. At least a roaring fire wouldn't melt stone. Such a necessity would undoubtedly be denied in case I set the palace walls dripping and warping, but I wasn't sure I'd survive the night without one.

Shivering and stewing over sleeping arrangements, I clambered from the sleigh on stiff legs. Sage followed, stepping slightly beyond me as she stared up at the palace, frosty breath clouding her face. We were at the head of a sweeping driveway. Blankets of snow covered what I presumed were lawns to either side, and tall evergreens stood like silent sentinels, spaced with precision beside the road. Between the trees, old-fashioned lamp posts burnt with a strange blue flame, lighting the way, but even with their eerie glow, the gate and walls were lost to the night.

Would the shades be able to find me here? I pressed closer to the light pooling around the palace, courtesy of its many frosted windows.

"This way," the guard said, gesturing away from the main entrance.

We followed him as he passed into the shadow of the wall, leading us away from the glowing lights. A path along the base of the building had been cleared of snow, and my boots crunched in the grit scattered over the ground.

Where was this beautiful fae creature taking us? Were we to be ushered in through a secret side door, far from prying eyes? Or maybe we weren't allowed in the palace at all. Maybe we were expected to sleep in the garden shed. As long as it wasn't made of ice, I didn't care.

Unsure of whether or not I was still supposed to be inconspicuous, I kept my head down, resisting the urge to gawk at my surroundings. My eyes stayed trained on my frozen toes as we rounded a corner and slipped through a narrow, metal gate cut into the ice. A small yard surrounded by tall walls greeted us. Crates stood in a precarious stack against one wall, and stone steps fell away to several basement doors. The guard made a beeline for one of those steep, narrow flights.

Perfect. The dank little side entrance it was, then. So much for being the chosen one.

We passed through a door of black metal, and at once, warmth poured over me, despite the corridor of ice stretching ahead. I stared around, searching for the source of the heat, but bar a few blue glowing lamps fitted to the walls, I found nothing. Our silent guard led us deeper into the castle before finally opening a door and spreading an arm in welcome.

Sage led the way, with me on her heels. The room we found ourselves in wasn't small by any means, but it certainly wasn't of palace proportions. The comfortable chairs lining the windowless walls gave it the distinct air of a waiting room, especially when the other three witches trooped in. Pansy shot me an excited smile from over her mother's shoulder.

"Please, take a seat. Lady Celyn will be along shortly." The guard departed without another word, and Sage lapped the room at a stroll, pausing to prod one of the chairs with an expression of immense distaste.

Not sharing her snobbery after days of walking, I sank into the nearest one with a sigh and tugged off my gloves. This room was warm too, and yet, the ice walls showed no signs of melting. I trailed a fingertip over the one behind my chair. Beneath a fine, powdery layer of frost, it was as smooth and hard as glass.

"Is it really made of ice?" I asked the room at large.

"Mother above," Sage muttered, giving no further answer.

"Yes, Aliza, it is." Hyacinth gave me a motherly smile. "Ignore Sister Sage, you will learn to trust your senses with practice."

There was nothing wrong with my senses. It was this world I didn't trust. "Then why is it warm?"

"There is fae magic at work here," Hyacinth said simply, as though that was all the explanation anyone could ask for.

Reluctant to give Sage any more reasons to question my intelligence, I lapsed into silence. The witches muttered amongst themselves. After a few minutes, the rest of our party arrived, pink-cheeked, and filled the remaining seats.

Silent minutes trailed by, and to my awe, I began to sweat gently beneath my layers. It hurt my head, to have my body telling me one thing and my brain telling me the opposite. I was surrounded by ice, and yet, I was boiling. It made no sense, but then, nothing did anymore. Before long, I unbuckled the belt holding my wrap in place and tugged the garment free of my shoulders.

My aching foot began to jiggle. As much as I appreciated a chair after days of hiking and sitting on rocks and logs, I was bored. I wanted a meal and a proper bed with immediate effect.

Warmth and comfort combined to tug at my eyelids. I propped my head on my hand and gave in, letting my eyes drift shut. Just a short rest, while we waited...

"It's true?"

The door burst open, and I startled awake with a jolt and an ungainly snort. A willowy fae female was silhouetted in the doorway, surrounded by a glossy mane of waist-length russet hair. Round eyes, as icy blue as the palace walls, fixed on me. Her pale, heart-shaped face broke into a smile, but her eyes flooded with emotion moments before a hand flew to her mouth, stifling a small sound that might have been a laugh or a sob.

"Forgive my outburst." She lowered her hand, taking a deep breath as she continued to stare. "We thought you would never come."

Lady Celyn's quarters were far more luxurious than the room we'd originally been shown to. My sleep-heavy eyes widened in wonder as I examined every inch of the decadent, frozen sitting room. Frosty white icicles, large enough to skewer an elephant, hung from the high ceiling. Nestled amongst them was an enormous chandelier that looked like falling rain, casting a haunting light over the room. I couldn't decide if it was hung with crystals, glass or yet more ice. Whatever it was, motes of light danced on the blue-white walls, drawing my attention from where I sat on a plush sofa scattered with cushions and blankets. Pansy sat beside me, her hands clasped tightly between her knees. I smirked. A plate crammed with delicate cakes rested on the nearby coffee table, but nobody had yet moved to take one.

Sage's haughty voice washed over me as she relayed her plan to a grim-faced Lady Celyn. The fae's impossibly smooth brow now bore a tiny crease between her perfect, upswept eyebrows as she listened to the witch.

I'd heard it all before, and my attention drifted.

A mesmerising fire burnt in the marble grate. Flames of every shade of blue danced and flickered, warming the room without making the ice weep. It had to be enchanted, there was no other explanation. Were the cakes enchanted too?

They'll almost never harm a guest who has been invited to dine.

Pansy's words crash-landed in my head, and my hand lurched for the cakes, snatching one up and stuffing it into my mouth whole. Pansy threw an incredulous glance in my direction before selecting a cake of her own with a daintiness I hadn't managed. I didn't care. My drowsiness had lulled me into complacency. The fae may be beautiful and even appear kind, but Pansy had made it quite clear that they couldn't be trusted. If I was to spend the night in a palace full of tricksters, I had to take precautions. Eating the cake was a necessary evil.

Lady Celyn's eyes snagged on me as I plucked up a second cake, but she turned her attention back to Sage. "I will have a team of my best warriors made ready to escort you."

"No, thank you." Sage shook her head. "Too large a group will draw unwanted attention."

Was she mad? A few burly fae soldiers were just what we needed as we headed into enemy territory. Monsters lurked around every corner, and as no human had survived the quest before, I'd take any help that was offered.

Never make a bargain with one.

Did this count as a bargain? Was that why Sage refused? Pansy should have been more specific because her warnings paled in comparison to the temptation of the fae's offer. Maybe that was the whole point. Maybe they made offers that seemed too good to be true, only to trick poor, unsuspecting souls into eternal servitude.

"I would request teleportation to Tir o Gaeaf, though," Sage continued. "I have coordinates."

"Of course," Lady Celyn replied without hesitation. I waited for the catch to come, but she only said, "I'm certain there are some amongst us who have travelled to the area you require. As soon as you are ready, we will deliver you. Though, perhaps a meal and a bed for the night would be in order."

"That would be welcome, thank you. We leave at dawn."

I stifled my groan, turning it into a yawn. Lady Celyn noticed and gave me a sympathetic smile. "Rooms are being prepared as we speak, Aliza. What is your favourite dish? I'll have the kitchens prepare it for you."

Don't make bargains, but do accept hospitality. My instincts warred against each other, but Pansy had definitely mentioned food offering protection. Besides, I was famished.

"I guess fajitas are too much to hope for?" At Lady Celyn's blank expression, I pressed on. "Madras? Thai green?" There wasn't as much as a flicker of recognition at any of the meals I mentioned, so I sighed, fixing a smile onto my face. "Whatever the kitchens have will be fine, but I don't eat any meat or fish."

Sage gave a tiny roll of her eyes, looking away as though I was something shameful, but Celyn smiled. "That can be arranged. Now, come, I shall show you to your rooms."

My room turned out to be another sprawling suite, grander even than Lady Celyn's. The style was the same, but it was larger, located on the top floor of the palace. The newly lit blue fire had yet to drive the lingering chill from the air, but huddled in a blanket before the enormous windows, I didn't care. Not when my room offered an unobstructed view of the wisps of green and purple light weaving across the black sky like an ethereal ribbon.

In only a few hours' time, I'd arrive in Tir o Haf, the kingdom where no free fae, witch or elf dared to wander. Only those trapped by Maelgwyn's wards, and those loyal to him, dwelt there. The last human to venture there had been Georgina, and I didn't need to know the details of her death to understand how slim my own chances of survival were.

That I'd made it this far was a miracle. In all honesty, I should have died in the caves. I should have cracked my skull on a rock or drowned in the river. I should have had my essence sucked out by a shade, or my blood drained by a vampire. I was no survivor. I was an indoor girl, a city girl, but against all odds, here I was. It was almost as though something wanted me to be here. Like I'd been protected and guided this far by something more than witches and vampires. Something mysterious and powerful. Fate, maybe. As terrifying yet comforting as that thought was, I couldn't bring myself to hope that I might really be the chosen one. That I might survive tomorrow.

What if I never made it home? Was this it? Were these the last hours and days of my life? Had everything been for nothing?

I would become just another name in history. Another ill-fated attempt. Two hundred years from now, would the witches assess a new woman while muttering 'at least this one has normal hair, not like Aliza with an A'? I'd be just another failure.

The weight of all my hopes and dreams settled on me, as though they knew they'd soon be scattered to the wind, lost in the ether. As though they wanted to be close to me, this near to the end. I clung to them, needing to pretend there was a future for me beyond whatever lurked in Tir o Haf.

Beyond the princes and their curse.

13

I Draw The Line At Spiders

Sage was true to her word. The sky beyond my window had barely begun to lighten when I was dragged from my bed and ordered to dress. Though my room had warmed overnight, it was Baltic outside as a pale, champagne light glittered on the snow. Mist hung in the air. I smoothed my glove over my hair. Wasn't it enough that I was going to my death? Did I really have to suffer frizz as well? Would the witches take my body back to Nairsgarth and tidy me up for my funeral, or would I be left to rot where I fell?

My breakfast churned in my belly. Maybe ladling all that sugar into my porridge had been a bad idea.

The palace was warded, which apparently meant we couldn't teleport from within its walls. As such, Lady Celyn, wrapped in an elegant coat trimmed with a fur collar and cuff, led us out of the grounds and into the city. The team of silent fae she'd brought along shot furtive glances in my direction. Every one of them was tall and beautiful, with clear skin and eyes that were just a little too vibrant to pass for human. The gleaming shades of blue, green, amber and brown made it hard to pretend I hadn't noticed the attention I was getting. Did any of them really believe I'd be the one to break the curse, or were they getting an eyeful before I was shredded apart by the howling creatures Jacques had warned me against?

Nobody spoke, not even Pansy. The thin, cold air pricked at my eyes, or maybe it was just my impending doom making them water.

The broad square outside the palace gates was quiet at this ungodly hour, and the streets were still. In the distance, through a sheer veil of mist, the dark shadow of the forest crowned the lip of the valley. I hesitated. Was it too late to change my mind? I might not be able to go home, but there was nothing to say I couldn't live out my natural life in Neath. There was no law that said I had to risk my life to break the curse that had absolutely nothing to do with me. I could sprint for the trees. Safety lay in that direction.

If I chose my safety, people would continue to die.

I turned my back on the trees and trudged after my companions.

A mane of burning red hair obscured my view, and my damp eyes shifted to Lady Celyn. The cold suited her, casting a rosy hue over her porcelain skin.

"This is where we part ways, Aliza," she said solemnly. "It has been an honour to meet you, and host you here at the palace. I wish you every luck on your quest. I have a parting gift for you."

One of her companions, a man–*male*–with honey-coloured hair, stepped to her side, offering her a long wooden box. Celyn opened it, revealing an ugly necklace. A grey-blue oval gem sat in an ornate twist of gold.

"This pendant belonged to the first queen of the fae, Claudia, who ruled sixteen thousand years ago. Each court was entrusted with safeguarding an heirloom of hers. This is Tir o Gaeaf's, and now, I entrust it to you."

Sixteen thousand years old, and they were just handing it over to me?

"Oh, it's lovely," I lied, "but I really can't accept it."

"You must. Queen Claudia was a seer, and she knew you would come. She left this to you. The other heirlooms are yours too, but of course, their courts and safekeepers have long since fallen."

"Oh." What could I say to that? If some batty, ancient queen had seen fit to foresee me in her will, it would be churlish to refuse. "What about all the other women who tried to break the curse?"

Had the fae palmed it off on them, only to pilfer it from their corpses when they failed?

Celyn lifted the necklace with care as she said, "None crossed the paths of myself or my predecessors, and more's the pity. The heirlooms are imbued with Claudia's own magic. This pendant will offer you protection."

Well, as I was facing the gallows, who was I to turn down a bit of protection, even if it was only a quarter of what Claudia had intended? Would her daggers, once more strapped to my hip, protect me too?

I barely had to duck my head to allow Celyn to place the chain around my neck, tall as she was. The cool metal settled against my skin, below my initial necklace. I lifted the ancient pendant as though it was made of glass, examining it closely. With the weak dawn sunlight shining through the stone, it looked slightly less hideous. I tucked it under my shirt with a smile. It was a nice gesture if nothing else.

"Thank you. It's an honour."

Lady Celyn sank into a curtsey. "The honour is mine."

My chilled ears heated at the attention. It might have been a welcome relief if I wasn't aware that they were also glowing beetroot.

"And now I bid you farewell. I hope we meet again, Aliza."

I pressed my lips into a thin smile, knowing I would never lay eyes on Celyn again. Before long, I'd either be dead or back in my own world. If I survived my quest, I'd leave the necklace with Sage. She could return it to its rightful place. It was the least she could do after dragging me into this mess.

The blond male slid the box into his pocket and spread his arms. His eyes shifted to me. "Take my hand. It's necessary for teleportation."

That wasn't right. I hadn't had to hold Sage's hand when she'd used her warp crystal. Maybe it was some ancient fae custom; they seemed the type to get their knickers in a twist over rules and etiquette. I wrapped my cold fingers around his. I glanced sideways to find Pansy beside me, her eyes glittering with excitement as she grasped her own escort's outstretched palm. One by one, the witches linked hands with the fae.

I opened my mouth to ask about the crystal, but before the words could form, darkness rushed in, obliterating Tir o Gaeaf in an icy crush.

My body became light, weightless, expanding and separating, until I was sure I was nothing but a cloud of atoms whizzing through a lightless wormhole. I couldn't move, couldn't breathe, I had no control over any part of myself. I wasn't even sure *myself* was a thing anymore. All I knew was panic as I unravelled on the dark, magical wind.

All at once, everything came crashing back together with immense weight. I was being squeezed, flattened. I was going to die.

Something slammed against my chest, forcing me to heave a great, sucking breath into my lungs. Warm air. Something cool tickled my cheek. I opened my eyes to find myself face down in the grass. My scrambled brain understood that I must have arrived in Tir o Haf, but that was all it was capable of. It certainly couldn't make sense of the muffled voices all around me. And my body? I couldn't so much as twitch my fingers.

Slowly, feeling came back, as did my wits. I blinked and pushed myself onto my trembling hands and knees.

"Easy now," somebody said, laying a hand on my back. "The first time can be something of a shock."

That was an understatement.

"That was not..." I broke off, panting. "That wasn't the same."

"What are you talking about now, girl?"

I shook my head, its contents swirling grotesquely. "The warp crystal."

Somebody tutted. Even in my state of disarray, I had no trouble guessing who. "Of course it's not the same. Warping and teleporting are entirely different. The crystals open a portal that we simply step through. Teleporting is fae magic. It is much more complex."

Why had nobody warned me just how horrible teleporting would be? If I'd been prepared... Honestly? Nothing could have prepared me for that. I much preferred the crystal method.

Nausea swirled in my belly, filling my mouth with saliva. No. No, I refused to part with my breakfast. I screwed my eyes shut and breathed through my nose, waiting for the sensation to pass.

Eventually, I composed myself enough to kneel upright, only to find all the witches and our fae escorts gathered around, watching me with trepidation.

Pansy sprang forward. "Water?" She thrust her skein at me, but my stomach churned. I waved her away.

"She looks clammy," somebody observed.

I felt clammy. I felt like I'd woken up with the world's worst hangover. I wanted nothing more than to crawl into my own bed, back home, and wait for the suffering to pass. But everyone was watching me, judging and waiting. We were in true enemy territory now, and sitting around feeling sorry for myself was practically inviting something to come and eat me. I summoned whatever strength still lingered in my poor body and rose carefully to my feet. The world swayed, but I kept my balance, and a few seconds later, everything levelled out.

"Are you well?" Sage asked. I couldn't say it was concern for me that tinged her voice, but there was definitely something there. Concern for her precious quest, probably.

"Never better." My voice came out dry and hoarse. Nearby, Pansy hesitated, still clutching her water, and I held out my hand with a small smile.

The water still carried the cold of Tir o Gaeaf, and as it tracked its icy path down my gullet, it dawned on me that the sweat coating my skin wasn't only a result of teleporting. It was *hot* here. Heatwave hot. The sun baked down on my head, making my scalp prickle. I swept my fingers through my hair in an attempt to rid myself of the part and protect myself from sunburn.

For the first time since my arrival in Tir o Haf, I took in my surroundings. There were plenty of leafy trees offering shade, but they were spaced too far apart to be considered a wood. Tall wildflowers blanketed the gently rolling ground, their colourful heads swaying and whispering in the balmy breeze. Bees and butterflies hovered, and wisps of fluffy white clouds dotted a blue sky blazing overhead. In the distance, mountains lined the horizon, their snowy caps glittering in the sunlight. It certainly didn't give off imminent death vibes. In fact, it was beautiful. Vivid.

My hand drifted to my pocket, itching to snap a picture, but then I remembered that my phone was dead, and that I might soon be joining it.

"I bid you farewell." The blond fae shifted his gaze to me. "Good luck."

He and his companions disappeared with a series of faint pops, leaving me to gulp away the lump in my throat. I only hoped his lucky tidings would be enough.

"Let's move on." Sage wasted no time in setting off through the flowers. They reached her chest, buffeting and swaying around her tiny form.

I took a deep breath and followed the witches deeper into Tir o Haf.

Just when I was beginning to consider digging out the sunscreen I'd packed for my ill-fated trek to the Fairy Glen, Sage veered away from the meadow, leading us into denser shade. I breathed a sigh of relief. I enjoyed the sun, but judging by its intensity, we were nearing midday, and I had no interest in burning to a crisp. It was cooler amongst the trees, but just as pretty. Large, creamy white mushrooms grew at the mossy bases of the trunks, and clumps of yet more flowers grew in the sun-speckled shade. A tinkling stream rushed over a rocky bed, and we took the opportunity to refill our skeins before following the spongy bank as it wove between the trees.

My stomach began to grumble, and I eyed the mushrooms with increasing interest. They were enormous, certainly enough to make a hearty lunch, but like everything else here, they probably wanted to kill me.

My questions and prayers were answered when Sage called us to a halt beneath a particularly thick tree, and the witches drew their knives and set about picking the mushrooms. Drawing confidence from their lead, I pulled out one of my daggers, crouched low and chose a particularly plump mushroom. The moment my black blade sank through its stalk, the whole thing withered, shrivelling up like crepe.

Interesting.

I eyed the dagger with renewed respect, turning it over to examine the blade. Did its cut turn anything into an old prune, or just mushrooms? The blade, though dark, reflected the branches overhead remarkably well. I watched the image of gleaming leaves sway over the blade, revealing dazzling glimpses of sunlight.

A hulking shadow blotted out the sun.

My skin froze, prickling with ice, and slowly, hardly daring to look, I lifted my eyes from the dagger to the tree top.

Eight round eyes stared back.

Fuck this shit.

I staggered to my feet, scrambling backwards. A rock struck my heel, and cool water splashed over me as I landed in the stream, but I barely noticed it. Didn't bother to look. The witches were exclaiming, but I couldn't hear their words. What I'd taken to be tree branches moved with predatory stealth. Eight great legs, each one at least as long as me, crept between the boughs.

My voice had abandoned me. I pointed, vaguely surprised to notice I still clutched my dagger, and mouthed wordlessly.

The witches followed my point, and all hell broke loose.

The gargantuan spider lurched, darting down the tree on scuttling legs, faster than even my worst nightmares could have imagined. I let out a wobbling scream, and the monstrosity clicked its pincers and scurried towards me. I wailed louder, and my back collided with a rock. I'd reached the far bank, and I was trapped.

This was hell. I was going to die. I was going to be wrapped in arse-silk and turned into human soup.

My scream turned to a shriek as the spider loomed over me, its awful feet splashing into the water. I was paralysed. I could do nothing but stare into those many, glaring eyes.

Of all the ways to die, not this, please not this.

A wall of water, far bigger than the stream warranted, collided with the spider, roaring as it tore past, leaving me untouched.

It wasn't over yet.

The beast hadn't been carried far. The wave flattened, sinking into nothing as quickly as it had come, leaving a jerking tangle of legs waving in the air a few feet away. The witches descended, swords drawn, and ear-splitting shrieks and furious clicks filled the woods as the blades rose and fell, sending blue liquid spraying into the air. In moments, the spider fell silent, its legs curling in on itself.

"Aliza!"

I only too gladly tore my gaze from the dead monster and found Hyacinth staring down at me.

"Are you hurt?"

My chest hurt, a crushing weight pressing against my sternum. My fingers grappled, but I found no wound, only furiously heaving ribs. I couldn't breathe. I couldn't get enough air. My skin was flushed and icy at the same time, and tears blurred my vision.

"Can you stand?" She eased the dagger from my grip, setting it down, and then her warm hands grasped mine, hauling against my weight, but I barely made it halfway up before my knees gave out and I landed on my arse with another splash.

"It's alright." Pansy's voice. "It's dead. It can't hurt you."

"I-I can't," I gasped between breaths. "I can't—do this."

Nobody answered. Of course they didn't. Nobody cared what I wanted.

"I'm going—home."

An impatient tut, followed by Sage's voice. "How many times must I tell you—"

"I know!" I shrieked, my voice burning my already raw throat. I was on my feet without meaning to stand. "You've told me plenty of times, *the rifts are sealed*. But you didn't tell me there would be *spiders!*"

A sob burst from my mouth, and I brushed my hands frantically over my sopping body, trying to rid my skin of the creeping sensations crawling over me. It was no use. I was going home, and if I couldn't get home, I was going to lock myself in my room in Nairsgarth and never leave it again. Fuck the princes. They could rot for all I cared. I was not going to die for them. I refused to deal with this bullshit for another second.

"Take me home," I demanded, but Sage opened her mouth to argue. "I mean to the castle! Take me back. I'm not doing this."

"Aliza..." Disappointment and worry warred in Pansy's eyes. I didn't care. I didn't want or need anyone's approval.

"Get me out of this fucking wood *now*," I snarled, not daring to look up, but convinced I could sense yet more giant spiders creeping closer. I hunched forward, making myself as small as possible. Nobody spoke. Nobody even made a move. "Get me out," I repeated. "Take me back. Now. *Now!*"

"No." Sage matched my glare with her own. "Don't you see? This"— she gestured in the direction of the dead spider, but I couldn't bring myself to look. A fresh wave of shivers cascaded over me — "it means we're close. That was no natural beast. It's one of Maelgwyn's creations, a guardian. The princes are near. We cannot turn back now."

I stomped to the bank and plonked down on a stone, crossing my arms. "I'm not taking another step until you get me out of here."

"You would turn your back on the crown that will be yours by right? On immortality?"

"I don't want to be immortal!" I snapped. Why was nobody listening to me? "I don't want to be a queen. I just want to go home and live my own life. I never asked for any of this. I didn't mean to come here. I don't care about the princes, and I don't want your bullshit rewards!"

My voice rattled through the trees, leaving ringing silence in its wake. Even the birds stopped singing.

The witch's hands balled into quivering fists. "Are you trying to bring more of those creatures down on us?"

"Sage," Hyacinth said soothingly. "The poor child has had a fright. Give her a moment—"

"We don't have a moment!" she all but shrieked.

I blinked, my anger temporarily forgotten. I'd never seen Sage so riled. Her moss green eyes glared, and her lips curled back from her teeth.

"We *must* do this," she insisted, her face whitening. "We cannot afford to dally. Aliza is the first human to come to these lands, willingly or not, in over two centuries. If we give up now, how long will it be until the next one comes? I—*we* cannot turn back. Aliza is our only hope."

I buried my face in my hands. To the surprise of nobody, they weren't going to listen. They couldn't care less about me or my life. I was a tool. A tool to get what they wanted. I was trapped.

"I hate spiders," I whispered, my body succumbing to trembles once more. "I can't do spiders."

Somebody wrapped their arm around me. "It'll be alright," Pansy murmured, stroking my shoulder.

It wouldn't. It was a disaster, and I was woefully unprepared. I was no *promised one*. I was no queen. I was just a pathetic human, trapped in a situation much too big for me, and I wanted to go *home*.

A pair of small hands cradled mine. Hands splattered with oozing blue liquid. The spider equivalent of blood. I snatched mine away, scrubbing them on my sopping trousers, but looked at Sage, half crouching to peer imploringly at my face.

"Aliza. I know you didn't ask for this. If I could wake the princes myself, believe me, I would have done it hundreds of years ago. But I cannot. We cannot do this without you. If the spiders are too much for you, I will scout the area and see to it that you never lay eyes upon another, but we need your help. Please, Aliza. Help us."

I swallowed. Moss green eyes held mine. They were using me. I, as a person, meant nothing to them, but… if I turned my back now, how many innocent people would die? Could I give up, live my life, with that weighing on my conscience?

I licked my lips and nodded. "Okay. But you have to keep them away from me."

Sage deflated, sagging with relief. "The spiders?"

I nodded again, my throat tightening. I didn't want to think about them, or even hear their name.

"Right." Sage straightened, all business once more. "Hazel, Meadow, with me. Pansy, can you, er…" She gestured vaguely in my direction with a faint expression of distaste.

Pansy snatched my hand, tugging me to my feet and up the bank to dry ground. I walked with my head low and my shoulders hunched, as though that would prevent anything lurking above from reaching me. "Tea. That's what you need." She leaned in and said in a conspiratorial whisper, "And a cookie."

I couldn't force my lips to curve. Not now that I knew exactly what stood between me and my freedom.

14

The End Is Nigh

Sage and her hunting party returned late in the evening, all heavily splattered in blue liquid. Hope of walking any further that day faded with the light, and we pitched our tents along the bank. The witches had burnt the monstrous body, and I was glad of it. I was certain I wouldn't sleep after the day's events, but I didn't need a dirty great spider shadow flickering over my tent wall as I lay awake all night.

I looked up from what might have been my hundredth cup of strong, sweet tea as Sage marched through the camp and straight to Hyacinth. They shared a whispered discussion before Sage headed to the river and began stripping off her stained clothes. Apparently, she had no qualms about privacy as she waded, stark naked, into the water. I averted my eyes from her slender but surprisingly muscular form. Nobody else batted an eyelid. Maybe nudity was the norm within witch covens.

Hyacinth approached the log I shared with Pansy, smiling.

"Sister Sage has done as she promised," she said, "but what's more, she has spotted signs of strange magic not far from here. It's likely, given the... *guardians*, that the princes are closer than we'd imagined. With any luck, this will soon be over, and we will be home in time for lunch tomorrow."

She gave another encouraging smile and hurried away, but the flame-roasted mushrooms I'd picked at curdled in my stomach. I could well be *dead* before lunch tomorrow. Still, it was an entire day later than I'd anticipated when that many-legged monstrosity had been coming at me.

"Isn't that exciting?" Pansy leaned in close. "You'll meet Prince Anwir tomorrow!"

"Hmm." Excited wasn't the word I would choose, but I thought of that painting, and that lopsided grin, and butterflies erupted in my belly. They were almost immediately squished by the weight of my dread, but still, they'd existed, however fleetingly.

Supposing I did manage to survive the following morning, what would the almighty immortal Prince Anwir make of me? I coiled the end of my plait around my finger. The fae I'd met so far had been beautiful beyond reason, and I was just a bog-standard human. Pretty, by our standards; everyone commented on how blue my eyes were, and how long my legs. But compared to the fae...

Urgh. I didn't care what the prince thought of me, did I? This wasn't me. I wasn't some preening fool whose only thoughts centred around impressing boys. I had a brain, and a good one at that. I was worth so much more than some man's–*male's*–opinions of my looks.

"I can hardly contain myself," I said in answer to Pansy's question. "I suppose I should get some sleep. Big day tomorrow, after all..."

In truth, I wanted to be alone. This could very well be my last night on earth, or wherever the hell I was. What if I *did* die? What if I never made it home, and my parents spent the rest of their lives in ignorance of my fate? What if I never got to see them again? Never got to graduate and give them a better life?

The ball of dread I'd nursed all afternoon tightened into a physical ache and tears welled in my eyes. I missed them. I couldn't leave them, not without a chance to say a proper goodbye. I had to live. I had to get through that rift.

I spent an extra few minutes checking the folds of my blankets for spiders. After the horrors of the day, it would take only one tiny beast to tip me over the edge, and I had enough to deal with already. I checked Pansy's too, just to be on the safe side, and finally crawled beneath my covers.

The camp was quiet. I might have found the snap of the fire and the tinkling of the stream soothing on any other night, but my body was heavy, weighed down by the thought of my parents wasting their lives searching for me. I slid my hand into my pocket and pulled out my phone.

"Please," I breathed, holding the power button down.

The screen remained stubbornly dark.

I hugged the phone to my chest and squeezed my eyes shut. Tears seeped into my hair.

Frigid wind whipped my hair across my cold-raw face.

Gliding.

I looked down.

Dark ice sped beneath my bladed feet. My lips curved into a beaming smile as I spun, noting the twirling white trail I'd left in my wake.

It wasn't the only one. Another set wove and intersected with mine, criss-crossing and spiralling under the starry sky.

Strong hands closed around my waist, hoisting me into the air. My head fell back, lifting my face to the twinkling heavens, and we revolved gently before my blades met the ice once more, gliding to a halt.

Those hands wrapped around my front, palms pressing into my flesh as they travelled up my torso. A warm, solid body pressed against my back, and when I rolled my head onto the waiting broad shoulder, feather-light lips found my neck.

I sighed, my eyes sliding closed.

Hands kneaded my breasts, sending an electric cascade of shivers over every inch of my skin. My panting breath drifted away in frozen puffs as that electricity pooled between my legs, pulsing and tingling.

I twisted, wrapping my arms around the neck of a tall, dark-haired male with skin as light as moonlit snow. An exquisite face stared back at me, too beautiful to be real, his pale eyes full of hunger as they flickered over my face.

"Aliza." His lips moved, but my name shivered inside me instead of drifting to my ears. A siren's call. A plea.

Lightning skittered across the cloudless sky, a blinding flash that threw his beautiful features into sharp relief. I lifted onto the toes of my skates and kissed him.

I woke with a gasp.

It took a good few seconds to realise I was still in the tent, not out on the ice, and that it was Pansy lying beside me, not a hauntingly beautiful prince...

My heart thumped against my ribs, robbing me of my breath.

God, what was wrong with me? I clenched my thighs together, trying to push away the throb between them. It was no good. I needed air. I needed... I knew what I needed, and I certainly wasn't going to get it.

The night air was cool on my flushed skin as I crawled out from under the flap and knelt on the ground. The camp was fast asleep, and thanks to my early night, I had no idea who'd taken watch. I peered through the dying glow of the fire, and saw Hyacinth's faintly glowing silhouette leaning against a tree with her back to me. As silently as I could, I crept between the tents and into the deeper dark of the woods.

I hadn't forgotten my disastrous afternoon, but I couldn't bring myself to look up. If I was going to be mummified and have my insides liquefied, maybe it was better to not see it coming.

I was only slightly surprised to find the vampire sitting on a half-fallen tree, his legs swinging idly. Had he always been that waifish-ly handsome, or was my mind well and truly in the gutter?

"Jacques," I said, my voice soft to avoid alerting anyone, or anything, to my presence.

He smiled, his lip ring dark against his stark teeth. "Aliza."

He pushed off the branch, landing without a sound, and prowled closer.

"I almost died today." I wasn't sure why I felt the need to share with him.

"I know."

What was the point of having a supernatural stalker if he didn't come to my aid every now and again? "Much use you were."

He huffed a breath through his nose and came to a halt before me. "You had your witches."

"Why are you following me if you're not going to protect me?"

"Who says I am not protecting you? My kind is feared by most. My presence here keeps you safer by night."

That explained why our camps had been left untouched so far. "We teleported here. How did you find us?"

"I am a hunter, faster and more efficient than any of nature's creations, and my kingdom lies beneath your feet, ma belle. A great spiderweb of darkness beneath the ground, allowing me to travel undetected and untouched by the sun."

"Don't talk about spiders." Shuddering, I wrapped my arms around myself. "I've had enough of them."

Jacques gave me a wicked smile. "Comme tu veux."

"The witches think we're close." I wasn't exactly sure why I volunteered the information when the vampire was basically a stranger, and a suspicious one at that, but I had few friends in this world. I was under no illusion that he was one, not with his penchant for human blood, but he made pretending easy. He was the first person I'd met in this God-forsaken place, and I was coming to enjoy our little chats, even if I didn't understand half of what he said. "I'll probably die tomorrow."

He stepped closer still, his star-bright eyes as sympathetic as I'd ever seen them. Had any other human glimpsed pity in a vampire's gaze?

"Non, ma cherie. Tomorrow you will break the curse." His nostrils flared, and his soft, gleaming gaze sharpened. "What have you been thinking about, ma belle?"

My thighs clenched again, my heart quickening. Could he smell me, and the dream I'd had? God, I hoped not. Then again...

"Why haven't you bitten me? Is it because you need me to break the curse?"

I expected him to deny any such thing, but his piercing gaze dropped to my neck, as though he was imagining his teeth piercing me instead. "Yes."

"Oh." My belly flipped, half fear, half insanity-fuelled excitement. "Then, you wouldn't hurt me no matter what?"

The muscles in his sharp jaw flickered. "I need you to live long enough to save us all."

I drifted closer. Did I have a death wish? Was I still dreaming? Whatever was happening, my mind had turned to candy floss, and the need between my legs grew more demanding with every beat of my heart. Cool breath fanned over my face, and my eyelids fluttered. My skin tingled, waiting to be touched by something other than air. I didn't care if I died. I was doomed either way, I may as well go out on my own terms.

"Is that all humans are good for? Food and curse breaking?"

"I too was human, once. I believe our kind are good for many things."

"Oh?" The word was nothing more than a sigh. I dared to slide my hands up his chest. Why shouldn't I? He'd touched me, the last time we met. I wanted him to touch me now. To relieve me of the need my dream had left behind.

Jacques' breath came heavier, but his hands remained at his sides.

"What would happen if you kissed me?"

Faster than I could see, his hand shot to my jaw, forcing my head back. A tree collided with my spine, knocking the breath out of me, and with Jacques' cool lips skimming my neck, I couldn't remember how to take another.

"If I kissed you..." His hissing voice fell silent.

I ground my crushed body against him, gasping at the sparkling sensation. A hissing sigh sounded at my ear, the vibrations travelling through my body.

"Do it." I couldn't stand another second of it. I needed lips and flesh. Maybe even teeth, as long as they didn't go too deep. Or maybe I wouldn't care as long as I was being touched. And if I died, so what? It was only a few hours earlier than the fate the witches had in store for me.

Jacques took a step back, freeing me from the prison of his body. I slumped a little, my legs weak.

"If I kissed you," he repeated, "your prince would have my head."

I bristled. "What?"

"You will be his queen. *The* Human Queen, promised millennia ago. He will be your king. I must not touch you."

"I don't belong to him," I protested, indignant and desperate for his lips on my neck once more. "I can do whatever I want, with whoever I want. He's not *my* prince."

Jacques' shrugged, giving me a half smile. "Perhaps, but it will not be me who tests your theory. Bonne nuit, Aliza."

He swept his tangle of waves back and disappeared into the shadows, leaving me hot and cold and bothered, in more ways than one.

15

What Did We Learn About Caves? Fuck All, Apparently

I was groggy and quiet over breakfast, my mind as far from my soggy bowl of porridge as it was possible to be. We were on the move before the sun had risen over the treetops, with Sage snapping at our heels like an energetic but bad-tempered sheepdog. I couldn't say I shared her impatience. Every step carried me closer to my doom. A substantial part of me wanted to turn and run before we ever reached the horrors King Maelgwyn had in store for me, but I knew I wouldn't make it far before something hunted me down. I was dead either way. Besides, where would I run to? The sealed rifts? Much good that would do me, even if I had the first idea where to find one. There was no place for me in this world.

I walked with my head low, not daring to look up from our path through the tangled roots and clumps of flowers. Even Pansy gave up her attempts to pry conversation from me. I had no more interest in the mysterious properties of the plants, or in learning about the creatures and people of this world. What did it matter to me? I would either succeed or fail my mission. If I succeeded, I was going home. If I failed, as was more likely, especially after such a terrible night's sleep, I would die.

"Aliza," Pansy whispered. "Are you well?"

How could I be well? I had no idea what lay ahead, other than that no human before me had ever come out of this mess alive. This wasn't some test that could be studied for. It was my life, and the fate of this world. I was woefully unprepared.

I forced myself to smile. "Just nervous."

Pansy nodded but didn't look convinced.

The trees ahead thinned out, revealing a towering, mossy cliff face, half covered with trailing ivy. Sage came to a halt, bracing her hands on her hips and staring up. If she thought I was climbing that, she had another thing coming.

After a minute, she told us to wait and veered off along the base of the cliff, trailing her hand through the vines. Pansy sank down onto a rock with a sigh, but, tired as I was, I couldn't settle. My blood fizzed in my veins, as though it had turned to lemonade. I crossed my arms and shifted my weight between my feet, watching Sage's progress. As much as I didn't want to climb, or do anything else for that matter, the cliff was pretty. Layers and ripples of different hues of grey and white, broken by the rich green of the vines. What would it feel like, to trail my fingers over the rock, as Sage was doing? I imagined the chalky residue it might leave on my skin, and rubbed my fingertips over my thumbs. I left Pansy on her rock and followed in Sage's footsteps.

When I pressed my palm against the cliff face, the stone was warm, from hours baking in the sun. It seeped into my hand, drawing out some of the tension from my body. It wasn't quite the same as the hum of energy the crystal tub back at Nairsgarth gave off, but, if I didn't know better, I could have sworn the rock was alive. I wouldn't have been surprised if it swelled beneath my hand, drawing in a breath. It was comforting, like coming home at the end of a long shift, to find the windows glowing in welcome.

"What is it? Do you feel something?"

Sage appeared at my shoulder, and I snatched my hand away, hiding it behind my back as I faced her. "What? No."

The witch gave a knowing smirk. "It's not the rock, it's the magic. It's *them*."

"Them?"

She rolled her eyes. "The princes, girl. They're here."

I gave the cliff a dubious glance from the side of my eye. "They're... in the rock?"

Did I have to chisel them out? Maybe it wouldn't be so bad after all. Maybe I *could* do it. Sure, it wouldn't be easy, but it didn't sound like something that could kill me.

"No. They're on the other side." She set off again, following the base of the cliff. I hurried after her.

"How can you tell?"

"I can feel the magic of the curse. It bleeds through the rock, trying to push me away."

"Away? I thought..." No, it was best to keep my mouth shut about the energies of crystals and rocks, even here, where such things didn't seem quite as ridiculous.

Sage frowned over her shoulder. "What did you think?"

Oh, whatever. Who cared if I was insane? I definitely wouldn't be the only one. "It's like it's... calling me."

Sage halted, narrowing her eyes in contemplation. "I see. Perhaps you should be the one to guide us from here."

"Oh no, I couldn't." I took a step back. "I wouldn't know what to look for."

"Nor do I. We have never searched this particular place before."

"Why not?"

Sage shrugged, her eyes losing their focus, as though she was journeying through her memories. "Other places seemed likelier. In the early decades, humans found their way through the rifts every other day. There was always a willing volunteer to test my latest theories with, but one by one, they failed, and I exhausted my options." And the humans died. I swallowed. "Now here we stand in one of the few places I did not have the chance to try."

"After so many failures, you truly believe that you've figured it out this time?"

"Yes."

"Why?"

"I can feel it, Aliza. The magic. It's... different. Not quite right. Maelgwyn has pushed the boundaries of magic far beyond any other, beyond what is natural. He should have stopped long ago." She placed her hand on the wall of rock. "It feels wrong. I know you feel it too."

I certainly felt something, but wrong wasn't the word I would use. I skimmed my fingers over the rock. The sensation that travelled up my arm was a summer breeze, or the first lick of ice cream, or slipping into pyjamas after a long day.

"What do I do?" I breathed, my eyes closed, the comforting sensation spreading up to my shoulder, so faint it was barely there at all.

"Trust yourself."

At Sage's simple words, I snapped my eyes open. She asked too much of me. This was all too new. This wasn't some test I'd studied for, it wasn't a practical examination I'd practised until I could do it blindfolded, this was the fate of the world, and I was just Aliza. How could I trust myself? Unlike Sage, I hadn't had hundreds of years to work with magic. It was unfamiliar. Alien. Everything in this world was. I didn't have a stream of volunteers willing to sacrifice themselves for their chance at a crown. I *was* the sacrifice, and I was far from willing. For once in my life, I was clueless.

Sage watched me expectantly with quiet hope in her eyes. Hope that finally, after all these centuries of searching and failing, her people would be safe, her world free. I heaved a sigh and let my eyes slip closed as I pressed my palm harder against the stone.

My mind wandered back to the Fairy Glen, and the cave that had ruined my life. I hadn't wanted to go in at all, and even when I succumbed to Isobel's nagging, I'd never intended to go beyond the puddle of grey light marking the threshold. I had done though. I'd gone deep enough that I'd wound up here. I'd taken step after step, even after my torch had flickered out and darkness had swamped me. At the time, I hadn't noticed, but with hindsight... had something called to me? Had I been drawn in by the pull of a magic I hadn't had the experience to recognise? Magic that spoke to me and only me?

Was I meant to be here?

My feet moved, wandering at a gentle pace. I kept my eyes closed and let my hand trail over the stone, maintaining that comforting connection. With the sun baking down on my skin, I could well believe I was back home in my own garden, enjoying a summer's day. A breeze stirred, lifting the loose strands of hair around my face.

The ground beneath my feet gave a satisfying crunch with every step. It became a rhythm, one foot and then the other, a gentle beat in my mind. A beat that was answered by the pulse of magic beneath my fingers.

My eyes snapped open at the realisation, and I swayed, blinking in the bright sunshine. Dazed, I turned to find not just Sage, but all the witches hovering at my back. When had that happened? How hadn't I noticed them? Behind them, the spot they'd rested in had vanished. How far had I walked?

"Anything?" Sage's question came out on a breath, little more than an expectant whisper.

"I don't know." I gave the rock a doubtful look. Was I really sensing magic, knowingly following its call when a few days ago I hadn't believed in it?

For all the walking I'd done, the cliff didn't look any different, but I closed my eyes again. The beat was still there, thudding through me like a second heartbeat, but my feet stayed still. There was no urge to move left or right. I opened my eyes to find the cliff face an inch from my nose. Had I leaned toward it? I took a hasty step back, severing my connection to the magic.

"Could they be here?" I regretted my question immediately. I was bound to be wrong. If all this came to nothing, the witches would think me the biggest fool to ever cross the rift.

Sage appeared at my side, running her hands over the stone as though my words weren't batshit crazy. She hummed in consideration. "The magic is strong here."

Okay, well, maybe I hadn't lost the plot completely. I retreated, making space for the witches as they rushed to examine the patch of wall I'd inexplicably chosen. Goosebumps pricked over my arms, and

I shuddered, hugging myself. I couldn't be right, but if I was, we were one step closer. To what? Success, or my death?

The witches muttered amongst themselves, leaving me to stew over my mistakes. Camping had been the first. If I survived this quest, if I made it home, I would *never* sleep in a tent ever again. It would be hotels only from here on out. Holidays would be spent in the sunshine, and would certainly not involve hiking or expeditions into caves.

"Aliza?"

Great. What now? I half hoped the witches were about to tell me I was wrong, that we should give up this ridiculous mission and return to Nairsgarth, never to try again, but the excitement simmering in Pansy's eyes told me otherwise. I approached on reluctant feet.

"We think this is it," Pansy muttered through teeth bared in a smile, "but we can't open it."

"Open what?"

"I suspect this is a hidden gate," Sage explained in an oddly strained voice. "I also suspect it can only be opened by a human."

"Oh. Well... that would make sense, I guess. What do I have to do?" I stared up at the cliff face, towering above us. I saw nothing to mark it as a gate, but then, if I was an evil wizard intent on hiding my cursed nephews, I wouldn't signpost it either.

"Give me your hand."

I did as Sage said, allowing her to turn my hand palm up. She stared down at it intently, as though reading my future. What did she see? Did my lifeline come to an abrupt end, marked with today's date?

Sage whipped a dagger across my palm.

Blood bloomed a moment before pain erupted. I tried to snatch my hand away, but she caught my wrist in a surprisingly strong grip considering her short fingers, twisting my palm toward the rock.

"What the fuck? A little warning next time!"

My blood smeared the stone, and I winced as my hand stung as though it had been dipped in acid.

With a ground quaking rumble, a crack split the wall. I staggered back, dragging Sage with me as the dark slice stretched taller even than me, before expanding into a pitch-black chasm. It stretched wide enough to admit one person, then fell still and silent.

Sage's incredulous, high-pitched laugh was so unlike her that it distracted me temporarily from the cave mouth that hadn't existed a moment ago. Was it some sick joke that my journey had started with a cave and now looked likely to end the same way?

"We found it," Sage muttered, dropping my wrist and advancing on the wall. "We actually found it."

By *we* I presumed she meant *I* had found it. The witch whipped around in a whirl of blonde hair, fixing her wild eyes on me. I retreated a step. "You're really her," she whispered. "It's you."

Well, this was weird. I couldn't decide if the jet-black cave was scarier than Sage's display of genuine emotion. Nor was her evident surprise at my small success reassuring.

"Your hand." She jolted into action, tossing her pack to the ground. Her hands trembled as she unbuckled the strap and began rooting through its contents.

"Aliza, you did it." Pansy laid a reverent hand on my arm, her mouth hung open in shock. Behind her, the witches all stared at me with identical expressions of awe.

So much for their belief in me being the mysterious Human Queen. They were as stunned as I was. I almost laughed, until a sharp throb reminded me of my injured hand. I clutched it to my chest as sticky warmth ran down my wrist. Was Jacques lurking? Would the metallic tang of my blood be enough to tempt him out into the sunlight?

"Here, Aliza." Sage staggered to her feet, reaching for my hand. I shied away, and she rolled her eyes. "Oh, come now, don't be ridiculous."

"You just sliced me open!"

"I had no choice, and besides, I'm about to patch you up." She brandished a jar containing thick green paste, the same concoction she'd used on me when I'd arrived at Nairsgarth. It *had* worked wonders.

Grudgingly, I allowed her to pour water into the wound, and smother it in paste, while I winced and ground my teeth, all the while trying not to look at the hulking cave. The pain eased beneath the cool poultice, and Sage wound a bandage around my hand. Her work wasn't as neat as it had been the first time, but it was done quickly.

Too quickly, in fact.

No sooner had she shouldered her pack once more than she marched me to the cave mouth. With a mutter and a click of her fingers, a little flame appeared in her hand. It wasn't much against the dense darkness awaiting us, but it was better than nothing. To my relief, she went ahead of me, picking up speed as she aimed for the narrow crack.

With a small oof noise, Sage collided with the darkness, bouncing off and stumbling backwards into my chest. Unthinkingly, I caught her, receiving a stab of pain in my hand as a reward.

"What happened?" I couldn't quite keep the hope from my voice. If we couldn't go any further, we'd have no choice but to give up.

Sage didn't answer. She shoved away from me, marching to the cave. She bounced back as though an invisible door protected the area, but she recovered her feet, trying again. Whatever was blocking her held firm. With a scream of rage, Sage whacked her fists against it. Where they should have arced through the air, they slammed to a stop.

The witch turned, seeking out her fellows, her shoulders heaving with every breath. "You try."

Hyacinth hurried forward, slowing as she neared the waiting hole. She lifted a hand, holding it before her. Her wrist bent back as her palm met something unyielding.

One by one, my companions attempted to enter the cave. All failed.

Sage turned to me, raising a questioning eyebrow.

Erm, no. Absolutely not.

Except, my feet moved, carrying me forward against my will. I didn't *want* to go in there, did I? Especially when Sage couldn't lead the way. No, definitely not. I much preferred the idea of staying in the sunshine, surrounded by my protectors, and yet there I was, strolling toward the cave mouth. I hesitated on the lip of the shadows. If I could go through, what did that mean for me? Did I go on alone? It wasn't too late to turn back. I could still run. I could become another failure in Neath's history.

Failure.

The word sat uneasily on my shoulders. I didn't know how to fail. I'd strived and worked for everything I had. Could this be the day I gave up without a fight?

With a deep breath, I took a careful step. My boot landed in darkness. Another step, and another. From the shade of the cave, I turned to face my party, my legs numb. They couldn't follow me.

I was alone.

Worried faces stared back. Pansy drifted forward, though she made no attempt to join me.

"Come back, Aliza," Sage said, her voice brisk and level once more.

As glad as I was to oblige, something, some strange, new awareness, grated over my skin as I emerged into the light. Something that clawed at me, trying to hold me back. I shrugged it off, rejoining the witches.

"You go on alone from here," Sage said, as though giving instructions on how to fold a bedsheet. "It seems we have taken you as far as we can."

I barked a single, flat note of laughter. She was joking, right? She couldn't possibly expect me to continue alone and live to tell the tale.

"Here." Sage fished something out of her pocket and pressed it into my uninjured hand. She cupped my upturned hand in hers, and I caught a glimpse of a white crystal before her palm laid flat over it. Her eyes slipped shut and she muttered a strange word under her breath.

Something spread over my skin, cool and hard, like a wafer-thin layer of ice. It moulded to my form, following every curve and contour of my body, then faded into nothing.

"What was that?"

"A protection spell." Sage raised her pale eyebrow, sliding the crystal back into her pocket. "It won't prevent major injury, but consider it a layer of armour against minor blows. Honestly, girl. When we get back you need to attend some lessons."

Major injury? My knees trembled, but before I could think of an argument for giving up this insane plan, another witch, Hazel, placed another rock in my hand. I was sick of rocks. I never wanted to see one again as long as I lived, starting right now.

Another strange word, another strange sensation. Tiny, champagne-like bubbles popped over me, starting at the crown of my head and cascading down to my toes. My body shivered involuntarily, though the sensation wasn't completely horrible.

"Luck." Hazel smiled shyly up at me, averting her blue eyes. "It will guide your choices."

I'd need more than luck.

Hyacinth came next, holding a small, glass lantern containing a tiny crystal. With a click of her fingers, a flame curled to life, engulfing the rock. Most unusually, she didn't smile as she handed it to me. Instead, she gave me a look Mum might have given if faced with the prospect of sending me to my death. "To light your way," she said softly.

Pansy came last, tears wobbling at her lower eyelids. "You have your daggers? And the necklace?" Her voice wavered. I nodded, and she sniffed before launching herself at me. I hugged her gingerly back, careful not to set her on fire, or snag my bandages. When she broke away, her cheeks glistened.

"It's going to be fine," she insisted, though I didn't know who she hoped to fool. "Just be careful, alright? We'll be waiting for you."

How could I promise to be careful when I didn't have the faintest idea what lurked in the darkness. Shades? Spiders? Maelgwyn himself?

"What if I find them?" I croaked. "How do I break the curse?"

Sage's green eyes swept over me, and she gave my dagger belt an experimental tug. When it held firm, she lifted her gaze. "Trust yourself,

Aliza. You are the Human Queen. I wasn't sure at first, but you are, beyond all doubt. You will know what to do, but be on your guard. You will not necessarily be able to rely on your senses beyond this gate. You must use your brain. Question everything you might see or hear. Trust nothing. The fae are notorious tricksters, and Maelgwyn is the worst of them. We'll wait until the moon sets on the second night," Sage said. "Be back by then, Aliza."

Shaking from head to toe, I nodded and walked into the darkness alone.

16

But Wait, It Gets Worse

Black pressed in from every side, threatening to obliterate my lantern's wavering puddle of light. In a matter of steps, the last traces of sunshine, the last whisper of birdsong and rustling leaves, faded into nothing. There was only me and my ratcheting heartbeat. My scuffing, tentative footsteps. My uneven breath. Blood hissed inside my head like I'd pressed a seashell to my ear.

Panic clouded my brain, making it impossible to think rationally.

Run. Go back. Scream. Curl up on the ground. Cry.

It was only sheer willpower that had me placing one numb foot in front of the other. As long as the lantern burnt, as long as it cast its light over me, I was safe from Maelgwyn's shades. This tunnel seemed just the place for them, creatures of shadow that they were. If they were here, they couldn't cross my glowing threshold. They could come close, though. They could press against the edge of the darkness, their eyes gleaming at me, waiting for a chance to snatch me and whisk me away to God knew where. I hooked my lantern over the wrist of my injured hand, careful to avoid snagging the bandaged wound, and with the other, I slid one of my evil daggers from its scabbard, holding it out in front of me. My arm trembled like a scolded dog.

If this was the place, if the princes were in here, I doubted Maelgwyn had left them unprotected. Centuries hadn't passed, countless hopeful humans hadn't died because of party tricks like nicked hands and hidden gates. Worse things were in store for me. Danger lurked. It stalked me, taking its time, relishing the slow, stealthy hunt.

I couldn't dwell on that. If I did, I'd turn back the way I'd come. I'd fail. Terrified as I was, I hadn't come this far to quit.

The princes were close. For over two hundred years they'd slept, waiting for someone, for *me*, to save them. Just because they were strangers to me, it didn't mean I didn't care. They were people. Not human, but people all the same. They'd had lives. Family. Friends. A future, which was more than I'd have if I gave up. The time to run had gone, if it had ever existed at all. By saving them, I was saving myself. Waking them was my only hope of going home. I could give all three of us our lives back in one fell swoop.

Hope countered my fear, soothing it, giving me a reason to keep going. I let thoughts of the princes fill my head. I *wanted* to save them. I wanted to help. All I had to do was keep placing one foot in front of the other. When I made the return journey, I wouldn't be alone.

By the faint light of Hyacinth's flame, a fork in the tunnel came into view. For the first time since stepping into the cave, I halted, holding my lantern aloft. There was nothing to distinguish between the paths, no markers to guide or trick me. I gulped down my rising swell of panic. I would not get lost. I would simply choose a path and remember the way. Easy.

Yeah, right. As easy as coaxing a cat out of its carrier without being savaged.

I screwed my eyes shut. I would not be defeated by this. When I opened my eyes, it would be with a decision made. I had Hazel's luck on my side. Claudia's necklace, too. I'd found the gate by listening to the magic. Why shouldn't I find my way here, too?

Still clutching my dagger, I reached out, pressing my skin against the wall of rock separating the two branches of the tunnel. The stone was cooler, having never seen the light of day, but surprisingly dry. I'd expected damp and mould, not chalky rock. My tight muscles eased slightly.

Right. I'd go right.

Opening my eyes, I forced my feet into action before doubt could creep in. Easy, I reminded myself. Nothing to worry about. Just a right turn. Just silence and darkness and imminent death. Nothing I couldn't handle.

I lost track of time, unable to tell if minutes or hours had passed since leaving the woods. Sage had promised to wait for two nights. How was I supposed to know how many times the moon had set when I couldn't see the sky? My phone was a weight in my pocket, taunting me with its uselessness. If only it worked, I'd have a clock *and* a decent torch. As it was, I couldn't even rely on my churning stomach to tell me how many meals I'd missed. Stress had a way of killing my appetite while simultaneously drying up my mouth.

I licked my lips, thinking longingly of the water skein in my pack. I'd save it though. For all I knew, these tunnels went on for days.

In the lightless depths behind me, a pebble skittered over the ground.

After such pressing silence, the sound was unnaturally loud, and my knees buckled slightly as I spun, lifting my lantern high.

My heart hammered against my sternum, my brain screaming *run* with every beat. If only they'd shut up. My ears strained to catch the slightest sound.

Nothing.

Nothing but stillness. No shades. No evil fae wizards. No giant spiders. Just me and my trinkets in this dusty, long-forgotten place. Maybe I'd imagined the noise. I blew out a breath, lowering my lantern slightly.

A milk-white shape shot out of the darkness.

I glimpsed huge, pale eyes and a mouthful of sharp teeth before it collided with me, sending me sprawling over the floor with a shriek. The creature, easily as large as me, landed on top of me, shoving the air from my lungs. Putrid, rotting breath smacked my senses as an overly large mouth snapped inches above my face. In a tangle of flailing limbs, I wrestled, twisting and writhing in an attempt to throw the creature off me. The flame of my lantern, still hung around my wrist, guttered, plunging the beast into shadow edged with flickering light. Strings of thick saliva splattered my skin as teeth clacked, closer to my face with each snap. It was no worse than a dog, I lied to myself. A vicious, bad-tempered dog who *hated* vets. All part of the job. In the absence of a collar to twist, my bandaged hand lodged at the creature's scrawny throat, straining to hold it at bay. Ignoring the throb of my wound, I squeezed, locking my joints to hold it at arm's length.

Long talons slashed across my stomach with a sharp flash of pain, knocking the breath from me. The thing would feast on my guts while I was still alive given half a chance. I would not die like that. I would take it with me.

I tightened my grip on my dagger. My arm strained under the weight of the monster, but I mustered all my strength and shoved it to the full length of my arm, giving myself room. The dagger plunged into its distended belly. Gloopy, slime-like blood tumbled over me in a series of wet slaps as the creature let out a rasping screech. For a moment, it went rigid, its hideous, oversized jaw straining wide, before it slumped, dangling over me.

I panted, my eyes darting over its hideous face. The monster wasted before me, as though the flesh was being sucked from its bones. Its waxy skin tightened over a large skull, its pointed ears curling in on themselves. Its overly long limbs contracted with its shrinking, wrinkling skin, leaving only a papery, bowed skeleton.

By some miracle, I was still alive and it was not.

Shoving it aside, I scrambled to my feet, panting as I pressed a hand to my slimy belly. I couldn't tell where my attacker's gloopy, paste-like blood ended and mine began, but my innards didn't tumble to the floor, which was always a good sign. There was no pain either, beyond a dull ache. If I died, it would be from some hideous blood-born pathogen transferred from the monster's guts to mine. Still, that would only be a problem if I survived these tunnels.

I examined the dark blade of my dagger. First the mushroom, now a creature, both reduced to husks. Without it, I'd be dead.

Heedless of the pain in my injured hand, my bandages now covered in thick, treacle-like blood, I palmed my second dagger.

The shock of the attack eased slightly, but panic barged in to take its place. I'd been attacked. I wasn't alone in these endless, lightless tunnels at all. I was being hunted. The monster surely had friends, but all I had were two cursed daggers and not much idea of how to use them. Forget the princes, I was going back. I couldn't do this. I wasn't prepared to die, not for them, not for the witches, not even for a chance to go home. I wanted to *live.*

My breath came in sharp, shallow pants. My legs wobbled violently beneath my weight. All I had to do was go back the way I'd come. Before I knew it, I'd be out in the sunshine and on my way back to a safe, peaceful life in Nairsgarth, with the entire coven and thick stone walls to protect me. Maybe I'd become a witch and spend my days making potions and polishing my crystals.

Averting my eyes from my silent, shrivelled companion, I took a few shaking steps back, away from the princes.

A distant shriek, identical to that my assailant had made as I buried my dagger in its belly, drifted down the tunnel. Ahead of me. There was another one, and it was blocking my way out. A second cry joined the first, and my skin prickled with icy terror. More than one. They'd heard the commotion. They were coming for me. My feet danced on the spot, torn between the stolen promise of safety, replaced with fanged, clawed horror, and the fear of the unknown. The dark.

My boots skidded as I spun, breaking into a sprint. Away from the protection of the witches. Away from freedom. I leapt over the dead monster and flew down the tunnel, as a chorus of hideous howls and screeches rose behind me.

The lantern's flame dipped and sputtered as I ran, never lighting more than a few feet before me. I pumped my arms, the glimpses of deadly, black daggers whipping in and out of sight my only reassurance. Faster. I had to go faster. Eyes straining against the wall of darkness, I sucked down breath after breath of dry, stale air. All the while, the screams grew louder, joined by the scurrying of many feet.

They were gaining on me. Two daggers would be no match against them. When I came to another fork, I let my momentum choose my direction. There was no time to feel the lure of magic. Death, gruesome, agonising, terrifying death nipped at my flying heels. Literally. I didn't need to look to know they were close, gaining with horrifying speed. Maybe even within my guttering puddle of light. They were no shades, and Hyacinth's lantern wouldn't slow them.

A sob burst through my teeth. I wasn't going to make it.

A bend came on me suddenly, and sprinting, I had no time to turn. I thudded against the rock, bouncing off, my feet scrambling for balance. No time. No time to feel pain. My light glowed brighter.

No. It was *daylight*.

To my right, at the far end of a long, low spread of tunnel, a window of sky beckoned, begging me to hurry. I'd done it, I'd found my way. I was almost there.

Throwing myself into action, my head filled with ear-splitting shrieks, I ran for the light. Pain erupted in my ankle, and I buckled with a cry. It was nothing. Just an old injury. I wouldn't let it kill me, not when I'd made it this far, even though every step was like wading through fire. Locking my jaw against the pain, I forced myself to run.

Light glared, scorching my eyes as I closed in on the finish line. I screwed them shut. I was going to make it. I *had* to make it.

Through my eyelids, burning white light engulfed me, and the ground disappeared from under my feet. For the second time in my life, I plunged from a cave and into open air.

Hard, unyielding ground crashed into me, forcing the air from my lungs in a puff. I rolled, limbs pinwheeling, body sliding, before skidding to a stop.

Cool, rough grass pressed against my face, and when I sucked down a breath, its musty, straw-like scent filled my nose. My eyes squinted open, watering in the piercing light.

I was out of the cave.

Trembling like a newborn kitten, I clambered stiffly to my feet. The pain in my ankle roared its protests, but after a few ginger attempts, it took my weight grudgingly.

I was halfway down a gentle slope blanketed in dead grass. Above me, cliffs rose high, identical to those I'd so foolishly gone into. A crack at its base marked my exit, and there, in the shadows, pale creatures writhed. Were they held back by the same barrier that had kept the witches out, or did daylight hurt their enormous eyes, made for living in darkness? Whatever the reason, I was safe, I'd made it. Elation swelled in my chest. I was alive.

Maybe Claudia's ugly old necklace was more than just a questionable fashion choice.

Limping, I revolved on the spot, taking in my surroundings. I found myself in a crater, walled on every side by high, sheer cliffs. The sun gleamed high overhead, still hours away from dipping below the horizon and robbing me of the protection of its light. It glinted at the tip of a sharp pinnacle.

There, at the bottom of the valley, surrounded by a dense forest of bald, twisting trees, stood a lonely tower.

17

What Is It With Me And Bottomless Pits?

My direction was clear. Maelgwyn had to be confident in the efficiency of his cave zombies because he hadn't made the slightest effort to hide the princes' location. Arrogant prick. Clearly, he hadn't known who he was dealing with.

I gave a dismal laugh at my own expense as I took stock of my body. He was dealing with an absolute mess.

Beneath the thick layer of dark, sludge-like gore splattered over my belly, my probing fingers found no trace of slashed flesh. My internal organs remained firmly in their allotted place, even if the aftershock of my near-death experience had them squirming like ferrets. Both my shirt and wrap were torn, four great slices cutting clean through both layers of fabric, but the flesh beneath was intact. I'd definitely felt talons rake across my abdomen. Had the protection spell cast by Sage, quite literally, saved my skin?

It certainly hadn't saved me from the aches and pains of my tumble down the slope. With one eye fixed firmly on the cave mouth above me, I limped up the hill, retrieving my daggers and lantern. By some miracle, my little flame still flickered and danced, though the glass protecting it had smashed clean out of its frame. Would I need it in the tower? I squinted at the top of the ugly stone structure, protruding from the dead forest. No glimmer of sunlight reflected on any windows. It would be just my luck that the building would be as black as the tunnels, maybe even guarded by more awful creatures like the ones still swarming the shadowy cave mouth, fighting each other for a chance to brave the sunlight and strip the meat from my bones. Whatever awaited me in the tower, I had to face those tunnels again if I wanted to get home. Would the princes be as burly as the fae guards of Tir o Gaeaf, or would centuries of slumber have reduced them to stick-thin waifs? Who would be protecting who on the return journey?

With resignation heavy on my shoulders, I hooked the battered lantern over my wrist once more, palmed my dagger in my shaking hand, returning its twin to its sheath, and set off down the slope of dead, yellow grass, my eyes fixed on the dead, black trees.

Only, they weren't trees.

My heart plummeted to my boots as the full scale of my latest obstacle drifted into sharper focus with every limping step.

Brambles. Thick, tangled brambles, as tall and broad as ancient trees, knotted and entwined with a density that prevented the glaring sun from touching the ground. I halted in their damp shadow, contemplating the wall of thorns. Some were as large as shark fins, waiting to shred my skin, others were shorter but still long and skinny, like oversized sewing needles, ready to pop an eyeball or sink between my ribs. Had they spent the past couple of centuries growing and snaking and twisting? In a couple more would they engulf the tower and fill the crater? What would become of the helpless, sleeping princes if I failed today? Would pain penetrate the curse as thorns squeezed the tower down around them, crushing them in a stony grave?

As it was, there was no way through the brambles for anything larger than a small cat. Maybe without the thorns I could have slithered and crawled between the narrow gaps left between the stems, but even then, I'd have risked tangling myself in a twisted tomb.

My grip tightened on my dagger. It had shrivelled a mushroom and a monster. Why not a bramble? Easing my arm between a cluster of deathly sharp thorns, careful to avoid skewering myself in the armpit, I scraped the tip of the black blade over the woody vine. With a bone-deep groan and a drawn-out creak, the bramble shrivelled, shrinking and slithering back into the mass like a retracting rope, whipping out of sight. In its place, it left a shadowed gap, large enough for a small child to fit inside–assuming they had an exoskeleton to protect from the thorns–and curled up in a ball.

Right, okay. Easy. I just had to nick enough branches to clear my path to the tower. I could do that. Sighing, I set to work.

One by tedious one, the brambles withered away at the end of my dagger, and I waded gingerly into the thatch they left behind. Hollow, husk-like brambles exploded into puffs of dust beneath my boots, while thick, healthy ones knotted overhead, beyond my reach. As long as they didn't fall down, I'd be fine, or that was what I told myself as I left all traces of daylight behind and worked my way deeper into the weaving thicket.

With my boots blackened by the puffed remains of my bramble victims, I halted my path of destruction. At last, a wall of dark stone blocked my way, the mortar crumbled with age. Smaller vines covered in hair-like thorns clung to the tower wall like the stone had been caught in a net. Beneath the web of stems and thorns, I glimpsed planks of wood so ancient they wouldn't have looked out of place on a pirate shipwreck. The musty scent of rotten wood drifted up my nose.

Perfect. It was a wonder this crumbling ruin was still standing. Health and Safety would condemn the building in a heartbeat, and yet, I had no choice but to go inside without so much as a hard hat. At least this ordeal was almost over.

It *had* to be almost over.

The canopy of dense brambles overhead left me with no sense of the tower's height, but it couldn't be that tall. Within the hour, I'd be on my way home.

Spurred on by the thought, I slashed the web of vines away. Without their support, the rickety door gave an ominous groan, tilting on its rusted hinges, the top half hanging free from the frame. There was no handle, but I transferred my dagger to my injured left hand and eased the fingers of my right into the dark crack the tilt had created.

Wood crumbled beneath my touch as I pulled on the door, using my entire weight to haul against it. After a moment of resistance, it gave a small jolt, almost throwing me off balance, and then began to move. My shoulder trembled as I dragged the door toward me, leaving a gap just wide enough for me to squeeze through.

Yet another dark cavern awaited me, and I hesitated, holding my flame aloft and letting my eyes adjust. The last thing I needed was another creature ambushing me. I'd been lucky once; I couldn't take any chances.

Nothing but silence and the lure of magic greeted me. It was stronger now, I realised with a surprised blink. Preoccupied with trying to survive, I hadn't noticed the warm, pulsing *something* in my sternum, a second heartbeat calling me onward. Now I acknowledged its presence, I couldn't believe I'd managed to drown out its strange loveliness. The sense of surety and calm that pulsed from its source. The feeling of home.

It was a trick. This tower was not my home, and calm was the last thing I needed to be. Danger stalked me, death clung to every shadow. I needed to be sharp and aware. I needed to survive. Only then could I go home.

With a shuddering breath, I eased through the gap and into the tower.

At once, flames erupted on either side of me, burning in brackets set into the walls. Ahead, another pair lit, then another, until my path was marked in a glowing trail, straight to the foot of a stone staircase.

No stalking creatures were revealed by the light, just plain stone walls and a floor coated in a thick carpet of dust. That was a good start, I supposed, but it did nothing to ease my nerves. Traps could be hidden anywhere, like some booby-trapped Egyptian pyramid. As Sage had wisely advised, I could trust nothing. I eyed the cobwebs that swayed in a non-existent breeze as I passed beneath them, but no spiders revealed themselves. Hopefully, they were long dead. Hopefully, I would not be joining them.

The hallway seemed to stretch far longer than it should have if my glimpse of the tall, narrow tower had been anything to go by. Or maybe it was my twinging ankle that made a short distance seem long.

I reached the stairs. Dusty, crumbling stairs, but otherwise, normal. They spiralled up and away from me, disappearing from view. Flexing my sweat-dampened fingers around the hilt of my dagger I took my first, careful step.

The walls didn't come crashing down. Ghouls didn't come whooshing from amongst the cobwebs. It was only me and a crumbling old tower.

I began to climb.

Thick dust muffled my footsteps, but in the dense silence, they boomed like a war drum. Around and around I went, clinging to the wall to ease my weight from my ankle. My thighs began to cramp as my skin grew hot under my layers. My breath rattled like the chains of a mournful ghost.

Around and up, and up and around. Over and again. A ceaseless climbing spiral.

Seconds turned to minutes, each one dragging on for its own eternity.

God, would it never end? Panting, I strained to see around the corner, hopeful I'd glimpse the top of the flight. Steps awaited me. No matter how high I climbed, how many steps I conquered, there were always more. The fire in my thighs grew with every step, and sweat slicked my spine.

A stitch seized my abdomen and I ground to a halt, buckling forward as I clutched the wall and waited for the cramp to ease. Ahead and behind, the stairs spiralled out of view, hidden by curved walls. My heart thudded frantically. At least it wasn't from fear this time.

What I'd give for a breeze, but the air was still and musty, undisturbed for hundreds of years. I stowed my dagger in its sheath and took a glug of water from my bottle, gathered from the icy stream I'd plunged into under the glare of an advancing spider.

The stream. When I made it back, I'd strip off and douse myself in that fresh, chilled water. But to make it back, I first had to make it up. I stowed my drink in the side pocket of my pack, drew my dagger, though it hung limply at my side, too heavy for my weary body to lift, and set off again.

I climbed for what felt like hours, until sweat ran in a river between my breasts. Until each breath was nothing but a short, sharp stab to the lungs. I was going to vomit. I was going to collapse and roll all the way back down to the bottom. I was going to combust into a ball of flames and become just another layer of dust on the endless, cursed steps.

Just when I began to seriously consider admitting defeat and sliding back down on my bum, a glimpse of faint light met the glow of my lantern, and the most beautiful breath of cool air kissed my overheated skin. A breeze. A window.

Swallowing my sob of relief, I forced myself to continue. With every step, the light grew brighter, until a landing slid into view, adorned with an enormous, glittering window. An open window, its glass criss-crossed with lead strips. Below it, near where it had been thrown wide open, a low, broad sill waited, inviting me to sink down and take the weight off my feet while resting my hot forehead on the cool glass.

Just for a minute. I could spare a moment to cool down.

Straightening my aching spine, I approached, my knees threatening to buckle in anticipation. The breeze danced over my skin. When had I ever felt anything quite as blissful?

Through the glass, I glimpsed the cliffs beneath a cloudless sky, and slopes of long, thick grass swaying in the breeze. The view was almost worth the climb. Despite what lurked inside those cliffs, the valley was beautiful from up here, lush and green.

Turning away from the view, I let my knees bend with a groan.

Green?

The grass had been dead. Yellow and as dry as hay. Not green.

Question everything you might see or hear.

Too late, Sage's warning clanged through my memory. My bum touched the sill as a chill that had nothing to do with the breeze that couldn't possibly exist shivered over my skin. The tower had no windows and the grass was dead.

The sill disappeared from beneath me just as I attempted to lurch back to my feet.

The world opened into a yawning chasm, and I threw my arms out wide, my fingertips skimming the velvety layer of dust encasing the walls. This was a trap, and I'd fallen right into it.

My stomach flipped, lurching to my throat as gravity dragged me down. The edge of the stone pit collided with my belly, and all the air left my lungs in a bark as my nails clawed at the floor, searching for purchase. They dug into the shallow crack between the floor tiles, clinging to the scant few millimetres of rock. Cold, stale air whooshed up around me, stirring my braid.

Visions of massive spikes and skewered skeletons filled my mind. Or maybe a starving beast, waiting for the first meal in centuries to fall into its enclosure. Whatever awaited me, it would not be pretty. The toes of my boots scraped the wall of the pit, searching for a foothold to propel me back to safety. I found none.

God, I was an idiot. Why did I have to be so fucking unfit? I was pathetic. If only I'd bothered to do a few squats now and again, the stairs wouldn't have left me desperate for a seat. If I'd curled a few dumbbells, my arms might have been strong enough to haul my weight from the lip of the pit, digging mercilessly into my lower ribs. Now I was going to die. I was still alive only thanks to my moment of realisation, the brief propulsion I'd given myself as I tried to stand. It was only a matter of time before my trembling, white-knuckled fingers lost their grip on the edge of the stone tile and I slipped into the waiting abyss.

Spikes would be quick, wouldn't they? With any luck they'd skewer my brain, killing me instantly. Or maybe my luck had run out. Maybe they'd spear through a shoulder, leaving me trapped and wounded, but not mortally so. Maybe I'd be left to bleed out slowly, alone in the dark. Or would infection or dehydration claim me first?

Would Pansy argue when the second moon set and the witches packed up their tents? Would she beg for another day, another hour, while I festered, far from help? Would Sage shoulder her disappointment at yet another human failure, putting on her impassive mask and doling out efficient orders? Would she claim she'd never believed in me at all, that her words at the gate had meant nothing?

You're really her. It's you.

It *was* me, Goddammit. I might not be the Human Queen, but I was going to break this fucking curse. Maelgwyn would not finish me off this easily. I would not allow it.

Grunting, I scraped the toes of my boots over the wall. The brief moment of resistance was enough to shift my weight forward onto my arms. I could do this. I had to. Again, I shunted my weight slightly in favour of survival. My knee scraped the wall, but I barely felt the sting. Sage would fix it with her magic paste. My arms trembled as, bit by bit, I shoved and scraped myself up the wall. By the time the lip of the pit dug into my belly, my fingers were numb and stiff, my elbows raw from taking my weight. With a last surge of effort, I swung my leg to the side, hooking my knee, and with trembling thighs, I hauled myself up and over.

With a sob of relief, I rolled away from the pit, collapsing on my back, the beautifully solid floor beneath me.

"Fuck you, Maelgwyn," I panted at the cobwebs, swaying innocently overhead. Hopefully the old bastard heard me with his weird magic. Actually, no. It would be better if he had no idea I was here until it was too late. Still, fuck him to Hell and back.

My body resisted my instructions to stand, reluctant to leave the solid safety of the floor, but I scrambled stiffly to my feet, the trap beckoning wide and dark beside me.

I'd almost died. *Again.*

Shivering, I retreated a step. That had been too close. A cat's whisker from disaster. Too easily I'd have become nothing but a broken skeleton, locked away in some lightless pit forevermore.

My legs began to quake violently. I was going to die here in this God-forsaken world. There was no point worrying about rifts, or monsters, or even making it back through the tunnels. This was it. This tower was the resting place of royalty, and everyone claimed I was destined to become a queen. It was my grave.

18

Yeah, That's Not Creepy At All

I hurried along the landing and away from the pit before my legs gave up and tossed me back in. All traces of heat had evaporated from my body, leaving a feverish chill in their wake. I wasn't sure which was worse.

The landing was long. Too long. A patterned carpet, its colours faded with dust and age, stretched endlessly ahead. More torches flickered on the walls. It was magic. Sorcery. The tower was round and not especially tall. There was no room for a corridor, and yet, there it was. Worse still, faint music drifted from the far end.

What now?

The hairs on my arms rose. I'd seen enough horror movies to know that approaching the strange, faint music was a bad idea, but there was no other way unless I wanted to give up. Did I? Could I turn around and crawl meekly back to the witches, telling them I'd almost made it but lost my nerve?

Shame curdled in my gut, and I set off, the carpet deadening my steps.

The music grew louder, its low, sultry melody becoming more distinct. New sounds joined it. Distant laughter, and moaning.

My damp brow furrowed, but I kept walking.

A door came into view, set into the right side of the corridor. It was thrown open, and light spilled into the hall. My steps slowed, my senses straining, alert for the clue that would tell me this was just another trap. I'd almost missed the last one, and though this was obviously another of Maelgwyn's tricks, I needed to pay attention if I planned to outwit it.

Another laugh rumbled, low and gravelly, and a woman burst through the door. I jolted to a halt, my muscles stiffening. She stumbled into the corridor, clutching a silk robe to her chest. Long, dark hair swayed around her as she found her feet, smiling and flushed. Dark eyes landed on me and widened.

"You made it." Her bare feet made only the slightest of muffled footfalls as she hurried toward me.

My knees bent slightly, primed to run, but she made no move to touch me. Besides, she was small, barely taller than a witch, with a slender frame hidden by her slip of silk and little else. I wasn't exactly a champion fighter, but my chances against her were good.

"It has been forever since anyone new came along," she continued. "The princes are waiting, come."

She seized my arm, and I was too slow to avoid her touch, but her skin was warm and soft and real. Normal. Not a ghost, or a vampire, as far as I could tell. Besides, I *did* need to find the princes.

"Come where?" I asked, my voice hoarse as I stumbled along beside her.

"To the princes, and your rewards." She shot me a grin. "We all came for the same reasons. Immortality, riches, the *princes*."

"We?"

"The humans, of course."

The music pulsed inside my head, thrumming through my body, merging with my heartbeat, seeping into my blood. The woman's hand, hooked around my arm, was firm but gentle. Following her was easy. The ache in my legs disappeared as I walked. In fact, I couldn't feel them at all. Was I floating? Did I care?

I drifted, dream-like and woozy, toward the door, the music within and around me growing louder and more insistent. Intoxicating. Feverish. The world was slow and clumsy, or maybe that was me. Should I be dancing? I certainly felt a little drunk. My skin heated and I eyed my companion's robe with envy. I couldn't remember why I was wearing ugly boots and a heavy wrap when I had perfectly good skin underneath. Beautiful, supple skin that deserved to feel the air.

We neared the door my friend had come through, stepping into a puddle of golden light, and I gasped at the sight awaiting me.

Naked bodies, more than I could even begin to count, writhed and ground together. Moans and pants of pleasure mingled with the music. I'd never seen anything like it, never imagined I could be a part of it, but my new friend's invitation had been clear. The princes were waiting for *me*.

As though on cue, an exquisite specimen of a man rose, extricating himself from the women pawing at him. He smiled as he approached, a beautiful lop-sided grin that revealed elongated fangs. That wasn't the only beautiful thing about him. My eyes widened as they travelled down the rippling muscles of his torso, to the defined V at his hips. Lower. I gulped. I'd never seen a man that big.

"I've been waiting for you," he said, drawing my attention back to his face.

Clearly. His body gave every sign of readiness. If only I hadn't worn so many clothes. They would only delay my reward.

Reward...

For what?

"Wait." I scrunched my brow, trying to remember the haze of events that had led me here. "Aren't you supposed to be sleeping?"

"Come here," he said, opening his arms, inviting me into them.

My knee bent, the weight shifting off my foot.

No.

The curse. I still had to break it. I gave my head a shake, and some of the fog dissipated. This was a trick. So much for being alert.

Before the spell had time to sink its claws back in, I wrenched my arm free of the woman's grasp and broke into a sprint.

Yells and roars of frustration echoed along the corridor behind me, but I didn't look back. An archway lay ahead, and I burst through it, skidding to a halt on the polished marble floor.

I found myself in a large chamber, lit by an enormous candelabra hung from the ceiling. Thousands of candles burnt amongst the crystal cascade, throwing an explosion of refracted light over the walls and floors.

Opposite, another, identical archway waited, but the way was blocked by a long banquet table, laden with dishes. Fragrant steam coiled into the air.

I groaned a sigh as my mouth flooded at the scent of garlic and spice. My feet carried me closer, eager for once, and my mouth fell open at the sight of a mountain of nachos, smothered in thick, melted cheese and sprinkled with coriander and jalapenos. Dishes of salsa and guacamole crammed into the gaps left between platters. A pile of tortillas, bowls of beans and rice and vegetables. And curry too! I hurried along the table, my stomach growling at a dish filled with rich, orange sauce topped with yoghurt. A stack of poppadoms. Even a platter laden with neat rows of inari sushi. My favourite. In fact, everything was my favourite, right down to the bowl of chocolate ice cream and the dish of rhubarb crumble. A feast made just for me.

What had Pansy said about fae food? Something about hospitality laws, and the promise of safety? It was too convenient that all my most beloved dishes were laid out waiting in a crumbling old ruin, fresh and steaming as though they'd come straight from the kitchen. Another trick, but how did it work? Was I supposed to be suspicious, bypassing the protection offered by the laws of the fae, or was I supposed to believe that? Was I supposed to eat, thinking I'd be safe, only to be poisoned, or cursed, or to choke to death?

I dithered while my stomach rumbled. How long had it been since my pathetic breakfast of gruel disguised as porridge? A million years, probably, and it had been even longer since I'd had the comfort of proper, human food. I circled back to the curry, swallowing my saliva. Maelgwyn was fae, and fae couldn't harm anyone who ate their food. It had to be protection. But why would he leave a protective banquet lying around when he clearly wanted me dead?

He wouldn't. That was my answer, as disappointing as it was. Besides, I already had protection, both from Claudia's necklace, and the witches. It had served me well this far.

The food was just another trick, even if I couldn't see why or how. Before I could give in to temptation, I veered off toward the arch, every step heavy with regret as I left the table behind. Soon. I would soon be home, and Mum would spoil me and make me as fat and happy as a pig. I didn't need Maelgwyn's offerings.

The delicious aromas faded as I set off up yet another flight of curving steps, my stomach aching with hunger and dread. A little nacho snack would have been the perfect fuel to get me to the top of yet another enchanted staircase.

This one, however, came to an end before I'd even got my heart pumping. I emerged onto another landing. There were no lights up here, bar the faint glow of my lantern. Cavernous stone archways opened on either side, but beyond them, I found only uninviting walls of darkness. Bypassing the luring voids, I set off down another impossible corridor.

My skin prickled, and though my lantern failed to light the hidden depths beyond the archways, I was certain that something hid in the darkness, watching me. Chills skittered down my spine, and I tightened my grip on the dagger, quickening my pace.

Where were these Goddamned princes?

"Aliza!"

I stumbled to a halt, my heart pounding as I turned to stare back down the corridor. I knew that voice. Knew it better than my own heartbeat.

"Mum?" I whispered.

"Aliza, come back, help us!"

"Aliza, we're here." That was Dad's voice joining Mum's anguished cry. "Don't leave us!"

The stale air was suddenly frigid as my parents' voices turned to sobs, interspersed with cries of my name. The sound grated over my heart, clawing and tugging at me, calling me back the way I'd come.

I screwed up my eyes. "You're not here. You're not real."

"Don't go, Aliza! We need you. Help us. *Help us!*"

Question everything you might see or hear.

Sage's warning hissed in my ear as though the witch was right beside me. She was right. Whoever those voices belonged to, they were not my mum and dad. My parents wouldn't try to lure me into the shadows, they'd tell me to run, to leave them.

"Fuck this," I muttered, shaking my head.

The rifts were sealed. My parents were not imprisoned in a lonely old tower in a magical realm. They were home. Distraught, but safe. Far away from here. Though it shredded my soul to do so, I turned on my heel and broke into a limping jog, leaving the haunting voices behind.

Another archway marked the end of the corridor, this one blocked by double doors rather than darkness. I burst through them with my parents' desperate cries echoing in my heart, slamming them shut behind me. The voices fell silent at once, and I slumped against the doors, my chest rising and plunging with every breath. Tears streamed down my cheeks, dripping to my collar.

It wasn't real. It was a trick, designed to lure me into whatever hideous fate awaited in the shadows. A trick, nothing more. Mum and Dad were far from here, safe. The only help they needed was for me to break this wretched curse and get home, relieving them of their torment.

Swiping my tears away with my bandage, I opened my eyes to see what fresh hell awaited me.

I was in a circular room, walled with yet more archways. These ones weren't full of darkness, or even blocked by doors, but filled edge to edge with swirling, white mist. Each was indistinguishable from the next, but for the one I leaned against.

Straightening, I took a step away from the doors. As I did so, something, some distant shadow, stirred within each window of mist. I froze, and the shadows fell still. They were barely distinguishable amongst the swirling vapours, but when I squinted, I could still pick them out.

My heart hammered a frantic beat against my ribs. How much more could I take before it gave up completely? It would be just my luck to make it this far only to die of heart failure.

I was close to my goal though. That pull, that magic, thrummed through me with renewed intensity, telling me this was it, the end, or the beginning. I was almost where I was supposed to be.

My foot slid into another careful step, and then another. The mist shadows moved with me, growing in size and clarity.

"Reflections?" I whispered, revolving on the spot.

Sure enough, the six dark figures moved with me. Relief crashed over me in a wave. It was me, just myself mirrored in the arches, not monsters stalking closer. I blew out a sigh, bracing my nerves, and marched the remaining distance to the archway directly opposite. Dagger poised, I forced myself to walk into the mist without hesitation.

White engulfed me.

My grip on my weapon tightened as fog obliterated my vision, but before I could do more than draw a breath, it faded away. I squinted as sunlight glared into my eyes, but there was nothing I could do to block out the screams.

Terrible, anguished screams, somewhere between a wail and a war cry echoed off the high ceiling. Beneath my feet, the ground was slick and dark with blood, and in the centre of the pool, a painfully small form lay still. Too still.

I lurched for the child, my hands outstretched, but the moment I lifted my foot, the room dissolved.

Weak sunlight, grey compared to that I'd become accustomed to, winked and rippled on the surface of a pond, stirred by a breeze. A group of women huddled on the bank. One had wine-red hair.

Abby!

I tried to move, but my feet refused to budge.

A police car trundled over the grass to the mouth of an all too familiar cave, joining a fleet of emergency vehicles already in place. Dogs in luminous vests sniffed frantically around the glen, darting in and out of the caves.

Isobel was standing with a pair of officers, sobbing into her hands.

The world shifted again. The Fairy Glen became an autumn woodland. People dashed between the trunks, sprinting past me with stricken faces. Fae. Some clutched children or small animals to their chests. Others threw terrified glances over their shoulders.

The leaf-strewn ground disappeared from beneath me, replaced by cold, endless blue. Clouds, like gold-gilded cotton wool, sped by, almost within touching distance.

A solemn-faced crowd filled a courtyard, a castle at their backs blocking out the sky. Flames roared to life, a wall of heat between me and them.

The visions sped by, gaining momentum. A snap of mighty jaws. A rain of feathers and blood.

A hulking, horned beast towered over me with skin like ash. Its leathery wings spread wide.

Jacques fled through a twilit wood, drenched in blood.

A frozen, starlit lake. A peal of laughter.

A dark-haired man carried a body through the night.

A tower of ice, melting and buckling as it burnt.

Diamonds scattered over the floor.

Rain battered down and thunder echoed, making the very air quake. Icy wind rushed by, whipping my skin. Blue-white light flared, and with a mighty crack, my muscles seized.

Everything fell away. I couldn't breathe. My heart refused to beat. My body bowed under the strain of my rigid muscles.

All at once, I went limp. I lay flat on my back, panting down the stale air of the tower. Above me, cobwebs dangled from a shadowy ceiling. No more visions. No more mist.

Gingerly, I hauled myself to my feet, only to find myself exactly where I'd begun, in a circular room. Where the archways had been, only dusty stone walls remained. Gone was the mist, and the shadows within. The doors I'd come through stood at my back, and a new set, carved with runes lay ahead. I approached, lifting my hand to trace a finger over one of the hundreds of carvings.

Something whimpered behind me.

The pitiful sound locked my muscles in place. My ears strained, catching the faintest hint of shallow, rasping breath.

God, what now?

Willing my hammering heart to ease, I turned slowly, squinting, afraid of what fresh horror lurked at my back.

Something, no, *someone* was curled up in the foetal position exactly where I'd lain only moments ago. My heart skidded to a halt, dropping to my boots at the sight of red-raw, melted flesh.

Every inch of twisted, steaming skin was burnt beyond recognition. All traces of hair had been scorched clean away from the splitting, blistered scalp, and the one ear I could see was nothing more than a pit in the side of the head. Smoke coiled into the air, filling the chamber with the putrid stench of roasted meat. I clapped a hand to my mouth, swaying on the spot, torn between the urge to run and help, and the need to turn away from such a gut-wrenching sight.

The person whimpered again, a tiny, rasping whine.

How were they still alive? Death would be a mercy. There was no coming back from this.

Except, it wasn't real. It was just another of Maelgwyn's visions, sent to frighten or trick me into turning away from my goal.

Comforting though that thought was, when the poor wretch stirred, attempting to shift their contorted limbs, pity swallowed me whole. Real or not, could they feel pain? I almost hoped the burns had gone deep enough to destroy the nerves, the only mercy in such horror. If an animal came to me like this, I'd end its suffering as soon as possible, but people were rarely lucky enough to be gifted a humane end.

Tugging my wrap over my nose, I took an absent-minded step closer.

As though sensing my presence, the person moaned, craning their neck to lift their head off the ground. Flesh sloughed away, sticking to the stone.

"Don't." I held out my hand, as though the poor thing could somehow see or hear my warnings.

Tears welled in my eyes at their pitiful yet desperate attempts to rise. There was nothing I could do to help. My knowledge was useless without the tools to implement it, but my soul thrashed, desperate to intercede, to help. I shook my head in an attempt to rid myself of the emotion clouding my thoughts. It wasn't real. It couldn't be.

The burnt person continued to struggle, fighting uselessly against the shrunken contraction of their flesh.

Shrunken...

Maybe I should use my dagger. A quick end had to be better than this. The hilt was slick in my sweating palm as I flexed my fingers, lifting the blade.

It would be no different to administering a lethal dose of pentobarbitone, would it?

My hand trembled and my breath quickened.

"Come on, Aliza," I hissed.

I couldn't. I couldn't do it. It was not the same as euthanasia, and I was no murderer.

My unfortunate companion writhed with renewed vigour, their tormented groans becoming louder. A ruined hand braced against the ground, and against all the laws of science and medicine, against the heat shrunken tightness of the muscles, the arm straightened, pushing them upright.

With twitching jerks of motion, the person sat, then kneeled, and as I stumbled back several steps, stood. Melted flesh smoothed, turning from charred red to pink to tan. Dark blonde hair sprouted from the healed scalp, growing at an alarming rate. Disfigured features regrew, smoothing into a woman's face.

My face.

The woman standing before me was... me.

As naked as the day she was born, my doppelganger stared. Her–*my*–blue eyes flickered over me before coming to rest on my face. Though she was undoubtedly my double, and though her hair was my natural colour, untouched by my beloved dyes, there was a glow about her that I'd certainly never achieved. A red mark bloomed between her breasts, spreading over her chest like fern leaves.

"You're close," she said, stealing my voice. I gulped. "The door behind you will lead you to the goal. The door behind me will lead you home. You have a choice to make."

"I can only choose one door?" I still had a voice after all. I massaged my throat, rubbing at the ghostly ache.

"No. Both doors will remain open to you."

"Then what do you mean? And what are you?"

"I am you, if you choose to go onward."

My eyes lingered on the boring hair. My double smiled knowingly. Immortality without my rainbow hair? Was it worth it? Of course not, but then, if she really was me, she'd know that breaking the curse didn't mean I'd accept the rewards. She'd know the only way home lay with the princes. I wasn't doing this for immortality or crowns or any of that nonsense. It was the flaw in Maelgwyn's plan, his assumptions that this world was better than the one I'd come from. His belief that I'd been driven here by greed and ambition, rather than necessity.

"Leave now, and remain as you are. Go on, and be forever changed."

"Changed how?" Despite my certainty that Maelgwyn had misread my motivations, I had to be sure. What if immortality was automatic? What if breaking the curse triggered my reward, not giving me a chance to refuse it? "Will it happen right away? Will I become... you?"

"It is a choice only you can make."

Hardly a straight answer. Typical fae trickery, I assumed. Veiled words. Hints. Lies.

"How do I break the curse?" Not that I believed for a second that Maelgwyn's creation would give me an honest answer, but it was worth a try. At least I could rule out whatever she said.

She graced me with a faint smile. "You must give your life."

I frowned, goosebumps peppering my skin. "You just said you're me, if I choose to go ahead. How can both be true?"

"Time will ravage and decay everything you love. Your heart will break relentlessly and the pain will never fade. You will be cursed to inhabit this world alone, for eternity, as it changes and lives and dies around you. You will lose everything for a crown."

I rolled my eyes. She sounded like a child's toy, spouting prerecorded phrases. Nothing she said made sense, or even linked to her last sentences, never mind mine. She wasn't real. If she really was me, she'd know that I had no interest in crowns. I was here to break a curse, and then I was going home. I wouldn't be in *this* world at all. Let the princes keep their rewards, I had no use for them. I'd save this God-forsaken world, but as soon as it was done, I was going home, mortal and free, to binge my favourite shows and eat all the fajitas I could get my hands on.

This was just a final diversion designed to make me doubt myself. More lies and tricks. I had no time for such nonsense, not now. I knew I was close.

"Let's get this over with," I muttered, turning my back on myself. I half expected my immortal self to grab me, or at least argue, but my hand reached the door unhindered.

"I tried to warn you."

I glanced back, but the speaker had vanished, leaving me well and truly alone, but for the chill creeping down my spine.

Just a trick, I reminded myself and pushed open the final door.

19

Well, Hello, Prince Charming

I'd expected to find a pair of neatly made beds, each with a handsome prince sleeping peacefully within, with not a hair out of place or a wrinkle in their blankets. Instead, two stone tombs stood side by side in the centre of the circular chamber, firmly closed and draped in cobwebs. There were no more stairs or archways or tricks. I had reached the top of the tower at last.

The rest of the room was eerily empty, as silent as a grave. More cobwebs hung from the vaulted stone ceiling, and motes of dust drifted in the dim glow cast by my lantern, but they were the only adornments.

I eyed the floor. A thick carpet of dust blanketed the stone, but I could still make out the shape of the tiles. If there were any traps, they were well disguised.

I licked my dry lips. The last thing I wanted was to test that floor for hidden traps and open a centuries-old tomb. What would I find within? A shrivelled husk? A skeleton? What if the princes weren't sleeping at all? What if they were dead? My hammering heart sank. Why hadn't I asked that question until now? Ancient bargains or not, it was blatantly obvious that an evil uncle who wanted to steal his nephew's throne would find a permanent solution to his problems.

He wasn't going to risk the curse being broken and his rule challenged. Had all this been for nothing?

I had to be sure. I had to see with my own eyes. The witches would be difficult to convince, and as they had no way of entering the tower, I would have to tell a compelling story, maybe bring back some evidence of the deaths. If only my phone still worked. I wasn't in the habit of photographing corpses, but it would have been helpful today...

I grasped the stone arch, my fingers biting into the crevices, and pressed one foot against a tile. Nothing happened. I pressed a little harder. The ceiling didn't cave in, neither did another chasm open beneath me, or poisoned darts fly from the wall. With my heart attempting to burst from my chest, I transferred all my weight onto my extended foot.

The room stayed silent and still. I blew out a slow breath and took another step, and another, all the while expecting death to come swooping from the shadows. But nothing happened, and in no time, I was standing at the foot of a tomb.

Now what?

I squinted in the faint light cast by my lantern. The stone appeared to be carved with yet more rune-like markings. A spell? The curse itself, keeping them sealed, maybe? I dipped my sweaty fingers into the dust, smearing it away from one such mark. Whatever it was, whatever it meant, I was none the wiser. If only Sage was here, I was willing to bet she'd be able to read it. But there was, at least, one carving I could decipher. A pair of crossed, curved swords marked the centre of the lid. Maelgwyn's way of saying 'ye be warned, me hearties'? I gave the swords a snort of disdain. As last ditch efforts went, it was a poor deterrent.

There was only one thing left for me to do. Discovering a skeleton was not top of my bucket list, but getting out of this mess definitely was, so I braced my hands against the corner of the stone lid and heaved.

For a long, horrifying moment, nothing happened. I held my breath, the pressure in my head building as I threw everything I had into my push. Just as I was about to give up, the lid shifted with a jolt and groan. It barely moved a few inches, but it was enough to expose an inner corner of the tomb. Neon green light spilled through the gap, painting my skin a sickly shade. I snatched my hands away, but my skin didn't bubble and melt from my bones. It was just... light.

With my nerves in knots, I approached the tomb again and dipped my fingers into the wavering glow. It rippled like sunlight shining through water, while my fingers cast dense beams of shadow. Motes of dust drifted through the neon glow. Mesmerising.

I was wasting time. The tomb was almost open. Assuming this wasn't some elaborate decoy, I'd almost found myself a handsome prince to send me home. With a deep breath, I shoved the lid again. It ground into motion a little easier this time, and I didn't let surprise stop me. My lips pulled back into a snarl as I pushed and pushed with everything I had, until all at once, the lid slid freely, and my momentum had me ploughing belly first into the rock. The crash of the lid hitting the floor was enough to set the entire tower quaking. I ducked my head, expecting the stone ceiling to cave in or the floor to give way, but when the echoes stopped rattling off the walls, I was still alive. There was only one thing left to do. If only I could bring myself to open my eyes and discover what lay within the tomb. Green glowed through my eyelids, coaxing me, but I wasn't sure I wanted to see.

"Come on, Aliza," I whispered to myself. "It's just a body."

I'd seen lots of bodies in my time. Not humans, or fae, for that matter, but what difference did that make?

Holding my breath, I cracked open my eyes.

The tomb was filled with light, ebbing and pulsing like a recently disturbed bathtub, but within the glow drifted the most breathtaking fae I'd yet seen.

My eyes widened and my breath left my body in a rush. The sleeping male was *gorgeous*, young and fair skinned, with a straight nose, and cheekbones I could cut my lip on, if I dared to try. His long, powerful limbs drifted as he floated in the light, so peaceful and beautiful. His hair wafted around his head in an ebony cloud, stained with streaks of neon light. The painting at Nairsgarth had failed to do him justice.

Who was he? Anwir or Idris? It would have been much simpler if they'd had the decency not to split into two separate embryos. What did it matter? Two princes or not, there was only one curse, and only one human stupid enough to contemplate breaking it.

But *how* to break it?

As tempting as it was to fall into a daze and stare at such masculine perfection, I had a job to do, and I didn't have forever. I needed to get out of this God-forsaken tower and back to the witches before something happened. The crash of the tomb lid had probably been heard by King Maelgwyn himself. A swarm of flying monkeys was probably heading this way, but as keen as I was to get this over with, I had no idea what to do next. Give my life? What did that even mean? Was I supposed to plunge my dagger into my own belly and shower the unsuspecting prince in the blood of a human sacrifice? Waking up to a bog-standard alarm clock was bad enough. Snorting at such nonsense, I worried my lip between my teeth. I wasn't supposed to kiss the prince, was I? It couldn't be that cliché. Besides, wasn't it always true love's kiss that broke the spell? I'd never laid eyes on this male before, not even the fleeting glimpse that was enough to set off happily ever after in most fairytales. And as pretty as the light was, how could I be sure it wouldn't melt my face off if I leaned in? Just because it hadn't harmed my fingers or my new immortal companion, it didn't mean something awful wasn't lurking. I was quite fond of my face, and I certainly didn't love the unfortunate stranger floating in the tomb, but I had to do *something.* I imagined returning to Sage, explaining I'd found the princes but had been too scared of a silly little light to break the curse. Then I thought of my parents, of me trapped on the wrong side of the rift forevermore. This male was my ticket home, if only he would open his eyes, and as for true love's kiss, well... all those fairytales had come from somewhere, hadn't they? To Hell with it.

I leaned over the side of the tomb, the stone digging into my belly. Green light washed over me, but apart from the burning as my eyes adjusted, nothing terrible happened. My face was inches from the prince's when I hesitated.

What if it worked? The rifts would open. I wouldn't be the only creature leaving Neath. Hungry vampires and lusty witches would flood my world, driven by centuries of deprivation. What if Mum invited a vampire in for a cup of tea? What if a witch got her claws into dad? Would I end up with a swarm of long-lived half-sisters?

What if I really did get to go home? What if, before the week was out, I was reunited with my parents? With my life?

I could warn people about the dubious visitors who followed me through. Maybe I could even convince this prince to seal the rifts anew, after I'd gone through, of course. He'd surely be grateful enough to bow to my every demand, if I ever got on with breaking this God-damned curse.

My mouth had gone dry. I swallowed, darting my tongue over my lips as I contemplated the sleepy perfection inches from my face.

"I can only apologise," I whispered. "I don't usually do this without permission..."

I pressed my lips to his.

I barely had a moment to register how cool his lips were before the light swelled, glaring through my closed eyes, then vanishing as though it had never been. The glowing shape of the prince's face burnt into my retinas, but his mouth jerked away from mine, and I scrambled back, opening my eyes in time to see him sprawled in the depths of his tomb, all traces of magic gone.

But his eyes. His eyes were *open*, and they flickered over me as he pushed himself up, before fixing on my own disbelieving stare.

"What have you done?" he hissed.

What? I opened my mouth with absolutely no idea of what I was about to say, but muffled yells and thumps filled the chamber. Shit. The other prince, still trapped in his tomb.

I made to move, but the prince moved faster. He leapt from his tomb with an ease I couldn't have managed, and I hadn't even been trapped under a curse for hundreds of years. In seconds, he was at his brother's resting place, shoving the lid aside with another groan and crash. A second male, identical to the first but for his long hair, rose from the tomb. The brothers clasped arms as the second clambered to freedom before finally looking at me. He fell still, his eyes widening.

"You," he breathed. "You're the Human Queen."

"Oh." I gave an awkward huff of laughter, my skin heating at their piercing attention. "I don't know about that."

The long-haired prince took a few steps closer, lifting his hand, but stopped short, as though he'd thought better of touching me. "You broke the curse. You saved us."

Oh, but he was gorgeous, with eyes of pale green, and strands of dark hair hanging around his face.

"I suppose I did."

I did. I *did*.

The princes were awake! The curse was broken. The rifts were open. I'd done it. I'd achieved what countless women before me had tried and failed to do. I was going home. Everything was going to be okay. I laughed again, half disbelief, half delirious elation.

"Prince Anwir, at your service." He flattened a hand to his chest and bowed. A prince, a future king, bowing to *me*.

"We need to leave," the first prince snapped, throwing me a scathing look, as though I'd wanted the attention. "Now."

He had to be Idris, the younger of the two. He wasn't wrong. Just because the curse was broken, it didn't mean this nightmare was over. He prowled around his empty tomb, examining it with an expression of distaste. When he reached the fallen lid, he stooped, and I followed his gaze. His long fingers brushed the carving of the swords, and at once, the stone crumbled away, revealing real weapons in their place. My breath hitched at the gleam of champagne coloured metal, but the prince snatched up the swords, deftly sheathing them across his broad shoulders.

I glanced away before he saw me looking, but my eyes only landed on his twin, who followed his lead, revealing a single but much longer sword hidden in the lid of his own tomb. His blade was an ordinary silver colour, but ornate and beautiful. My daggers, hidden in their sheaths, seemed uglier than ever, not to mention *small*. Still, they'd gotten me this far.

Now all they had to do was get me back through the tunnels. "The witches are waiting to warp us to Nairsgarth castle. Come on, it's this way."

I wasn't keen on leading the expedition, but the company of two tall and hulking fae males was a definite improvement on my lonely journey through the tower.

"Witches?" Anwir hurried to my side as I led the way back into the passage lined with dark archways. To my relief, no tortured voices called out to me.

"They've been helping me. I—"

Whatever words I'd been about to say died in my mouth. A sharp crack split the air, and the stone at my feet opened, a dark, jagged split bolting between my feet. The floor rumbled, the walls shook, and dust streaked down from the ceiling. The tower...

"Run!" Anwir snatched my hand and dragged me forward.

I stumbled after him, ignoring the stab of pain in my ankle, twisting to be sure Idris was following. The three of us hurtled down the winding stairs, dodging and leaping the cracks that hunted us. No matter how fast we ran, the cracks kept pace, appearing beneath us, sometimes darting ahead, or veering off to split the wall. Anwir's grip on my hand was painfully tight, but I clung to him as though he was my lifeline.

We burst into the grand dining chamber, the prince never slowing his pace as he hauled me around the table. Crystals rained down from the trembling chandelier, clattering over the banquet. I was only faintly surprised to see that the delicious feast had been replaced with decaying bones and lumps of mould.

The music in the corridor had ceased. I didn't dare glance into that den of lust as we hurtled past the room. The tower gave an ominous groan, the sound rumbling deep within the ancient stone.

The cursed staircase appeared at our feet. Down and down and round we went, passing the haunting, dark chasm I'd escaped on my way up. The journey to the top of the tower had seemed to take a lifetime, but this... this was worse. How long would the ancient stone hold? The quaking of the building grew more violent with every passing second. Crashes sounded overhead, and I knew the roof was coming down somewhere above us. I couldn't let it end like this, not when I was so close to going home. I hadn't come this far to be buried alive.

I pushed my burning legs harder, throwing myself down the stairs with a recklessness that would have broken my neck any other time, but adrenalin made me surefooted, burning away my dizziness as we spiralled down into the dark. Dust and grit streamed down onto my head, larger chunks bouncing off me like hail.

When the first hint of pale light reached my stinging eyes, my knees wobbled with relief, but I hurried onwards, letting go of Anwir's hand and taking the last few steps at a leap, staggering across the hall and out into the open air. I didn't stop there, or look back at the groaning, cracking tower. I broke into a sprint, speeding through the tunnel of deadly vines I'd carved, then into the sunshine and toward the tunnels. The witches were waiting on the other side, probably watching the cave mouth with baited breath. They'd be ready for whatever followed me out. I would be safe when I reached them.

A stitch burnt in my side, growing stronger and more insistent with every pounding step, but I ignored it, fixing my attention on the fissure in the cliff face. I was too far away to see clearly, but I caught no glimpses of those cave-dwelling monsters waiting to strip the meat from my bones. Maybe they'd grown bored, or maybe the imminent collapse of the tower had scared them off.

I skidded to a halt on the dead grass outside the tunnel, doubling over and pressing a hand to my stitch.

The princes were barely a step behind me, and neither appeared even slightly flustered by our mad dash. Panting, I forced myself to straighten.

"There are things," I said breathlessly. "Monsters. In here. We have to go through."

Anwir swept his long hair back from his face, eyeing the cave warily. Behind him, in the valley basin, the tower gave an almighty rumble. We all turned in time to see its dark walls collapse inwards before the structure tilted, and surprisingly slowly, sank beneath the sea of brambles. The ground quaked beneath my feet as a cloud of dust billowed into the air, blocking out the sky. A minute slower, and we'd all have been dead.

It wasn't nearly as shocking as it should have been. Had I been desensitised to near-death experiences? If I had, it did nothing to lessen my dread at the looming prospect of facing those blind-eyed beasts again.

I turned to Anwir, a brilliant idea unfurling in my mind. "Wait. Can't you teleport us out?"

He'd only have to take us to the other side of the cliffs, then we could rendezvous with the witches and warp to safety.

It was Idris who answered. "No," he said, his voice flat and cold. "Our magic is dead."

"What?" Dismay made my voice shrill. "What do you mean, dead?"

"Wards." His pale eyes flickered skyward, then he lifted both arms over his head, drawing the curved swords with a delicate shivering ring. Free of the gloom of the tower, the blades were somewhere between silver and gold, as pale and lovely as dawn light. "They're nullifying our power. Let's go."

Without any further hesitation, he strolled into the tunnel as though he was off for a walk in the park. I shot a panicked glance at Anwir, who grimaced, gesturing for me to follow his brother. Hoisting my pathetic lantern higher, I hurried after Idris. Behind me, metal hissed as Anwir drew his weapon. I followed suit, sliding a dagger free of my belt.

"The witches didn't say anything about wards," I whispered as I caught up with the prince. "Will your magic come back when we get past them?"

"Quiet, human."

I blinked, my mouth falling open at his rudeness. I'd just saved his sorry life, and that was how he spoke to me? If I'd known what a prick he was, I'd have gone to the other tomb, kissed the other prince. Would it have made a difference to anything but my dignity? Was that why the wards were up, because I'd somehow broken the curse wrong? How was I supposed to know the difference between identical twins? It wasn't as though Maelgwyn had carved their names onto their tombs. Still, Idris was right. I knew what lurked in the dark, and the last thing

I wanted was to draw them out with idle chatter. Not that my horror at the magic-deadening wards could be classed as idle. The curse was broken, the tower had fallen, yet there was no magic here?

Maybe Idris was wrong. Maybe his power was just taking its time to reawaken after such a long slumber. The witches' magic would work, and even if it didn't, the warp crystal would. Wouldn't it? The words Sage had muttered as she used it couldn't have been a spell. We had to get back to Nairsgarth.

I chewed my lip as we crept through the dark. The fae made barely any sound as they prowled ahead of and behind me, but my lantern lit up Idris' silhouette, gleaming softly on his wicked, curved blades, reassuring me that, this time, I wasn't alone. I'd survived the journey in without help; the walk back would be a piece of cake in comparison.

"It's a left here," I breathed as quietly as I could as we came upon a bend.

Idris stiffened at my words, and irritation sparked in my chest. Had he ever been in these tunnels before? Did he think he knew better than me, the *human*? That he could find his way without me?

"I told y–" something huge and pale and horribly familiar barrelled around the corner, leaping at Idris.

20

Mistakes Were Made

Monster and fae collided, tumbling sideways and crashing into the wall with an ear-splitting shriek and a yell. Together, they veered backwards and I, lingering too close to my escort, took the full force of their momentum as we collided with the ground.

With a clatter, my lantern skidded away, and we were plunged into pitch darkness. Footsteps pounded past my head. Deafening shrieks drilled into my eardrums as, for a moment, bodies writhed on top of me, robbing me of my breath, but then the weight disappeared, and something hit the wall with a sickening crunch. I scrambled away, back to where I'd last seen Anwir, and staggered to my feet.

Ahead of me, the fight continued, the stale air full of shrieks and thumps, the hum of metal slicing through the air and the wet hiss of flesh splitting open. Though the creature made a lot of noise, Idris was silent.

Was he winning? Was he silent because he was dead? His attitude hadn't endeared him to me, but that didn't mean he deserved to be slaughtered within minutes of waking up. If only I could see, I'd be able to help, but my eyes widened blankly, nothing but black pressing against them.

Where was Anwir? Had he joined his brother, either in victory or defeat? What if they were both dead, and it was just me and the monster?

I tightened my grip on my dagger. Wait, I had two! Without a lantern to hold, I plunged my injured hand to the second dagger. My palm stung and throbbed, but I didn't care. I'd rather be in pain than dead. I held my blades before me. I might not be able to see, but if anything attacked me, it would have to get past my cursed daggers first.

A wet choking noise bubbled ahead of me, the sound of imminent death. The fight fell silent, and something heavy hit the floor with a thump.

My ears strained and my eyes stung. Who'd won? Was Idris bleeding out on the floor while that *thing* crept toward me? The fae's name formed on my tongue, but I bit it back, willing my ragged breath to quiet. The last thing I needed was to attract the monster when it might yet overlook me.

Something touched my wrist.

I screamed.

A large hand clapped over my mouth, silencing me, as metal clattered to the floor, and I collided with the wall with a thud, one wrist pinned, my hands suddenly empty of blades.

"Shut up!" a voice hissed, inches from my face.

Not a monster. The breath that fanned over my face was crisp smelling, like a winter morning, with not a hint of rot.

My body went limp, and when I was released, I sagged against the wall. "Idris?"

"Human." His voice oozed disdain as his breath fluttered over my skin once more.

He was still close then. Could he see me? Of course, he could, he'd found my mouth easily enough. All I could see of him was a vague, hulking shadow towering over me, but then, I was just a *human,* with pathetic human eyes.

"Pick up your daggers, but *do not* wave them at me again."

Easier said than done. "I can't see anything," I whispered, wishing I still had my lantern or even my torch. Or a working phone. Anything to light my path out of this mess. "Why did you take them off me?"

"You were pointing them at me."

"Not on purpose," I hissed. "Are you okay?"

I knew I hadn't cut him; he'd be desiccated by now if I had, but that didn't mean he hadn't been wounded by the monster. The phantom ache of claws slashing my belly throbbed.

Idris was silent, and though I couldn't see a thing, the intensity of his contemplating gaze was evident even in the darkness. The words he'd spoken when I broke the curse came back to me.

What have you done?

What *had* I done? There'd barely been a spare second to interact with him, but the way he'd disarmed me just now left me in no doubt that he couldn't care less about me, or any of my kind. Had I awoken some sort of monster? Was he just like his uncle? A human-hating piece of shit? Would he leave me to die in these tunnels? Or worse, was he weighing up the benefits of killing me himself?

When he finally spoke, he somehow managed to make his whisper clipped and hateful. "Keep your mouth shut."

The hilts of my daggers reappeared in my palms, and I gripped them tight. The prince grabbed a handful of my wrap and half dragged, half shoved me along the tunnel.

"Stop it! I can walk!" I tried to shrug free, but his grip tightened.

"You can't see, and I told you to shut up."

"Wait, where's Anwir? Is he following?" He seemed nice enough. His first instinct when the tower began to quake had been to grab my hand. Was he going to allow his brother to manhandle me?

"He fled the moment that thing attacked, now stop talking before you bring more of them down on us."

What? He'd just left us? Abandoning me, I could understand. He didn't know me. But to leave his brother...

Anger bubbled in my belly, overtaking my fear. Without Anwir to direct it at, I turned on his twin. "First of all," I hissed, glaring at the shadowy outline of him. "You don't get to tell me what to do. Second, dragging me along isn't exactly quiet, if that's what you're hoping to achieve."

"Do you want me to get you out of here alive, or not?"

"Well, obviously, but you don't have to manhandle me. I can walk."

He was silent for so long that I expected him to abandon me and leave me lost in the dark, but instead, he released my wrap, a little roughly, I had to say, and waited.

What an absolute crank. Still, my escape options were limited. Taking a deep breath, I sheathed a dagger and lifted my hand, groping blindly at the prince. Was that an arm? I squeezed. Yes, that was definitely a bicep, and a very nice one at that, as far as I could tell. The fae stood perfectly still as I slid my hand into the crook of his elbow.

"See?" I whispered. "Isn't this civilised?"

I could almost see that unnaturally perfect face twisting into a sneer. "Fine."

"*Fine*. Lead the way."

The sulking prince set off at a steadier pace, a silent, prowling stroll. I gripped his arm, hating myself for finding comfort in his presence. He might be a piece of work, but he was here. I wasn't alone. I slid closer, until my shoulder pressed against his arm. He didn't complain. He was no doubt biting back his reprimand, driven by his need for silence, but I honestly couldn't care less, as long as he got me out of here alive.

We crept through the tunnel in silence, pausing while Idris peered around pitch black corners with his stupid fae eyes. The only sounds were the soft padding of my feet, and my uneven breathing. The prince was so silent that, if I hadn't had a firm grip of him, I wouldn't have known he was there. I was glad he was, even if I suspected he was hating every second of my company. To think, everyone this side of the rift expected me to marry one of these stuck-up royal brats. A life sentence. No, an eternal sentence, if Sage's claims of me being given immortality could be believed. No, that was nonsense. These creatures might live forever, but I was human, and mortal. I belonged to a mortal world. I would return to it and live my natural life with people who loved me for who I was, not revered me for what I had been forced to do.

I allowed my mind to drift far from the dark, twisting tunnels, across woodlands and meadows and mountains, back to the human world. To my little house, with Dad busy in the garden, pruning his hydrangeas, and Mum fussing over me, telling me I worked too hard and should put my feet up. I *would* put my feet up. I would sink down onto that squashy, faded sofa and stay there for weeks. I'd eat my meals on trays, and I'd binge TV, and drink all the coffee Mum could make. I'd saved the world. God knew, I deserved a break.

Idris stopped so suddenly that I bumped into his shoulder. I fell still too, my daydreams melting away into the darkness. My skin prickled.

"What—"

"Shut up!"

But too late.

A screech pierced the still air, and Idris wrenched away from me. I threw myself to the floor, scrambling until I found the wall and pressed myself against it. Something scuttled in the dark, and metal rang, that beautiful shivering sound, almost like a note of music. My eyes strained wide, but I could see nothing. I felt more than heard something move nearby, followed by a soft whoosh and an ear-splitting shriek. Something wet pattered on stone. Shuffle, thump, scratch, hiss. I screwed my eyes shut, for all the good it did me. Splitting flesh. The familiar scent of blood filled my nose, and something crumpled to the ground with a thump.

Oh God, please don't let Idris be dead.

If he was, I was next.

Something grabbed my arm, and I sucked in a breath, but instead of devouring my bones, my captor hauled me to my feet. "There are more. Move."

I couldn't find the voice to argue as I stumbled along beside him, his fingers biting into my wrist. We didn't need to be quiet anymore, apparently. Idris dragged me along at such a speed that the soles of my boots slapped the floor, echoing along the tunnel.

We whipped around a sharp turn, Idris dragging me, but no sooner had we rounded the corner than the fae skidded to a halt, shoving me in another direction.

"Shit, they're everywhere. Run. *Run!*"

I didn't need to be told a third time. Clinging to his sleeve, my grip tight with terror, I ran blindly at his side. What sounded like hundreds of scurrying footsteps pounded along behind us, my ears full of chittering and shrieks. If only I could see, if only there was the slightest light, I'd be able to run faster. I was slowing us both down. If it came to it, would Idris leave me behind?

My insides hollowed out at the thought. Even with my daggers, I had no hope of fighting them off when I was blind. I'd still be alive when those things started eating me. How long would it take for me to die?

Something unyielding caught the toe of my boot, and I lurched, losing my grip on Idris. Pain bolted up my knees before my belly collided with the floor. My knuckles, gripping my dagger, cracked against stone. Something clattered beside me. Something small, a sound I recognised.

I groped my empty pocket.

"My phone!"

I scrambled, patting the floor in the dark. I couldn't leave it. I needed it. My only connection to my world, my family. My frantic fingers scrambled over the rough rock, even as the thundering of many feet closed on me. Panic tightened around my throat. I couldn't breathe.

Where was it?

My fingers brushed something smooth, and I let out a sob of relief as I snatched my phone up. A shadow darted over me, landing softly on my far side, and a heartbeat later came the whoosh of metal and the slice of flesh. Warm, sticky liquid sprayed over me.

"Get up!" Idris roared.

I couldn't see him, but I sensed him, flitting through the endless dark, his swords swinging and slashing. Shrieks and screeches curdled. Bodies fell.

Someone grabbed the scruff of my shirt, half choking me as I was hauled to my feet. I was released, and I'd barely sucked down a breath before I was shoved away. I staggered, and almost fell.

"Run, you fucking fool!"

I ran. Or rather, I shuffled awkwardly, my hands held blindly in front of me, my feet wary of another fall. At my back, the fighting continued. Those *screams*. They slashed along my bones, making my hairs stand on end and my ear drums shrivel. But worse than that, I was alone. I might not be able to see, but I could sense it. Idris had stayed behind to fight, giving me time to get away.

I hesitated.

I shouldn't leave him. I was a liability to him, but I shouldn't leave him to fight alone in the dark. But what could I do to help?

"Get help," I whispered to myself.

If I could make it out, I would find the witches and Anwir. The prince could help his brother, the witches too, if the wards could be broken. They were brave and fast. Useful. They were everything I was not.

I squeezed my phone, the phone I had gambled my life, and Idris', to retrieve. What was wrong with me? The stupid thing didn't even work, and now it would be my fault if Idris died...

Gradually, the shadows grew clearer, until I realised I could see. Only faintly at first, but then a sob burst from my lips as I rounded a corner and saw the tunnel mouth opening to reveal a world of green.

I'd made it.

I broke into a real run, blinking in the blinding sunlight as the stone beneath my feet turned to gravel then grass. Squinting, I spotted the witches lurking just beyond the treeline, and I veered in their direction, stumbling to a stop before them.

"Idris," I gasped, buckling over.

My stitch was back with a vengeance. I needed to speak, to send them back into the tunnels, but my throat was too tight. God, I was unfit.

Stomping steps approached. Before I had a chance to straighten, a hand closed around my neck, forcing me upright. Idris' blood-splattered face appeared not an inch from mine. All I could see was fanged teeth.

"What the fuck was that?" he spat.

"Your Highness!"

"Unhand her!" A male's voice, barking a command.

I lifted my eyes to the pale green ones glowering down at me. They were so close my vision blurred.

"You almost got us both killed, mortal," Idris snarled, but his hand dropped, and he spun away from me as though I was some dirty, contaminated beast.

My fingers brushed my throat, though I wasn't hurt, only shocked.

I'd been stupid, risking everything to save my dead phone. The princes had only just awoken, and one had already brushed death because of me. Further proof that I wasn't meant for this world.

"Are you alright?"

I blinked up at Prince Anwir. He hadn't come as close as Idris had, and I was able to focus on the utter perfection that was his face. There was no revolting gore splattered over his fair skin, probably because he'd fled at the first sign of danger. Worry shone in his beautiful, pale eyes, quite at odds with his cowardly actions. Despite my annoyance, relief flooded through me. He was alive. The heir I'd almost died to save had made it out of the tunnels unscathed. I hadn't killed the only known person capable of fighting Maelgwyn's shades.

Pansy appeared at my side, concern shining in her eyes as she laid a hand on my arm.

"I'm fine." I let my hand fall away from my neck to prove it, but my trembling fingers gave me away. I wasn't fine. Not at all. "Can we go home now?" My voice sounded pathetic, whining. Like a child.

"Soon enough," Sage replied in her usual brisk tone. "We need to get beyond this ward and then we can warp."

"There are definitely wards then?" I'd hoped that things might be different on this side of the cliff.

Sage gave a brisk nod, her eyes sweeping the trees. "We must reach the border of Tir o Haf with all haste."

God, would it never end? It was supposed to be over by now. This should have been a moment of elation. I battled down my turbulent emotions, forcing myself to focus on the birdsong overhead, and the golden beams breaking through the branches. We may not be safe yet, but at least it was peaceful. At least I could see. The sun was warm on my skin.

Sage approached Anwir and sank into a curtsy. Such a show of deference didn't suit her, but Anwir smiled, inclining his chin. "Sister Sage of Nairsgarth, isn't it? I take it I owe my freedom to you?"

Indignation bristled along my spine. Okay, so Sage had done her part, but I was the one who'd risked life and limb to wake his ungrateful arse.

"My coven and I have worked tirelessly these past centuries, Your Highness. I must apologise for our late arrival, but it seems we were waiting for the right human."

The witch nodded in my direction, and heat hummed in my ears. At least someone appreciated my efforts, though that someone being Sage was almost as disconcerting as my many brushes with death. Pansy squeezed my arm in silent appreciation.

The prince didn't look at me. Instead, his face grew several shades paler. "Centuries? How long has it been?"

Sage pressed her lips into a thin line before answering. "Two hundred and seventy years."

A flurry of emotions crossed Anwir's face. Shock, dismay, confusion. "I thought... it seemed an eter–" he cleared his throat and his face settled on simmering rage. "My uncle will pay for this."

"An eternity?" Sage asked in a hushed voice. "You were aware of time passing?"

I grimaced at the idea of being trapped, fully aware, inside a useless, unresponsive body. An hour would be torture, never mind centuries.

"Almost," the prince answered, his brow knotting in contemplation. "Not all of the time, but it was like trying to wake from a dream."

A memory of my recent dreams popped, unbidden into my head. Kisses and teeth. Hands around my neck. My fingertips brushed my throat, the same spot Idris had grabbed. I glanced at him. To my relief, he lingered at the edge of the group, staring between the trees and paying no attention to me or anyone else. Beneath his crossed swords, his shoulders sagged. My heart twisted in pity. Just because he was a piece of work, it didn't mean he deserved such a miserable fate. Neither of them did.

But pity, both for them and myself, turned slowly to pride. I'd done it. I'd freed them from their nightmare. Now they could rid the world of Maelgwyn, and I could go home. It didn't seem the right time to smile, so I quashed my giddiness by pressing my lips together and fiddling with the sharp point of the letter A nestled against my chest. The fine chain whispered against my skin, a familiar, grounding sensation.

"You're sure you're alright?" Pansy whispered, peering up at me.

I nodded, and tears rushed to my eyes. I was alive. I was free. I was going home. Pansy threw her arms around me, squeezing tight.

"I knew it was you," she whispered.

I laughed. "I wasn't so sure."

The witch beamed up at me, breaking the hug but still gripping my arms. "You did it, Aliza. You really did it."

She was right. The weight of the last few days lifted from my shoulders, leaving me as light as a bubble. If not for Pansy, I might have drifted into the sky.

Sage and the prince continued to talk in low tones, but my head was too full of my own dreams to listen. Dreams of reunions, of graduation, of ordinary, everyday life. I had no interest in the prince's future plans. My job was done.

Anwir sidled up to me, interrupting my idle reverie with a small smile. Pansy made herself scarce.

"I never caught your name," the prince said.

I snorted a dismal laugh. "There wasn't really a chance for introductions. I'm Aliza."

"Aliza," he repeated, testing the word.

Ahead of me, Sage stiffened, and I wondered if she was about to offer up the rest of my title. Aliza with an A, the human.

"Well, Aliza," the prince continued. "I believe I owe you my freedom. Thank you for breaking the curse, and waking me and my tedious little brother."

My lips curled into a grin. Only that morning, I wouldn't have believed myself capable of such a thing, not today, but it was done. The curse was broken. I was free, or at least, I would be, just as soon as we escaped Tir o Haf. "I wasn't given much choice, but for what it's worth... you're welcome."

Even if he had abandoned me and his own brother at the first opportunity. Still, maybe it was understandable. Those cave zombies were pretty scary. I'd have run too, if I'd been able to see.

We fell into silence, but Anwir stayed at my side. I didn't bother to look back to see where in the line Idris might be.

21

Please, Not The Bunnies

Sage drove us through the woods without a break. My limp grew more pronounced with every passing hour, and I could barely put one foot in front of the other by the time the witch finally admitted defeat and ordered us to make camp for the night.

"No fire," Sage ordered. "We don't know who it might attract."

Or what. I shivered, but not because I was cold. In truth, my skin was damp with sweat after trekking through a world of eternal summer for hours on end. What I'd give for a cool shower.

No fire meant no cooking, and after the tents had been hastily erected, with me proving more of a hindrance than a help, we all gathered in a circle and Hyacinth handed out cheese and bread that was long past its best. When she smuggled me an extra parcel, I blinked up from the log I'd collapsed onto.

She bent low, whispering in my ear, "An extra portion for our saviour."

I wouldn't call myself that, but when I unwrapped the waxy paper to find a little block of cheese dotted with cranberries, I smiled. Who was I to refuse such a reward?

"That's not fair," Pansy hissed at my side. "I'm your daughter!"

Hyacinth flicked Pansy's nose. "And I'm your mother, but you never thought to share your secret cookies with me, did you?"

She winked, moving along to where Prince Idris sat a little way away, not quite in the circle, staring unseeingly. He stirred when the witch spoke to him, but gave a brief, close-lipped smile as he took the food she offered. As though he sensed my stare, he looked straight at me. His eyes shifted from mine to my hair, and a tiny frown creased his brow. I was used to the way people barely glanced at my face before inspecting my hair, the same way they always looked at my feet to see if I was wearing heels. Idris' obvious distaste brought a smile to my lips, just as the awed comments of little girls usually did.

"How did she know about the cookies?" Pansy asked in disbelief. "Did you tell her?"

I pulled my attention from the frowning prince. "No! As if I would."

"She knows everything," Pansy grumbled.

"At least she didn't tell us to share."

The witch giggled, pressing a hand to her mouth. She was pretty, with her dimples and the splatter of freckles over her brown cheeks. How she managed to continue looking cute after trailing through what felt like the entire magical world, I had no idea. I dreaded what I'd find when I finally had a chance to look in a mirror. Still, there was no point worrying about it now. I took a bite of cheese. It was still soft, and the flavours rich. I chewed slowly, savouring my hard-earned treat.

Nearby, Sage and Prince Anwir were arguing. Or rather, Sage was.

"I insist," she said in a tone that left no room for disagreement. "I will not have our king sleeping on the forest floor."

"Then allow me to ease your conscience by taking watch. My brother and I have been sleeping long enough. I have no desire to take to my bed this soon."

"But—"

Anwir held up his hand. "I will take the first watch, Idris the second. It's decided."

Sage looked as though she would very much like to continue arguing, but the prince clapped a hand to her shoulder and turned away. Turned to *me*. He strolled with his shoulders thrown back and an easy smile pasted across his face, someone well used to having all eyes on him. He certainly had my attention. He was beautiful, and confidence rolled off him in gentle waves. The old ladies at the practices I'd been placed at would have loved him.

"Aliza," he said as he settled himself on the log beside me.

"Oh, I've just remembered," Pansy said in a bright voice. "I promised my mother I'd, um, help her with dinner."

"It's just cheese," I said hurriedly, but too late. Pansy sprang up and away, leaving me and Anwir as alone as it was possible to be in the camp. Traitor.

"She seems a lively sort," Anwir observed, but it was me he was watching.

Why did he have to be so gorgeous? It put me at a distinct disadvantage. I could barely arrange my thoughts, and I didn't like it. I was too smart to go to pieces because of a handsome face, but however much I told myself that, I couldn't force my pulse to slow.

"Are you alright, after today?" he asked. "It can't have been easy."

What? What on earth was he on about? The walk had been long, but it hadn't been that bad.

"Breaking the curse," he prompted.

"Oh! Oh, yeah, that. It seems like forever ago," I said in a rush, heat rising in my ears. Thank God my hair covered them. They always turned beetroot when I was embarrassed, which only made things worse than they had to be. "I'm fine."

"You're sure? And, well, I couldn't help but notice that my brother was a little short with you after the tunnels. You must excuse him. He's been through a lot."

"Haven't we all," I muttered. As far as I could see, I didn't have to excuse anything.

"Some more than others."

I didn't care what Idris had been through. Poor privileged prince. What was a two hundred and seventy year nap when you were immortal? Was I supposed to feel sorry for him? God, there were days I could kill for a twenty minute snooze. He didn't know how lucky he was, yet he had the audacity to treat me like dog muck stuck to the sole of his expensive boot. He had saved my life, I supposed, but I'd broken his curse, so we were even. I took an angry bite of my cheese.

"You have an extra portion, I see." Anwir smirked, and I forgot why I was anything but perfectly happy, basking in the attention of such a hotty.

"It's a treat. You can have it, if you want."

What? *What*? Was I giving away cheese? That was it. It was confirmed. My brains had been scrambled by Maelgwyn's curse. It was the only explanation.

To my immense relief, Anwir refused. "Thank you, but no. You keep it. You deserve your treat. If truth be told, I'm more of a sweet tooth."

"Really? Go on then, if you could have any dessert right now, what would it be?"

I was always interested in talking about dessert, especially when it felt like forever since I'd had ice cream.

"Definitely lemon and lavender muffins."

My eager smile turned flat. "Muffins? Really? Have you never heard of meringue? Or chocolate cake? Or even strudel?"

"Chocolate cake is too sickly."

"In that case, we can no longer be friends."

His perfect smile widened. God, his teeth could be on a toothpaste advert, even with those deathly sharp fangs glinting. Still, his portrait back in Nairsgarth hadn't been entirely accurate. There was something about that smile, something different. Not wrong, exactly, because how could such good looks be considered a flaw, but something that hadn't been conveyed in the painting. Not that I knew anything about art. Whoever had painted it had clearly possessed more talent in their little toenail than I had in my entire body. I could forgive one small inaccuracy.

"We were friends?" Anwir enquired, his tone playful. "Until I offended you with differing opinions, that is?"

For some reason, my ears began to warm again. I touched my hair to be certain they were hidden. "I don't go around breaking curses for just anybody, you know."

He'd called me the Human Queen, so he had to be aware that I was supposed to be his bride. He'd been suspiciously nice to me since we'd met. Had it really only been that afternoon? He was going to be a king. Surely, he'd have a lot to say about a bride being predestined for him? He wouldn't stand by and let some whispers decide his fate, not when he could have his pick of potential queens. Why would he choose a human? Why would he want me?

He wouldn't. Which was lucky, because I didn't want him. Yeah, he was gorgeous, and kind, and charming, and maybe he'd be good for a night, but I didn't want the life he offered me.

That was what I told myself as I lay sleepless that night, wedged between Pansy and the tent side. I didn't want this life. I wanted mine. But... what would it be like to be immortal? To know my days weren't numbered? There would be heartbreak, of course. I'd lose my parents one day, but I'd lose them either way. It was the normal way of things. Children buried their parents. What could I do with *my* life if I had eternity? What would I learn? What would I master, if time was no obstacle? The possibilities were endless. The world opened up to me as I stared at the canvas, but it wasn't the tent I was seeing. It was a whole new set of fledgling dreams. Dreams I didn't want, that I had no intention of fulfilling, but that nevertheless kept me wide awake and simmering with wild, foolish hope.

When the riotous birdsong began, signalling dawn's coming, I gave up my fitful attempts at sleep and crawled from the tent. The forest air was as cool and fresh as it ever got, and I pulled my wrap around my shoulders to keep away the slight chill.

My ankle took my weight with only a twinge of protest, which was always a good start. Apart from the birds, all was quiet. The witches still slept. Lucky them. I'd barely closed my eyes all night, too preoccupied with foolish fantasies, and now I was paying the price. My eyes stung with tiredness, and my groggy head felt too heavy to carry. God knew what I looked like. Not a beautiful immortal queen, that much was certain.

Was it immortality that made the fae so gorgeous, or just the luck of genetics? If I did accept immortality, which I wouldn't, but *if* I did... would I become as beautiful as them? And speaking of fae, where was Idris?

I frowned as I swept my eyes over the peaceful camp. Anwir had trusted Idris with the second watch, and as far as I could see, the younger prince was nowhere to be found. He hadn't left our sleeping camp unguarded, had he?

I glanced up at the dark trees, afraid of the creeping monsters I might find lurking amongst the branches, but all I could see were leaves, their outlines painted in the first grey light of dawn. A few softly glowing fairies winked in the darkness. As quietly as I could, I crept to the edge of the camp, peering through the gloom.

Nothing. Nobody.

Where on earth was Idris?

"Have you lost something, mon amor?"

I jumped as though struck by lightning, but somehow managed to strangle my scream. I spun, and sure enough, a vampire lolled against a tree he most certainly hadn't been leaning against a second ago.

"Stop doing that," I hissed, massaging my chest. "You'll give me a heart attack one of these days."

He tsked, eyes glittering like diamonds. "Poor old Jacques would not be up to such a task."

Old? Of course. He might look to be in his mid-twenties, but Jacques was a vampire, and likely at least as old as the princes, if he remembered a time before the curse. "Not when King Maelgwyn's monsters could not."

"Why are you still following me? The curse is broken," I grumbled. I hadn't forgotten his refusal to kiss me the last time we'd met, nor his claims that I *belonged* to another male.

"Yes, but that doesn't mean you are safe. You are in more danger now than you have ever been. The false king knows the curse is broken. He knows you are here."

My blood chilled. Was Maelgwyn hunting for me, even now? Was he descending on the camp that Idris had left unprotected? Were shades lurking in the copious shadows?

"But it's done," I insisted, trying to convince myself as much as Jacques. "Killing me would be pointless. The princes are awake, nothing can change that."

The vampire shrugged, examining his chipped nail varnish idly. "Still. I will keep an eye on things until matters are settled."

Maybe it was a good thing he was lurking. At least *someone* was keeping watch in Idris' absence. Not that Jacques' protection had done me any good so far. I'd still been attacked and almost killed at every turn, and it certainly hadn't been him who'd saved the day.

"You're not in a rush to get through the portals and start slaughtering humans? That's why you needed me to break the curse, isn't it? It's why you didn't kill me?"

Jacques chuckled, the sound clattering over my bones. It was an evil thing that set my hair on end. "We are not as uncivilised as you might believe. It would not do for all of my kind to storm the human realm at once. People would notice so many deaths. It might cause... a stir."

I folded my arms. "Then you're going to sneak through in pairs and just kill a few at a time?"

"My people need to feed."

That old chestnut. "You've survived this long. Why kill people at all? I don't eat meat. It doesn't mean I don't miss chicken nuggets; it just means I value life over my own tastebuds. You don't need to kill people, you just want to."

Jacques' eerie eyes sharpened as they focused on me, his features tightening over his sharp bones. He pushed off from the tree, inching silently closer, until his breath, as fresh and cold as a winter breeze, fluttered over my face. "Yes, I want to. I have survived, as you say, but I am *starving*, Aliza. I am weak. I am eaten up by hunger, and yet, I cannot die. I am plagued by my want, night and day. It is endless."

Panic tightened my throat, but not for myself. Of all the things that wanted to kill me, Jacques was the least of my concerns. I almost trusted him, as stupid as that was, but I knew his restraint would not extend beyond me. People were in danger, people would die, and it was my fault. I had broken the curse. I had opened the rifts to allow a swarm of blood-sucking monsters through to my own world. Without the superstitions of the olden days, nobody would be safe. My selfish, human desire to return home had endangered my entire world and everyone in it.

"Can you go in the sunlight?" I asked. Not that it would make any difference. The world was twenty-four hours now.

"I can, but it is uncomfortable, and harder to hide."

"What about houses? Can you go in without permission?"

He laughed again, chilling the already cold panic rushing through my veins. "What is this? An interrogation? I must be invited."

Relief almost had me sagging against a tree. That was something, at least. It wouldn't stop the deaths by any means, but it was a layer of protection.

"Now it is my turn to ask a question, belle fille. How did you break the curse?"

Was this a trick? Was this sensitive information that needed protecting, or had I learnt to see danger in even the most innocent scenario? Whatever it was, my ears grew warm. "A kiss. That's all it was in the end. There was a vision that said I'd have to give my life, but it was just one of Maelgwyn's tricks."

I laughed. The trials had been easy once I'd made it out of the cave. Nothing but tricks and illusions. Maelgwyn had underestimated humankind. He'd underestimated me.

Despite my cleverness, Jacques' expression softened, something like regret dimming the glow of his eyes. He trailed a cold finger down my cheek. "Which prince did you give your life to, mon amor?"

Ice spread from his touch, coating every inch of my skin as the vision's warning took on a new meaning. What if she hadn't meant instant death at all? What if I'd cursed myself instead? "I didn't. I told you, it was just a kiss." It was, wasn't it? Just a quick little peck. Nothing more. Nothing profound. Though, Idris would probably be only too glad to take my life after my performance in the caves.

What have you done?

" Bien sûr. Forgive foolish Jacques. I misheard."

My breath of relief hissed out as I smiled. It was nothing to worry about. I was still alive, wasn't I? Idris' unwilling kiss hadn't been the brush of death for me, and he had saved my life. He didn't want me dead. The vampire could keep his questions to himself if this was how it was going to be. My turn. I opened my mouth to ask about garlic and wooden stakes, but Jacques' eyes widened, his head tilting as though listening for something I couldn't hear. He whipped around, hissing, and leapt into the branches of a tree with the speed and agility of a cat.

"Jacques?" I squeaked, but it wasn't him who answered.

"What are you doing out here?"

I yelped, spinning, and found Idris prowling silently in my direction, his arms full of sticks.

Oh, thank God.

The prince looked slightly dishevelled, a lock of dark hair falling into his eyes, and his shirt rumpled, though he'd washed most of the gore from his perfect face. He looked much better than I undoubtedly did.

"I could ask you the same thing," I snapped, my frayed nerves getting the better of me. "Shouldn't you be keeping watch?"

"I am."

He drew level with me, and I fully expected him to pause and argue, but he walked right past me as though I was of no importance.

"That's not what it looks like to me." I hurried after him, keen not to be left alone in the gloomy woods now I knew Maelgwyn was after me. "I woke up to find the camp completely unprotected."

"It was not unprotected." His voice was flat and bored. Arrogant prick.

"Where have you been?"

"None of your concern."

"It is my concern! When you're supposed to be keeping us all safe and you just disappear and—"

He turned, quicker than my eyes could follow, and brought his snarling face inches from mine. I blinked, stumbling back a step. "You were safe, mortal. Now please, stop talking. It is far too early for your screeching."

Screeching? *Screeching*? The cheeky bastard. He turned away and continued into camp. I followed, stomping my feet louder than was wise in enemy territory. The prince crouched and began arranging his precious sticks in the centre of the circle of tents.

"Sage said no fires," I reminded him.

He ignored me, continuing to stack the wood just so. Irritation warred with unease.

"Somebody might see the smoke." Maelgwyn might see, but as I couldn't admit to my secret rendezvous with vampires, I kept that thought to myself.

"Do you ever shut up?"

The urge to march over and kick the stupid stick pile had my muscles clenching, primed for action. "I see your servants didn't manage to teach you any manners."

Idris ignored me, and a tiny flame appeared amongst the sticks, spreading until it was burning brightly. The prince sat back, drawing a knife. It was then I noticed three dead rabbits hung from his belt. My heart twisted in pity.

"You killed them?"

"I'm hungry. Everyone is hungry. We need more than cheese."

Everyone was hungry but me. My stomach churned as Idris unfastened the corpses from his hip and laid them before him. The small, sharp knife, made from the same dawn-bright metal as his swords, flashed in the glow of his fire. I looked away quickly. I might not be squeamish, but as far as I was concerned, he was barbaric. Those poor bunnies. I retreated to my tent, unable to find any more words to waste on the prince.

With Pansy snoring softly beside me, I stared at our canvas ceiling, my guts churning.

What have you done?

What *had* I done?

I faked sleep for as long as I could, but the smell of cooking meat had the witches stirring, and before long, the camp was filled with the sounds of life. I preoccupied myself with removing the bandage from my hand and silently marvelling at the thin, pink strip of perfectly healed skin cutting across my palm, but when I couldn't reasonably fake it any longer, I headed out into the open, only to find myself face to face with a prince. For a second, I thought it was Idris standing before me, but then I noticed the long hair tied in a low ponytail, and I relaxed, smiling.

"Good morning." Anwir held a little metal plate, and my stomach dropped at the sight of slightly charred meat. "Breakfast."

He pushed the plate toward me, but I clamped my teeth together and shook my head, unable to rid myself of the image of those adorable little angels with dead, staring eyes.

"What's the matter?"

"I don't eat meat," I managed, my jaw tight. "I'm a vegetarian."

I grimaced in apology. It was sweet of him to think of me, and I wouldn't have been so affected by the sight of meat if I hadn't seen Idris settle down to skin the rabbits.

"What? You don't like meat?" Anwir, to my disappointment, reacted the same way most people did when learning of my preferences. As though not eating meat was unthinkable.

"I don't dislike it; I just don't want anything to die for me. Thanks anyway."

He looked slightly crestfallen, so I took pity on him. "You have mine. I don't like a heavy breakfast anyway."

It was an outright lie. I was often pulled from sleep by the insistent complaints of my stomach, but for some reason, I wanted to make Anwir feel better. He'd only wanted to show me kindness, after all. It was more than could be said for his brother.

The prince was quiet as we headed to the log we'd shared the previous evening, me grabbing an apple from Sage as I passed. Idris' fire was still burning, much to my annoyance. I'd hoped Sage would admonish him, but apparently, being a royal arsehole meant he could do whatever he liked. The prince himself sat nearby, leaning against a tree trunk and staring unseeingly at the flames. His own plate of murdered rabbit lay untouched beside him. I scowled. What had he killed them for, if he wasn't even going to eat them? So much for being hungry.

"I've never met anyone who doesn't eat meat before," Anwir mused.

Nearby, Idris stirred at the sound of his brother's voice. Great. Was he eavesdropping? Though his eyes remained trained on the campfire, a tiny line appeared between his dark eyebrows. He was probably the type of person who would judge me for being compassionate to innocent creatures. He'd probably make a point of moaning and groaning in ecstasy as he devoured those poor bunnies, just to offend me.

"You don't mind others eating it?" Anwir prompted, pulling my attention from his surly brother.

I smiled encouragingly. It was refreshing when people didn't go on the offensive, and instead showed interest in my diet. A lot of people took my choices as a personal attack, when I really couldn't care less what they did, as long as it didn't involve skinning their prey in front of me. It was rare to meet someone who spoke without judgement, and rarer still to have them consider my comfort.

"Not at all. Tuck in." I took a bite of my apple. It wasn't that bad. I might be hungry again sooner rather than later, but it was crisp and fresh.

Following my lead, Anwir ate a piece of meat, though he chewed tentatively. The wary way he met my gaze from the corner of his eye had me stifling a laugh. I swallowed with difficulty.

"Honestly, I don't mind!"

He relaxed, smiling with his lips closed as he chewed. Even with a mouth full of food, his face was the very image of symmetrical beauty. It was distinctly unfair.

"You have a good heart," he said at last. "Compassionate."

"Thank you. It's a blessing and a curse."

"How so?"

"Well, I'm a vet, or a student, for now. I should be graduating any day now, but instead, here I am, saving you two. Anyway, I care for sick animals, try to make them better, but it's not always possible, and losing a patient is... painful."

"A healer. I should have guessed."

My ears heated. "I try my best."

"You've never considered healing people?"

Irritation licked at my veins, a swift flip from the glow I'd felt moments ago. It wasn't uncommon for people to learn of my profession and immediately judge it less worthy, as though performing surgery on an animal was somehow easier, requiring less skill than the human equivalent. "Animals are better company than most people."

"I have offended you, please forgive me." Again with the wary eyes.

I softened slightly. "I only meant to say... healers are cherished in my kingdom, or they were. Before..."

"Before your uncle?"

"Yes. They are extremely rare amongst the fae. My mother was a healer. Perhaps she still is. I don't know if she still lives."

"She does," Sage piped up from near the fire. "Though we receive little news on our side of the ward."

My heart squeezed tight, oozing pity and shame. I'd been so preoccupied with my own plight, wrapped up in how my own parents might be feeling, that I'd never considered what the curse must have meant to those who had known and loved the princes. To have them taken away, to have hope wither with every passing day. Century, even. The poor queen. She had lost her husband, then had her children betrayed by their father's brother. She had lost everything, and suffered for longer than I could comprehend.

I laid a comforting hand on Anwir's forearm. He tensed, his muscles hard beneath my palm, but after a second or two he relaxed. "You'll see her again soon enough."

Anwir looked at my hand, still resting on his arm, then lifted his eyes to mine. I hadn't realised how close we were until those beautiful, golden-green orbs were before me. My breath stilled at how utterly gorgeous he was.

Flushing, I snatched my hand away. "What sort of magic do you have?"

"Lightning." His voice was gruffer than it had been a moment ago. "Almost as rare as my mother's gift, but much more dangerous."

Of course. The crown prince was the only fae capable of wielding lightning, the only one capable of fighting back against the shades. I already knew that. Why wasn't my brain working properly?

"I'd like to see it, when we've crossed the wards."

Anwir shook his head. "I never use it. It's not worth the risks."

Something gnawed in my gut. "You'll use it to get rid of the shades, though, won't you?"

What if he refused? How could the fae fight Maelgwyn if their best warrior refused to wield his unique weapons? Had my efforts to wake him been for nothing?

"Time to go."

I blinked and found Sage staring down at us.

"If we want to reach the border by nightfall, we need to make good time. Pack up." She turned on her heel and stalked away, issuing orders.

Anwir stood, extending his hand. I couldn't bring myself to look him in those stunning eyes as I took it, and he pulled me to my feet.

What would that enormous hand feel like on other parts of my body? I gulped. Did he hold my hand a little longer than necessary, or was it wishful thinking?

Why was I wishing anything of the sort? My task was complete. I was going home. But I didn't pull my hand away. I let him hold it, his skin warm against mine, until he gave me a small smile and dropped it of his own accord. Was it my imagination, or where his cheeks pinker than they had been a few minutes ago?

Nearby, Idris clambered to his feet and wandered off between the trees, disappearing from sight. Why didn't he stay with the group? Was he off to murder more innocent animals, or was he up to something much worse?

22

Years Of Academy Training, Wasted

Sage really did mean business. By my calculations, lunch should have been hours and hours ago, and my measly apple felt like it belonged to a different lifetime. I'd been light-headed and jelly-legged for ages, my stomach long since past the stage of rumbling. Instead, it felt like it was trying to implode.

My brain might have been full of starving fog, but I hadn't failed to notice Idris slipping away from the main group several times during our long trek, only to return without fanfare or fuss an hour or two later. In fact, he was absent when Sage finally took mercy and called us to a halt beside a chatty stream. For all I knew, it was the same stream I'd fallen into during the spider attack on our journey to find the princes, but my senses had given up caring hours ago. I felt more than a little drunk as I sank down onto a rock while the witches busied themselves behind me.

I should have eaten more at breakfast, but I hadn't expected to skip lunch completely. My rock was located in a patch of sunlight, and I tipped my head back, letting the light warm my face. If Sage hadn't been such a tyrant, and if the world wasn't full of monsters, I could have gladly stayed there for hours, basking in the early evening glow.

Before long, the scent of smoke and roasting meat drifted up my nose. The no fire rule had obviously been abandoned completely. The stream burbled past, and birds twittered overhead. I couldn't bring myself to worry about spiders, or anything except the very real possibility of me fainting and falling face first into the water.

When the sun sank too low to break through the treetops, I gave up my sunbathing and watched my companions with fuzzy eyes. Nobody bothered me. Even Pansy kept her distance. True, she was busy, but I couldn't help but feel she was making herself scarce deliberately, leaving room for a certain prince to speak with me. But Anwir was busy too, helping to prepare dinner.

I admired his broad back as he prodded and poked the fire. It was a miracle that his glorious physique had survived hundreds of years suspended in a tomb. The curse had clearly frozen its victims, preserving them in perfect condition. Had they truly been sleeping, or had they been aware of every second? Either way, it seemed a foolish way to go about things. If I'd been a villain, I'd have gone for something a little more debilitating, or permanent, but I wasn't complaining. The view was really quite miraculous.

My gaze drifted, landing on an equally beautiful form. I blinked in mild surprise. Idris was back. I hadn't noticed him sneaking back into camp, but there he was, lurking slightly away from the rest of the group, silent and sulking as usual, but helping. He knelt in the dirt, sleeves rolled up and knife in hand, chopping away at something I couldn't see. A lock of black hair fell into his eyes, and he swiped at it with his bare forearm before returning to chopping. Muscles and tendons flexed under his skin as he worked. Had he been hunting again? Was that what he was doing during his absences?

What if he was a traitor?

The thought slid down my spine like an ice cube, and goosebumps erupted over my skin. What if he *was* a traitor? What if he was sneaking away to meet with his evil uncle? No, it made no sense. Why would he work for someone who had cursed him? Idris might be standoffish and rude and downright unpleasant, but he wouldn't betray us, would he? Not his own brother, not the woman who'd broken his curse?

I'd kissed him.

Heat licked at my neck, chasing away my chill. My lips had touched his, and the curse had broken. God, I still couldn't believe that it had actually worked. It was such a cliché.

Which prince did you give your life to, mon amor?

Did the vision's message mean Idris would betray me? Did he remember the kiss?

As though he read my gut-twisting thoughts, Idris' whipped his head around, eyes snapping to me over his broad shoulder. I looked away hurriedly, pretending I hadn't been admiring his muscular forearms while remembering my lips on his. I hoped I hadn't turned beetroot. I felt like I was about to spontaneously combust from the shame of it. If I did, it would be a mercy.

Abandoning my rock, I rose on wobbly legs. The world swayed, and it was a few seconds before I was steady enough to attempt what I hoped was a casual stroll over to the fire. Some poor little soul was roasting over the flames, but I averted my eyes before I could make out what, exactly, had been slaughtered.

"Can I help?" I asked nobody in particular.

I wasn't sure what use I could possibly be, but I didn't want to sit around looking shifty.

"You've already done your share." Anwir smiled up at me from where he crouched over an assortment of metal plates and bowls. He offered one to me. "Here, this is for you."

My plate was crammed with food. Carefully sliced cheese, including some of that delicious cranberry one, a mound of nuts piled on top of a bed of leaves, an assortment of juicy berries, buttered bread, and taking centre stage, an apple. Not just any old apple though. It had been sliced into delicate, wafer-thin strips, which had been skilfully arranged to look like a rose in full bloom.

"Oh my God." I took the plate, a smile spreading over my face. "This is amazing! I almost don't want to eat it."

"Eat," Anwir said firmly. "You look like you're about to keel over."

Well, that was always good to hear, especially from somebody who was too handsome to be allowed. Still, he was probably right.

"Thank you. This is really thoughtful, and pretty."

"It suits you then."

My blush bypassed my ears completely, igniting my entire face. I tried to speak, but the only sound I could make was an awkward high-pitched laugh. I retreated to my rock before I could embarrass myself further, but not before Pansy could give me a wink and a sneaky grin from where she sat, turning a stick of skewered mushrooms over the flame.

What was wrong with me? I had never been the type of girl to get tongue tied and swoony over a handsome man, but Anwir was beyond handsome. He blew all my conquests out of the water with his sheer perfection, and his charm, and his kindness. I looked at the plate balanced on my lap. The apple must have taken forever to carve and arrange. Such delicate work, and he'd done it for *me*. He'd obviously marked my choice of apple at breakfast and decided I liked them. And I did. I mean, I'd rather have a croissant, but apples were okay, but it was the effort that made it special. No man except my dad had ever done anything as sweet for me, mainly because I'd never given them the chance, unwilling to allow anyone or anything to distract me from my studies, but... My heart glowed at the sight of that apple rose.

Smiling to myself, I layered the cheese onto my bread and began to eat.

I'd all but finished when Pansy approached, clutching two mushroom kebabs. She handed one to me and sat on a nearby rock, grinning like a fool.

"What?" I demanded, but I had a feeling I already knew the answer.

Damn her to hell. I didn't have a clue how to deflect her implications, so I tore a mushroom from the stick with my teeth. It was glorious to fill my belly after all those hours of starvation. The shaking limbs had already begun to subside.

"Come on then, tell me what you think."

"Mmph." I nodded, swallowing my food. "Yeah, tastes amazing."

"Not the *mushrooms*, Aliza!" She dropped her voice to a whisper. "I'm talking about Prince Anwir."

"Oh. I mean, I don't know him very well, but he seems alright."

Pansy rolled her eyes. "He seems to like you."

"He's polite."

"Don't you find him handsome?"

God, she was relentless. I narrowed my eyes at the prying witch, deciding if I could trust her. I knew I could. "Fine. He's gorgeous."

Pansy squealed, drawing the attention of the entire camp. I hurriedly busied myself with my mushrooms, trying to look innocent and unconcerned. When she continued, she lowered her voice, leaning in.

"Mother above, I knew it! I knew there was something between the two of you. I've been watching."

"There isn't anything," I sighed. "Just because I think he's good looking doesn't mean there's anything there."

What if Pansy was right? What if Anwir looked at me and saw beauty? It wasn't possible, was it? I was just a human. I had no idea how old the prince was, but he'd undoubtedly spent his life before the curse surrounded by stunning fae females. The apple glared up at me. Kindness, or something more?

"Oh, please. I've seen the way he's drawn to you."

"It doesn't matter," I insisted, unable to deny that the prince had shown me a fair amount of attention. "I've done what I needed to do. I'll be able to go home as soon as we get back to Nairsgarth."

It was true. Just because I found the princes attractive, it didn't change anything. It didn't make me waver. I would bask in the attention until it was time for me to leave. Maybe I'd enjoy Anwir's company for a night, scratch the itch my illicit dreams had awoken in me, but no more than that. After all, it wasn't every day a girl had the chance to take an obscenely handsome prince to bed.

The scandalised delight on Pansy's face faded into disappointment.

"Don't look at me like that, we always knew—"

A snarling bark shattered the peace of the woods, sending my plate and skewer splashing into the stream as I scrambled to my feet. I spun in time to see something huge and black careen into the midst of the camp, skidding through the flames in a blur of snapping teeth.

Screams erupted, but not enough to drown the snarls.

My eyes glued to the creature. It was a red-eyed wolf, easily as large as a carthorse, with a shaggy black coat and overlong fangs flashing in its snapping mouth. The witches bolted like zebras in the midst of a lion attack, screaming and reaching for their weapons, but the wolf was faster. Before I could do more than open my mouth in a scream that never came, the beast mowed down Meadow, those awful teeth snapping at the back of her neck.

Almost in slow motion, the pair tumbled to the ground. The momentum carried the wolf too far, and it rolled over the fallen witch, but its jaws remained clamped around the base of her skull. A spray of red mist arced through the air, and the wolf regained its footing, plunging back to finish the job.

The sinewy crack of bone snapped me from my horrified trance.

Pansy tugged on my arm. I stumbled into step beside her, my feet numb, my mind reeling. We'd barely staggered a few faltering steps when a second, identical beast leapt from the shadows, with a third close behind.

"Run!" somebody screamed.

I didn't need telling twice.

I burst into a sprint, careening along the riverbed, leaping rocks and tree roots. The screams faded with every pounding step, but I couldn't tell if that was only due to the blood blaring in my ears. Pansy darted along at my side, though with her short legs, I had to check my pace.

"Come on," I encouraged, waving my hand.

I ran until my lungs threatened to burst out of my mouth. The woods were quiet when we staggered to a halt, with nothing to hint at the oversized beasts prowling its shadows. The last of the day's sun glowed golden through the canopy of green leaves, reminding me of the princes' eyes.

I shook my head. This was no time to be thinking—

A wolf leapt from the bracken, soaring straight at me, fanged jaw wide.

A streak of darkness launched into the wolf's side, knocking it off course. Pansy screamed as the beast went down. I snatched her hand, dragging her away as the wolf tussled with...

"Jacques!"

The vampire didn't look up. I barely caught a glimpse of his features, contorted with rage before he moved again, too fast to follow. One moment the wolf floundered to its feet, the next it was thrown onto its back with a yelp that dislodged leaves from the trees overhead. Jacques launched at its throat. Teeth snapped, and the beast snarled and writhed. I pressed a hand to my mouth, dancing on the spot.

With a wet tearing sound, the wolf gave up its fight. Jacques rose, the grotesque innards of the beast's throat clutched in his blood-drenched fist. He threw it to the ground, where the wolf lay twitching and gurgling through its death throes. Blood spurted, pooling around the dying animal before sinking into the ground.

The vampire turned to face us. I gasped. Enormous, angry blisters covered his moon-white skin.

"Oh my God." I darted toward him.

Pansy's hand closed around my arm. "Aliza, that's a vampire!"

"It's okay, I know him." I shrugged her off, hurrying to Jacques' side.

I'd never seen him in daylight before, never been able to guess at the colour of his eyes. What should have been the whites were dark, threaded with black veins, and his irises were lightest grey and white, but for the red corona around his pupils. The star-bright gleam was even more striking against the raw red of his skin.

I took an awed step closer. "You actually saved me."

Through cracked lips, he said, "Bien sûr, mademoiselle."

I didn't have the heart to tell him I didn't have the faintest idea what he was saying. "Will you be okay? Will this" — I waved a vague hand at his face — "heal?"

He huffed a small laugh. "Do not fear for handsome Jacques, all will be well. Now hurry back to your camp, there are worse things than barghests in these woods."

Barghests? Was that what the oversized dog was? Before Jacques could disappear at the speed of light I caught his blood-drenched sleeve, holding him in place. His eyes dropped to my hand, but I didn't give him time to protest or escape before folding him into a hug. Somewhere behind me, Pansy gave a great shuddering gasp. Though I was careful to avoid Jacques' burns, his nose went straight to my neck, and his protruding ribs expanded in a deep breath beneath my arms.

I stepped back hurriedly, only to find his focus had sharpened. He stared at the spot he'd sniffed with all the intensity of a cat about to pounce.

With a nervous chuckle I said, "Thank you, Jacques."

The vampire blinked rapidly, as though coming out of a trance, then he gave a brief bow before leaping into the branches overhead, leaving me staring at the body of the monstrous wolf.

"Aliza?" Pansy asked doubtfully.

"Come on." I turned away from the beast, veering back the way we'd come. "You heard him. It's not safe out here alone."

Pansy's silence was almost as unnerving as the knowledge that at least two more barghests prowled the woods. The witch trudged beside me, but I couldn't decide if her lack of speech was down to shock, fear or judgement. Somehow, I suspected the latter. What had she said about vampires? That she'd hoped the curse would starve them?

"I know what you're thinking," I said at length, keeping my voice low. In truth, I had no idea what was going on inside her head, beyond that it couldn't be good. "You don't need to worry. Jacques' alright. He's been protecting me since the first night I arrived in Neath. He hasn't tried to, you know... eat me."

Pansy shot me a sharp look.

"He's actually helped keep me alive."

"He's a vampire, Aliza. Do you understand what that means?"

I bristled. I might not know much about this world, but I wasn't as naive as everyone seemed to think. "Of course I do, but the fact is, he just saved our lives. The curse is broken, he doesn't need me anymore, and he still saved me. He's alright."

"Never trust the undead! I don't know why he saved you, but I'd bet my life he's helping you for his own reasons."

My voice was cold as I retorted, "Not unlike the coven, then. Let's not forget that I didn't actually want to come on this God-forsaken mission."

"That's different," Pansy gasped, her eyes widening in shock, but it wasn't. As far as I could see, none of my so-called friends would have bothered to keep me alive if I hadn't been their only hope.

"Look, it doesn't matter. I just want to get home, and if that means befriending Maelgwyn himself, I'd do it."

"You don't mean that."

I heaved a sigh. "No, but I do trust Jacques to an extent, and nothing you can say or think will change that."

"Just... be careful, Aliza. He's dangerous."

"Who's dangerous?" Anwir strolled out from between the trees, sword in hand. His blade was an ordinary silver like those of the witches, not the beautiful metal of Idris' weapons. No hint of blood marred the blade, and I breathed a sigh of relief. After everything the witches and I had risked, losing the princes on the way home would be far from ideal.

"Nobody," I said hurriedly. "Are you okay?"

"I'm unhurt. I was separated from the others. The two of you?"

"Fine. We're heading back now."

Anwir dropped his eyes frowning. "You have blood on your arm. You're sure you're unhurt?"

I glanced down, and sure enough, a smear of red marred my skin. Probably barghest blood, transferred from Jacques to me when I'd hugged him. "One of the barghests is dead. We... found it, back there. That's all it is."

Anwir peered through the trees at my back, his eyes narrowing. "What killed it?"

"We don't know," I lied, praying Pansy would support my dishonesty. If Jacques' earlier reaction to Idris had been any indicator, fae disliked vampires almost as much as witches did. "But one down, two to go. Come on, let's find the others."

After a moment's hesitation, Anwir fell into step on my far side, and I led him away from the barghest and any evidence of Jacques.

The walk back to camp took an eternity. Pansy resumed her earlier silence, and Anwir wasn't his usual charming self. I was glad of his presence though, and the way his eyes swept our surroundings, alert to any dangers lurking in the growing gloom. He stayed close to me, and his tall, solid presence was reassuring, especially as I wasn't entirely convinced Jacques still haunted my steps. I caught no glimpse of the vampire amongst the shadowed boughs, nor those strange eyes disguised by the stars winking slowly into life above us.

Finally, voices drifted to my ears, and I quickened my pace, but as we grew nearer, and the voices clearer, the unmistakable notes of panic rang through the dusk. The witches shouting was interrupted by a ferocious snarl.

I shared a worried glance with Pansy, only for our brief eye contact to be broken by a scream.

Anwir flung out his arm, blocking our approach. "Wait here."

He didn't give me time to answer before he broke into a run. Drawing my daggers, I ignored his advice and followed, Pansy's footsteps close behind.

The moment we broke through the trees, the moment I saw what awaited us, I regretted not following Anwir's order.

Another barghest lay dead, multiple stab wounds littering its body, but it was the smaller, second form, sprawled in a pool of blood, that made my stomach lurch.

Hyacinth. Hyacinth grappling with a gaping wound on her thigh, bleeding profusely. Too much. Far too much.

"Move!" My daggers thudded to the ground as I darted between the cluster of witches and threw myself to my knees, unbuckling my belt as I went. "It's okay, Hyacinth," I said. "You're going to be fine."

Blood spurted between Hyacinth's shaking fingers, splattering in the rapidly growing pool.

My nerves and panic evaporated, leaving only a numb sense of purpose. Emotion had no place here, and my body knew its job. My hands were deft as I wrapped the belt around the witch's thigh, pulling the buckle as tight as I could. Her thigh was much slimmer than my waist, and there were no holes to fasten it.

"Someone hold this," I ordered, my voice calm and steady. A large, pale hand took the belt from me. "Pull it as tight as you can. We need to slow the bleeding."

Much good it would do out here.

"Okay, Hyacinth. I'm going to apply pressure to the wound. This will hurt."

Pansy dropped into place opposite me, seizing her mother's hand. Her desperate eyes fixed on me, silently pleading. Unable to offer even a hint of a smile, I lowered my gaze, gathering up my wrap.

When I pressed it against the wound, Hyacinth screamed. I'd heard somewhere that dying patients didn't scream. It was a lie, and I suspected I had lied when I'd told the witch she would be fine. With no hospitals, and no magic...

"I need a hot blade," I yelled, to nobody in particular. It might be a long shot, but if I could locate the artery amongst the mangled flesh, if I could cauterise it...

"There's no fire," somebody answered in a panicked voice.

Fuck. "Sage, the paste you used on me, have you got any left?"

"It won't work quickly enough." The witch's voice shook as she spoke, wracked with as much emotion as I had ever heard from her.

I looked up at her, at her colourless face and white ringed eyes. "Let's try, shall we?"

Because it was all we could do. Because however faint that glimmer of hope, without it, Hyacinth would be dead in minutes. I could slow the bleeding, but that was all I could do. I couldn't seal the artery or stitch the wound. I was buying time. Seconds, minutes. But for what?

Because, in the face of suffering, I didn't know how to do nothing.

Sage pressed her white lips together, nodding, and slid her pack off her shoulder. I turned my attention to Hyacinth. Her clammy brown face was a sickly shade, losing colour fast. Her eyes fluttered on the edge of consciousness. At her side, Pansy muttered a string of high-pitched attempts at cheery reassurance. I couldn't stand the wild desperation in her voice. This was no calm, sterile surgery, with an impassive team. There had never been loved ones present as we battled to save a life.

My hands grew sticky and warm. Blood soaked through my wrap. I checked the tourniquet. The prince's hands held it tight. His white knuckles were streaked in blood. My eyes trailed up his straining arm. Idris stared back at me.

I swallowed, hooked by eyes almost identical to Anwir's, but bleak. He knew. I looked at him, and I could feel it down to my bones. He knew how fruitless this was, and still, he held the belt. Still, he tried.

"I've got it." Sage interrupted my moment of hopeless clarity. She crouched beside me, a pot of that same thick green paste she'd mended me with clutched before her.

"Okay. In a second, I'm going to move my hands. I want you to slather that paste on as quickly as you can, nice and thick. Get into the wound, don't worry about hurting her. Then I'm going to put pressure on again. Yeah?"

Sage nodded, scooping a gloopy dollop of paste.

"Idris, you keep that belt pulled tight, okay?"

"Understood."

"On three then. One, two, three."

To Sage's credit, her shaking hands didn't falter as she smeared the paste into the gaping wound, but just as quickly as she worked, fresh blood pooled. Shit. I could feel Idris shaking with the effort of pulling the belt. As soon as Sage moved, I slammed my wrap back down, throwing my weight forward onto my arms.

Please, please, please.

It had to work. There was no other option. It didn't have to leave a perfect limb, but if the paste could just seal the edges, close the severed artery...

It would be enough to get Hyacinth home, to the magic. That was all we needed.

Though Hyacinth's chest rose and fell, the movement was barely discernible, growing fainter by the second. I didn't believe in any god, but I silently begged somebody, anything, to intervene. Nobody did, of course. The only gods were us, and we were powerless.

Inevitably, despite our useless efforts, Hyacinth's chest fell still.

"Sage," I barked. "Take over from me."

"What is it?" Pansy wailed. "Aliza?"

I scrambled, sliding my hands from underneath Sage's as they pressed down, and shuffled around Idris to Hyacinth's chest. I lowered my ear to her mouth, hoping against the cold, sinking sensation in my chest that warm breath would flutter over my skin.

Nothing.

Shit.

Locking my hands together, I rose onto my knees and thrust the heel of my hand down onto Hyacinth's chest, beginning to count the rhythm in my head. I'd never performed CPR on a person before, and while I was confident that I knew what I was doing, I also recognised the creeping heaviness of futility spreading through my body. But I had to try. I couldn't just sit back and let Hyacinth die, knowing there was something, anything, I might have tried. I couldn't live with that.

"Stop it!" Somebody shrieked. "Get off her!"

My rhythm faltered, and I found Pansy, teeth bared, eyes wild, glaring back at me.

"You're hurting her!"

"I'm helping her," I muttered, trying to return focus to my beats. "I'm trying to help."

Thirty. Despite Pansy's continued arguments, I pinched Hyacinth's nose, blowing two deep rescue breaths into her mouth, before returning to her chest. I'd barely managed a full compression before an arm wrapped around my neck, dragging me away.

"Leave her alone!"

The arm released me, and I tumbled to my arse, blinking up in shock. Pansy, for once, towered over me, glaring down at me.

"Stop hurting my mother!"

"Pansy, I would never! I'm trying to save her life. I know it doesn't look nice, and it's not, but if I can keep her blood moving through her body, and get her breathing again, if the paste works..."

If. So much depended on if.

"Please, Pansy. Let me try."

My friend's lip trembled, and I wanted nothing more than to wrap her up in my arms, to squeeze her and let her cry, but that could come after. Right now, her mother needed me. Maybe the calm, reassuring mask I'd spent the past few years perfecting slipped to show exactly how dire this situation was, or maybe it did its job exactly as intended, because Pansy's face crumpled, and she gave a nod of assent.

"Hold her hand," I said, trying to inject some gentleness into my tone. "Speak to her. Let her know you're there."

"She can hear me?"

"Of course she can." I didn't know if that was true, but what harm could a little white lie do now?

By the time I sank down beside Idris, surrounded by silent, watchful faces, my limbs had begun to shake. My arms trembled as I resumed chest compressions, and Pansy's voice drifted through the silence.

"Mother, it's me, it's Pansy. Can you hear me? Everything is fine. Aliza and Sage have fixed you up. All we need is for you to wake up, and then we're going home. Come on, Mother. You can do it. I know you can."

I tuned her out, fighting against the tears welling in my eyes. I narrowed my attention to my sickeningly bloodied hands, to counting. Thirty compressions, two rescue breaths. Thirty compressions, two rescue breaths.

I repeated the cycle over and over, until my own breaths were harsh as they burst from my mouth, until my shoulders ached and my arms trembled. Then I repeated it some more. I lost count. I had no way of knowing how long I'd been working, but I knew the mantra. I couldn't stop until I was exhausted, or until help arrived, but this wasn't my world, and no help was coming. We were alone.

Eventually, Pansy's imploring mutterings turned to quiet sobs. I tried not to notice when she curled up on the ground beside her mother, clutching the older witch's hand to her chest. I tried not to notice that the other witches had begun to turn away, that some were crying. I tried not to notice that, despite my best efforts, I was slowing, my body betraying me. Every pump was weaker, shallower than the last. A sob burst through my clenched teeth.

"Aliza."

A large hand settled between my shoulder blades. "Aliza, it's time."

No. It couldn't be. Yet though I knew it was, I still couldn't stop. I couldn't be the one to quit.

The hand slid around my shoulder and down my arm, closing firmly, preventing my next compression. I didn't have the strength to fight. Another sob shattered from my tight throat.

"It's alright."

It wasn't. How could he not see?

I blinked through my tears at Anwir. He released my arm and pulled me to his chest. His heartbeat was strong and steady in my ear, an awful reminder that, beside me, Hyacinth was dead.

Dead.

I had let her die. At the thought, I began to dissolve, drowning in guilt and disbelief.

"We need to move."

It took me three full seconds to make sense of Sage's words. I disentangled myself from Anwir's arms. Sage looked, for the first time ever, lost. Unsure. Her whole body trembled, and her face was a sickly shade of grey. Wet streaks spilled down each cheek, but despite it all, she held her head high as she gathered her control. Of us, and of herself.

"This is it," she said, her voice growing stronger. "We need to reach the border. We're out of time. Pansy… say goodbye to your mother. It's time to go."

I didn't want to look, but I couldn't prevent it as Pansy's terrible, animalistic wail howled through the gathering dark. In the seconds since Anwir had pulled me away, she'd half laid herself over Hyacinth, her head nestled beneath her mother's chin. Now she clung to her, her whole body heaving with sobs.

"We can't leave her," I said, even as I thought of Meadow, the first witch to die, torn apart by wolves, and left behind as we fled. This was different though. This was my friend's *mother*.

"She will only slow us down." Sage spoke with no room for argument, but her voice cracked, betraying the emotion she held at bay.

Idris stirred, snagging my gaze. He'd been at my side throughout my failed attempts, but he'd moved away since, maybe to allow Pansy whatever shred of privacy we could give in these God-forsaken woods. Now, he prowled close once more, crouching, and muttered words I couldn't hear.

After a moment, Pansy released her mother's body, clambering stiffly to her feet where she was immediately embraced by Hazel, but it was Idris I watched.

Watched as he scooped up the dead witch as effortlessly as though she was a child. He rose, turning to Sage, his face set with challenge.

Was it my imagination, or was that a glimmer of gratitude on Sage's face?

“Keep up, Your Highness,” was all she said before turning away, fading into the failing light.

23

The Prince Is A Prick

For the first time in my life, I wished my brain would just *stop*. I wished it would stop analysing, looking for ways I might have done better. Ways I could improve. I didn't want to know, not this time. I didn't want to remember it all. Yet, I could think of nothing else as we trudged silently through the woods.

It was fully dark by the time we reached the border of Tir o Haf. Thousands of stars winked overhead, and the moonlight gilding the wildflowers made them look like a shimmering sea of silver, rippling in the balmy breeze. I marvelled briefly that beauty could still exist, even after the events of the evening. Even with the dead witch still clutched in the prince's arms. Idris carried his burden without a word of complaint. He hadn't slowed, or faltered, or asked to rest. An alien bubble of admiration had lodged itself in my chest, and my darkly swirling emotions were unable to burst it. I'd doubted him, mistrusted him, but he'd wordlessly knelt in the dirt beside me and tried to save a life. Maybe carrying Hyacinth was the punishment he inflicted on himself for what he saw as his failure. I wanted to tell him that none of it was his fault, but finding such words would mean absolving myself of my own crushing failure, and I wasn't ready to free myself of it just yet.

Instead, I chose to walk at his back as we crossed the sleeping meadow, my silent show of support. Of shared guilt. Whatever he felt, it could be nothing to my own failure. I knew that Hyacinth's cause had been hopeless from the moment I'd seen the blood gushing from her thigh, but that didn't ease the weight of my guilt. Of how useless I had been, when it mattered most.

I couldn't summon surprise, or even relief, when we reached the border unhindered, and Sage pulled out the same dark void of a crystal she had used to take me from her cottage to Nairsgarth. When she muttered the incantation, and the crystal turned into a swirling black hole, sucking in the silver of the night bathed meadow, I found no awe to spare.

"The princes first," Sage insisted, standing back to make way, "then Aliza."

I kept my eyes on Idris' back until he vanished into the void, and I followed him as though the portal was nothing but an ordinary door.

The all-engulfing darkness was nothing compared to that inside me.

Pansy was gone.

No sooner had she spilt out of the portal onto the castle floor, than the witch had staggered to her feet and fled the room. Nobody had followed her. I'd wanted to, but Sage had dragged me through the corridors to meet with Granny.

Now I slumped in an armchair staring at my hands draped limply in my lap while Sage relayed the whole sorry tale to the High Priestess. I hadn't even been given time to scrub Hyacinth's blood from my skin. It stained my cuticles almost black, clinging to the crevices of my knuckles.

Sage's voice hummed in my ears, barely making sense. As far as I knew or cared, she was giving the old bat a blow-by-blow account of our journey to the tower. Prince Anwir was standing at her side, filling in the details of what had occurred after his waking. Idris had disappeared almost as quickly as Pansy. What had become of Hyacinth's body, I didn't know. I couldn't care about any of it. I was numb, inside and out. The only part of me with any feeling was my palms, where I could still feel Hyacinth's sternum. Feel the lack of a heartbeat.

I flexed my finger. Dry, powdery blood flaked free, drifting to my lap in a gruesome cloud. An unbidden, shuddering breath sucked into my chest, and before I could stop them, tears rolled down my cheeks.

Hyacinth was dead. I had failed to save her. It wasn't my fault. I wasn't a people doctor, and I'd done everything possible given the circumstances. That didn't change the fact that Hyacinth would still be alive if I'd stayed on my side of the rift. Pansy would still have a mother.

My vision blurred but I didn't dare wipe my eyes with blood-stained hands. I gave myself over to my guilt, letting it manifest as ugly sobs and sniffs and unchecked tears.

Warm hands closed around mine. I tried to shift away, conscious of the blood, but whoever it was held on, squeezing gently. That small comfort, that show of support, opened the floodgates, and I wept until I had nothing left to give, and then some more.

When my tears finally ran dry, I found Anwir crouched before me, clasping my hands in his. This close, his eyes were stunning. Pale apple with little flares of gold around the pupil, all framed in lashes as dark as his raven hair.

"Are you well, Aliza?" he asked, his voice as soft as velvet.

I shook my head. "I've never lost a person before."

Who did I think I was? Of course I hadn't lost a person before, I was a vet, or near enough. I'd witnessed countless lives ending, and I'd spend the rest of my life easing the passing of others. It was my job. My duty. My heartbreaking honour to bring peace when no cure could be found. But no matter how painful all of that had been, no matter how many evenings I'd gone home and cried into my pillow, this was worse. I'd lost a *person*. My friend's mother. I'd been helpless. I had failed.

"Hyacinth knew the risk."

I blinked, searching, and sure enough, I found Sage watching me impassively. Did she feel nothing? Had she already buried the death of her friend beneath a marble smooth surface?

"She chose to support you on this quest, knowing full well it might mean her death."

"You did all you could," Anwir offered his own, rather more effective brand of comfort. "Look at you. You have no magic. You are so young, and yet, you did what none of us could do. You tried."

I nodded, swallowing. He was right. I knew it well enough, just as I knew that, eventually, time would soothe my emotions, and bolster the logic that was all too easy to ignore tonight. I'd done all I could. Even in the human world, with paramedics and doctors and surgeons on hand, Hyacinth's injuries would have been critical. Nobody could have done more given the circumstances. But for now, it hurt. I would let it hurt, and eventually, I would let it heal.

Sliding my hands out of Anwir's grasp, I rose to my feet. I needed a bath, and maybe even some sleep, if my brain would allow it, before…

"I'd like to go to the rift tomorrow."

Sage betrayed not a flicker of emotion, but her eyes darted to Anwir. Mine followed, finding the prince frowning up at me from where he crouched.

"Why?" He stood, his eyes still fixed on me.

Oh, God. Not now.

I sighed. I didn't have the energy or the headspace to justify my choices again. Was he actually expecting me to claim my prize by marrying him? If only I'd kept my mouth shut.

"Aliza does not wish to be queen." There was the faintest hint of mockery in Sage's voice.

"I beg your pardon?" Granny interjected, stomping her stick from where she lounged in her throne-like chair.

"I want to go home," I said flatly. I felt like a parrot, doomed to repeat the same phrases for all of time. "I never wanted any of this."

"Nonsense!" The old bat said the word like it closed the matter. "You are the Human Queen. You broke the curse. It's expected."

"I don't care what's expected," I snapped. "I never wanted to come here. It was an accident. I never wanted to marry a prince, or rule a kingdom, or even live forever." Though, admittedly, that particular reward was pretty tempting. "I never wanted to break a curse that had nothing to do with me. Everything I've done has been so I can go home."

"You won't marry me?" Anwir sounded… hurt.

I almost rolled my eyes. Had he been expecting my love? Had his efforts at kindness, at friendship, been forced, all because he believed in some prophecy nonsense? Had it been an obligation?

"Of course I won't. No offence, but I don't even know you. I have a life of my own. Family, friends, a job. I won't give that up for someone I just met."

"But... you broke the curse."

"Yes." My tone oozed impatience. I was sick to death of everything and everyone. "So the rifts would open and I could *go home*."

"That is no manner in which to address a prince," Granny decreed indignantly, but Anwir held up a placating hand.

"I never expected—"

"What?" From somewhere, deep inside, I managed to pull a sardonic smirk. "You never expected a woman would refuse you? A prince? We're not all desperate for a husband anymore, Your Highness. We have our own minds. Our own lives. Freedom. We don't rely on men anymore."

"No, that's not what I meant. I only thought to say... the thing is, Aliza, queen or not, I need you. Your role didn't end when I awoke."

Oh great. That did not sound promising.

"Even before my uncle cursed me, for thousands of years in fact, there have been whispers of a prophecy. The first fae queen saw a great evil befalling her line. The only way to scourge it is with the Human Queen. I don't know exactly what that means, nobody does, but you are the key to me taking back this kingdom. I cannot do it without you at my side."

"No." I was sick of this. Sick of being used. "I will not marry you."

"I'm not asking you to," he insisted. "I have no wish for a wife who holds me in such disdain, but would you not consider staying a little longer? Pretending? The people will want you at my side. I need their support. I need *yours*. I can't win back my kingdom without it."

I turned my glare on Sage. A faint smile played at the corners of her mouth.

"You knew." I barely recognised my low, hate-filled voice. "You knew and lied, every step of the way. You swore I could go home."

"I swore nothing."

"And *you*!" I turned my anger on the undeserving prince. "If you can't take back your kingdom without my help, then maybe you're no king at all."

I didn't give Anwir a chance to reply. Following Pansy and Idris' lead, I stormed from the room, slamming the heavy door as hard as I could.

My walk through the castle and into the surrounding grounds revealed one thing. Everybody was surprised to see me alive. Shocked faces turned in my direction, whispers and exclamations following me like the smell of a rabbit hutch. They all wanted to know if it was done, if the curse was broken. I ignored them all. As far as I could see, the curse was very much intact.

Sage was a lying bitch, but I was angry at myself. I should have known better than to trust her. I'd known she was using me. Maybe even Jacques was in this elaborate deceit. Why hadn't I heeded my doubts about the rifts? I'd bet my life they'd never been sealed at all. All this time wasted, and now the princes were awake, and King Maelgwyn would be hunting me. There was no way I'd make it to the rift alone.

I'd missed my chance.

I hesitated in the gardens, staring down the long path I'd walked down not days ago on my journey to find the princes. It seemed like a different life, not mine at all. In the distance, the castle walls rose in a protective circle, only they looked more like prison walls from this side of the curse. If I made for the gate, would anyone stop me? And if they didn't, how long would I last out there in that terrible world? An hour? A day?

Sighing, I veered off the path and stomped towards a little copse of trees, and the glittering lake beyond. With every step, a little of my anger leaked out of me. Maybe I was too tired to hold on to it, or maybe it was just that the lake looked so pretty, glinting silver in the moonlight with a rainbow of fairies scattered amongst the reeds. Either way, I felt slightly less murderous as I ducked under a low branch and wove through the trees.

I was not alone.

As I neared the lake edge, a pair of bare feet, crossed at the ankle, appeared behind a tree. I fell still, and in the absence of my footsteps, a faint scratching drifted to me.

"I know you're there, human." Idris' voice was bored. "You walk with all the grace of a rampaging dragon."

I continued my stomping, and the prince came into view. He sat leaned against a broad tree trunk, a pencil in one hand and a small, battered leather-bound book in the other. As I passed, he angled the book carefully, hiding it from me, but didn't bother to look up from its pages.

Fine. What did I care what he was up to?

Pebbles shifted and crunched underfoot as I made my way to the water's edge. Maybe I'd dip my feet in the cool water. They'd been stuffed inside hiking boots for far too long. I focused on the starlit ripples gliding across the lake. I snatched up a pebble and hurled it at the tranquil pool. It plunked beneath the surface and sank like a house brick.

"If you were trying to skip stones, that was abysmal."

Ignoring his remark with all the dignity I could muster, I sat on the lumpy ground, hugging my knees to my chest. Idris could go and boil his head for all I cared. Gone was my former admiration. Well, no, I couldn't fault him for his efforts, or his actions tonight, but the fact remained that he'd been nothing but an arse since the moment he'd opened his eyes. He had none of Anwir's manners, and though I was still furious with the latter, I couldn't help but compare him favourably to his sulking, bad tempered twin.

"What do you want?" The prince's deep, cool voice was edged with impatience, but the low chesty rumble eased some of the tension in my shoulders all the same. It was a pleasant voice, one that I might have enjoyed listening to if every word that had passed his lips so far hadn't been condescending and downright rude.

"Don't pretend to care what I want. Nobody else does." I wanted to cringe at my petulant remark, but I was still too angry. Besides, I was right. The witches and now the prince had made it perfectly clear that I was a pawn, and they would take and take with no regard for me or my feelings.

"I'm not pretending," Idris said. "I genuinely do not care in the slightest, but as you're intruding on my space, you could at least explain yourself."

"I didn't realise you owned the grounds, Your Royal Highness," I mocked, my foul mood blooming once more. "And besides, didn't you want me to 'shut up'? Why bother speaking to me now?"

The scratch of his pencil resuming was the only answer I got. It mingled with the chirp of insects and the hum of late-night fairies, a rhythm of rapid scratches followed by a pause, repeating. Was he drawing?

I propped my chin on my knees, staring unseeingly over the lake.

"What were you doing earlier," Idris asked at length, "with the witch's body?"

I stiffened. I didn't want to talk about that. The last thing I needed was to end up crying in front of this unfeeling prick. But as ever, I couldn't resist elaborating. Science and medicine were wonderful things, as good as any magic. Just because it didn't always yield the desired results, it didn't take away from my amazement. Maybe it had no place in this world, but knowledge was power, and maybe Idris could learn something from me. The thought almost made me smile.

"CPR," I offered, keeping the spark of passion in my voice to a minimum. God forbid the prince knew how much of a nerd I was when it came to this stuff. He'd only use it against me somehow. "Cardiopulmonary resuscitation. It's a lifesaving emergency procedure. Or, at least, it can be... Why?" I twisted to look at him, only to find him studying his drawing. "Don't you have CPR here?"

"I would have thought you could guess as much from the reaction of the daughter."

"Yeah, well. I had other things on my mind."

"Indeed."

"Anyway, the idea behind CPR is that it keeps oxygenated blood flowing through the body after a cardiac arrest. It's even been known to restart the heart, or at least keep things moving until a defibrillator can be used."

Idris finally deigned to look at me. He raised a questioning eyebrow.

"A defibrillator sends an electric shock to the heart. It can restore the rhythm."

I thought of Hyacinth, bleeding out on the forest floor. A defibrillator would have made no difference, not with that amount of blood loss. I looked at my hands again, still stained red. I scrambled to the water's edge and dipped them into the lake. I rubbed and twisted, trying to free myself of Hyacinth's ghost. Who was I trying to fool? It would haunt me until my last breath. I swiped my hands on my trousers. They weren't clean, but they were better than they had been. I turned to the prince.

"What are you drawing?"

He'd resumed his sketching and didn't pause or look up at my question. "None of your business."

"I answered loads of questions."

"And yet, I asked only two, one of which you failed to answer. You like the sound of your own voice, human."

"I have a name."

"So I've heard."

"Fine, *fae*. What are you drawing?"

He snapped the book shut, fixing me with a glare so similar to his brother's and yet lacking all of his warmth. "Nothing. Not anymore."

"What are you doing out here?"

"Trying to get away from you."

I scowled.

"And everyone else," he conceded, losing some of his waspishness but assuming an air of extreme boredom.

"I'd have thought that after a few centuries sealed in a box you might be glad of company. Especially after tonight."

"Perhaps I grew fond of the silence."

I couldn't relate. He was right about one thing; I did love to talk. Maybe not as much as Pansy, but I enjoyed the company of other people. Most of the time. Except when they were Idris.

"Are you... okay? After what happened?" I dared to ask, bracing myself for a stinging reply.

None came. Instead, he asked, "What are *you* doing out here?"

I picked up another pebble and threw it at the lake. It did no better than the first. "The witches lied to me."

I wouldn't mention Anwir, not to his brother. It probably wouldn't go down well. But what had Anwir called Idris? Tedious? I snorted. He wasn't wrong.

"About?"

"About everything, I think." I heaved a sigh, my shoulders sagging. "Ever since my first day here, all I've wanted was to go home. They said the rifts were closed, and that the only way to open them was to wake you two. Is that true?"

"As a victim of said curse, I wasn't privy to its inner workings."

"Oh. Well, anyway. Now they're asking me to stay longer, to pretend I wan—I mean, to pretend I'm going to marry your brother and be this ridiculous Human Queen."

"You don't want to be queen?"

"No."

The scratch of his pencil resumed. "You seemed to be enjoying my brother's company. Do you mean to tell me you're not falling over yourself to put on a pretty dress and marry the charming prince?"

I smiled. I actually smiled. For the first time, Idris and I seemed to be on the same page. "Believe it or not, no. I want..." I trailed off, my throat restricting, my eyes stinging. My earlier numbness had long since vanished, and it was only in its absence that I realised what a blessing it had been. There were too many emotions fighting for space inside me. Hope was still there, though it dimmed with every passing day. I missed Mum and Dad, and the cramped house that I'd desperately wanted us to escape from. I missed my friends and the future I'd toiled for and earned with my own sacrifice and determination. A future I could be proud of because I'd forged it myself. Not this one. Not this glittering, magical prophecy. I looked up at the smattering of glimmering stars beyond the canopy of leaves, so beautiful, so vivid, compared to the night skies of the human world. "I want to go home."

"Anwir will win back his kingdom soon enough. The palace of Tir o Haf is quite something."

"What?" I turned to give him a questioning look. Was it my imagination, or were his eyes rimmed in red? I couldn't quite tell in the dark, but the skin around them looked darker. He looked exhausted. I'd never seen such dark shadows hang beneath anyone's eyes before. "No, I mean, *my* home. The human world. I want to go back."

"Oh really?"

He didn't even look at me, the ignorant prick. He just lounged against the tree trunk, sketching away, his dark hair flopping into his eyes, his long legs crossed at the ankles.

"I know you don't care, you arrogant, immortal bastard, but you insisted I answer your stupid question. I won't bother next time."

He made a small breathy noise as one side of his lips curved, revealing the slightest glimpse of teeth. The nearest thing to a smile I'd seen from him. "It's not that I don't care, I just don't believe you."

He really was a tit. I should have left him locked away, sleeping off his curse, where he couldn't sneer at any of us.

"Well, I don't care what you think," I retorted, turning my attention back to the lake.

"Snappy."

I ignored him, and the lick of indignation. I should have turned away the moment I'd spotted his feet sticking out from behind the tree.

"Humans are all the same," he drawled on. Apparently, talking wasn't such a chore when it involved assaulting me with an endless stream of snide comments. "They only consider what they can gain from us. The others have told you you're special, have they not? Not at all like every other desperate mortal woman to crawl through that gate. But they're lying. You're no different, no better."

"I didn't choose to come here, you know."

"Perhaps, but you certainly didn't put up a fight when Sage promised you immortality as a reward for doing the right thing, did you?"

"I begged and begged to go home," I countered, but he was right.

I hadn't put up much of a fight. Had I made any real attempts to get home? No. Was it really because I'd wanted to help, or because of the shiny promise of immortality? The worst part was, I could barely remember. Those days seemed to belong to another life already, another person. I wasn't sure who I was anymore. Surely not the same woman who had slipped on a wet stone and ruined her entire life.

"Then you would have left us to rot in those tombs?"

God, I couldn't win with him, could I? Whatever I did, whatever I thought, it was wrong.

A pair of pale feet appeared silently on the pebbles beside me. "Isn't that so?"

To my immense surprise, he bent his knees and sank into a crouch, fixing me with his calculating gaze, so similar to his brother's, but different somehow. I couldn't put my finger on it yet. It was like a forgotten word, hovering on the edges of my brain. Infuriating. That wasn't the answer, but it would do until I figured it out. Yes, the way he looked at me was *infuriating*. He hadn't looked in my direction this long since meeting me. I turned away, focusing my attention on the ripples.

"I don't know," I admitted. "I really don't. What does it matter? You're awake now."

He rose gracefully to his feet, and when he spoke, his voice was cold. "Who says I want to be?"

It took a long moment for his words to register. When they finally slogged into my brain, I whipped my head around, my mouth falling open to release a tangled spill of words that never came.

He'd gone.

24

The Horrors Persist

I should probably move.

My hair drifted, floating around my shoulders in the now lukewarm water of the second bath I'd taken that night. God knew what time it was. I'd been exhausted for long enough that I could no longer trust my body's internal clock, but my many candles had burnt low, and the window beside the crystal tub was velvet black, the moon glowing like a fat pearl beyond. The combined candle and moonlight was enough to drive any traces of darkness from the cavernous bathroom, leaving no shadowy corners for shades. Not that I cared. Let them take me. Much use I'd be. When it came down to it, when it really mattered, I was useless. Besides, I'd probably have a better chance of escaping Maelgwyn than I did the witches.

Tonight should have been a triumph. I should have been giddy with relief and excitement, and I should have fallen into bed with a groan, glad my days of camping were well and truly over and anticipating my imminent return home. I shouldn't have taken two baths, the first to scrub myself raw, ridding my skin of any trace of Hyacinth's death, the second to soak away my shame. My clothes shouldn't be dumped in a grimy, blood-stained pile in the corner of the bathroom. My friend shouldn't be sobbing into her pillow, somewhere in the depths of the castle.

Everything was wrong.

I had failed.

I sank beneath the surface, blowing out a sigh in a stream of bubbles. The soft beat of power coming from the huge crystal bowl seemed stronger under here, thrumming through the water in a peaceful, barely discernible pulse. My eyes grew heavy, stinging slightly in the soapy water. I should get out. Go to bed. If not sleep, I needed rest, at least.

Before I could change my mind, I emerged from the water with a slosh and dried myself off with a fluffy towel. I was squeezing my hair when I heard a muffled knock coming from the corridor.

Pansy.

Had she come to talk? To cry? I threw on my robe and dashed into the bedroom and to the door, wrenching it open.

Anwir lurked in the hall, looking sheepishly back at me.

Oh. A warm flush spread over my scandalously attired body. I thought of my thick, fluffy dressing gown at home. Not as stylish, but certainly less revealing than the thin, elegant material I'd haphazardly draped myself in.

"I apologise for disturbing you at this hour." Anwir's voice was hushed and soft. A night-time voice, something a secret lover might use upon scaling the trellis and climbing through the window. "I'd hoped we might talk."

Did I want to talk? No, not after his earlier request. I wanted him and the witches as far away from me as possible, on the other side of a rift, in fact. Maybe he'd come to apologise. Maybe he'd try to convince me that he'd make a perfect husband. I wasn't willing to be swayed, but if he wanted to try, if he wanted to show me exactly what kind of husband he could be… It had been a while since I'd been with a man. Anwir might be exactly the kind of relief I needed. A good, angry fuck might send me to sleep when all else failed. I wasn't convinced I could wrangle my tongue into forming words, but I nodded, stepping back to let him in.

He surveyed the dark room.

"I was just getting out of the bath," I said needlessly, considering my wet hair and floral scent, not to mention my convenient state of undress. "Sit down."

The prince sank into a chair before the empty grate. "Thank you. This can wait until tomorrow, if you're tired?"

"It's fine." And besides, I'd never sleep a wink after such a statement, even at the best of times. I'd spend the night chewing over every possible scenario, anything and everything he might have to say. I plonked down into the chair opposite, arranging my robe carefully over my thighs. "What did you want to talk about?"

"You. Us." He swallowed, leaning forward and bracing his elbows on his knees. The glow of the candles brought out the golden tones in his eyes, making them almost yellow. "I wanted to explain myself."

I doubted I'd hear a single word he said when he had the audacity to look so sickeningly perfect, but I nodded. An apology was the least I would accept before, well… anything else. "Okay. Explain."

"I like you, Aliza. I like you a lot."

Well, that was a promising start. I shifted in my chair, hyper aware of just how naked I was beneath my robe.

"And yes, I assumed you'd want to marry me. After you woke me, the witches explained what had happened since my uncle's betrayal. How the humans flocked to break the curse because of the promise of a marriage. Becoming my queen. I assumed you'd come for the same reason. I know now I was wrong."

"Yes," I said, trying to sound firm despite the hoarseness of my voice. "You were. I came here by mistake. I didn't even know this place existed. I didn't believe in... *Creatures*. Fairies and witches and fae and v—" I stopped short, remembering how Jacques had avoided contact with other species. "It was just an accident, and everything I've done has been so I can get home to my family."

"Tell me how it happened. How you came to be here."

I heaved a sigh. My tumble in the cave seemed like forever ago, and my bump to the head had made things hazy, but I told Anwir about the Fairy Glen, about how I hadn't wanted to go into the cave at all, how, for whatever stupid reason, I'd wandered deeper than my friends, losing myself in the dark. How I'd slipped, and the next thing I'd known, I was here, in Neath. Lost and alone, with no way back.

"Then... your family..." Anwir began hesitantly.

I pressed my lips together in a cheerless smile. "They probably think I'm dead. That's why I have to get back, Anwir. I can't leave them like that. I can't just disappear and leave them without answers."

"You love them."

"Of course I do. It's just me, Mum and Dad now. My grandparents are all gone, and my auntie lives abroad. I'm an only child, and my parents gave up everything to have me. I have to get back to them."

"What do you mean, gave up everything?"

"Well, they couldn't have kids naturally, so they had to pay for IVF." Anwir's brow knotted in a questioning frown. "Oh, it's a medical thing. They take the egg and the, um, sperm" — God, how had I got into this? Why was I talking about sperm with a gorgeous, rich, immortal prince but *not* falling into bed with him? — "and they basically make a foetus in a little glass tube, and then transfer it into the mother. Anyway, it didn't work the first few times, but they desperately wanted a child. They ended up selling their house and spending every penny they had on this treatment, until they got me."

"You are a baby from a tube?"

"Yep. A miracle, according to my mum and dad."

Anwir's lips quirked in a smile. "I would have to agree with them. That you made it here, against all odds, that you woke Idris and I... The fact that you did all that without intending to be here... I would call that a miracle."

My ears began to burn. I ruffled my damp hair, shifting it so the wet clumps fell over my ears, hiding them from view.

"Just a girl, trying to get home."

Anwir's smile dropped. "About that. Aliza, I know you want to leave. I know you *will* leave, and I understand. I do. But I must beg you. Please, consider staying a while longer. I expect nothing of you, and you've already given more than I deserve, but my people are in danger, and without you, I cannot save them. Will you hear me out?"

No. Absolutely not. I wanted to clap my hands over my ears and scream at the top of my lungs. This late-night tryst wasn't playing out as I'd expected. I didn't want to be roped into another scheme that had absolutely nothing to do with me. And besides, what use could I be? I'd already saved the princes, and now I was expected to save the kingdom? Nope, nope, nope.

"Okay," I said.

What? *What*? No! Anwir's tragic expression crumpled with relief, and he dragged a hand down his exquisite face as it broke into a smile. More guilt dolloped on top of everything I was already wrestling with. Letting the prince down would be nothing compared to the burdens I'd shouldered tonight, but I didn't relish the thought of doing so, especially now I'd stupidly given him a shred of hope. I should have said no. I should never have allowed him to believe there was even the slightest chance I'd agree to whatever he was about to say.

"It's nothing awful, or dangerous, I promise you that," he insisted, maybe glimpsing my dismay. "I will allow no harm to come to you. All I want is for you to attend a few events. Balls, parades, that sort of thing. I want people to see you at my side. I want them to believe us united."

"Balls? Why? What difference will that make?" I was no expert, but it didn't seem like the most direct route to taking back a kingdom.

"It will bring them hope, Aliza. For millennia, we have heard whispers of the Human Queen who will rid this world of evil, a promise derived from a prophecy made by our first queen, sixteen thousand years ago. The Human Queen would rid my bloodline of evil. We tell our children bedtime tales about her. She has always been a part of who we are, a symbol of hope. When my uncle betrayed me and cast his curse, I'm certain he believed it an amusing quip to name a fragile, mortal human woman as the only one who could break the curse. An impossible caveat. *He* made it impossible by driving out your kind, slaughtering them until none remained. The day I fell asleep, it was in a thriving kingdom, brimming with all kinds of people, humans included. Your kind were as much a part of this world as mine. Then I wake to find hundreds of years have passed, and the humans are long gone. And yet, here you are. You came, just as we've always believed you would. You've already begun to fight the evil by breaking my uncle's curse. Don't you see? After all these years, glimpsing a human at my side, one who woke *me*, no less, will convince my people that redemption is at hand, that my uncle's downfall has come at last. The prophecy has come to pass. The Human Queen has arrived."

"So... You want me to be your mascot?"

"My rallying cry." He leaned closer, skewering me with his golden-green stare. "Dance with me. Sit at my side. Smile. If you act as though you love me, my people will love me too. They will rise for me, fight for me. Fight for *themselves.* They have lived too long without hope of a better world. I can give it to them, but only if they believe in me. If they believe in *us*."

Dancing at a royal ball didn't sound *that* bad.

"And if you wish it," Anwir continued, "when this is over, I will escort you back to the human world myself. You will go with my blessing and, I hope, my lasting friendship and... gratitude."

I did wish it. More than anything. I had no hope of surviving my journey to the rift alone. "How long will I have to stay?"

"Not long at all. How about this? One ball. We'll throw one ball, right here in Nairsgarth, a week from now. You and I attend together, a chance for the free fae to come and see us with their own eyes. We'll dance and laugh and eat, and we'll see it as nothing more than a celebration of the curse being broken. A chance to have fun. You can give me your answer after that."

"And if I want to go home after that ball?"

Anwir reached out, taking my hand in his own. The warmth of his skin sent a jolt through me, and I squirmed in my seat. "Then I will be sorry to see you go."

It wasn't an unreasonable request, and when would I ever have a chance to attend a proper ball, if not here and now? I might not be in the mood for dancing, but I could pretend. A week wasn't that long. Mum and Dad would understand. Saving the world was pretty important. More important than me or even them. It would be selfish of me to refuse such a simple yet important task.

"One ball," I said sternly. "I can't promise more than that."

The prince smiled, a wide, glorious smile. It was real and raw, the most genuine gesture I'd seen from him. For a moment I glimpsed a lonely, desperate male beneath the smooth veneer of a prince. A male who, for the first time in God knew how long, had found hope.

He slid out of his chair, kneeling at my bare feet, and lifted my hand, pressing it to his lips. His eyes slipped closed, and he held my knuckles to his mouth far longer than he had any cause to. My heart skittered about my chest like a dizzy butterfly, and as for breathing, it seemed I'd forgotten how. But I couldn't sleep with him now, not after agreeing to stay a while. He'd take it completely the wrong way. He'd think there was hope of a more permanent solution. He'd be wrong. Handsome or not, he wouldn't be sharing my bed tonight.

At last, but far too soon, Anwir pulled back, only enough to allow himself to speak. His breath brushed my fingers as he said, "Thank you, Aliza. You truly are a miracle."

I couldn't find my words as he rose gracefully to his feet. He dropped my hand, only to touch his fingertips to my cheeks. "Rest. We'll talk more tomorrow."

With a slow blink and one last smile, he departed, leaving me staring at the door he'd disappeared through, my skin still tingling from his touch.

The witches wasted no time.

I was summoned from my bed at midday, having finally managed to doze off as the sun was rising. A witch I didn't recognise hovered at my bedside, an apologetic look on her face.

"I'm sorry to disturb you, Your Majesty, but the funeral will take place in one hour at the cove. Your presence has been requested."

"An hour?" I parroted, the words wading through the grogginess of sleep deprivation. How could a funeral be arranged in only a few hours? The witches must have worked through the night while I floated in my bathtub. While Hyacinth's body cooled.

How had Pansy spent her night? Sleep must have proven impossible.

"Yes," the witch said, heading for the door. "I've left a small breakfast on the table."

Had it only been yesterday that I'd been starving, or a hundred years ago? Alone in my room, I padded from the bed to examine the meal. My stomach soured at the sight of scrambled eggs and buttered toast.

The thought of eating when only a few hours ago Hyacinth's heart had beat its last beneath my hands...

I dashed to the bathroom, plunging my hands into the sink. The blood had been washed away, but I could still smell it, still sense it coating my skin. Tears plopped into the water as I soaped up my hands, the evening's events playing on a loop in my head. I couldn't block it out, couldn't stop questioning myself or my actions.

What if there'd been a way? What if I'd missed it? What if I'd never gone into that fucking cave?

Only when my skin was stinging did I rinse the soap and splash my tears away with a handful of water. I had to get it together. I had to be strong for Pansy. She had no father and now, no mother. I was no substitute, but at least I could be her friend for another week. The silver lining to agreeing to Anwir's request.

Taking deep, soothing breaths, I left the bathroom and peered into my sparse wardrobe. The lilac dress was too cheery for such an occasion, but I couldn't show up in clothes drenched in Hyacinth's blood. Thinking longingly of the high-necked, form-fitting black dress hanging in my bedroom back home, I donned my shorts and t-shirt, shrugging Jacques' jacket over the top. At least it was black. With my hair brushed and my feet stuffed back into my wretched, filthy hiking boots, I made my way down through the castle.

I'd never been to the beach before, but I had no problem finding my way thanks to the steady stream of forlorn witches, all dressed in muted colours, leading the way out into the grounds. I followed them past the neat lawn and toward the wilder clifftops, where tall, whip-like grass swayed, and enormous daisies were buffeted by the brisk wind. The choppy sea stretched as far as the eye could see, glittering in the afternoon sunlight, breaking through the grey clouds. It might have been beautiful any other day. A dirt track led the way down a steep slope, zigzagging back and forth, and at the bottom, a small beach of golden sand waited. Plentiful white rocks scattered the shoreline, some slick and green with seaweed, others as smooth as eggs. Nestled amongst them, laid out on the sand, was a muslin-wrapped body. Pansy huddled at her mother's side, shoulders hunched and head bowed. She clutched a candle in her hands, her body turned to protect the flame from the wind. Sage waited at her side, her face smoothed of any emotion, and clinging to her arm, leaning heavily on her stick, was Granny.

How the old witch had made it down the slope, I had no idea, and I certainly couldn't imagine how she'd make it back up, but at least she'd come. As High Priestess, would she conduct the ceremony?

I accepted a candle from a group of witches handing them out and picked my way between the rocks to Pansy's side. She lifted her wet, red-rimmed eyes to me and attempted a smile, but her lip quivered, and she dropped her gaze, tears splashing down her front. My own eyes pricked with moisture and my throat tightened. I couldn't find any words, and wouldn't have trusted myself to speak regardless, so I took Pansy's hand and squeezed. She returned the gesture.

Before long, the princes appeared, taking their places opposite me, with Hyacinth laid between us. Anwir gave me a small, close-lipped smile, but Idris stared down at the wrapped body, his face paler than usual. Was he plagued by guilt too? Had he spent his night wondering if things might have somehow been different if only he'd pulled the belt tighter? Though placations would have done nothing to lessen my own guilt, I longed to tell him that he'd been brilliant. Unexpectedly so. That nothing he could have done would have changed the outcome. That he should be proud of himself for trying, but with the crowd around us building, and with his red-rimmed eyes firmly downcast, I had no opportunity to relay my empty comforts.

A shadow passed over the beach, and I glanced up at the gathering clouds, greyer than they had been on the walk down. Rain seemed appropriate for a funeral, somehow, but for Pansy's sake, I hoped it held off. Maintaining candles in a downpour might be problematic.

When the last witch had taken her place, Granny hobbled forward to stand at Hyacinth's head, refusing Sage's offer of support.

"My sisters," she said in her thin, reedy voice, her eyes making a slow sweep of the assembled crowd before pausing on the princes, then me. "Honoured friends. We have come together today to say our final farewells to two of our own.

"Sisters Meadow and Hyacinth bravely gave their lives for a cause we can all consider our own, and though Hyacinth leaves behind her much-loved daughter, Pansy, both our sisters will live on through the continuation of our work, which would not have been possible without their sacrifice."

Her voice faded as a buzzing filled my head. Whatever pretty words she found to explain it, the deaths were pointless. The curse had already been broken when the barghests attacked. Both witches should be alive and well, spending today relaxing and recuperating, preparing for a celebration, not beginning their eternal rest.

Idris seemed to be struggling to accept it too. His shoulders rose and fell in deep, sharp breaths. Beside him, Anwir was the very picture of respectful sorrow. Calm, collected, yet mournful. I didn't dare look at Pansy, who clung to my hand as though, if she let go, she might be forever lost.

When Granny had finished her rambling, she called Pansy forward. The witch extricated her hand from mine and stepped to her mother's side. She looked much smaller than usual. Even her bun drooped under the weight of her sorrow. Pansy muttered something, too quiet for me to catch over the wind, then placed her candle at Hyacinth's side.

Sage went next, her eyes fixed on the body. "You were a true friend when I needed one." She placed her candle beside Pansy's.

Anwir stepped forward. "Thank you for your sacrifice, Hyacinth. It will never be forgotten." He laid his candle, returning to his place.

Distant thunder rumbled, and a drop of cool rain burst on my forehead. I ignored it, too transfixed by Idris, who followed his brother's lead, his jaw clenched. The little flame wavered as his hands shook. "I'm sorry." His voice cracked on the simple words, and when he placed his candle down beside Anwir's, he was clumsier than I'd ever seen him. He'd really taken the death badly, worse even than I had.

"Aliza, would you like to say a few words?"

I startled at Granny's voice, pulled from the puzzle Idris had presented, and lurched to Hyacinth's side.

What to say? I hadn't thought I'd be called upon like this. I hadn't had time to prepare. If the rolls had been reversed, Hyacinth would have known exactly the right words. She'd have been ready, just like she'd readied me to break the curse.

"Thank you for lighting my way," I said. If not for her lantern, I'd never have made it to the princes at all. They'd still be sleeping, and I'd be dead in the tunnels. Hyacinth would be alive and well.

The injustice of it threatened to engulf me as I crouched to tuck my candle into the forming cluster. The wetness of my eyes blurred the flames into one dancing light, not unlike that which had protected me on my journey to the tower.

As I stood, I dashed my tears away, resuming my place in the crowd.

One by one, the entire coven spoke their final words to their sister, until the sea of candles grew, forcing us to step back. By some miracle, though the wind tugged and dragged the flames, they all remained lit. Even the threatening rain held off. After the last witch had paid her respects, the crowd began to disperse.

"I think I'll stay for a while," Pansy whispered at my side.

"Do you want company?"

She shook her head, setting more tears loose. "No. No, I think... I need to be alone."

My face threatened to crumple under the weight of my pity. Instead, I pulled Pansy into a hug, squeezing her tight. "You know where I'll be if you change your mind."

She sniffed, nodding, and patted my arm. I took it as my signal to leave, joining the crowd filtering onto the narrow path.

Something dark caught my attention on the far side of the cove. Idris, sneaking off alone.

I hesitated. Maybe he wanted to be alone too, or maybe he was up to something. Though I no longer suspected him as a traitor, he certainly had a shifty habit of sneaking away. It was none of my business, as he'd undoubtedly remind me if I asked him where he was off to, but the thought of returning to my room, of stewing over my guilt and misery, was intolerable.

Before I could talk myself out of it, I abandoned the queue for the path and set off after the prince.

25

I'm Flying, Jack!

The cliff path on this side of the beach was much steeper and more precarious. In places, I was forced to my hands and knees to avoid falling to my death. I lost sight of the prince, but with tough grass and thorny shrubs growing on either side of the trail, there was no way he could have veered off course.

Breathing heavily, I stomped higher, trying to ignore the burning of my thighs. I'd definitely made the right choice in not wearing a dress.

I rounded a bend in the track and there was Idris, lounging idly on a rocky outcropping with his face tilted to the sky. I dropped low, grimacing, hoping he hadn't noticed me.

"Are you going to tell me why you're following me, or just skulk behind that bush?"

Oh.

Blushing furiously, I stepped sideways, pressing my lips into a thin smile and raising my hand in an awkward greeting. "Hi."

He studied me from beneath his floppy, dark hair. "Care to explain why you're stalking me?"

"Why are you sneaking off again?" I countered.

"An answer for an answer."

I narrowed my eyes but said nothing. He shrugged, hopping down from the rock, and continued walking, his long legs making short work of the slope.

"Oi, wait!"

I stumbled after him, my ankle aching with the effort of my climb. Idris ignored me, neither waiting nor slowing, but he hadn't told me to go back, so that was something. My knees were shaking, and my skin was hot by the time the dirt track levelled out. To my immense surprise, Idris was waiting for me, his arms folded in a haughty show of impatience. He was as cool and flawless as ever, completely unruffled by the climb that had almost finished me off, even if shadows still hung beneath his eyes.

"There better be something good at the end of this walk," I panted, clutching a stitch in my side.

His lips twitched, the only sign he gave of having heard me. Cranky old bastard.

It was alright for him, with his immortal legs and lungs, but I was winded and aching in places I hadn't even known I had. Days of hiking and climbing billions of stairs, and now this?

When I straightened, he was staring at me from beneath a frown. "I thought making it to Nairsgarth would afford me a little privacy."

"Nope." I managed a brief smile between breaths. "I'm determined to be a thorn in your side until I find out what you're up to."

His lip curled in distaste. "Fine. Just remember, mortal, you asked for this."

"Asked for what?"

I caught the briefest glimpse of a venomous smirk before he seized my hand. In an instant, the castle, the sky, the sea, everything vanished, replaced by a crushing darkness I knew all too well. The weight of the universe crushed against me, and my bones threatened to buckle under the intense pressure.

I spilled back into the world like a newborn giraffe, sprawling over the ground with a thud.

That *bastard*.

Rising on trembling arms, I fought down the wave of nausea that swelled in my throat. Idris stood nearby, adjusting his jacket and staring around without a shred of concern for my well-being.

Nairsgarth was gone. Instead, we'd arrived in a woodland horribly similar to that we'd escaped the night before, only the ground was blanketed in fallen leaves, and the canopies were a rainbow of reds, oranges and yellow-green. A distinct autumnal chill lingered in the air.

"Where—" I broke into a fit of breathless coughs.

"Tir o Hydref," Idris answered my unfinished question, the strange words rolling off his tongue like music. He drew a deep breath in through the nose and his entire demeanour softened on the exhale.

I hadn't heard much about the other courts, but I did remember that Tir o Gaeaf was the only friendly one. Was he a traitor after all? Was he planning to hand me over to Maelgwyn?

"Why?" I gasped.

He finally spared me a glance, and something like irritation passed briefly over his face at the sight of my kneeling in the dirt. "Get up. We're here because I want to be, and because you can't keep your nose out of other people's affairs."

I'd well and truly learnt my lesson. From now on, I was going to mind my own business and not give in to curiosity. It only ever led to trouble. Still, I was in this mess now, and I wouldn't get out of it by shivering on the ground. I forced myself to my feet, dusting bits of decaying nature off my bare legs.

"And why, Idris, do you want to be here? Isn't this enemy territory?"

He snorted. "Technically, it's my brother's territory, which makes it mine by extension."

The same could be said of Tir o Haf, and we both knew how that had ended. With a sharp stab of guilt, I realised that Pansy was probably still at her mother's side.

"Come on," Idris prompted. "You're wasting my time."

Like he didn't have enough of it. The fae set off as though he fully intended to abandon me if I failed to keep up, so I pulled my jacket tighter and stumbled after him, swallowing down the lump in my throat.

"At least it's not raining here," I offered in a feeble attempt to strike up a civil conversation. "It looked like it was going to pour down back at Nairsgarth. I hate the rain."

The prince threw me a sharp look. Had I offended his almightiness with my opinions on the weather, or was it only my presence that did that? But his scowl faded as he looked away from me and said in an uncharacteristically soft voice, "Me too."

He didn't elaborate further.

We walked in silence for a while, and in the absence of Idris' disdain, my thoughts returned to the beach.

"Idris?" I hurried to catch up, veering alongside him. He closed his eyes, drawing a deep breath in through the nose, as though searching deep within for a scrap of patience. "What will happen with Hyacinth's body now? I've never been to a witch's funeral before."

There had been no burial, after all. No hint of a cremation. Poor Meadow's body had been left behind altogether.

"Do I look like a witch?"

I raised an eyebrow. He certainly had the attitude of something that rhymed.

"I don't know," he admitted. "I believe the candles represent her spirit here in this world. When the last flame dies out, her spirit will move on."

No wonder Pansy had wanted to stay behind. Not long ago, I'd have sworn I didn't believe in such nonsense, but now, if it had been my mum, I'd have waited as long as it took, savouring every last moment of her presence.

At long last, the trees began to thin, the clear blue sky visible in broad patches above them. Idris threw out an arm, too fast to see. I collided with the surprisingly solid, steely limb and staggered backwards, clutching my chest.

"What the hell? A little warn—"

"Quiet."

A low command. I obeyed.

He pointed two fingers at my eyes, and then pressed one to his lips, and pointed between the trees ahead.

I followed the movement, and when he began to edge forward on slow feet, I followed that too, doing my best to mimic his silent steps. When we reached the last tree, he slipped behind it, pulling me with him.

I opened my mouth to protest, but found him barely a hair's breadth away. I made to step back, but his hand, gripping my arm, didn't yield even an inch.

“Wait here,” he breathed, and suddenly, he was gone, leaving me glaring at empty air.

Immortals, urgh.

I peered around the tree, the rough bark biting into my sweaty palms, and the breath left my body in a rush.

Idris strolled, his shoulders loose, looking somehow smaller and less threatening than he usually did, towards a herd of horses, grazing on the lush grass plain stretching before me.

Horses with *wings.*

Some of them raised their silver heads, snorting nervously and backing away as Idris approached. They were going to bolt. Would they run, or take to the skies? I stifled a laugh and shook my head. That I was here, that I was even considering such things... I was lucky. For the first time since I'd woken in that sunlit pool, I felt lucky to be here, to see such wonders. Whatever happened, whether I found my way home or not, however quickly my life blazed by, I could not regret being here and seeing this.

Idris stopped a healthy distance away from the nearest horse. The herd watched him, heads high, ears pricked, glorious wings flared. All but one.

One horse tossed its mane and gave a high, whinnying cry. Idris whistled, and with an almighty beat of wings, the horse propelled itself into a prancing trot. It was only after the beast skidded to a halt before the prince, after it nudged him with its head, sending him staggering harmlessly back a few steps, only after Idris wrapped his arms around the beast's neck, that I realised my mouth was hung open.

The prince turned to where I still hid behind the tree, beckoning, and without hesitation, I walked to him on hollow legs.

The horse watched me with piercing blue eyes. It was much bigger up close, and I saw it wasn't white at all, not really. It gleamed a light, metallic grey, almost blue where the sun shone. Its wings, folded loosely at its sides, skimmed clear of its hind legs, the blue-tipped feathers trailing on the ground behind the tail.

"Meet Saeth," Idris said, and he smiled, actually smiled. If I hadn't been so preoccupied with the impossible animal before me, I might have paid a little more attention to how that beautiful, lopsided grin transformed his face into something quite breathtaking.

"Saeth, meet Eliza."

I'd never heard my name come out of his mouth before, even if his pronunciation wasn't quite right. It was always 'human' or 'mortal', or some other insult.

"I didn't think you knew my name," I said without looking, too mesmerised by Saeth, who extended his neck to sniff my outstretched fingers. "But it's *A*-liza. With an A." The difference was minor, but it mattered to me, now more than ever, just like it had mattered to Mum when she'd scoured the book of baby names. Not that the prince or his horse knew the difference between the spellings. "It means joy."

"My apologies." Idris faced me, his eyes sliding to my initial necklace, resting just below my collar bones. He lifted his hand to my chest and my lungs simply gave up, refusing to draw another breath as his fingers slid along the metal, tracing the golden A. His skin never touched mine, but my ears heated all the same.

"I assumed it was A for Annoying." His lips twitched into another smile, this one more reluctant than the first, as his hand fell away.

"Oh, I didn't realise you were funny." I tried to sound scathing in an attempt to hide exactly how flustered I was, but it was futile. I could barely hold his unnervingly beautiful gaze. Instead, I turned my attention back to the magnificent horse.

The horse whickered softly, coaxing a grin from me. This, talking about animals, I could do. "He's beautiful. I didn't know they really existed. I've seen them on TV, but humans think they're a myth."

"TV?"

I couldn't resist a sideways glance to confirm I'd scored a point in this imaginary match I'd started. He'd teleported me and embarrassed me, but at least I wasn't stuck in the medieval days. That had to count for something. "Oh yeah, I forgot, you're an antique. A TV is a sort of... mirror humans use. It has moving pictures. We use it to tell stories and share news and stuff."

He pulled a bemused face. "You mortals have come a long way while I was sleeping."

Saeth, seemingly satisfied with me, turned his attention back to Idris, nuzzling his neck and making small, low noises.

"You have been missed, friend."

"So, are you going to tell me what on earth is going on?"

"This is my horse," he said simply. "From before. I've been tracking him ever since I awoke, and here he is at last."

"But you were cursed hundreds of years ago, doesn't anything here ever die?"

Idris' broad, pale hand, sweeping down the silver neck, fell still at my question. He didn't answer, but the air between us chilled. Had I said the wrong thing? Trust me to put my foot in it as soon as he started to thaw toward me.

"Well, at least I know where you've been disappearing to now." At least he wasn't a traitor. I dared to run my hand over Saeth's shoulder. The hair was silken and surprisingly springy, almost like feathers.

Idris fixed his clear green eyes upon me. For once they weren't haughty or bored, they were... alive. "Well, human, do you want to taste the sky?"

"Erm, what?" I backed off a step, panic coiling around my stomach.

Idris placed a foot on the folded wing, and sprang, cat-like and agile, onto Saeth's back. The horse didn't so much as flinch, though the others nearby snorted uneasily. A pale hand unfurled, palm up, waiting for me. An invitation.

"I can't," I croaked, throat dry. Despite all the evidence to the contrary, I didn't have a death wish.

"Which frightens you more? Me or the horse?"

It took me a moment to register his words, but then I scowled. "I'm not scared of you."

He gave a low, elegant laugh. "You mortals were always terrible liars."

I snatched his hand, glaring up at him, but he made no move to help me, only gave a slow half-smile as his cool fingers closed around my palm.

Seconds ticked by, and he continued to survey me with the corners of his eyes lifted by that crooked, villainous smirk. My ears began to burn.

"You need to put your foot on his wing."

"Oh, right."

Blushing, I placed my boot gingerly on the waiting limb. If I snagged a feather, I doubted the horse would hesitate to kick me from here back to the trees. I might be doomed to the mortal trappings of age and death, but I didn't fancy bringing that inevitable end forward.

Before I had time to think any more on the subject, to see sense and change my mind, Idris hauled me upwards, and I grabbed onto his jacket, swinging my leg over Saeth's broad, silver rump.

His flanks were warm and silken beneath my bare thighs. Slippery. Oh shit. This was a bad idea, a very, very bad idea. I was already too high off the ground, and the horse's hooves were still firmly planted in the grass. What was I thinking? I'd never done anything more daring than riding a donkey at the beach. I should get down, now. I was going to—

"Hold tight!"

I'd barely adjusted my seat, wedging my knees into the back of Idris' thighs, when enormous, beautiful wings spread, each at least twice as long as the horse itself.

With a great whoosh, they beat the air, and I shrieked as the ground sank away, just for a moment. The horse surged into a gallop, the wings beating again, and again, each time lifting us momentarily into the air, before a belly-swooping drop back to the ground.

I clung desperately to Idris, my nails aching with the force of my grip. The wind rushed past, snapping my hair back as we gained momentum. Ahead of us, a ravine that I hadn't noticed earlier raced closer and closer.

What if we didn't get airborne? What if two riders were too heavy? Idris wasn't exactly dainty, and neither was I for that matter. What if we plunged over the edge of that cliff? I didn't even know what waited at the bottom. Jagged rocks? The broken bones of those fools who'd attempted this before us?

The drop was upon us, and the horse sprang into the air, wings snapping wide, and for a moment, we were flying. My heart swelled.

But then Saeth arched, and we were going down. Down, down, down. Plummeting. Faster and faster. My organs floated up to my throat, horribly weightless. We were falling. Free falling. Plunging to the wild river I now saw speeding towards us.

A scream ripped free of my chest, and I buried my head against Idris' back. I was going to die. We were both going to die.

The world tilted sideways, and an icy spray hit my stinging face. Idris gave a howling whoop that turned into a cackle of wild laughter.

I opened my eyes.

The river raged not inches below my dangling feet, white plumes and glistening spray leaping around us, around the wings, spread wide and strong, the feathers rippling in the wind.

I lifted my head.

We sped through the ravine, sheer, grey cliffs rising tall on either side of the wild river cutting through the land. A bend rushed upon us, and we banked, tilting sideways again. I dug my knees in and held my breath, but this time, I kept my eyes open.

We began to climb in a gentle curve, the river falling away with terrifying speed. We rose past the cliffs, the woods, the plains spread out below us, a distant blanket of rolling green.

With a boom, the wings beat the air, and the clouds, which had been tiny, scudding across the vast blue sky only moments ago, loomed.

Clouds.

A laugh tore from deep within my chest and my eyes streamed, from the wind, or awe, or maybe both.

We were *flying*.

Booms and whooshes sounded all around, and I whipped my head around, hair streaming across my eyes, to see the rest of the silver herd soaring joyously along with us, manes flying, the sun blinding on their metallic feathers.

My heart swelled, threatening to burst through my ribs in a supernova of delight. I *loved* this. I, Aliza, the boring human woman, loved *flying*.

My cheeks ached as I smiled as I never had before, and when I turned forwards again, the clouds were close enough to touch. I gasped, but the wind tore the sound away before I had a chance to hear it.

The tips of Saeth's feathers grazed the cloud, sending rippling wisps pluming free. I dared to loosen an arm from Idris' waist and stretch it out into the open air, reaching.

Idris shifted his weight slightly, and we tilted, drifting closer and closer until my outstretched fingertips skimmed the impossible.

I was touching a *cloud*.

My fingers came away wet and numb. I held them up, marvelling at the crystalline drops of water clinging to my skin.

Then Idris tipped his head back, his hair whipping me in the face, and threw his arms wide like wings, with only his legs gripping the airborne horse.

"Don't do that, you stupid bastard!" I bellowed, clamping my own arms around him again.

The shaking of his shoulders was the only sign he'd heard me. I didn't even know why I held him so tightly, when he was the idiot not holding on. If only I could reach the mane. I should have been in front, would have been if I'd known he had a death wish. Or maybe I'd have stayed on the ground.

What was I thinking? I didn't love this at all. Humans had no business flying anyway. Maybe in an aeroplane, with lifejackets and seatbelts and in-flight snacks, but not on the back of a horse, with nothing but a dim-witted immortal to prevent me falling to my death.

Idris lowered his arms obligingly, twining his fingers into the mane again. I let out a breath of relief, but it took a few seconds more to relax my vice-like grip on his shirt, and even longer to let enjoyment weave between the tight coils of fear once more. But it was impossible not to enjoy this. Even though the cold wind all but skinned my bare hands and legs, even though my eyes streamed continuously. It all faded into insignificance as we soared through endless blue. I could have stayed up there forever, huddled against Idris' warmth, with Heaven within my reach.

My body disagreed.

When at last we landed, surprisingly smoothly, all things considered, I could barely pry my stiff arms from the prince's waist. I was frozen. My whole body trembled with cold and adrenalin, and the ground spun beneath me. Idris swung his leg over the horse's neck, sliding gracefully to his feet, and turned to lift me down. Though I tried to help, my legs wouldn't cooperate, and I suspected I resembled nothing more than a sack of gravel as he dragged me from his glorious steed. My legs immediately buckled, and I flopped onto my back, shivering violently and staring at the sky I'd soared from only moments ago.

Saeth wandered away with a snort, his cold, damp feathers skimming the length of my leg. I couldn't even bring myself to roll away from his thudding hooves. Idris' face appeared above me, blocking the light, his mussed-up hair a faintly glowing halo in the sunlight. Ironic, given he was the devil incarnate.

"Are you well?"

Well? *Well*? I'd just had my hand inside a *cloud*. A peal of hysterical laughter erupted from me.

"I'll take that as a no."

He disappeared from my line of sight, but a faint rustle alerted me to movement at my side. I lolled my head to find him draped on his side in the grass, his temple propped on his fist. His hair really was a disaster, and his skin was flushed, but there was a light in his eyes that I'd never seen there before. That hair though...

My trembling, numb fingers patted my own head, and I grimaced at the tangles I was unlikely to ever fully comb out.

His eyes followed the movement. "It's worse than you can possibly imagine."

I chuckled, my hand flopping onto my belly, which still swirled and somersaulted and plummeted. "It was worth it. That was sik."

My words slurred over my numb lips.

"Sik?"

I could practically hear his disapproving frown.

"I forgot you're a dinosaur. It means... amazing. Incredible."

"What is a dinosaur?"

I squinted my eyes against the sun to look at him. "Something even older than you, if you can imagine." I felt drunk, like I couldn't make my words come as quickly as they should, my tongue slow to form them.

His lips tightened ever so slightly. "What's the matter with you?"

As though in answer, my body gave a violent shudder. "Cold," I breathed through numb lips. "Freezing."

His frown deepened, his green gaze raking over me. How had he avoided hypothermia? Was it something to do with being immortal? Not fair…

My eyelids flickered, and then the ground was moving, jolting, and heat washed over me. I opened my eyes to find myself nestled to Idris' chest, his arms cradling me. My frosty brain registered dim surprise and I wriggled, trying to free myself. He shouldn't be doing that. He didn't even like me. Idris' arms tightened, pressing me close.

"I forgot how pathetic humans are." His voice came from far away, seeping into my consciousness like warm chocolate sauce drizzled over ice cream.

"I miss chocolate," I mumbled.

"And strange," Idris huffed. "Pathetic and strange."

My eyelids drooped again, too heavy to resist the warmth pressing against my cheek. I curled into it, savouring it as it sank deeper into my frozen flesh, and I sank into dreams of feathers and clouds and wild, unbound laughter.

When I stirred, I found myself back in my room at Nairsgarth, wrapped in a toasty cocoon of blankets. The fire roared in the grate, and on my nightstand stood a plate of luxuriously decorated chocolates.

I took my breakfast in the communal dining hall the next morning, hoping to bump into Idris, but the prince's dark hair was nowhere to be seen amongst the heads of many witches, all gleaming in the sunlight streaming through the doors, thrown open to the courtyard.

When I was accosted by a seamstress, mere heartbeats after swallowing my last mouthful of porridge mounded in brown sugar and laying down my spoon, and dragged along to a studio brimming with rolls of fabric in every colour of the rainbow, he wasn't there either.

Maybe the princes already had more than enough regal costumes fit for a fairytale ball, but I couldn't show up dressed in denim hotpants, and so I endured the measuring and prodding and poking while mindlessly agreeing to every design suggestion the witch threw my way, all the while itching to escape, my head full of clouds and feathers.

Had yesterday been a nightmare turned into the loveliest of dreams? I'd started the morning at a funeral, only to end up as close to heaven as any living soul had ever been.

No sooner had the seamstress dismissed me then I leapt down from the crate she'd insisted I stand on, despite my already prominent height advantage, and dashed away down the corridor, barely noticing the direction my feet carried me in.

My fingers flexed, the tips rubbing together as I passed a window and glimpsed the fluffy white clouds beyond. I'd touched one of those. I'd held out my hand, reaching, and Idris had done something with his body weight in response, steering the horse closer until my fingers had trailed through the swirling mist. Such a small gesture, but the gift he'd given me... it was profound. A core memory. I would *never* forget that moment. Which was precisely why I wanted to see him today, to thank him, and to apologise. I'd misjudged him.

Maybe it was because I was already thinking of him, but when I came across him, lounging in a secluded oriel window, sketching in his little black book, I walked straight past, too lost in thoughts of him to sort memories from the present.

Realising my mistake, I halted, glancing over my shoulder, only to find his eyes already pinned on me beneath surly eyebrows. A tiny crease formed between them at my attention.

Smiling, I retraced my steps and trilled, "Morning."

One of his long legs was propped on the window seat, leaving no room for a second person to sit, while the other trailed on the floor, the picture of princely arrogance. He made no effort to budge, nor did he return my smile. Instead, he dropped my gaze, resuming his sketching, and said, "It is indeed morning."

My spirits, which soared on feathered wings, dipped slightly, jostled by sudden turbulence. The scratch of his pencil filled the awkward silence.

"Drawing anything good?"

"Why are you here?" he asked without looking up, his cool, irritable tone negating the need for a glare or filthy look.

So much for misjudging him. But no, he'd been nice yesterday, hadn't he? Civil? More than that. He'd made sure I made it safely to my warm bed, and he'd left chocolates on my nightstand. That definitely hadn't been a hallucination, because I'd eaten them as a sneaky little pre-breakfast starter, and they'd been as delicious as they were beautiful.

"I was just walking," I lied, unsure whether I was still in the mood for gushing gratitude, "and I saw you sitting there and thought I'd say hi. I've just come from a dress fitting. For the ball."

Idris looked up from his book. The sunlight caught his eyes, shrinking his pupils to tiny black specks and enhancing the striking yellow tones of his irises, all but obliterating the green. He really was a gorgeous creature, even if his attitude left a lot to be desired. Those lovely eyes flickered over my body, taking in my outfit and no doubt deeming me unworthy of whatever magnificent ballgown the witches were running up. They lingered on my bare legs just long enough for me to grow conscious of his attention before they lifted back to my face.

"What a thrilling life you lead." This time, he held my stare as my mouth fell open in mildly offended surprise.

Maybe it was a bit boring compared to his, but we couldn't all be born into vast wealth and spend our days prancing over the rainbow on pretty ponies.

"Has anyone ever told you that you're incredibly rude?"

He smirked, basking in my insult as though I'd told him how handsome he was. "As a matter of fact, yes, but it means so much more coming from you, human."

I bristled at the condescending nickname. I wasn't ashamed of being human, but the way he said it... he obviously expected me to be. "Oh, pretending you don't know my name again, are you?"

"Perhaps I've forgotten."

I rolled my eyes. What did I care? He could go and gaslight somebody else, just as soon as I'd proven myself to be the bigger person. "Anyway, *Idris*, I was hoping to run into you. I just wanted to say thanks for yesterday, I really enjoyed it, and the chocolates were lovely." The temptation to add 'unlike you' almost got the better of me, but

I pressed my lips together in an attempt to maintain the moral high ground.

Idris' eyebrows lifted. In surprise? Did he really think so little of me that I wouldn't bother to thank someone for a once in a lifetime experience? Maybe it wasn't the speech I'd imagined, maybe I hadn't expressed just how deeply the flight had marked me, but it was better than nothing, and more than he deserved, evidently. Yesterday's kindness had apparently been nothing more than a little blip in a consistently piss-poor personality.

I flicked my loose hair away from where it had fallen forward over my shoulder. The prince tracked the movement, his unusual eyes lingering on the colourful strands. I wasn't about to give him the opportunity to insult my pride and joy. "See you around."

Before he had a chance to say something else to sour my mood, I walked away, making an extra effort to walk in a perfectly straight line and avoid scuffing the soles of my boots. The last thing I needed was to make a fool of myself when I knew the absence of his pencil scratching meant he was watching my retreat. Maybe I even swished my hips a little, remembering the way his undeserving eyes had lingered on my legs. Maybe.

26

New Dress, Who's Dis?

The girl looking back at me from my dressing table mirror wasn't quite a stranger, but she was somebody I no longer knew. It wasn't just the way I looked, polished to an almost fae-like perfection in preparation for Anwir's ball. It was how I *felt*.

Excited. Brimming with anticipation at the prospect of a fairytale ball. That in itself wasn't unusual. I was no stranger to blowing off steam at the end of a long week by donning a slinky dress and hitting the clubs until the early hours, but the Aliza I'd thought I knew would have been wracked with guilt at leaving my parents in agony for a week longer than necessary.

I should have been preparing for my graduation. My robe should have been hung in my bedroom, a thrilling reminder that all my hard work had finally paid off, that my future had arrived at last. Had Mum and Dad cancelled the rental, or had they collected it in the hope that I would show up in the nick of time? Would my friends feel like celebrating when they received their own degrees, or would the occasion be marred by my empty seat? My guts writhed. They would celebrate. They'd cheer for each other, they'd smile, and when it was all over, they'd raise a shot to me before drinking the bar dry. They'd dance and laugh and make lifelong memories. Without me.

My gaze drifted from my reflection to the explosion of glittering golden tulle hung from my wardrobe, and my belly did a little flip. Tonight, I'd make my own memories. Never in a million years had I imagined a chance to wear such a thing. Maybe if I'd ever met someone worth marrying, but even then, I'd have had to marry in a cathedral to pull off such a dress. I could hardly believe the witches had created it in only a week. Somehow, the gown filled me with more fizzing anticipation than a dowdy old graduation robe ever could. What did that make me? Some sort of vain, selfish monster? I could accept that title, just for one night.

What would Anwir think of me in my dress?

I do not care what any man thinks.

Except... I did. I cared, and I hated myself for it. Tonight was an act, my last night in Neath, but I wanted the prince to see me and wish it wasn't. I wanted him to see what I could look like when I wasn't covered in blood and dirt and a week's worth of grease and grime. I wanted him to want *me*, not the idea of the Human Queen with the power to stoke the flames of uprising in his people. When he saw my fairytale transformation, maybe he'd forget his kingdom long enough to sate the need my nightly, illicit dreams had awoken in me.

Maybe, just maybe, I had a chance.

A pair of witches had spent the past few hours transforming me. After all my baths, my hair had faded into the palest of pastel ombres. It shimmered like an opal in the candlelight. The witch had curled and pinned it into a low knot at the nape of my neck, leaving a few loose coils to frame my face. A diamond tiara, shaped like an explosion of stars, nestled on top.

I'd worried about how I'd look without access to my makeup bag. I was a fan of winged eyeliner and bold, pink lips, and I'd never attended an event without them. But a smothering of magic lotions had given my skin a glassy glow, and with the barest hint of colour applied to my cheeks and lips, and a dusting of kohl around my eyes, I looked naturally radiant. Not as beautiful as the fae, with my too-human face, but a damn sight better than I'd looked since I'd arrived in this awful place, or any day since.

Except, I was finding Neath less awful with every day that passed. It was all too easy to shove the memories of giant spiders and wolves the size of horses to the back of my mind when I was safe behind the witches' walls. Ever since my flight with Idris, I'd been struck anew with the beauty and magic this place had to offer. I couldn't make myself believe that this, however brief my stay might be, was my life. I'd have to go the rest of my years pretending none of it had ever happened, so what was the harm in enjoying it while I still could?

Not that Idris had bothered to take me on any more flights to the clouds, or even to glance in my direction since he'd scooped me into his arms and saved me from the clutches of hypothermia. I'd seen him about the place, lurking in a quiet nook, or hidden in the grounds, sketching in his little black book. On those occasions, he didn't bother to look up, though I thought I might have seen his shoulders stiffen as I drew near. Not that I cared. What could we possibly have to say to each other? I had nothing in common with the haughty prince. I was glad that he was absent most of the time. Probably riding his pretty little horse through the clouds without a care in the world, making the most of his freedom now he was awake.

Who says I want to be?

I hadn't forgotten his words at the lake. I played them over in my mind whenever I had a moment between party plans and soul-crushing guilt. Poor pampered prince. He was right. It had to be a difficult life, born into immense, unearned privilege, to have the world at his fingertips. Though my tiny mortal mind couldn't even begin to fathom such torment, I could at least grasp that it must be simply horrific to have everything I desired brought to me on a silver platter. No wonder he preferred being cursed to soaring amongst the clouds.

The witch at my back slid one final diamond pin into my hair and smiled at me in the mirror.

"Done. What do you think, Your Majesty?"

Your Majesty.

I'd been getting called that all week, and it still made me want to snort with laughter. Anwir had spread the story that, after my temper tantrum the night we'd returned to Nairsgarth, I'd decided to stay, to become his fabled Human Queen. We had agreed that our ruse should be complete. Nobody, not even the witches could doubt us. All it would take was one too many glasses of fairy wine, and somebody might say the wrong thing to the wrong person, and our deception would come crashing down. As far as anyone but the prince and I knew, a coronation was all that stood between me and the throne. That, and a psychotic male intent on my death, of course.

I couldn't be scared of King Maelgwyn tonight. I smiled at my reflection, turning my head to admire my hair, and the stunning diamond starburst hovering above.

"It's gorgeous. Thank you."

The witch curtsied, blushing furiously. My heart sank a little. If only Pansy could have been the one to help me get ready. If only her heart hadn't been broken into thousands of pieces. If only my hands weren't smeared by the phantom stain of her mother's blood.

I'd tried to visit Pansy, but my friend was deep in the first days of grief, and she'd turned me away each time. It was only grief, I reminded myself several times a day, only grief that had her refusing my company. She couldn't possibly blame me for her mother's death. Could she?

I snatched my hands to my lap, remembering too late the second witch kneeling beside my chair, buffing my fingernails to a shine.

"I'm sorry, did I hurt you?" She looked horrified and terrified all at once.

"No. No, I'm fine. I just..." How could I say that, in certain lights, I thought I could still see blood in my cuticles? "I just can't sit still. I'm too excited."

Relief washed over her face. "It *is* almost time to get dressed."

There it was again, that all-consuming, jittery excitement. I snatched up my as yet untouched crystal flute and took a deep swig of the bubbling, golden liquid within. Fairy wine. It fizzed over my tongue, an explosion of citrus and sweet notes that tickled the back of my nose.

I swallowed, marvelling at how smoothly it went down. "Wow. I thought prosecco was good!"

Polite, if confused, smiles answered me. Of course. They had no idea what prosecco was. They were ignorant of my life. Of my world. Sometimes, I felt like an alien here, but tonight, I was determined to be a happy alien. Anwir's guests had swarmed to Nairsgarth, mainly from Tir o Gaeaf, the last free kingdom of fae, but others had come from far flung locations, not kingdoms as such, just little clusters of those who'd been lucky enough to escape the three fallen kingdoms. There were witches too, from the other covens dotted about this magical world. And there were other magical beings I was yet to meet. All had come from far and wide to celebrate the princes' awakening and glimpse their rightful king and the legendary Human Queen. Would there be vampires in attendance? Somehow, I doubted it, though I could all too easily imagine Jacques lurking in the shadows, watching me with too bright eyes.

I took another swig of wine, and my body lightened delightfully. God, I should have eaten more at lunch. There was going to be a fancy buffet this evening, but I had to make a good impression first. I put my flute down with a too loud clink. I'd drink my share after I'd successfully navigated the dancefloor.

Dancing. God, I was going to dance with Anwir. If my luck was in, we'd be doing more than dancing before the night was out. My last night.

I suddenly wished my hairstyle did a better job of hiding my burning ears, but it was too late to start making changes now.

"Right. Let's get this dress on, shall we?"

At Anwir's insistence, I was to arrive fashionably late. It would be his grand reveal. I could see the logic and the appeal of being the centre of everyone's attention, but now that I stood before the closed double doors that led out into the grounds, where the ball was being held, my belly tumbled and flipped at the thought of all those people, strangers, waiting for *me*.

How could I live up to their expectations? They'd waited millennia for their Human Queen. She'd been woven into legend, into fairytale, but I was just... me.

Muffled music and laughter drifted to me. I hoped everyone had managed to drink at least three glasses of fairy wine by now, so they might overlook my nerves and shivering limbs. Maybe *I* should have drunk more wine.

What if I tripped on my hem? What if I forgot my dance steps? What if everyone thought I was a hideous frump next to the stunning fae females I'd seen in Tir o Gaeaf? Maybe Anwir would change his mind about the whole thing, leaving me looking like a fool in a ridiculous dress. Now the moment was upon me, I wished I'd gone for something simpler, and foregone the tiara altogether. I was no queen. I was nobody. What right did I have to be here, with all eyes on me?

My legs itched, the impulse to run growing stronger with every second those doors barred my way. It wasn't too late. I could change my mind.

If I did, Anwir would never win his kingdom back. I wasn't going to stay, but maybe this one glimpse of me, of *hope*, would be enough to bolster his people. Maybe he could carry the lie on without me, after tonight. After this one, small thing.

I took a deep breath, stilling my nerves. I could do this. I'd done worse. This was easy. All I had to do was walk to Anwir, smile and dance.

Dance with Anwir.

The thought made me dizzier than any prosecco ever had. God, those dreams had really gotten under my skin.

Beyond the doors, some sort of trumpet sounded, and the music and laughter died. A voice rang out, and I knew they were announcing me, but I couldn't hear the words over the blood rushing in my ears. I rolled my shoulders back and pasted a smile on my face, not a moment too soon.

The doors swung open.

At the sight awaiting me, I forgot my nerves. The grounds, pretty enough before, had been transformed. I couldn't see far beyond the sea of eager faces turned in my direction, but I glimpsed towering flower arrangements, ice sculptures, and intricately carved topiary trees. Fairies drifted overhead, a rainbow of glowing colours. Fairy lights. They reminded me of Christmas. Had humans retained some memory of the magical world we'd once been a part of? How else could we have named our Christmas decorations so accurately?

But there was no time to admire any of it.

The music started up again, accompanied by a roar of applause as I took my first uncertain step over the threshold. I was alone. Completely alone as I made my way down the stone steps. The crowd parted, clearing a path for me, and there, at the far end, was Anwir.

My fixed smile became real.

He looked like a dream. Like something from a fairytale. He wore a perfectly fitted jacket of peridot green, an exact match for his eyes, embroidered with an elaborate pattern of golden thread running down his front, either side of his buttons. His close-fitting trousers disappeared into polished, knee-high boots that gleamed in the fairy light almost as much as his sleek, black hair, tied in a low ponytail.

But his expression was what really caught my attention. The slightly stunned, wide-eyed way he drank in my approach. My smile grew as

I basked in his evident admiration, glowing beneath his gaze. This was fake. He had to look at me like that if he wanted all these people to believe they stood a chance against the sorcerer king. I was their salvation. Little did they know, I would be gone come morning, and Anwir was merely acting, the way I was sure he'd had to do every day of his princely life.

Still, fake or not, I couldn't help but return his smile. I couldn't help but blush as I stopped before him and he took my hand in his, bending low to kiss it, exactly as he had a week ago in the privacy of my room. Just as they had that night, his lips lingered, heating my blood in anticipation of where else they might touch.

"To King Anwir, and his bright young queen!"

The ball erupted into cheers, whoops and the occasional explosion of flame or light. Petals materialised from thin air, flurrying and twirling around us. I laughed in delight at the sight of such flamboyant outbursts of magic. Anwir turned to me, evidently struggling to contain his smile.

He twirled a lock of pastel hair around his finger. "Exceedingly bright."

Something in his tone had my guts twisting. "You don't like it?"

"It is... strange." His gaze flickered over my hair, the smile melting away. "Pretty, in its own way, but I have never seen anything so... I'm just not sure how suitable it is for a queen."

My steaming blood cooled, becoming glacial. All my hopeful ideas of where the night might lead cracked and shattered to icy dust. It was a good thing I had no intention of becoming anyone's queen, let alone his. Who did he think he was, to deem any part of me unsuitable? I'd survived hideous ordeals and overcome impossible odds to save him. All he'd done was get himself cursed, and then run away at every whisper of trouble. Besides, I thought my hair would look amazing with a crown, if I ever gave it the chance. Not that I would. "Maybe, but I'm not like all those other queens, am I?"

"No." He gave me an indulgent smile, nudging his nose against mine as though he'd missed my venomous tone. A show, that was all it was. A performance for his people. "You are most definitely *not* like them."

A few seconds ago, my stupid heart might have stuttered as I stared up into those peridot eyes, but now its pace quickened only with irritation.

"It's time," he whispered, his minty breath filling my nose.

"For what?"

A low chuckle rumbled through him. "Have I dazzled you? It is time for the opening dance."

Oh. That.

I dropped his gaze gladly, looking around at the watching crowd. They smiled back, faces alive with happiness. Hope. The floor had cleared expectantly, leaving Anwir and I alone in a vast, empty circle, and I saw that the grass had been hidden beneath a now petal-strewn marble slab. Where it had come from and how it had gotten here was beyond my imagining. Smiling, expectant faces stared back at me; the witches and fae and other strange creatures I didn't recognise had crowded around the two of us. Music drifted on the simmering air.

Anwir squeezed my hand. It was all I could do not to snatch it from his grasp. "There's nothing to worry about if you follow my lead. I've done this thousands of times. I'll guide you."

I turned back to the prince. He'd danced with thousands of women, had he? Or maybe just one woman thousands of times. Was that why he thought he was entitled to an opinion on my appearance? Did he think I'd fall over myself to compete with them? Just because he was handsome, just because he'd been kind? Or because he was a prince? Whatever the reason, my foolish fantasies were as dead as my world believed me to be.

Smiling slightly, he laid his hand on my waist. I stiffened, my spine going rigid. A poor start to any dance. I needed to be poised yet flexible. Liquid and solid at the same time. I forced my lungs to draw a deep, slow breath.

At the lightest pressure from his hand, we began to sway in time to the music, on the spot at first, but then he steered me into the steps, revolving us around one another. His eyes bore into mine, looking for all the world as though he was besotted with me. He was quite the actor, I'd give him that. Well, I could act too. Putting on a brave face was part of my job. I donned my mask, letting a wide smile spread across my face.

Anwir, with his free hand, lifted my arm, guiding me into a spin. My feet moved effortlessly as I turned, the stunning dress swishing around my legs as I extended my free hand, fingers poised, and stepped back into his hold.

I noted with pleasure the faint surprise on his face.

"What?" I whispered, smirking. "You think mortal girls can't dance?"

I was picking up the rhythm now, starting to anticipate the swell and fall of the music, and the movement that went with it. Maybe I didn't know the steps as well as I'd like, but my instincts merged with Anwir's guidance, creating something passable, maybe even pretty.

Soon, I lost myself, my annoyance ebbing with the pulse of the music. My body responded to Anwir's lead and the music's guidance. Whatever imperfections lingered in my steps were surely masked by the swell of my skirt. We twirled around the dancefloor, my dress swishing magnificently, past a blur of faces almost as happy as my own.

All too soon, the music faded out, and Anwir steered me to a halt, bowing low. I curtsied on numb legs, my chest rising and falling breathlessly. Around us, the music began again and Anwir's guests filled the floor around us, beginning the next dance.

The prince, however, stepped closer to me.

"That was... not terrible," he said.

God, what had I ever seen in him? I kept my waspish tones to a minimum as I said, "Wow, you'd better stop there, or the praise will go to my head."

He grinned. "I didn't know you could dance."

"You never asked. I used to be a figure skater, you know, on ice? It's not so different to dancing, really."

"Used to be?"

My fake smile became real but sad, accompanied by the tug of regret deep in my belly. My skating days were long gone, but I still missed them fiercely. Still couldn't so much as look at a skin of ice forming on a puddle without suffering a stab of longing. "Injury. Broke my ankle when I was seventeen. I think my parents might have been secretly relieved. I was obsessed, and it was so expensive, but it was my only hobby, and they wanted to give me the best life they could. Even if they couldn't afford it. But that fall was the end of my dream."

"You could have a new dream," he reminded me. "A better one."

While becoming a queen was undoubtedly a more ambitious dream than being a professional figure skater, better wasn't the word I would have chosen. The promise of untold riches, of fabulous dresses and diamonds the size of eggs, of eternal life, were undoubtedly tempting, and up until a few minutes ago, Anwir had been too. Not enough for me to consider marrying him, but certainly enough that I would have made a fool of myself. At least I could leave in the morning without regrets. Speaking of which, I wasn't going to let an opinionated prince spoil my night. I would likely never have the chance to dance at a ball again, and I intended to make the most of it. Starting right now, with someone, anyone, else.

"I'm thirsty," I lied, trying to sidestep Anwir.

His hand closed around mine, firm and unyielding, halting me in my tracks.

"I have a better idea." With a sharp tug that sent a twinge of discomfort up my arm, he pulled me close again. "How about another dance?"

27
I Hate Them Both

Anwir led me through four consecutive dances, leaving me breathless and flushed and increasingly irritated. Finally, he pulled me aside, weaving between still dancing couples and to the edge of the floor. With tender fingers completely at odds with the biting grip he'd maintained on my waist, the prince grazed a loose lock of hair back from my face, tucking it neatly behind my ear.

"We've put on quite a show," he said with a smile, "but I should probably mingle with my guests. Go and enjoy yourself. This is a celebration of you, after all."

Finally. "Okay." I nodded, unhooking my hair and trying to pretend I was deeply disappointed to leave his side.

His grip on my hand tightened. "Just remember to make a good impression. It's probably best to avoid the fairy wine. It's... potent, and we don't want any foolishness, tonight of all nights."

So much for enjoying myself. What was a party without a glass of wine? "I've already had a glass. It was fine."

"What? Who gave it to you?" His face hardened as he scanned the crowds, as though searching for some imagined assailant.

"Relax, I had a few sips while I was getting ready."

His lips thinned. "Well, no more. Trust me, I only want my people to think highly of you, and humans rarely behave well after a few glasses of wine."

The last vestiges of my patience evaporated. Did he forget that the only reason I was here at all was because he'd begged me to deceive the people whose opinions he valued above mine? I fixed a simpering smile on my face. "Don't worry about me. Go, mingle."

Anwir kissed my hand again, and I fought the urge to snatch it out of his grasp. Without another word, he was gone, strolling through the crowd with his shoulders back and his head high. Everywhere he went, bright-eyed, hopeful faces turned in his direction. He paused here and there, bestowing a word or two to over-exuberant laughter. As charming as Anwir could be, he wasn't exactly a comedian. Oh, the things people would fake for the powerful. Was it flattering or annoying to have everyone he ever met fall over themselves to please him? I'd seen a side of him tonight I didn't like, and it left me in no doubt he was lapping up the admiration.

When I dragged my eyes away, it was to find myself surrounded by a gaggle of breathtakingly beautiful fae females, dressed in equally stunning gowns with quirky, elaborate details, all staring expectantly. The moment I noticed them, they rushed to curtsy, rising with eager smiles. Was this it? My opportunity to wow and amuse with the dullest of words?

"Lovely party," I said, spotting a passing tray laden with fizzing wine. "Excuse me."

I darted between their reluctantly parting shoulders and snagged a glass. The rim had barely touched my lips when I spotted a familiar head of dark hair.

Idris, loitering near a floral arrangement, held a crystal flute in each hand. I wouldn't exactly call him a friendly face, but at least I knew him. I lifted my hem and hurried to his side.

"Hi." I took a deep swig of fairy wine, grimacing at the bubbles exploding at the back of my throat.

Idris swayed as he turned to look at me, his eyebrows lifting in surprise. His misty gaze travelled from the hem of my gown, all the way to the tip of my tiara, before finally dropping to my face. He didn't smile, never mind offer a compliment. Maybe this had been a bad idea.

The prince tipped the entire contents of one flute down his throat, gulping and grimacing. Judging by his unsteady stance, it was far from his first drink of the evening.

"Maybe you should slow down," I suggested, instantly hating myself for it. "Anwir doesn't want *any foolishness*."

Why was I parroting him as though I cared what he wanted? To hell with Anwir. I took another gulp of my own wine. Idris downed his second glass as though he'd read my thoughts and agreed wholeheartedly.

"Well, now look at what you've done. You've got nothing left," I observed, nodding at his empty glasses.

As though summoned, a serving tray passed by, and Idris seized two fresh glasses. The look he gave me was complete and utter challenge, daring me to admonish him. He held my gaze as he lifted the wine to his lips and drained the flute, swallowed and licked his lips.

Despite myself, I laughed. "Okay, fine. Is the party really that bad?"

He blinked, swaying on the spot, but opened his mouth to answer. Finally. At least I wasn't talking to a wall.

"It's not th–"

"Pansy!" I glimpsed a familiar head of coils in the crowd. "Sorry, Idris. My friend..."

I dashed between laughing, chattering ball goers, my stomach flipping. I hadn't expected Pansy to attend, but I wasn't going to pass up the chance to spend some time with her before I left.

My stomach tightened at the sight of my friend's face. It had only been a week, but the weight had dropped from her previously plump cheeks, ageing her. Or maybe it was the dull skin or swollen eyelids. Whatever it was, grief cloaked her like a veil.

"You came," I said, catching her up. "I wasn't sure you would."

The witch's smile was heartbreakingly small. Unlike the other witches, she hadn't bothered to dress up. Her deep aubergine dress was pretty in a hippy kind of way, but as unadorned as ever. "Neither was I, but I thought I should show my face to support your victory."

I shouldn't be wearing a ridiculous ballgown or a starburst of diamonds. Hyacinth had died, and we were celebrating. I gave my best, disinterested shrug. "Anwir insisted on it. Apparently, a party is going to help him win back his throne."

I glanced at the sky. Between a dark patchwork of clouds, stars winked down at me. What did witches believe about death? Had the candles burnt down for Hyacinth's soul to drift to the stars or the heavens or wherever else?

"I heard you're going to stay?" Pansy asked, bringing my attention earthward again. "To help him?"

Ruse or not, I could trust Pansy with the truth. I shook my head. My tiara tugged gently at my hair as it swayed. "No," I whispered, leaning in so only she could catch my words. "I should have gone home already, but Anwir asked me to stay just for this, and promised he'd take me home afterwards. Don't tell anyone, will you?"

"Of course I won't. I'll miss you. I know I haven't been the best friend lately, but I will. I'll miss you a lot. I wish there was a way you could stay."

As reluctant as I was to admit it, there was a tiny part of me that wished that too. Returning to normal, mundane life would be strange after this adventure. Leaving these people... a fortnight ago, if anyone had told me I'd miss them, I'd have laughed in their face, but now... I didn't need to be told. "We'll find a way to visit," I insisted, my throat growing tight. The rifts were open now. Why shouldn't I come back? Why shouldn't Pansy visit my world?

My friend nodded as though she didn't really believe it. All the fun, all the spirit had sapped out of her, leaving a hollow shell of the girl she had been only a week ago.

"I appreciate you coming, but if it's too soon, I really don't mind if you want to sneak away. If I'm honest, I feel like doing the same."

Surprise flitted over Pansy's face, a momentary spark of life. "You looked like you were enjoying yourself."

"I thought I would," I admitted, "but it turns out balls aren't all they're cracked up to be. Now I'm supposed to *mingle*." I grimaced at the word, giving a little shudder for effect. For my theatrical efforts, I won a single, quickly strangled chuckle.

"I'll keep you company for a while. It's probably good for me to be out of my room, even if it doesn't feel like it." Her voice trembled as she spoke.

I pushed my glass into her hand. "You need this more than I do. Shall we go and have a look at the food?"

God knew, she could do with a decent meal. Pansy looped her arm through mine and together, we wove our way through the crowd.

I had to hand it to the witches, they knew how to work fast. From healing wounds in record time, to creating ballgowns, to pulling together a party, it seemed they didn't let a little thing like the passage of time get in their way.

Elaborate floral arrangements peeked over the head of even the tallest fae in the crowd, all brought to life by a rainbow of fairies. The music drifted along on the night air, and here and there, fragrant fires burnt, warding away the slight chill. The only flaw in their arrangements was the view from the buffet table.

Though obscured slightly by the guests who crowded its edges to watch, I had a clear enough view of the dancefloor. Of Anwir, as he held a fae beauty in his arms. And then another, and another. It seemed his idea of mingling involved close physical contact with the prettiest of guests. Though the battleaxe didn't break a smile, he even took Sage for a turn, the height difference making them faintly ridiculous. Lady Celyn, who came next, made a better-suited partner.

Nibbling my food without tasting it, I watched the pair dance. Celyn was as graceful as she was beautiful, and when she smiled, she put my artificial glow to shame. What did Anwir need me for? The brave and beautiful steward of Tir o Gaeaf would make a better queen than I ever could. At least she knew how to rule a kingdom while holding Maelgwyn at bay.

I could never measure up to Lady Celyn.

Beside me, Pansy watched the dancing through vacant eyes, sipping the fairy wine I'd forced upon her. My idle thoughts of how to get it back came to an abrupt halt when Celyn disengaged herself from the prince and made a beeline for me.

Her porcelain skin was flushed a pretty shade of pink as she curtsied. "Your Majesty, congratulations on your success. This is a joyous occasion."

My arm grew chilled as Pansy drifted away from my side.

"It is," I agreed, trying to muster some enthusiasm. "Not without its losses, though."

Celyn arranged her face into a solemn expression. "I heard that a number of witches were lost."

"Two. Meadow and Hyacinth were killed by Maelgwyn's barghests." It seemed important that people should know. That they remembered.

"A terrible fate, but a worthy cause to give one's life to." Celyn's voice became cheery again. "The princes are awake. Our Human Queen truly has come, just as the prophecies foretold. It is only a matter of time before Maelgwyn is forced to answer for his crimes and our people are freed."

"Yes," I agreed, my teeth clenching into what I hoped was a smile rather than a grimace. "If you'll excuse me, Lady Celyn..."

I caught no glimpse of Pansy as I picked my way through the throng. I couldn't blame her. The urge to disappear to my own room grew stronger with every passing minute. My search for a friendly face was hindered by enthusiastic fae and witches, none of whom I recognised from my time in Nairsgarth, and the curious stares of other creatures. Some, with colourful hair and ridiculously elongated pointy ears, I took to be elves. Pansy had told me about them when I'd fished for information on vampires. As surprising as it was to see them here, I couldn't summon much interest in them. Where had they been while Hyacinth bled out?

I couldn't I take a step without being congratulated, without someone begging for the tale of how the curse came to be broken at last. I forced my smile until my cheeks ached and tried to remember that these people had lived without hope for centuries. My presence was the reason they might be reunited with long-lost loved ones. They had every right to be excited and hopeful. If only they knew I would abandon them all come morning...

When the first drops of rain fell, turning quickly into a torrential downpour, it came as something of a relief. Nobody was willing to spoil their hairdos or muddy their hems just to speak to the Human Queen. Tipsy, shrieking guests ran for the cover of the castle, a perfect opportunity for me to sneak away from the crowd and return to my rooms.

Hiking up my skirts to avoid the rapidly forming puddles, I hurried to the castle steps, squinting through the rain soaking my face. Someone had the same idea as me, but he was using the chaos to sneak away from the castle altogether.

Idris.

I hesitated at the foot of the steps, watching as witches, elves and fae streaked past. The prince walked with his head bowed against the downpour, disappearing around the corner of the castle. Where could he possibly be going in such weather? Not flying, surely? Or for a clifftop stroll? Not when he could barely stand straight. Was it any of my business?

Probably not, but if he was going to do something stupid–and I wouldn't put it past him–I had to put a stop to it. I no longer suspected him as a traitor, but seeing him sneaking off under the cover of darkness was enough to have my innards churning with unease. Teetering in my heels, I jogged after him, cursing his name with every soggy step. Freezing rain pelted my bare face and shoulders with all the ferocity of hailstones, and when a particularly deep puddle sloshed right over my shoe, the flame of my curiosity sputtered and almost died. Almost.

What could be important enough to lure the prince further out into the waterlogged grounds? If he was planning to teleport into enemy territory again, I had to at least try to talk him out of it. What if an ambush was waiting for him? What if he didn't have the reaction time he needed to escape?

Clinging to the meagre shelter offered by the ivy-riddled walls, I quickened my pace. When I turned the corner Idris had disappeared around, I squinted, spotting him meandering in the direction of the cliffs, and the path that led to Hyacinth's cove. This was no weather for a beach stroll. Was it the wind that whistled like that?

Through a shimmering sheet of rain, something large and ghostly pale moved in the distance, speeding toward Idris.

28

Who Turned The Tables And Can We Put Them Back?

My eyeliner was probably already streaking down my cheeks, but on the off chance I didn't yet look like some sort of grunge panda, I carefully swept the rainwater from my face, squinting through the deluge.

The white shape pranced to Idris' side, ruffling enormous wings.

Saeth.

How on earth had the horse gotten from Tir o Hydref to the sodden grounds of Nairsgarth? Was this the reason for the prince's frequent absences this past week? I'd assumed he'd been hiding, maybe even avoiding me, but it looked as though he'd been flying his horse across the island instead, without a thought to spare for discretion.

He wasn't going to fly him now, was he? Not when he could barely stand straight. Somehow, I wouldn't put it past him, and no other idiots lingered in the rain, waiting to intervene. It looked like it was down to me.

Sighing and grimacing, I hoisted my hems and squelched through the soggy grass.

When I reached them, my suspicions were confirmed. Idris was trying to fly. Saeth stood with his head hung low in resignation, his mane plastered to his neck, while the prince took several failed attempts at placing his foot on the waiting wing joint. He eventually managed the feat, but immediately lost his balance, swinging sideways and thumping against Saeth's shoulder.

"Shush, Saeth," Idris reprimanded in the loudest whisper I'd ever heard. "Keep still!"

It might have been funny if it wasn't a disaster waiting to happen. The poor horse gave a dismal snort and threw me a look that quite clearly said, 'I get this all the time.'

"Idris," I barked. The prince jolted, spinning and stumbling. His wide, alcohol clouded eyes took several moments to focus on me. "What are you doing?"

"Oh." His brow lowered almost to his dark eyelashes. "It's you."

With a rumble that shook the ground, lightning cracked overhead, momentarily illuminating the low, petulant clouds. Electricity zinged over my skin and quivered in the air. My heart leapt to my throat, urging me to duck or retreat, but I held out my hand.

"Come on, it's not safe to be out in a storm." Especially in the middle of such open grounds. I had no interest in being barbecued.

Idris laughed, a low, joyless chuckle and, ignoring my outstretched hand, turned back to Saeth. This time, his foot planted on the lowered wing.

I moved without thinking, my wet hem slapping against my legs as I closed the distance and grabbed fistfuls of Idris' jacket. He staggered as I dragged him, but kept his footing, twisting out of my grasp. I launched a fresh attack, this time seizing his wrist with both hands and clinging on for dear life.

Idris blinked, as though mildly surprised that I hadn't given up, and laughed. Mean-spirited amusement sparked in his eyes as he raised his arm above his head, stretching me to my full height and then some. I teetered on the tips of my toes, while he just grinned down at me, completely unperturbed by the weight of an entire human dangling from his arm.

"You won't win, you know," he mused.

The urge to slam my knee into his balls, just to prove that he wasn't as all-powerful as he thought he was, had me grinding my teeth.

"Maybe not," I panted, "but I'm not letting you fly like this."

He lowered his arm, twisting it free of my grasp. Too easily. It was laughable and humiliating in equal measure. As I attempted to grab him again, he caught my wrist, and then the other, with a precision he certainly hadn't possessed while trying to climb onto Saeth.

"*Stop*," he hissed, his grip tightening slightly as he forced my arms down to my side. The movement brought him close. Close enough that his warm breath fluttered over my freezing skin, filling my nose with the light, fruity scent of fairy wine. I wriggled and squirmed, to no avail.

"No. You can't fly like this." Giving up my escape attempts, I glanced around Idris' broad shoulder, to where the horse waited dutifully. "And shame on you, Saeth, for letting him."

The horse tossed his head with an indignant snort, as though he'd understood me. Maybe he had. I'd given up declaring things impossible. If fairies and vampires were real, why shouldn't animals understand human speech?

"Don't be mean to him," Idris reprimanded, frowning again. "He's a good boy."

I blinked, momentarily thrown off balance by the prince's choice of words. I'd never heard him sound so... soft. But I rallied, determined to put an end to this stupidity. "I'm sure he is, but you're not. You're drunk."

"So?"

"*So*, you were going to fly, weren't you? Flying under the influence is against the rules." I didn't know if that was true, but if it wasn't, and if I ever became queen, I'd make it a reality. "You could fall and die. Come with me, let's find your brother."

"I don't want to."

That made two of us. I shivered, eager to get inside and out of my soggy dress, if only the wretched prince would stop being a disagreeable old dinosaur. "Idris, please."

"No, Aliza." The prince said my name like he was tasting it, some unfamiliar, exotic thing. The fact that he'd remembered it, that he'd pronounced it properly, knocked me senseless, as did the way it sounded on his tongue, his melodious accent twisting it into poetry.

I didn't notice he'd released one wrist until his finger hooked through the string of diamonds around my throat. He gazed down at the glittering stones, before lifting his eyes to my face. His soaked, alabaster skin shimmered, and his hair, plastered to his forehead and dripping into his eyes, was as black as the darkest night. It was distinctly unfair that, even drenched, he looked every bit the fairy prince, while I probably looked like a sewer rat.

"No name tag today?" he purred, a hint of mockery in his voice.

"It didn't go with my dress."

His lips twitched, and he blinked, slowly enough that I thought he might fall asleep where he stood. Taking it as a sign of his weakening, I said, "Let's go inside."

I regretted the words as his expression hardened in cold marble. He let go of me, retreating a step. "You go."

I planted my hands on my hips, fighting down my shiver. "Oh, come on. You're being ridiculous. You can't fly like this. You don't really think I'm going to let you, do you? You're drunk! What if you fell to your death?"

Idris avoided my glare, staring down at the dark grass. He seemed smaller, somehow. "Please... just leave, Aliza."

Gone was all the music of his voice. It flatlined, dull and hollow, not the bored tones he usually reserved for me, but something worse, something that had my stomach clenching with oily dread.

The cold air twisted around me, stealing the last warmth from my body. "Idris? Are you okay?"

For a moment, I thought he would ignore me, but then he lifted his eyes. Bleak, desolate eyes, utterly devoid of the spark I'd seen earlier. I gulped. Pansy had looked at me like that at her mother's funeral. I knew that darkness. Idris was not okay at all.

"What's wrong?" I demanded, my voice rising in panic. I cast my mind around for anything that could have caused such apparent misery. Had his part in Hyacinth's dying moments affected him? Had tonight been an attempt to drown his guilt in the bottom of a bottle of wine?

Idris shook his head, blinking and looking away as he did so. The muscles in his jaw feathered, and then he said, "You were right earlier."

That was unsurprising, but what in particular had I said? Had I caused this?

He blew out a long breath, lifting his face to the sky, heedless of the rain pattering over his skin. "I have nothing left."

A cold veil of panic settled over my already frigid skin. Had I said that? If I had, I didn't remember, and I certainly hadn't meant whatever *this* was.

Idris squeezed his eyes shut, swaying again. He leaned into Saeth, who braced his legs and supported the drunk prince without complaint. I waited for him to say more, but he maintained his silence.

Should I get Anwir?

I would, but I couldn't leave Idris alone in such a state. He'd try to fly again the moment my back was turned, and there was only one way that would end.

Idris hiccoughed, winning my attention back. He pinched the bridge of his nose, then opened his eyes, his gaze settling on me again.

"I don't hate you, you know," he slurred.

Oh, wow, what a compliment. "I know. Nobody leaves chocolates for people they hate. Unless they're poisoned chocolates."

To my knee-buckling relief, he huffed a laugh through his nose. "Who says they weren't?"

My queasiness after stuffing the treats into my face had little to do with poison, and everything to do with my lack of restraint. I spread my arms. "Still alive, aren't I?"

His faint smile fell away, revealing that darkness again. Damn me, and my stupid mouth, straight to hell. Was this really about Hyacinth? I'd played a bigger role in her demise, but I had no inclination to take my car for a drunken spin, even if I'd been able to. There had to be something else at play.

I casually stepped to his side, though I didn't lean on poor Saeth the way he did. Maybe if I wasn't looking at him it'd feel less like an interrogation. Maybe he'd tell me something. "So… why did you want to hate me?"

There was no humour in his laugh. "Isn't it obvious?"

Was it? Was I *that* bad? "Not to me." My voice came out weaker than I'd have liked.

Idris was silent for so long that I almost gave up hope of an answer. Finally, he sighed and croaked, "You woke me up."

A chill skated down my spine. "That's a good thing, isn't it?"

What have you done?

He blew out a long breath. "Is it?"

Who says I want to be?

Maybe it was wrong of me to take advantage of his drunken state, but further prying was needed, starting with the sleep he hadn't wanted to wake from. Sage and Anwir had talked about it briefly once we'd escaped the tunnels, but I hadn't paid much attention. "Did you dream, while you were under the curse?"

"Yes." His voice somehow cracked in that one syllable word.

"Good dreams?"

Silence. Great. This was getting worse by the second. Warning bells clanged in my head. This male was in real trouble. I peered through the dark, searching the grounds for another person, someone who could help me. Unsurprisingly, given the relentless weather, the prince and I were alone.

"Idris," I whispered, unsure of what to say next, but unable to say nothing.

The silence stretched, broken only by the pattering rain and the occasional rustle of feathers. There'd been no further bolts of lightning, at least.

"You shouldn't be out here," Idris said into the quiet.

"Well, I'm here now, and I'm already wet, so I might as well stay a while."

Maybe it was the cold and rain, or maybe it was the unexpected turn my evening had taken, but a dull ache started deep in my chest. I pressed my fingers to my sternum, massaging the pain. In my peripheral vision, I saw Idris bow his head before turning his face to me. Forgetting my no eye contact plan, I peered sideways.

The moment my eyes met his, pain barrelled into me, snatching the air from my lungs.

I buckled forward, clutching my chest, but the sensation vanished as quickly as it had appeared, leaving nothing but that faint ache, and a wave of tears mingling with the rain soaking my cheeks.

What the hell?

Straightening cautiously, still massaging my chest, I turned an accusing glare on Idris. *That* hadn't been an attack of indigestion, that much was certain. It hadn't even been a physical pain, not really. It was the pain of learning Nan had passed away in her sleep, of losing Grandad to a heart attack just months later, neither giving me a chance to say goodbye. The pain I saw in people's eyes as their beloved pet slipped away in their arms. It was that heartache that no drug could reach, and it certainly wasn't mine.

Idris surveyed me with a detached curiosity, as though mildly interested in how I'd react to whatever the hell he'd just done to me.

"What was that?" I demanded, my voice hoarse. "It hurt!"

Idris sighed, averting his gaze. "I know. That's why I didn't want to wake up. It's why I tried to hate you." His voice was steadier than it had been, but his words still came slow and slurred. Still lacked life.

I took the opportunity to study him; the sag of his shoulders, the misery clinging to every feature. It had been hidden before, by a brittle, cold veneer, but that had fallen away, revealing the truth. He was hurting.

All that animosity, all those waspish words… Everything made sense now. He wasn't some heartless, unfeeling monster. Something was eating away at him, and if the brief bolt of pain his clever little magic trick had shared was anything to go by, it was *bad*.

Maybe even bad enough to do something unthinkable.

"Why were you trying to fly tonight?" I forced the question out, terrified of the answer. Once this particular truth was spoken, acknowledged, there would be no escaping it. Maybe I was already ensnared.

Idris sighed, still avoiding my gaze. "I think you already know, don't you?" He shrugged. "But now you're here."

Did I know? For once in my life, I wanted to be wrong. I didn't want to know why he would choose to fly alone at night, when he could barely stand, never mind ride. I didn't want to know what that awful pain might drive him to. But I did know, and I *hated* it. Fresh tears sprang to my eyes. I had to do something, say something, anything, to make him see sense. I had to tell Anwir, or the witches, anyone who might know how to help him.

"You're right. *I'm here.* Of course I am. And so is Anwir. He loves you."

Idris laughed coldly, shaking his head and blinking at the sky.

"Did you lose somebody?" I blurted the question before I could talk myself out of it, my words leaving in a rush. Maybe there was a lost love, from the days before the curse. A beautiful fae female, as ethereal and lovely as those who'd danced at the ball. I massaged the ache in my chest again.

Idris just stared at the sky. As though on queue, a break formed, revealing the moon. Its reflection gleamed in his overly bright eyes. When he spoke, his voice was so quiet that I felt the words more than heard them. "I have nothing left. Nobody."

I couldn't stand it. I couldn't take it. My heart was crumbling, and it *hurt*. I stepped in front of him, and before he could stop me, no matter how inappropriate it might be or how much he might despise it, I threw my arms around his neck, squeezing tight, hard enough to push back against the hollow he'd somehow carved into my chest. His sodden clothes were freezing against my bare arms, and he stiffened beneath me, but I didn't care. He needed this. He needed the comfort of knowing he wasn't alone. I didn't know exactly why he needed it, but I'd figure that out later. Right now, all that mattered was that he was close to someone, even if that someone was me.

I don't hate you.

I screwed my eyes shut against his chest. "I don't hate you either. It'll be okay, Idris. I promise, one day, everything will be okay."

How could it be? How could my words bring comfort when I didn't even know if they were true? But Idris sagged against me, all the tension draining from his hard muscles. His arms wrapped me up so completely that there was nothing but his warmth seeping through our chilled skin, and the blinding beat of pain pulsing from him to me. A second, poisoned heartbeat.

How had this happened? How had I wandered away from the dancing and the music, only to end up here, with him? How had he gone from such blatant hostility to broken in my arms in only a few glasses of wine?

With his massive arms crushing me against him, I could barely move, but I stroked my fingertips through the wet hair at the nape of his neck.

With the rustle of feathers and the shifting of a hoof in the grass, Saeth leaned against Idris, gently pushing him upright. The angle shifted, and though he towered above me, he curled, enveloping me, his cheek pressed against mine. His ribs expanded and deflated with shallow yet desperate breaths, much like mine did when I was trying to hold my tears at bay.

I wouldn't be the first to break this contact, not when I suspected he was in desperate need of it.

"I want you to make me a promise," I whispered in his ear.

He stiffened again. I knew what he dreaded, and I longed to say it anyway. To demand that he never let this pain get the better of him. To insist that he struggle through, every day, for eternity. I wanted to scream at him to agree to my demands, but I couldn't. I had to start small. If I was going to help him, as my soul insisted, I had to tiptoe.

"No flying tonight, okay?"

He had me pressed so close that I felt him gulp. A few heartbeats later, his cheek rasped against mine as he gave a brief nod.

I smiled weakly. It was a start. One night, one day, one step at a time.

29

I Didn't Sign Up For This

The rain eased, the relentless, icy pounding against my bare back fading to drizzle. Wrapped in Idris' arms, I barely noticed the chill. His body heat soaked into me, and I clung to it, to him, unwilling to let go and brave the cold again. He held me right back.

I didn't count the minutes as I trailed my fingers up and down his spine, trying to ignore the impressively muscled expanse, the dip running up its centre, and the little bumps within. It was strange to think that our two species were so similar, right down to the vertebrae, and yet so different. This male would live forever, long after I'd withered to dust. There was magic, *actual magic* in his veins. And yet, he felt pain just as much as any human. What had happened to the person who'd caused this grief? Had life simply taken her in a different direction, or had she died? The witches claimed fae were immortal, but I knew Idris' father had died, leaving the throne vulnerable. I knew countless fae had been lost at Maelgwyn's hands. Death came for them too, sometimes, and when it did, the people who loved them cried, just like the many stricken families who had brought their ailing pets to me, over my years of study.

Eventually, Idris' breathing slowed, deepening, and it was only then that some of the tightness in my chest eased. He straightened at last, and if I'd expected him to pull away completely, to become awkward or full of bravado, I was wrong. His hands hovered at my ribs, as if he was worried I'd back away, but his eyes were soft.

"I haven't been very nice to you," he observed.

My mouth twitched into a smirk. Understatement of the century, or given his lifespan, the millennia. "That's okay." I'd glimpsed who he was under that cool, indifferent facade. Tonight, and the day of the funeral. He wielded his pain like a weapon, turned his sadness into a shield, but beneath it, I suspected someone sweet and caring lurked, waiting to be uncovered. Someone I could grow to like.

He shook his head. "No, it's not. I'm sorry." His hand drifted to my face, and when his fingers grazed along my jaw, to my ear, blood rushed to burn in their wake, a glowing trail.

I could barely breathe as I said, "Take me flying again when you're sober, and I'll forgive you."

"Are *you* sober?" The disgusted accusation in his voice enticed a laugh from me.

"Yes, as a matter of fact, I am."

"Why?"

"Anwir said–"

A long, cool finger pressed against my lips, silencing my voice and every thought in my head.

"I'm going to tell you a secret." He blinked, as though struggling against the fairy wine for control over himself. When his eyes opened again, he leaned closer, and that finger still held my mouth. "It doesn't matter what Anwir said."

I huffed and dared to pull his hand away from my face. His fingers curled around mine, not squeezing, but sure and firm as our hands dropped, suspended between us.

"Try telling him that," I groused. Why couldn't I slacken my hold? Why did I make no move to let go? Why did my lips tingle with cold in the absence of his touch?

"Do you want to know another secret?"

Did I? Another dark revelation might be enough to tip my sanity over the edge. My mouth dried up at the thought of what new horror I was about to discover.

His eyes lifted to my hair, or maybe the tiara atop it. He peeled a sodden lock from my face, twirling it around his finger. "Your hair..."

I clenched my jaw, bracing myself for another insult or lecture on practicality, and readied my well-used retorts.

"It's mesmerising."

Surprise parted my lips. Idris let my sodden strands slide free of his grasp. He followed its movement, before shifting his drowsy gaze back to my face. "I don't know how to look away."

His hand, still held in mine, was a burning brand against my skin. I knew I should pull away, but I could have sooner sprouted wings and flew back to the human world. *My* world, I reminded myself. And I was going back to it.

Idris' thumb swept over my knuckles as he gazed down at me. Was he going to *kiss me?* Something fizzed in my belly, some misplaced thrill that surged through my veins, chasing away all common sense. My eyes, my stupid, foolish eyes, fluttered to his lips.

A faint, tinny whistle filled the distant recesses of my mind. A warning. A far-away siren's wail. It brought with it a million reasons to put a stop to… whatever this was, not least that he was sozzled and probably had no idea what he was doing. Whatever regrets he had come morning, I would not be one of them.

I cleared my throat, taking a hasty step backwards. His hand slipped out of mine.

"Now I *know* you're drunk." I injected my voice with a hefty dose of cheer. "Sober Idris would never say anything flattering to me."

"S'because he's an idiot," the prince observed with the solemnity of someone describing a different person entirely. "Drunk Idris is smart."

I raised my eyebrow, crossing my arms over my chest. Nothing about this encounter had been smart. "I think drunk Idris needs to sleep it off before he says anything sober Idris will regret."

The prince grinned sleepily. "He won't even remember."

My lips twitched. He was probably right. "Come on. Let's leave poor Saeth to get his beauty sleep, and get you to bed? I think you've had enough partying for one night, haven't you?"

"What about you? You haven't had any wine!" He straightened, his outrage teasing a laugh from somewhere within me. At least I still had some humour left.

"I don't mind, I'll have some next time."

He peered blurrily at me. "Don't let Anwir tame you."

I really did laugh at that. I was hardly a wild child. I might enjoy a good night out, but I was a model student and a perfect daughter. My life's ambition was to deserve my parents misplaced pride, repayment for all they'd given up for me. I was far from needing taming.

I grasped Idris' wrist, wrapping his heavy arm around my shoulders. "Don't worry about me. Come on, but remember, don't squish me. You'll have to walk."

"I'm good at walking," he declared, staggering and dragging me sideways as he set off towards the shadowy castle.

I bit back my smirk. "You certainly are."

What anyone would have made of us if they'd seen us weaving and staggering through the hallways, leaving a trail of muddy footprints behind us, I had no idea, but we passed nobody. Distant music drifted through the empty halls, signalling that Anwir's party had continued indoors. I had no desire to rejoin the celebrations.

It was slow going, despite Idris' bold claims of talent. We stepped sideways just as much as we did forwards, and more than once, he slumped against a wall or a bannister, and stayed there long enough to have me worrying that he wouldn't get back up. My spine was aching by the time we arrived at the door to his room, only a wing away from mine.

Maybe I should have left him there, but the gnawing worry in my belly had me hauling him through the door and to the foot of his bed. The next thing I knew, Idris gave up completely, and dropped face down onto the mattress like a sack of boulders, with me still clamped under his arm.

A face full of thick blankets muffled my squeal. I twisted and squirmed, but Idris draped half on top of me, his arm wrapped around my neck and a long, heavy leg tangled with mine. He made no effort to release me, damn him.

"Idris," I spluttered, managing to get my arms under my chest and push back against his immense weight enough to breathe. "Let go."

No response.

A glance over his shoulder confirmed he was indeed asleep. Great. Just perfect. Well, I certainly wasn't going to allow myself to be found in his bed come the morning. I mustered all my inconsequential strength and wriggled backwards, freeing myself from his arm. My beautifully styled hair hung tattered and limp around my face, the pins pulling uncomfortably at the back of my head, but I was half free. Without his arm strangling me, I crawled further up the bed, pulling my leg out from under his.

My shoe landed on the floor with a thump.

Panting, I twisted and surveyed the disaster before me. Idris slumped face down on the bed, his legs hung off the end, the arm he'd trapped me with twisted awkwardly. He looked as uncomfortable as it was possible to be.

For whatever reason, a soft smile curved my lips at the sight of such a mighty fae prince, looking incredibly, vulnerably human. No, we weren't so different at all. The last traces of any lingering wariness, any justified dislike, had already melted away during our earlier hug, but I softened further as his deep, slow breathing filled my ears.

Was his sleep a peaceful one? It looked it, but then, the cursed slumber had seemed peaceful too. I knew differently now, but if he'd resented me for waking him, then surely his dreams were better than his reality? Surely this sleep would be a respite from the pain?

I shook my head, my ruined hairdo flopping from side to side. The prince might be good at walking, but I was supposed to be good at healing things. It was my job. My life. Physical wounds were a different beast entirely than the mental sort, and this suffering was beyond me, but I couldn't turn away. If the only way I could help him was by giving him a good night's sleep, then so be it.

Sighing and standing atop the mattress, I kicked off my remaining shoe and hitched my voluminous, sodden skirts around my knees as best I could. This wasn't going to be easy. Idris was enormous. If only I'd shown the slightest interest in the gym back in the real world.

I began by untwisting the prince's arm, laying it flat at his side, and then with much wriggling and pinching, I forced my hand under his shoulders and hooked them in his armpits. What people would think if they walked in now...

Crouching low, I hauled with all my inconsiderable might. Idris shifted maybe an inch. Great. Now what? Taking a deep breath, I heaved again, throwing all my weight back. Just when I thought I was going to give myself a brain haemorrhage, he moved, sliding up the bed. I staggered backwards, dragging him with me for a few ungainly steps. His feet still dangled over the edge of the mattress, but it was an improvement. It would do. I waded to the edge of the bed and hopped down, removing his boots from his limp, uncooperative legs.

My skin was hot and flushed by the time I tossed them aside, my hair like a bird's nest. I had no choice but to abandon the party, even if I'd wanted to go back. Anwir would just have to carry on dancing with everyone else. I gazed at Idris' pale, perfect face, so similar to his brother's, but different, somehow. I couldn't put my finger on it. There was no difference I could see, but maybe it was just a feeling. A sense. I knew Anwir better, and I'd thought I knew Idris as well as I wanted to. But now...

I'd been wrong about him. If he was cold or cruel, it was only because he was trying to push people away, to protect himself, or maybe them. Who was he, really? Someone who'd risked his neck to save me in the caves. Someone who'd hunted to feed his hungry campmates. Someone who'd knelt in the blood beside me and fought to save a life. He'd taken me with him to Tir o Hydref when he really hadn't had to. He'd taken me flying, and cared enough to make sure I was warm afterwards. *That* was who he was, and no amount of pained lashing out would change that.

Poor, sweet prince.

I sank down beside him, rolling him onto his back. He stirred, muttering, his head flopping to the side. An errant tendril of dark, damp hair fell into his eyes. I reached to smooth it away, but he grumbled again, and closed a hand around mine, pulling it to his chest. He rolled onto his side, cradling my hand, curling around it, and my heart spasmed once more. Only this time, the sorrow I felt was all my own.

30

Opening Pandora's Box Was Not My Finest Idea

When I woke the next morning to sunlight streaming into my room, it was with a clear head and a renewed sense of purpose. For the first time since I'd gone into that God-forsaken Fairy Glen, I was doing something that *I* had decided to do, for reasons that belonged only to me.

I would stay.

Not forever, but at least until King Maelgwyn was defeated. And while I certainly applauded Anwir for his determination to right his kingdom, it wasn't the only factor for me.

Idris was.

I couldn't leave him.

Whatever haunted him, I would be there for him while he worked through it, whether he wanted me or not. At least for a little while. His early anger toward me was nothing more than him lashing out in pain at the worthiest target. I had woken him. I had brought his senses back. While I didn't regret it, while I knew it was right, it was also my undeniable responsibility to support him, even if all I could do was hold his hand while he found someone better qualified to help. Before I could do that, I needed answers to my questions, and I doubted I was going to like them.

I dressed in a hurry, throwing on my trusty shorts and t-shirt and dragging a brush through my hair. I'd had the good sense to remove all the pins last night, even though my hands had been clumsy and shaking as I played over the evening's unexpected turn in my mind. I'd barely noticed what I was doing, so it came as something of a surprise when I saw the beautiful, tousled head of curls I'd been left with this morning. I combed my fingers through the thick waves, smoothing the strands with a drop of oil, and left my hair loose.

Presentable, I dashed from my rooms in search of Anwir.

I didn't need to look far.

The prince's room was located in the same wing as Idris', a short walk from my own. Nervous anticipation fluttered in my belly at the sight of his door. As Anwir wanted me to fool the world, he would have to agree to my requests. And answer my questions, however prying.

I knocked once, letting myself in.

Anwir was standing at his window, staring out at whatever his view might be. I'd never been in his room before, but a quick peek showed it to be almost identical to mine, even down to the closed door leading to what I presumed to be a bathroom. Was his bath made of rose quartz too, or did princes get something a little less pink?

The door closed behind me, and I turned my attention back to Anwir. He was still staring out of the window. Had he even noticed my arrival?

"Hello? Anwir?" I took a few steps closer.

At the sound of my voice, he turned, grim-faced. He held something glittering in his hands. I looked closer.

My tiara.

My mouth fell open, and I touched a hand to the top of my head. How hadn't I noticed it was missing?

"Oh my God, where did you find that?"

"Perhaps you should tell me."

His tone was cold. I frowned in confusion. "Anwir, wha—"

"Imagine my shame when the servants delivered this to my room this morning" — his voice rose steadily with every word, until he was shouting — "and told me that my queen's tiara was found in my brother's bed!"

He hurled the tiara. It hurtled past my head before I had time to do more than blink, close enough to ruffle my hair, and crashed against the wall behind me. Though my muscles tensed, I didn't turn to look, but judging by the clatter and tinkling, some stones had fallen loose and scattered over the tiles.

"What the hell do you think you're doing!" I screeched, my hands balling into fists. "That nearly hit me!"

"What was your jewellery doing in Idris' bed?" he countered, his face alive with fury. "If your jewellery was there, then you were too!"

"Yeah, I was, and what? That's actually why I came to see you, but if you're going to be such a dick, then you can go fuck yourself." I made to turn away.

"Because my brother is fucking *you*, is that it?"

"How dare you?" I rounded on him. I didn't care that he towered over me. I'd never let any man scare me, and I wasn't about to start now. "Not that I have to explain anything to you, but I'm pretty sure your precious brother was trying to kill himself last night. I stopped him, and I put him to bed. I guess my tiara got knocked off while I was struggling with an unconscious male twice my size. I was coming here to see if you knew anything about it, but if this is how you think you can speak to me, then as I said, *go fuck yourself*."

I snarled the last words, before spinning away with every intention of leaving, but Anwir snatched my wrist.

"Aliza, wait. What did you say?"

The touch of his hand had my skin crawling. "Get off me."

He didn't. "What did Idris do?"

"Ask him yourself," I said in a slow, simmering voice. "And get your *fucking* hands off me."

He dropped my wrist. All traces of anger had gone from his face. "I'm so sorry, Aliza, I thought—"

"You jumped to conclusions." To be fair, I probably would have jumped to the same one, in his position, but that didn't lessen my outrage. "And you threw a fucking crown at me!"

"Not *at* you." He dragged a hand over his face. Shadows hung under his eyes. I'd left the party early, but it was clear he hadn't. Had he spent all night dancing with any woman who'd have him? Had he brought his favourite back to this very room, and then had the audacity to challenge *me*? "I didn't mean... I was angry and humiliated. I thought..."

"I know what you thought." And it didn't justify assault.

"It's just that... It's vital that people believe our relationship is real. What if the witches talk? I can't—I can't have people thinking you're dallying with Idris."

"Maybe it'd be better if you take me home, like you promised," I suggested coldly, knowing full well how vital I was to his plan.

"No, please. Aliza, I'm sorry." He reached for my hands, but I shifted away. "Please forgive me."

"No," I said flatly. "I won't." I dodged him, walking further into his room, and halted before the window, turning to face him as he'd done to me. "If this is going to work, we need to lay some ground rules. First and foremost, I do not, in any way, shape or form, belong to you. You don't get to police me. If I want to fuck your brother, or anyone else for that matter, I will, and there's nothing you can say or do to stop me."

The colour drained from his face.

"This is a *ruse*," I went on, relentless. "I'm not yours. I never will be. I have no intention of marrying you. You already know that, so please understand, you can leave your possessive bullshit at the door where I'm concerned."

"Aliza—"

"Secondly," I raised my voice. "Tell you minions to stop calling me 'the Human Queen'. I'll be known as *the queen*, or I'll go home. Do you understand?"

"Aliza, please."

"I said, do you understand?"

"What if I want you to belong to me?"

For half a second, I faltered at his words. Did he actually want me? Had the discovery of my tiara riddled him with jealousy? *Him*, a prince, pining over *me*?

"Then you're about to get a crash course in disappointment." As though I would ever want to be with anyone who could blow up like that. Maybe his abusive tactics had worked on other females, but not me. It didn't matter how beautiful he was, I knew my worth. "This is the last time I'll ask you, Anwir. Do you understand?"

"Yes," he relented, his tone desperate. "I do, but... do you-do you *want* to... My brother—"

For some reason, my ears began to warm. "Not that it's any of your business, but no."

He deflated, relief washing over his face. God, he was pathetic. How hadn't I noticed it before? Was I really so easily blinded by a pretty face?

"Speaking of your brother." I folded my arms, leaning against the windowsill as I glowered at Anwir. "What happened to him? Why does he want to die? Do you know?"

"Yes." My stomach flipped as Anwir heaved a sigh. I'd half expected him to deny all knowledge, to insist I was mistaken, but he crossed to the bed and sank down on the edge of the mattress, burying his face in his hands. "I do know. I should have... I've been so preoccupied with my kingdom, I never thought—"

"What happened?" I didn't care about what Anwir thought. I cared about what had happened to Idris. I cared about answers.

Anwir looked up at me, his green eyes full of grief. He looked so much like his brother that it was like a slap to the face. They were identical, but I was beginning to tell them apart. Not just by their hair or attitude, but in little ways, ways I couldn't quite place. I couldn't explain it, but I could see the difference, most of the time. But when he looked at me like that, Anwir may as well have been Idris staring up at me. Apart from the smile. It was the slightest of differences, but Anwir's was cover model symmetrical, while Idris' was endearingly lopsided. Not that anyone was smiling now.

"He had a child," the prince said, his voice soft and tinged with regret. Ice cascaded over my skin. *Had*. "A boy. My uncle, he... In the last days before the curse, he'd taken us prisoner. He had the boy killed. Idris was forced to watch."

"Oh my God." I pressed a hand to my chest, where last night I'd been hit by a stream of agony. It hurt again now, a pulsing pain that robbed me of my breath. "Oh God, that's terrible."

No wonder. It was no wonder poor Idris had tried to fly. Tears blurred my vision, but I fought them back. I couldn't let Anwir sense weakness. He'd use it against me somehow. I wasn't sure how, but I didn't trust him, not after last night and this morning. Fae were clever. Manipulative. Tricksters. I would keep him at arm's length, even now, when the world was crumbling beneath my feet.

"Indeed. He was barely two years old."

Every breath was like fire in my constricted throat. I had to get a grip of myself. "I thought-I thought fae couldn't harm blood relatives?"

"Not all fae, just my bloodline, and unfortunately, the protection doesn't extend to half-fae. Idris' wife was a human, like you. Queen Claudia was not specific enough in her wording, and her protection did not extend to the child."

Fae and their stupid bloody word games.

"I didn't know he was married," I said, trying to steer the conversation into slightly less turbulent waters.

Anwir gave me a sad smile. "Idris has always been a law unto himself. Don't misunderstand me, he took his duties seriously, but in his downtime... he was untameable. Nobody could tell him what to do. He spent half his life out in the wilds with our border patrols. He learnt how to track and hunt. He loved to fly. He joined the aerial cavalry the very day he was old enough." Anwir shrugged. "I never liked flying much, but from the moment he was assigned to a drift, his feet barely touched the ground. Anyway, I suppose he met a common girl, and not even a year later, a half-fae baby was bawling in the cradle. He married her, this woman, against everyone's will. He was young and reckless, determined he knew best. My father was furious for the longest time, but he came around. Idris had his son at court more often than not, which is how my uncle came to know of Taryn's existence. And now he's dead."

"What about his wife?"

Another shrug. "Who knows? We were put to sleep not long after the murder. Whatever happened, she's long dead too."

I'd never wanted children. I'd seen first-hand how my parents had given everything in their quest for a family, how they had put their lives on hold, emptied their savings account, how they had struggled ever since. I didn't want that for myself, but I also knew how much Mum and Dad loved me. How much Idris had loved his little boy. My heart bled for him.

I dashed a tear from my lash line, sniffing.

"That's why he hates you, I think," Anwir went on. "He blames you for bringing us back. And you're human, like her, but you're alive and she's not."

"He doesn't hate me," I said without thinking. He'd told me as much himself. He wanted to, but he couldn't. God, if I was in his shoes, I'd want to hate me too. "Why didn't she become immortal when they married?"

The question of immortality hadn't been far from my mind since I'd woken the princes, but somehow, I'd never put much thought into how it would happen. There'd always been something more pressing to stew over. If I had to guess, I'd have said it was part of the wedding ceremony, that when I, theoretically, married Anwir, I'd become like him. After all, the promised reward for breaking the curse was immortality *and* a royal husband.

Anwir frowned up at me from his bed. Maybe I'd guessed wrong.

"Nobody told you how this works?"

"Not that part, no," I admitted grudgingly. There was nothing worse than ignorance. I should have asked more questions instead of being blinded by my desire to get home.

"If only it were that simple. Immortality is not something to be doled out like grain to the poor. It is a rare gift, and those in possession of it guard it fiercely. Idris is one of those few, but he didn't use it on his wife. Rhodd Anfarwol we call it. The everlasting gift. It can only be given once. Idris and his wife agreed to wait. Their son was half-fae. Some take after their immortal parent, others... do not. Idris and Jane were waiting to see if their son was immortal. Most children begin to show magical tendencies in the toddler years. If Taryn did not, they planned for my brother to use Rhodd Anfarwol on the boy."

"And did he?" I asked, barely daring to breathe.

Anwir shook his head. "Taryn was killed and Idris imprisoned before he had a chance to use it one way or another. Jane is dead, and we'll never know if Taryn would have needed it at all. For all we know, he was immortal, and Idris missed his chance to save his wife. He will not use his power on you, Aliza. I'm sorry."

He would not... what? I scrunched up my brow. "Me? What do you mean?"

"I don't have it," There was remorse in his eyes. Was it real? "I can't make you immortal, even if you did choose to stay. To be mine."

That wouldn't happen, even if he could bribe me with eternal life. Despite that, disappointment settled over me like a cloud of fog. I'd always known my idle dreams of living forever had been just that... dreams, but the certainty that they were out of reach, an impossibility, hammered home just how much foolish, irrational hope I'd pinned on them.

"Idris could," Anwir went on, "but he won't. Not after he failed Taryn and Jane."

It didn't matter. I didn't want it. If I said it enough, I might even start believing it.

"How do you know you don't have the power?" I mused.

Anwir stared at me like I'd sprouted another head for long enough that I began to give up hope of an answer.

"Power must be balanced," he said at last. "You've heard too many stories of my uncle, I think. He is unnatural. The rest of us are never as overpowered. I have my lightning. I suppose nature spent all of my power on that, leaving no room for Rhodd Anfarwol."

It was just as well that I was going home, eventually. I wouldn't have accepted immortality, especially not from Anwir, not when I had my normal, human life waiting for me. First, however, I had matters to take care of.

I rubbed my temple, massaging away the ache that had taken root. "Right, okay. Listen, I think I've decided to stay for a while. Do not think it has anything to do with you. But I'll help you if I can, while I'm here."

"You'll stay?"

"For now. But... Anwir?" I hated asking him for anything, after what he'd done. "I want you to take me home, just for a visit. It's just that, I've been gone so long already, and my parents don't know what's happened to me. If I could go back, just for a night, I could—"

"I can't, Aliza." Anwir stood, inching closer. "I wish it were different, truly, but fae have never been able to cross. I couldn't take you. I couldn't ensure your safety, or that you'd find your way safely back to Neath. The rifts are treacherous. It's a miracle you made it here at all. I cannot risk you not coming back. I'm sorry."

My stomach plummeted. He'd promised he would escort me home after the ball. What had changed? "A witch then, if you can't go. I'm sure if you asked, one of them could–"

"Witches aren't powerful enough to protect you."

"They were powerful enough to keep me alive long enough to find *you*." With every passing minute, my regret that my kiss had woken both princes grew.

Anwir gave his head a regretful shake. "Not in the human world. Magic is weaker there. I'm sorry, Aliza, but until my uncle is defeated, I can't allow you to take unnecessary risks."

No doubt he classed drinking wine as an unnecessary risk too. It was only a matter of time before he suggested that my shorts didn't offer enough protection for my legs and decreed that I wear sensible trousers or a dowdy skirt.

"You will go home soon, I swear," he pressed, his voice imploring.

Had he forgotten that I was the one who'd decided to stay? I could have gone home a week ago if I'd pushed for it. I could go home now. I would, if it hadn't been for last night. I couldn't fix Idris' trauma or grief, it wasn't in my professional repertoire, but the fact was, he needed someone to be with him while he navigated his grief. Though he'd tried valiantly to push everyone away, this wasn't something he should face alone. The thoughts he'd had last night were normal for someone in his position. He just needed time, and a friend. As far as I could see, he didn't have one here, but maybe he knew some of the fae in Tir o Gaeaf. Maybe he just needed time to reconnect with his support network.

I wouldn't be here forever.

"I'm offering to help you, Anwir. You need me, apparently. If crossing the rifts is too dangerous for me, the least you can do is send a witch to pass on a message," I insisted. He would agree, or I would leave under my own steam. I couldn't stay if it meant abandoning my parents. I'd only send them spiralling into the same depression I wanted to guide Idris through, if they weren't already in it. What if they had the same thoughts as Idris? My innards turned to ice. No, they wouldn't go down that road, not while my body was still unaccounted for. They wouldn't give in, not while there was still the slightest ray of hope. "I could tell the witch where to find them. I could send something of mine, and a letter, to let them know I'm okay."

Anwir eyed me doubtfully, but I could almost see the cogs in his mind turning. I'd have liked to picture them straining to turn, lodged with rust from lack of use, but in reality, his mind was a well-oiled machine. He was scheming and manipulative. His doubtful expression was probably fake, part of his deception. I waited with bated breath.

"Very well," he conceded. "I can agree to that."

My strangled sound that burst from my throat was half laugh, half sob. With a violent wobble of relief, my knees threatened to buckle, and I slumped against the windowsill. They'd know I was alive, that I was coming home. A tear plunged down my cheek. I dashed it away before Anwir could see.

"Okay," I breathed, barely able to get the word out. "Good. Find a witch, and I'll bring a letter to your room this afternoon."

With news of my continued existence, my parents could wait a little while longer to see me in the flesh. They'd understand, when I got back and explained everything. They'd probably have me committed, but they'd understand. I straightened, sliding past Anwir.

"In the meantime, make a start on overthrowing your uncle."

"Wait," he called. "Where are you going?"

I didn't bother to look back as I marched across the room.

I had another prince to find.

31

Did We Just Become Best Friends?

I hovered in the shade of the stone archway leading out to the courtyard, unnoticed by Idris, who lounged on a nearby bench, sketching. I couldn't see his face, but there was no mistaking him. The sun bounced off his raven hair, revealing subtle shimmers of deepest purple and green in the dark strands. I'd never noticed the colours before.

My stomach flipped, telling me to abandon my plan and turn back, but I clutched my parcel and forced myself to approach.

"Hi," I said softly as I drew near.

He slammed his drawing book shut before turning to squint at me, the sun hitting him full in the face. His peridot eyes were bloodshot, rimmed in red and purple shadows. Too much wine, or crying? As I hadn't seen him shed a single tear last night, I guessed the former.

"I brought sustenance. Can you stomach it?"

I didn't wait for an invitation to sit. Just because he'd let his guard down once, I wasn't fooled. He would likely push back harder because of it, assuming he remembered anything of the previous night. But to my satisfied surprise, he took the parcel without a fight or sly remark, unwrapping the warm baguette. I'd never paid much attention to what he ate, so I'd gone with trusty bacon, sausage and eggs, a popular choice with the carnivores in my life. My own sandwich contained egg, cheese and a green substance that I sincerely hoped was avocado.

"Thank you," Idris muttered, staring blankly at his breakfast. I took a bite of mine, letting the silence stretch as I ate.

"As tempting as it was, I didn't poison it," I added eventually, winning myself a tiny hint of a smile. Idris took a tentative nibble, confirming my suspicions of a delicate stomach.

I waited until he'd finished, screwing his napkin up in his fist, and asked, "How are you feeling after the ball?"

He shot me a sideways, quizzical look, like he couldn't work out why I was there and being nice.

"As rough as a buzzard's crotch," he admitted, still watching me warily.

Ordinarily, I might have laughed at his phrase, but I was in no mood for amusement today. "Do you remember any of it?"

He heaved a sigh, straightening, and for a moment, I thought he might flee. My heart spasmed, but he remained seated.

"I remember you," he said softly. I met his sheepish, yellow-green eyes. "I'm sorry if I spoilt your evening."

A lock of dark hair hung over his forehead, the same one I'd touched last night. The urge to brush it out of his eyes seized me, just as it had as I'd gazed down at his sleeping form, but I kept my hands still. He'd held my hand while he slept, held it cradled to his chest. What would he say if he remembered? What would he say if I took his hand now? I wanted him to know that I was here for him, and that I would stay for him, even if I was the last person he wanted, but still, I didn't move.

"Anwir told me about your son."

His whole face tightened, muscles flickering in his jaw as he turned away to stare across the courtyard. I knew he wasn't really seeing it.

"Idris... I'm so sorry for your loss." Words I'd spoken countless times, but suddenly carried a whole new weight. "I can't even imagine how you're feeling."

His breath wavered, his only response. Thanks to the curse, this was still raw for him, even if it had happened hundreds of years ago. He'd never been allowed to grieve properly, except in haunted dreams.

"We don't have to talk about it if you don't want to." I injected a little cheer into my voice, casting around for a lighter subject. "Listen to this. Anwir and I had a fight this morning. Apparently, you knocked my tiara off. He didn't take it well when the witches went in to tidy and found it in your bed."

"What?" I had his attention again. Unflattering panic widened his eyes. "How was it in my bed?"

I pressed a hand to my mouth, stifling my chuckle. "Oh God, you don't remember that part? You were unconscious, I guess. Do you remember me escorting you back to your room? Well, as soon as you saw your bed you just gave up using your legs and fell on top of me. My tiara must have been lost in the fray."

"You took me to bed? Wait, no, I think I'm remembering." He groaned, burying his head in his hands, but he peered sideways at me through his fingers. "Did I brag about being able to walk?"

I fought against my smirk and lost. "I don't remember the details."

"Liar."

My grin widened. "Your secrets are safe with me, though, just between us, I think you'd better tone down your walking before anyone else notices."

"I do like to keep my talents under wraps."

"I've noticed." I looked pointedly at the black book perched on his lap. He stiffened. "Are you good at drawing?"

"Not bad."

"I'm terrible. I'm very much a stick figure sort of girl." My artistic abilities had ceased to develop since the age of five.

He blew an amused breath out of his nose, but didn't rise to the bait.

"Can't I see one of your pictures?"

"No."

And there I was, thinking I'd made progress. Unfortunately for him, I didn't know how to fail. "Is it because you're not as good as you say you are?"

"It's because you're an irritating mortal who doesn't know how to mind her own business."

"Just one picture." It wasn't as though I was asking for access to his royal bank account. My request was perfectly reasonable.

"No."

"Please."

He ignored me.

"Pretty please with sugar and a cherry on top?"

He furrowed his flawless brow questioningly.

"It's what my nana used to say. You can't say no to it. It's basically law." It had certainly ensured my grandad was wrapped around Nana's, and by extension, my little finger.

"I can."

"But you won't. It's impossible."

"*Fine*," he hissed, and I fought down my smile of triumph.

He angled the book away from me, his glare shifting between me and the pages he turned. Finally, he settled on a suitable image and turned the book.

"Oh my *God*."

The page was yellowed with age, but from edge to edge it was full of feathers, a study of a wing, maybe. It was incredible. Lifelike. Almost like a black-and-white photograph.

"Idris, that's amazing." I leaned in closer, studying the tiny, intricate details that I couldn't quite fathom a person creating. Every barb was shaded and defined, and yet impossibly soft. If I touched the page, I could almost believe it wouldn't be paper that brushed against my fingertips. It must have taken him hours. Days. Who was I kidding, I had no idea how long such masterpieces took to create. The prince's knuckles whitened as he tightened his grip on his precious book, as though afraid I'd make a grab for it. "Is that what you were drawing before?"

"No. It's an old one. I drew it a few... well, a few hundred years ago, I suppose."

I met his eyes. "I don't understand. Did you have this with you? In the tomb?"

"No. I went home for it."

"What? When?"

"The night we got to Nairsgarth."

"But—"

"As you know, fae can move between places," he explained before I had a chance to pry. "As long as we know where we're going. The castle itself is warded against such movement, but I left the grounds and went home for this. It's how I was able to take you with me, the day we flew Saeth. Technically, that beach isn't protected by wards as it's a border line."

"But, Idris, going home was really dangerous. What if there'd been a trap waiting for you?" It was bad enough that he'd frequented Tir o Hydref in his hunt for the horse, never mind returning to his *house*.

"If I'd gone to the palace, I'm sure there would have been, but that's not my home. Anyway, I needed this. It was worth the risk."

Where was his home if not the palace? Did he have a castle of his own, or did he mean wherever his wife had lived? Anger mingled with belated panic swirled in my veins. "It's just paper, it's not worth your life. I've got paper in my room. I'm sure if you'd have asked—"

Idris flicked through the pages, catching my attention. My words dried up in my throat when he stopped on a sketch of a smiling little boy with a shock of dark hair and wide, round eyes.

"Is that..." I whispered.

Idris nodded silently. I reached for the book. He allowed me to grasp it, but didn't let go as I steered it closer.

"I needed this with me." His voice was little more than a broken croak.

I pressed my lips together, fighting the dreadful sadness rising inside me. I didn't dare risk meeting Idris' eye, and not just because my own were suddenly watery. I hadn't forgotten the rush of pain he'd sent into me last night, and I was struggling to hold my tears at bay as it was. I was under no illusions that the prince would forgive me if a teardrop landed on his drawing, ruining it forever.

"He was beautiful." Was. *Was*. I *hated* that word at times like this. It felt like kicking the grieving person in the gut when they were already down, but what else could I say?

I drank in the image, the little peg teeth revealed by a cheeky, lopsided smile. Tiny fangs. The gleaming eyes that Idris had somehow managed to make shine like light on water. The round cheeks, rosy even in their grey shading. "He looked like you."

Past tense to talk about such an adorable little boy. God, the world was cruel. No, *people* were cruel. How could King Maelgwyn, Idris' own uncle, have ordered the death of such a sweet angel? I couldn't even begin to fathom the evil of such a mind, and I didn't want to. For the first time, Anwir's whole 'saving the world' spiel felt personal. I finally had a real stake in the game. I wanted justice for that little boy, and for Idris. I wanted it with a burning fire I'd rarely felt before in any of my endeavours. This wasn't mere obligation. *I* wanted justice.

"His name was Taryn."

"Taryn," I repeated, my voice soft, pretending I didn't already know. "I like it. It's beautiful, like him."

We lapsed into silence, each still clinging to the book, balanced between us. Finally, I loosened my hold.

"I've decided to stay, just for a little while," I whispered. "I don't want to be queen or anything. I know Anwir can't give me immortality, and that's fine." I felt rather than saw Idris' gaze drift to me, felt it brush over my skin like feathers. "I just want to help in any way I can, so I'll stay for a bit, see if I can get Anwir on the throne somehow. Mum and Dad will understand."

"You love your parents." It wasn't a question.

I nodded. "Of course I do. I wish I could show you a picture of them." I reached into the back pocket of my shorts, retrieving my long-dead phone. "This used to be full of pictures of everything I loved. Now they're all gone. Or maybe they're not, but ever since I came here, it doesn't work anymore. I can't give it up though. I guess what I'm saying is... I might not be a parent myself, and I don't know the pain of losing a kid, but... I understand why you went back for that book."

"That's the thing you almost got us killed for in the tunnels."

"Yeah. Sorry about that, it was stupid and irrational. Thank you," I looked up, meeting his red-rimmed eyes, "for not abandoning me."

I wouldn't abandon *him*.

Idris closed his book with all the tenderness of a father kissing his son goodnight and laid it on the bench between us. I tried not to marvel at that tiny gesture of trust. Not only had he let me see his work, and his child, but now he left his most treasured possession, which he'd guarded so fiercely, where I might grab it and run. How far we'd come. I should probably thank the fairy wine.

"What is it? That thing?" He jerked his head at the device in my hands.

"This? It's a phone." It was easy to forget just how little these people knew of modern humans and their conveniences. Electricity hadn't even been invented when Idris was cursed. The thought boggled my mind. "It's basically my whole life in one little rectangle. I can use it to take pictures, or speak to my friends and family, organise my calendar, pay for things. Most importantly, I can look at cute animals on the internet."

"What's the internet?"

"It doesn't matter," I said hurriedly, unconvinced I was capable of explaining such things. "The point is, this little thing is like my window back to my own world. My life. But it's broken, so the window is dark and I can't see."

"What happened to it? How did it break?"

"Well, I don't think I ever told you how I got here, but it involved a lot of water. Phones aren't supposed to get wet, but I hoped it'd dry out and start working again. Only, the battery drained too, I guess, and I have no way to charge it to see if it's broken or just dead."

Too late, I realised my choice of words. *Just dead?* I cringed, shifting in my seat as my skin heated. What an idiot. But Idris either didn't notice, or chose to overlook my faux pas. I ploughed on, determined to move away from the topic of death. "I left my charger back in the tent I was staying in, you know, in *my* world. If only I'd put it in my bag. Still, I don't suppose you have electrical plugs here."

"It charges with electricity?"

I blinked at the surprised tone of his voice, like he was as shocked as I was that he'd finally understood a word I'd said. "Yeah. You don't have electricity, do you?"

He gave another small smile. When would I get to see another wide one? "May I?"

I placed the phone in his waiting hand, hope swelling inside me, even as I tried to stamp it out. I knew better. Good things didn't happen here. But I thought of Saeth, and taking to the skies with the dishevelled prince now sat trustingly at my side. I was wrong.

There was *some* good in this world.

Idris examined my phone, turning it over and over in his long, white fingers. It was dwarfed in his enormous hands. A joke phone. I held my breath, terrified he might drop it, but he treated it with the same care he'd shown his drawing book.

The hairs on my arms rose, standing on end.

I'd barely had a chance to notice the strange reaction of my body when a faint simmering crackle emanated from Idris' *hands*. My mouth fell open as white fronds of light spread over his skin, reminding me of the little strobes inside the plasma ball I'd had in my room as a kid. The blue-white light extended to my phone, streaking over the screen.

I stifled my gasp with a hand clapped to my mouth when a symbol appeared on that stubbornly dark surface. A battery, filling before my eyes.

"Idris!"

The battery filled in record time, and the electric light faded into nothing, leaving only my phone lying in the most extraordinary hands I'd ever seen. I forgot my manners, snatching it back and pressing the power button down.

I sobbed, half in delight, half in dumbfounded disbelief when the screen fired up. "Idris, you fixed it!"

My hands shook as I keyed in my password and my background appeared, a close up of me and my friend, Abby, both a little drunk and clutching cocktails, beaming back at me. I'd almost forgotten what she looked like. I stared at the image for a long moment before my watery eyes drifted to the symbols in the top corner. No signal. Not that I'd expected there to be. Even that couldn't dampen the sheer joy I drowned in. I flicked through my apps and clicked the gallery.

Tiny square glimpses of the life I'd left behind unfolded in my hands. "Oh my God. *Oh my God!*"

Without thinking, I twisted, throwing my arms around Idris' neck, my phone still clutched tightly in one hand. "Thank you, thank you, thank you!"

An awkward pat landed between my shoulders, nothing like the bone crushing squeeze I'd been enveloped in last night. My smile widened, even as tears tumbled down my cheeks.

I let him go, dashing the back of my knuckles over my wet face. "How can I ever thank you?"

"You just did. Three times, in fact."

"No, but really. This means everything to me." My words ended with a squeak, and I stopped talking before I dissolved completely.

"Consider it payment for me ruining your ball."

"You didn't ruin anything." He blinked at my words, as though he didn't quite believe them, but excitement rushed through my veins like the magic undoubtedly rushing through his. "I had no idea you had electric magic. Isn't Anwir's power lightning? Do you have it too?"

I could have sworn I'd heard that Anwir was the only fae with lightning powers, but I must have jumbled the facts somewhere along the way. There had been a lot of unbelievable information to take in, after all.

"Only a tiny bit, not enough to do anything useful."

Was that why he had the power to grant immortality? Because his lightning magic was weak? Anwir had said fae couldn't have too much power. Weak or not, Idris' power was a gift.

"It *is* useful," I insisted. "Honestly, this means *so* much to me, you have no idea."

One side of his mouth curled up as he nodded at my phone. "Do me one favour? Don't tell anyone I did that. I have an image to protect."

"Ah yes, the brooding, bad-tempered prince image. I would never dream of spoiling it for you."

"Good." He smiled. A proper smile, showing all his teeth. My belly flipped again, and my breath hitched. I'd done it. I'd won a genuine smile. Pride swelled in my chest. This was worth more than any good grade. "Now, I believe you promised to show me photos of your parents?"

My parents. I scrolled eagerly, my heart swelling with such happiness that it threatened to burst out of my chest and soar on silver wings.

"Look," I said, shielding my screen from the sun. "This is my mum. We went out for breakfast on Mother's Day. We had the best waffles *ever*."

Idris leaned in close, as I showed him picture after picture. My family, my friends, my life. He smelled faintly of wine and bacon, but I didn't mind a bit as he let me share my world with him.

A human and a fae who had lost everything but their memories.

32

In My Defence, It Was Hot

My pillow was drenched. I couldn't remember ever crying as much. I was half joy, half crushing heartbreak. Idris had given me the most precious of gifts, and at the same time, shattered my soul. We'd parted ways with a promise to charge my phone whenever needed and, I thought, a tentative *something* growing between us. Maybe not friendship, but understanding.

But just because he'd promised to charge my phone, it didn't mean I had to go skulking back that very same day, so reluctantly, I closed my screen, hiding my photos and videos from view. I'd spent much of the last few hours laid on my bed, quietly weeping over my camera roll, remembering half-forgotten faces, listening to voices and laughter I sometimes believed I'd never hear again. Interspersed with images of my own life came flashes in my mind of Idris' son, smiling up at me, eternally two years old.

I couldn't wallow forever. There was pressing work to be done.

Pocketing my phone, I slid from the bed and donned my shoes. A glimpse of my reflection showed blotchy, red skin, and eyes swollen from crying, but I merely splashed a few handfuls of cold water over my face and smothered myself in the magical dewy cream I'd used the previous night before I left my suite. My pride was unimportant in the face of bringing a modicum of peace to Mum and Dad.

On my way out of the door, I picked up the sealed envelope containing my letter home. Several ruined drafts littered the desk, some discarded because my shaking hands had taken a long time to steady, others because I'd struggled to convey my continued existence while also justifying my absence without leaving my parents to question my sanity. In the end, I'd left out any mention of Neath, settling for simple assurances that I was safe, and would return home as soon as I could. I'd explain the rest in person. They wouldn't believe a word of it, but I owed them the truth. Until then, my handwriting and promises would have to do.

For that, I needed the rightful king.

For the second time that day, I found myself outside Anwir's room. Faint voices drifted from the crack in the slightly open door, and when I raised my fist to knock, I paused at the sound of my own name.

"Aliza told me what you attempted last night. Are you a fool?"

I'd never heard Anwir sound like that, not even when he'd raged at me over the tiara. His voice wasn't raised in anger, but dripping with loathing and disgust.

"No more than you believe her to be," a second, almost identical voice retorted. "Why did you lie to her?"

Anwir had lied to me? My hand dropped to my side, and I edged closer to the door, pressing my ear to the crack.

"About what?"

"Immortality."

"You don't know what you're talking about."

"I know that she believes you can't do it."

My stomach dropped, goosebumps peppering my skin.

"What does it matter? She's mortal. A few decades and she'll no longer be a problem."

"Then all of that, last night... that was an act?"

"Of course it was. You didn't seriously believe I would lower myself to immortalise a human peasant? I can only do it once, Idris, and I don't intend to waste it."

"This is about the witch?"

Witch? What witch? Anwir didn't answer.

"She broke the curse." Idris' voice was low but simmering with barely contained rage. "You parade her as the Human Queen. Do you think our people will stand for her being set aside as soon as a crown is on your head?"

"*My* people. Remember that, brother. And of course I don't think that. I'll do my duty to them and marry her, make a few princes of my own, and when she's dead, there'll be a new queen."

"A witch queen?"

"Yes. But in the meantime, I have a prophecy to fulfil."

"You need to tell her the truth. She won't care. She doesn't want to be queen."

"Idris, how many times." Anwir sounded beyond exasperated. "I need living heirs, and I cannot get them from a witch. Aliza will come round, she'll marry me. But not if she knows the truth."

"By our own laws, a marriage based on deception would be invalid, you know that! What if someone discovered your lies?"

"I don't need it to be valid. I need heirs, and a disposable queen. Aliza will be dead before anyone can question its legitimacy, but she'll leave a brood of princes and princesses behind."

"And what if those princes and princesses inherit their mother's mortality? Did you think of that?"

"Oh, please. Of course I did. Never fear, Idris. Humans are fertile little whores, as you well know. There's bound to be at least one immortal amongst the children."

An icy silence followed Anwir's statement. When Idris spoke again, his voice oozed venom. "You don't care about the others?"

"I suppose I'll mourn them when the time comes, but as long as I get an heir, all will be well."

"What if you don't? What if they're all mortal?"

"Then I'll pick my favourite and use my gift. It would be regrettable, since I plan to use it on my future queen, but we all have our priorities. Not that it will come to that."

I'd heard enough.

One foot. Then the other. I concentrated on that simple action as though I was learning how to walk again after a terrible accident. I couldn't feel my body. Only my heart, thudding like a war drum in my ears. But with every step along the stone corridors, feeling seeped back in.

Shock. Anwir's ruse had been grander than I'd ever imagined. I'd thought I was in on it. I'd believed him when he'd said he'd take me home.

Hurt. He'd tried to make me like him, and shamefully, he'd almost succeeded. If not for his comments at the ball and his subsequent actions, I'd still be eyeing him up. I'd been fooled by his handsome face and charming act, but that was all it was. An act. He was already counting the days until my death, leaving him free to marry some *witch*. Not before I'd pushed out a few little princes for him, of course.

But worse than any of that, Idris was in on it. Idris had listened to me repeat Anwir's lies, and he hadn't said a word. Not to me, anyway. And to think I'd wanted to help him. To think I'd wanted to ease his pain.

By the time I made it back to my rooms, I was trembling, trapped in a cyclone of raging emotions, threatening to break me into pieces.

"Hello, belle fille."

I couldn't even find it in me to jump.

Jacques sat outside my open window, his legs dangling over the sheer drop to the sea far below.

"What are you doing here?" My dull voice came as a surprise, considering the strength of everything I was feeling.

"I heard about your little party. Did poor Jacques not warrant an invitation?"

I turned the lock of my door, determined to keep lying fae and witches on the other side. I was exhausted. Hours of crying and utter betrayal were a potent mix. I plonked down on the edge of my bed and lifted my eyes to Jacques' over-large ones, prominent in his starved face.

"I didn't have your address."

The vampire tutted idly. "You know where to find me."

"Yeah, lingering behind bushes and lamp posts. It wouldn't surprise me if you were at the ball."

He grinned his toothy grin. "Perhaps I was."

I wasn't in the mood for whatever this was, some game or dance with words. I wanted to lie on my bed and think. I wanted to down a bottle of wine. I wanted to put on a nice dress and find a nice man and work out my rage.

I might not have the dress, but a man had delivered himself to my room.

"Jacques," I said. "Come in."

"Quoi?"

"Come in. I'm inviting you in."

Maybe I was an idiot, letting a vampire into the coven. Maybe I didn't care anymore.

Slowly, his eyes fixed on me, Jacques lifted one leg, then the other, over the window frame, and hopped down to the floor.

For a heartbeat, I felt like prey. A rabbit facing down a wolf. Maybe I didn't care about that either. I shoved myself to my feet, closed the distance, and kissed him.

His back collided with the windowsill as I cupped his face, holding his lips against mine. He didn't fight, but he didn't reciprocate either.

I pulled my lips from his, barely. "Bite me," I breathed.

"Aliza, no."

"You're hungry. You're starving. Let me help you." I had to help *someone* in this horrible world.

"I cannot."

"You can. I want you to." I tilted my head, exposing the side of my neck. He stiffened, tension rolling off him in waves. "I trust you."

"Oh, mon amour, you shouldn't." His pierced lip brushed my skin, the metal hoop cool and smooth, sparking a glittering cascade of shivers over my body.

"You want to." My voice was pleading and breathy.

He didn't deny it. Hands drifted to my waist, featherlight. I squirmed, pressing the length of my body against his. My hand slid into his long hair, closing at his scalp, and I turned his head to me.

Our eyes met.

His lips crashed to mine, and for the first time, I registered the chill in his skin, in his tongue as it lapped against mine. I didn't mind. All I cared about was hiding from the betrayal I would eventually have to face. About freeing myself, proving that I made my own choices. That I was nobody's pawn.

Jacques twisted, and then I was the one pinned with my back to the open window. The twilight breeze caught my hair, teasing it out over the ledge. He arched me onto the sill, his mouth travelling down over my throat. A thrill of fear surged through me, swirling headily with the touch of his cold hands as they swept down my hips. I squirmed beneath his touch, my skin warring between trying to evade the chill and wanting to feel *more*. Feeling won. I lifted one leg, wrapping it around his hips, pushing my body against his. He gripped my thigh, his nails biting the flesh exposed by my shorts.

His other hand dragged up my top, and I lifted my arms as it slid like liquid over my head. Thank God I'd worn a pretty bra when I went hiking. I felt everything through the lace as Jacques dropped his head lower, kissing and nipping, and a moan slipped past my lips.

As though the sound broke whatever restraint he still clung to, Jacques ground his leather clad hips against mine, and before I could so much as gasp a breath, he was at my neck.

Sharp, white-hot agony erupted as his fangs sank into my flesh. I tried to move, but I was pinned, his hands holding me like vices, one still gripping my thigh, the other pulling my head to the side. But as sticky warmth spread over my shoulder, the pain died away, making room for a strange, weightless pleasure. I was floating, cut adrift in a bubbling sea of need. It rose inside me, drowning my hurt, my anger, my fear. There was only Jacques, and his mouth at my neck, and the blood flowing from me to him. I wanted to give him more. Give him *everything.*

I whimpered and his fangs sank deeper in response.

How long I ebbed, I couldn't say. Forever, maybe. I grew limp, the urge to move fading from my limbs. My head might have lolled if Jacques wasn't holding it in place, cradled in the crook of his wrist. I was as light as a feather, and as heavy as a rock. The world swirled gently around me, blurred and soft as night pressed in, carried on the soothing breeze that danced through the open window.

Distantly, I thought I heard a roar.

Sharp pain cut through my tranquil daze, followed by a spill of warmth down my chest. Jacques was gone. Without him to hold me up, I slid down the stone wall, slumping, half sitting, half sprawling.

My eyes were heavy. I wanted to sleep, but shrieks and hisses drifted slowly between my ears and my brain. My eyelids fluttered. Idris was there. And Jacques. Fighting.

Fighting?

No, they couldn't do that. Through a veil of mist, I watched the vampire and fae battle, as though in slow motion. Idris was a head taller than Jacques, and I suspected he might be winning. His face was contorted with rage. I couldn't let him hurt Jacques.

I stirred, trying to shift a little more upright, but without the vampire's floaty magic, my body wouldn't cooperate. What was that, shining on the floor? I blinked. Shards of glass. My bleary gaze followed them. Someone had tipped over my dressing table, shattering the mirror.

Irritation flickered somewhere beneath the fog. That was *mine.* Why did people keep breaking my stuff?

A shadow soared over me. I tried to lift my eyes to follow, but my lids flickered and almost closed.

"Aliza? Aliza!"

It took a long time for my muddy brain to recognise my own name. With immense effort, I shifted my eyes.

Yellow and green and black.

Idris.

"No," I sighed. I didn't want him here. The door was locked. Or was it? I thought I'd turned the key... I tried to see past the bulk of him hovering in front of me, but I slumped sideways, sliding further down the wall. I never hit the floor.

"It's alright. Stay with me."

I wouldn't.

I didn't want to.

"Hold on."

I couldn't.

33

Well, Well, If It Isn't The Consequences Of My Own Actions

Stab. Stab. Stab.

I screwed up my face, tossing my head in an attempt to rid myself of the piercing pain in my neck. My efforts earned the sharpest throb yet, and my eyes snapped open as I cried out.

"Be still, Your Majesty. You're safe now."

A blurred figure hovered over me, and the stabbing pain resumed. The pain sharpened my focus, and a witch drifted into relief, dabbing my neck with a warm cloth.

Jacques.

The bite.

I bolted upright, knocking the witch's cloth aside. The room immediately swirled, like colours mixing in a pot. Hands seized my shoulders, easing me back onto the soft pillow.

"You still have venom in your system, Your Majesty, and you suffered terrible blood loss. I've replenished you to a safe level, but you need to lie still until the bleeding stops."

I was flat on my back in a strange bed, bare from the waist up but for my lacy, blood-stained bra.

"Where am I?" The brief glimpse of the room had revealed little, other than it being somewhere I didn't recognise. I could barely bring myself to wonder what magical concoction of herbs was capable of replacing a blood transfusion.

"The sick ward. His Royal Highness is here too. He got to you in the nick of time."

"Hello, Aliza." Idris' voice drifted from beside me. I blinked, turning my head. Pain speared down my neck and into my shoulder.

Sure enough, the prince occupied the bed beside me, his expression forlorn as he offered me the smallest of smiles. He too was shirtless, and as my eyes strayed to his god-like form, I found numerous nasty cuts and slices, still bleeding freely, peppering his body. Two more witches caught the rivers of blood with their cloths, pressing them to the wounds. Idris didn't flinch as he stared at me.

I lifted my gaze to the ceiling.

"What happened?" I asked nobody in particular. I remembered some of it. I'd invited Jacques into the castle, all but forcing him to bite me in a moment of rage-induced madness. The witches couldn't know that though. Nobody could.

"You were attacked by a vampire. His Royal Highness fought it off and brought you here. Unfortunately, the vampire got away, but we are conducting a thorough search."

Did it count as an attack if I'd pushed for it? Not that I'd wanted him to take me to the point of collapse, but still. I couldn't find it in myself to be angry at him. Not now that my mind had cleared, and I remembered all the reasons I had to be angry with the male whose eyes I could feel burning into the side of my face.

Biting back the pain, I rolled onto my side, away from Idris. I had nothing to say to the male who'd listened as I made a fool of myself. Who'd said, and continued to say, nothing. How long would he have gone along with his brother's deception? Until the prophecy was fulfilled? Until Anwir fooled me into loving him? Married me? Fathered a child at my expense? Or would he have carried it to my graveside, holding his tongue even as dirt was thrown down on top of me? The precious Human Queen. Human sacrifice, more like.

Not that it mattered. I had never intended to stay that long, and after everything I'd heard, I wasn't going to spend another night in this castle, surrounded by liars and users.

"Aliza!"

I jumped at the shrill voice calling my name, but my nurse pressed her hand to my shoulder again, keeping me still. Pansy hurtled around the end of my bed. Despite everything, my face softened into a smile.

"Hi."

"Mother above, are you alright? I just heard. I can't believe it." She all but threw herself onto the bed beside me, her dark eyes widening as they took in the blood seeping from my neck. "Is that where..."

I nodded and was rewarded by a stab of pain shooting down my shoulder all the way to my fingertips.

"I heard Sage telling Granny that you'd been bled almost dry. I was expecting..."

She was expecting to find me as her mother had been. My heart squeezed tight, and I reached for her hand, biting back the pain of that small movement. "I'm fine. Sore, but fine."

"You'll feel much better after this," the nurse said, brandishing a spoon at me.

I sat up awkwardly, accepting whatever magic potion they'd concocted this time. A magic potion that hadn't been available to save Hyacinth, not that it would have prevented the renewed blood from pouring straight out her severed artery. It was enough to help me though, apparently. Despite Sage's melodrama, Jacques couldn't have done *that* much damage.

Pansy dropped her voice to the faintest whisper. "And Prince Idris saved you?"

My teeth clenched. I didn't want to admit that I was yet again in his debt, not even to Pansy. I gave a terse nod.

"The vampire. Was it..."

I threw her a sheepish, imploring glance, silently pleading with her not to spill my secret. Of course she would know the truth of what had happened. What were the chances of some random vampire finding his way into my bedroom? I'd let Jacques in, I'd put the lives of everyone in the castle at risk, but she couldn't know that I'd pushed him. That it had been me who'd caused this particular mess.

Behind me, Idris snarled at a witch attempting to clean him up.

My nurse glanced at him briefly, lowering her voice as she said, "It certainly put up a fight. The prince could barely stand by the time he arrived here." At my questioning eyebrow, she elaborated. "Vampire venom induces a temporary paralysis, to prevent the victim from fighting back. Fae are more resistant than humans, but with that number of wounds, I'm astonished he made it here at all, never mind carrying you. The bite also prevents blood clotting, which is why you're still bleeding. The potion will counter that."

Idris snarled again, a guttural, vicious noise deep in his throat. Did he feel the same slicing pain that I did every time I moved? I'd done that to him. I didn't want to care, but I did. And what had I done to Jacques? If Idris was covered in injuries, what state was my unlikely, undead friend in? Could he even bleed?

"Why did he do this to you?" Pansy whispered under her breath as my nurse took the spoon away. "I thought he was protecting you."

I couldn't answer that without admitting my petulant moment of weakness. I couldn't tell her about Anwir's lies, or Idris' duplicity. I couldn't tell her I would be gone come morning, not now I knew the prince intended to hold me here for life. One whisper of my change of heart and he'd have me locked away in a tower just like the one I'd freed him from.

"I guess he was just hungry." Was that it? The best I could come up with.

But Pansy seemed content to drop her line of questioning. She brushed some hair out of my face. "You look pale. Shall I fetch something sweet from the kitchens?"

It was good to see a glimpse of my old friend, who'd smuggled cookies and cakes and fussed over me like a mother hen. "That sounds amazing. Could you leave it in my room for me? I think they're going to let me go soon."

"Of course. Do you want company?"

More than anything, I wanted to say yes, but I needed to be alone. I had no idea how late it was, only that it was fully dark outside the windows. It had been dusk when Jacques appeared. I'd wasted precious hours.

"To be honest, I'm knackered. I just want to sleep. Tomorrow though."

I hated lying. I was sick of feeling guilty. This had to end. I needed to get home, once and for all.

"Tomorrow. Rest well." Pansy gave me a last squeeze before scampering from the ward. I braved facing Idris to watch her puffy buns disappear from sight one last time. My heart sank, and I turned to stare at my lap before Idris could notice the tears filling my eyes.

The prince's nurses left, leaving us alone. The air grew thick. His gaze burnt into my back, imploring me to turn around. I could all but hear the words he held on the edge of his tongue, admonishing me. I didn't need to hear it. He'd lied to me, or at least, he hadn't told me the truth, which was just as bad. After all we'd been through together, he'd lied. Tears lined my eyes. His criticism meant nothing. I didn't care what he thought of me. Didn't care if he was furious that I'd tangled with a vampire when I was supposed to be falling desperately in love with his lying brother.

My nurse returned, and I endured her prodding and poking while studiously avoiding Idris' gaze. She tutted over the two perfectly round puncture holes, before applying a generous dollop of green paste and a dressing. Finally, with one last check of my pulse, the nurse smiled. "You're doing much better, Your Majesty." I wished they'd stop calling me that. "I'm happy for you to leave, as long as you keep that paste on until tomorrow."

"I will. Thank you."

I slid cautiously from the bed, unsure whether my wobbly legs would hold. The last thing I needed was to crumple in a heap and be forced to spend the night in the ward.

The nurse smiled encouragingly. "Send for one of us if anything changes." And with that she bustled back to what I assumed was her office.

I edged around my bed, holding the footboard until I was sure my body remembered what to do.

"Aliza."

My muscles tensed, attempting to hesitate at the sound of my name spoken so softly by a male who rarely used it, but I forced myself to keep walking.

He didn't speak again.

Somebody had been in to tidy up my room. The glass scattered over the floor had disappeared, but an empty mirror frame perched atop my mysteriously righted dressing table. A valiant attempt to clean up the blood smattering the wall had been made, though a pink tinge remained. I averted my eyes quickly. My room was otherwise as it had always been, apart from the door. Idris had all but shattered it when he'd broken through. It hung crookedly from its hinges, with several buckled, splintering planks, and a hole blasted through the middle. Had the fae prince punched his way through, injuring himself before he'd even entered the fray? And why? How had he known I needed him?

No. I didn't need anyone, least of all someone who'd hidden a pretty important truth from me.

I did what I could to close my door, wrestling it into the frame. There was nothing I could do about the hole. It was a good thing I wouldn't be sleeping here tonight. I turned away.

On my bed lay a little round plate, topped with an iced fruit bun. The sight had my shoulders sinking. If only I could take Pansy with me, but there was no sense dwelling on that. I crossed to my wardrobe. A deep scratch slashed diagonally down one of the doors, and I raised my eyebrows. What, exactly, had those males done to each other?

Dragging the door open, I changed my shorts for the trousers I'd worn for the curse-breaking mission, freshly laundered and free of stains, but stowed my trusty denim inside my backpack, along with my gloves. I hadn't forgotten how chilly the nights could be without a tent to huddle inside. With no alternative available, I had no choice but to keep my bloodstained bra, but I tugged my hoody over my head, wincing as it caught on my dressing. I hesitated at the sight of Jacques' leather jacket. He wouldn't have bitten me if I hadn't pushed him to it, and he'd warned me not to trust him, but still. Had there been any need to try and kill me? Uncertainty flickered in my gut. Without Idris' interference, would my vampire stalker actually have left me for dead? According to Sage, he'd almost bled me dry. Almost, because he'd been interrupted.

It didn't matter. I'd never see any of them again. As though the thought had been an order, I snatched up the jacket, stuffing my arms into the delightfully long sleeves before closing the wardrobe, hiding my ballgown forever.

I spent the next few minutes rummaging through my room, stowing anything that might prove useful into my bag. By some miracle, I still had my hand-drawn map, and the starburst tiara might be broken, but the diamonds and white gold were probably worth more than my parents' entire house. I'd consider it payment for my weeks of service in Neath. Legally, I was probably entitled to danger pay anyway.

The black daggers were no more, returned to whatever witch's trove they'd come from, but if all went to plan, I wouldn't need them. Besides, they were an ancient relic, and taking them felt a lot more like thievery than the diamonds did.

Finally, once I'd laced my hiking boots and wrapped my iced bun, placing it carefully on top of the other junk stowed in my bag, I slid my phone into my pocket. I regretted spending my afternoon draining my battery, because there was no way in hell I was asking Idris for a top-up. I'd just have to avoid the temptation to look through my pictures and hope it lasted long enough to call someone once I was back in the distinctly unmagical Fairy Glen.

Outside the window, the moon shone like a ghost, alone in an ocean of black. I blew out my candles.

34

The Bane Of My Existence

Like the castle, the dark grounds were deserted. I marched in silence through the damp grass, my attention fixed on the glimmer of silver I'd spotted in the distance.

I'd searched everywhere, and had begun to despair of ever finding Saeth when I'd glimpsed him grazing at the edge of the little copse of trees where I'd first seen Idris drawing. It made sense that the horse would linger near his master's hiding place.

The impossible creature lifted his head at my approach, pricking his ears and nickering softly.

"Hi," I whispered, despite not having seen another soul but me and Saeth. "Want to go for a ride?"

I swept my hand down his long, softly gleaming neck, and as though in answer, he nudged me with his velvet soft nose.

I smiled, but a rush of butterflies burst into flight in my belly. This was it. I was breaking free at last. "Just don't let me fall, okay? I'm a bit of a novice."

That was an understatement. I had no idea how to ride, let alone fly, but Saeth wasn't an ordinary horse. Not for the first time, I got the distinct impression that he understood every word. He wouldn't let me fall. As though proving my suspicions about his intelligence, he shifted his neatly tucked wing, lowering it for me.

"Okay." I blew out a breath, shaking the tension from my arms and shoulders. I could do this. I'd flown with him before. Maybe this time I wouldn't have a burly escort to cling on to, but I could do it. "I'll just climb up, yeah? Don't take off yet."

Saeth snorted. I'd take that as a yes

Before I could talk myself out of it, I clamped one shaking hand in his mane, planting the other on his broad back. My legs turned to jelly, but I somehow managed to climb up onto the wing joint as Idris had shown me, swinging my leg over Saeth's round rump.

I was up. Just like my first ride, the ground was horribly far away. Trying not to look down, I shifted myself forward, positioning myself in what I hoped was the best place to sit, and wrapped the surprisingly coarse mane around both hands. With my knees wedged behind the wing joints, I was as secure as I was ever likely to be.

"Right." Now the moment was upon me, I could think of a thousand reasons to slither down from my silver perch and march straight back to my room with its delightfully solid floor. "Okay."

Saeth's ears flickered in my direction, and the great wings inched low and wide. Oh God, I was going to throw up. I was going to die. What was I thinking?

A few decades and she'll no longer be a problem.

My excuses fell silent.

"East," I said, my voice as flat and cold as steel. East until dawn."

When I'd ridden with Idris, Saeth had launched straight into a gallop, flapping his mighty wings until he gained the air, but this time, he broke into a steady, if bouncy trot. My fingers tightened, clinging to his mane as I jolted about on his back. After a few strides he picked up his pace, moving into a gentle, rocking gait. Though faster, it was easier to sit to, though my bottom shifted about hopelessly, and after a few strides, my confidence grew. I leaned forward, as Idris had done, and the wind caught my hair, tugging the downy strands around my hairline as the horse eased into a gallop.

Okay, this was fast.

I screwed my eyes shut, pouring every ounce of will and focus into staying aboard. My arse thudded relentlessly up and down, even with my knees wedged tight. The wings shifted on top of them, and I felt them beat a moment before we lifted into the air. The thud when we landed jolted through me, knocking me forward, but before I had time to panic, Saeth flapped again. And again.

An impossibly smooth motion, rising and falling gently like a boat on calm waves, replaced the thunderous rhythm of hooves. The wind roared in my ears, growing colder with every passing second. I squinted through my lashes and saw nothing but inky black sky and a ghostly mane, streaming before my face.

I'd done it.

I was free.

Despite my long sleeves and trousers, I was frozen solid by the time Saeth landed on a ridge, halfway up the side of a mountain. A dark cave yawned on one side, and a sheer, deadly drop plunged away on the other.

I slid down beside the cave, still clinging to the now tangled mane.

It was a relief to find solid ground, even if it was a little higher than I'd have liked. On the horizon, a faint peachy glow warred against the black of night. The sun was rising, and I was dropping.

Trying not to think of the disgustingly comfy bed I'd left behind, I crept into the cave. Saeth followed, the clop of his hooves echoing off the walls. God, I hated caves, but this one wasn't the worst I'd ever been in. It was cold but dry, and it kept the freezing wind at bay. There was nothing I could use to light a fire, and the mountainside was barren and, truth be told, a deathtrap, but I could have stumbled upon a stack of firewood and still had no clue what to do with it.

Resigning myself to living with the bone-deep chill caused by several hours soaring through the night sky, I shrugged off my backpack and sank to the floor. My thighs ached and wobbled. Saeth hadn't flown as high as he had with Idris, which was probably the only reason I didn't have hypothermia.

"I'm going to try sleeping for a few hours," I said. Saeth watched me with gentle, blue eyes as I dug my gloves out of my bag, stuffing my numb fingers inside. "Maybe you can fly down and find some grass, if you're hungry?"

He swished his tail but made no move to leave.

I shrugged, diving back into my bag. "Here." I tore my iced bun in half and tossed it at Saeth's feet. He dropped his head, sniffing, and ate the treat in one bite.

I picked at my own half, trying to make it last. I hadn't dared venture down to the kitchens for supplies, but, with Saeth's speed, I hoped to be back in the human world by tomorrow. I wouldn't starve to death in that time, but if I did, well... As Anwir had said, I was mortal. I was only hastening the inevitable. At least if I died now, I'd die free, which had to be better than spending my life living a lie with someone who was counting the days until he could be rid of me.

Sighing, I hugged my knees to my chest and watched the light creep toward my feet. Saeth had chosen an excellent spot. The sunrise bled across the sky, and I had an unrivalled view as the burning orange turned to peach, then gold before finally settling on blue. Only then did I curl up on the bare ground, propping my head on my arm, and try to sleep.

Tired as I was, sleep wouldn't come. Not proper sleep anyway. I drifted on the edge of consciousness, never quite losing awareness of the unforgiving rock pressing against my hip, or the steady pulse of pain in my puncture wounds. Jacques' jacket creaked every time I tried to squirm into a more comfortable position, tipping the scales in favour of wakefulness. But I did dream. Nonsense, for the most part, but nonsense that brought unease to my gut, even if I couldn't grasp why. In the midst of aimless chaos, some parts made sense. I was being hunted. Foes lurked on every side, unseen, unheard, but felt. It was only a matter of time before someone caught me. I wandered, lost in pitch darkness, trying to find my way. Trying to avoid my assailants. Trying to get home.

But I wasn't alone.

Jacques.

Thank God. I almost wept. A friend. I stumbled toward him, but when he reached out to catch me, his hands were tipped in claws. He lunged for me, opening his mouth wide. A mouth full of razor-sharp fangs.

I gasped, startling from my half-slumber, and found myself inches from a shadowy wall. The cave. I was safe. I'd broken free, and up here in the mountains, nothing would find me.

I took a few deep breaths, slowing my racing heart and taking stock of my body. I huddled in my jacket, curled against the wall for what little warmth I could find, but still chilled to my core, and stiff. Everywhere ached, and I was, if possible, even more exhausted than I'd been before I laid down to sleep.

Screwing my face up at my too-tight muscles, I pushed myself upright. I found myself face to face with a pair of yellow-green eyes.

"Jesus fucking Christ!" I scrambled away, earning myself a crack to the head as I collided with the wall. "What are you *doing here*?"

Idris, leaning against the mouth of my cave, his hair ruffling in the wind, seemed supremely unconcerned by the situation he'd found me in. He didn't so much as blink as he said in a slightly accusatory tone, "You stole my horse."

Massaging my head, I allowed myself a few seconds to compose myself. The prince was dressed for travelling. Gone were the fine, embroidered jackets. He wore a dark green cloak, and the hilts of twin blades peeked over each shoulder, strapped to him by way of a leather harness buckled over his chest. My gaze drifted to his hands, folded in his lap. His split knuckles had all but healed, leaving shiny, raw red skin, but I couldn't help but notice the bandages peeking out from beneath his leather cuff. Maybe it wasn't just pathetic mortals like myself who had a hard time healing venomous vampire bites. Satisfaction shot through me.

Idris had no right to accuse me of anything. I was the one who should be angry, and yet, after my unsettling dreams, I couldn't help but breathe a little sigh of relief at his presence. It was idiotic, really. He was going to drag me back to Nairsgarth and force me to marry his brother, but even as he skewered me with his disapproving glare, I felt safe.

"Borrowed." I shrugged with all the nonchalance I could muster. Saeth himself stood near the back of the cave, watching the exchange with doleful blue eyes. "How did you find me?"

Ignoring my question entirely, Idris said, "You're lucky you didn't fall to your death. Tell me" --he shifted, uncrossing his ankles and leaning forward, the better to glare at me-- "was it desperation or stupidity?"

Why should I answer his questions when he hadn't bothered to tell me the truth? I folded my arms. "It was none of your business, Your Royal Highness."

"I found you because I know you. Your room was empty. My horse was gone. There was only one place you could have gone. Home."

I rolled my eyes at his assumption. He didn't know me at all. "Well, *obviously*, but how did you find this cave?"

Idris' smile was almost sympathetic. "It's mine. Saeth knows all my favourite camps, and as this one lies near your route to the Blood Gate, it seemed the obvious place."

He even knew which rift I'd used? "What are you? Some sort of mind reader?"

He huffed in amusement. "Just observant. You told me your arrival involved a lot of water, and I knew Sage had been the one to find you." He shrugged. "It was obviously the Blood Gate."

Arrogant bastard. I wished I'd never spoken a word to him if he was going to use them as ammunition.

"This is your cave then? You've camped here?" I couldn't picture it. This fancy, polished prince, roughing it in a hole in the mountainside when he had palaces and castles at his disposal. Though, admittedly, he looked considerably less fancy in his travelling gear, but it only enhanced his unearthly good looks. How was it fair that he looked like *that*, and I probably looked exactly like I'd flown through the night and slept in a cave after having most of my blood drained by a vampire? I felt terrible and probably looked infinitely worse. Fleeing Tir o Haf had been one thing, but I couldn't understand why anyone with a choice would want to sleep out in the wild. "Why?"

"It's your turn to answer my question."

I scowled, trying to summon some of my earlier anger, but whether it was exhaustion or my inexplicable relief at his presence, I failed. My shoulders sagged. "I overheard you talking to Anwir yesterday. I know everything. That's why I left."

Idris's already fair face paled. "I didn't want you to find out like that."

"You didn't want me to find out at all," I snapped, but even as the words left my mouth, I knew they were false. Idris had told Anwir to tell me. Maybe not with any real conviction, but he'd advocated for me. It was more than anyone else would have done. "How long have you known he was lying to me?"

"Since you told me what he'd said about immortality. And, Aliza? I wanted you to know the truth. I wanted Anwir to be the one to tell you, but he refused, so I took matters into my own hands. That's why I came by your room yesterday evening. I was planning to tell you myself."

Instead, he'd found me half naked and half dead, with a vampire at my throat. My ears began to burn, but I wasn't about to let my shame get the better of me. "What, exactly, did you plan on telling me?"

That I'd been wasting my time these past weeks? That the whole marriage fiasco didn't matter because Anwir, pathetic liar that he was, was too cowardly to save the world? He'd bailed at every whisper of danger; how did anyone expect him to defeat Maelgwyn, even with me as a mascot? He was too afraid to use his lightning, even against the shades. Any children he'd tricked me into birthing would have no throne to inherit.

None of it mattered, and nothing would change. I'd risked my life for nothing. Hyacinth and Meadow had died for nothing.

Idris dropped my gaze, suddenly intensely interested in his hands. He flexed his fingers, stretching out the shiny red marks. "Anwir could give you immortality if he chose to. *I* could. Any fae. We all have the ability to do so, it's an inherent magic, but it has its limitations. It can only be used once. In our long lives, we can only choose one person to bestow it on."

Anwir's words rang in my ears. "He didn't want to waste it on me." The human peasant. There was a witch he intended to immortalise, as though they didn't live long enough already. Either that or the heir who had no hope of ever being conceived but who was already more valuable than me.

Idris grimaced and looked up. "When a mortal is changed, it creates an unbreakable bond between themselves and their fae. Many believe it to be a boon from our first queen, a chance to share our entire lives with anyone we choose. Historically, it has been used when a fae fell in love with a mortal, which was common enough before the curse. Not only would Anwir have, as you put it, wasted his gift, but he would have bound himself to you forever, and as you heard, he doesn't want that. He loves another, and intends to use it on her. I'm sorry, Aliza."

Well, that explained everything, except who this witch was. I opened my mouth to ask who, exactly, had stolen my promised reward, but before the words left my mouth, I decided I didn't want to know. What difference did it make? "It's fine. It doesn't matter. I'm going home to live my mortal life with my mortal family and friends. That's the way it's supposed to be. I never wanted to marry him. I don't even like him as a person. There was no chance I was going to go along with his plan to breed me. I don't want kids with anyone, let alone him." I gave a thin-lipped smile. "Even a crown and immortality couldn't sway me on that."

"I would have done it," Idris said softly. "I would have made you immortal, but I knew you wanted to leave eventually. I knew you wouldn't want to be tied to somebody like me."

I blinked. "You would have used your gift on *me*?"

That couldn't be right. Anwir had said Idris would never use it on me, not after he'd missed the chance to save his human wife. Then again, Anwir had said a lot of things that turned out to be stinking, great lies.

Idris nodded, once, his expression heartbreakingly tragic. "If you wanted it."

My heart thudded against my ribs. My brain stalled. Idris, who wanted to hate me. Idris, who was mean and rude and wanted to throw himself out of the sky, would have given his one gift to me.

"But..." I gulped, reining in my rush of tangled emotions. "What about you? Why would you waste it?"

"You have a good heart. Do you forget that I knelt beside you while you battled to save the witch? And you were a friend to me when I had all but given up. You offered to stay, to free my people. You broke the curse, and immortality was to be your reward. My brother refused, but I would not consider it a waste."

"Idris," I breathed. I didn't know what to say, how to respond. He was all but offering me eternal life. The gift that was meant for the woman he loved.

Who didn't dream of living forever? My mind raced with all the things I could do with all that time. I would never get wrinkles. My hair would never turn white. My body would never sag and grow brittle and painful. But... Mum and Dad would die. My friends would grow old. Everyone I ever loved would eventually leave me to face the world alone, just like my vision in the tower had warned me. It was a bleak prospect. Lonely. A curse, not a gift.

"I wouldn't want that," I managed at last. "I mean, it's an incredible offer, and so kind, don't get me wrong, but I was never in this for the prizes. I only ever wanted to get back to my old life. It's not that I wouldn't want to be tied to you, I don't want to be tied to *anyone*. I want to be free. I want to live my own life, even if it's a lot shorter than yours. I don't want to be left alone when everyone I love has gone."

"I know." Idris gave me a rare, if sad, smile. Who could understand the pain of loneliness better? "That's why I'm going to help you leave instead. I'm going to make sure you get home. Let that be my gift to you."

What remained of my defences crumbled, and tears filled my eyes. "You're not here to take me back to Nairsgarth?"

The prince rose to his feet, unbuckling his cloak as he moved. He crossed to me, holding his head low to avoid grazing it on the cave roof, and sank down at my side. With a flourish, he draped the cloak around my shoulders, tucking it under my chin.

With his face only inches from mine, Idris met my gaze. He touched a finger to the point of my chin, his lips curving into a small smile. "Anything to piss off Anwir."

I grinned, basking in the heat of his cloak sinking into my skin as giddiness bubbled inside me. I was going home. I was really, finally going home. Before I knew it, I'd be in my own bed, in my own room, and everything would be back to normal. Except... I'd be different. However unexpected and unwanted this adventure had been, it had changed me. I would carry the scars and memories with me for the rest of my life, never able to breathe a word of them to anyone, unless I fancied a stay in a psychiatric ward.

Maybe the thrill of my excitement was infectious, because Idris' smile grew until I glimpsed his fangs. It lingered for a moment before fading into solemnity at the same time mine did, at the moment I considered the reality of leaving all of this behind.

"Would you like to teleport to the rift?" He peered into my eyes from beneath his errant lock of hair.

Would I? It would be quicker, but I was in no particular hurry to experience the crushing pressure and all-consuming nausea that came with teleportation. "How far away are we?"

His lips twitched into a ghost of a smirk, no doubt remembering how pathetic I'd been when we'd teleported the first time I met Saeth. "A few more hours of flying, or seconds of magic."

"I'd rather fly, if that's okay?" Let him laugh at my expense all he wanted, I wasn't going to be here for much longer. Besides, as ready as I was to go home, a niggling part of me recoiled at the idea of saying goodbye now, when I'd thought I still had hours left.

"Of course it is. We'll wait for nightfall, then continue under the cover of darkness. Try to get some more sleep," he said softly. "This cave is warded. You're safe here."

I didn't need to be told. I'd known I was safe the moment I'd opened my eyes.

35

Forgiveness Can Be Bought With Food

When I awoke, the first thing I noticed was the throb in my neck, courtesy of Jacques' fangs. The second was warmth. A little fire crackled at the cave mouth, casting a dancing glow over the dark rock, and filling the little space with heat. I got to my feet, pulling Idris' cosy cloak snugly around me, careful to avoid my punctured neck, and wandered to the fire, staring out at the dark sky beyond. A window to the heavens. Out here, with none of the light pollution I was used to back home, the stars were clear and bright, undimmed even by the flames. Beautiful. I itched to take a picture.

"Wait," I breathed. I *could* take a picture.

Grinning, I fished my phone from my pocket and edged out of the cave, pressing myself against the stone wall. I snapped a few photos, none of which really did justice to what I saw with my own eyes, but that I knew I'd treasure, nonetheless. I turned, planning to thank Idris again for saving my phone, but I found the cave empty.

Even Saeth had gone.

"You bastard," I snarled.

He'd abandoned me. He had no intention of taking me home. He'd lied to me, yet again. And now I was stuck halfway up a mountain with no transport, and no supplies.

"Shit." I stalked beyond the lip of the cave, and out onto the ledge.

Icy wind grabbed me, ripping my hair and cloak out into the void. I swayed and threw myself back against the wall. The ledge I'd landed on yesterday suddenly seemed impossibly narrow. Darkness stretched below me. I couldn't even see the foot of the mountain, and worse, I could see no way down. The ledge was just that. A lip of rock, jutting out of the sheer face. There was no path sloping gently down. No stairs carved into the rock. I was trapped. Panic's frozen fingers slid around my heart, squeezing tight, and I retreated back into the safety of the cave, cursing Idris with every step.

Something rustled underfoot.

Glancing down, I found a sheet of aged paper beneath my boot. I frowned. I hadn't noticed it yesterday. Shifting my boot, I plucked it up.

Aliza. I have gone to find food and will be back soon. DO NOT go anywhere. Idris

As if I could go anywhere, even if I wanted to. I read the short note again, the anger and panic leeching from my body. My eyes snagged on the angry underline. He'd gone over it more than once, etching the mark into the thick paper. I smiled at the mental image of him furiously scribbling into his precious sketchbook.

"Fine," I said out loud, as though he'd spoken the words to me instead of writing. "I suppose I'll stay."

Sitting down, I made myself as comfortable as I could, arranging the over-long cloak around my legs, and returned my attention to my phone. I had to pass the time somehow, and now that I was reunited with my living, breathing phone charger, there was no reason why I couldn't use a little battery.

I'd made it halfway through my camera reel when a clatter outside the cave had me leaping out of my skin, but it was only Saeth landing on the ledge.

Idris appeared a moment later, carrying a parcel wrapped in cloth and tied with string. I raised an eyebrow. "When you said 'find food' I assumed you meant hunting down poor, innocent, defenceless bunnies. I'm glad to be proven wrong."

"I hunted down an inn." He threw himself down beside me and set about unwrapping whatever it was he'd brought. My stomach grumbled in anticipation.

He smirked without looking at me. "Patience." Handing me a fat little pie, still warm from the oven, he said, "Don't worry, it's cheese. No meat."

"Oh." I couldn't hide my surprise. He really was observant. "Thank you."

"It's nothing."

He was wrong. To be seen, to be noticed without judgement, to be cared for, even with so simple a gesture. It was far from nothing. Though he tried to hide it under an air of aloof boredom, he was an angel. An outrageously gorgeous sweetie with a heart of gold.

I leaned against the wall, shifting closer to him under the pretence of getting comfortable. My shoulder brushed against his, but he didn't move away. I hid my smile by biting into my pie.

We ate in silence. I couldn't have spoken even if I'd wanted to. In all the turmoil of the past day or so, I hadn't had time to register just how hungry I really was. And cold. The hot cheese pie went down like the nectar of the gods, soothing my achingly empty stomach and warming me from within. Try as I might to savour it, I wolfed it down in record time and slid my eyes sideways to Idris' half-finished meal, straightening.

He narrowed his eyes. "Don't even think about it."

"I wasn't."

"Good, because mine has meat."

"Oh." I slumped back, but Idris chuckled, nudging the bundle of cloth he'd brought.

"Help yourself."

I dove forward, flipping open the folds of fabric. A selection of cakes and pastries greeted me. "Oh, you absolute sweetheart," I muttered, snatching up a sticky pastry roll and taking a bite. With a contented sigh, I leaned back, stretching out my legs. My stiff thighs ached horribly from my ride, and I didn't relish climbing onto Saeth's back and heading out into the sky again, but it would all be worth it when I emerged into the Fairy Glen.

And then I'd have to say goodbye to Idris.

It was hard to believe I'd been furious at him only a few hours ago. With a full belly, I was feeling a lot more forgiving toward the world, and toward him. Somehow, his secret keeping stung more than Anwir's lies. He should have told me the truth the moment he realised I'd been lied to, but if he'd really been planning to tell me when he'd come to my room, then I couldn't stay mad at him. He *had* saved my life, I supposed. Again.

"How are your vampire bites?" I asked tentatively between mouthfuls. My insides squirmed with guilt. All those cuts peppering his body were the direct result of my stupidity, and like a child, I'd refused to speak to him in the ward. He'd said my name, and I'd ignored him, after he'd saved my life. Had he wanted to tell me the truth about Anwir then and there, or had it been something else? I couldn't summon the nerve to ask him.

"If I'm honest, they're fucking terrible."

I stifled my snort, but not before Idris shot me a disapproving glare.

"Sorry, I'm not laughing at you. It's just... You're so fancy, it's a surprise to hear you sound so..."

"What?"

"Well... human, I guess."

His glare softened. "We're not all that different, are we? Apart from you being much more annoying."

I grinned. "Well, you know, I've got to keep you on your toes."

"Aliza, I'm hiding in a hole in the mountainside, defying my brother and king, and potentially sealing the fate of my people, and all the while, my vampire bites are stinging like a bitch. You are more than keeping me on my toes."

Well, that was sobering. "You don't have to do this."

It was too much to ask of him. Of anyone. He had enough to deal with. And yet, as the words left my mouth, I held my breath, hoping against hope that he wouldn't see sense and leave.

He shifted, turning to face me. "And yet, here I am," he breathed, his voice impossibly soft and low.

Something in his breathtaking eyes shifted, pinning me to the spot as he gazed down into my soul. The whole world stilled, centring on that little cave, high up in the starry sky, on the male before me, so beautiful and broken. I couldn't remember how to blink or draw breath. I only knew how to exist, here and now, with him. My skin tingled as though his magic was sliding over every inch of it.

"There you are," I breathed.

My gaze dropped to his lips.

Idris turned away, breaking the spell by busying himself with unwrapping a parcel of cakes. I adjusted my hair, loosening strands from my bobble to hide the tips of my ears as best as I could. What on earth had just happened, and why had it made me feel all tingly and light?

It didn't matter. None of it mattered. He wasn't mine, and this wasn't my world.

I snatched up a cake, stuffing it whole into my mouth to smother my unease. Idris twisted slowly, one amused eye peeping over his shoulder.

"Wha?" I managed to say around a mouthful of cake, hoping against hope that he wouldn't notice my unfortunate blush.

The one eye I could see crinkled as he smiled, and I couldn't stop myself from attempting to return the gesture, twisting my overfull mouth.

"I underestimated your appetite."

"Ooh werth payn ah-enshun."

Idris laughed. A real, proper laugh, not just a chuckle. His shoulders shook as the rough yet musical sound filled the cave, and my heart. How long had it been since he'd last laughed? Hundreds of years? And I'd been the one to cause it. I might not be staying, I might be unable to help him, as I'd wanted to, but maybe I'd reminded him that there were still little moments of happiness to be found. That they were worth fighting against the darkness for.

"Let's take a selfie?"

"Let's—what?"

That had his attention. I retrieved my phone and opened my camera, leaning in close enough that Idris' body heat washed over me. "Look at the screen and smile."

"Absolutely not." He tried to shy away, but I hooked my arm around his neck, pressing our temples together.

Forcing myself to ignore the warmth of his face pressed against mine, and the cool, crisp scent that filled my nose, I beamed, while he glowered. I snapped a picture. The bastard looked incredible, even when he was sulking. "Look, now I'll be able to remember your cheerful face forever."

He blinked again, and I realised what I'd said, and what he'd offered. Immortality.

"By forever I mean, just for the rest of my life."

Idris' lips twisted, and he dropped his eyes. "We should finish up and move on."

Oh.

I'd almost forgotten that we still had to travel. That I was on my way home. Idris tidied away the debris of our meal, but while his back was turned, I folded up the note he'd left me and slipped it into my backpack.

36

What If I Just... Stayed?

Despite my jelly-thighs, my next flight was infinitely more comfortable.

Idris allowed me the honour of riding up front, though one successful solo flight did not a qualified pilot make, and the prince insisted on reaching around me to take hold of Saeth's mane. I couldn't complain, not when his arms acted as safety barriers and his chest pressed against my back, blanketing me in his warmth. Maybe it should have been awkward, and maybe it was for a few minutes, but as we leapt from the ledge and soared into a pastel orange sky, I forgot that anything was less than perfect.

It *was* perfect, or so I told myself. I also told myself that the tears welling at the corners of my eyes were only because of the wind. Definitely not because some insane part of me didn't want to leave this life behind. No, it couldn't be that at all.

This would be my last flight. Never again in all my life would I experience anything like this. Oh, there were planes and helicopters, but I'd never have the wind tearing at my hair while feathered wings spread on either side. I'd never be part of the sunset in the same way. I'd never feel the swell of Idris' cheek skimming my jaw, betraying the smile I couldn't see, coaxed free by the sheer joy of the sky.

A smile as rare and precious as this flight.

Idris' chin settled on my uninjured shoulder, heavy as he relaxed against me. I wished he wouldn't. When my tears eventually escaped my eyes, he'd be right in the firing line. He'd know.

Maybe I wasn't sad at all, maybe it was just this moment being all ridiculous and emotional, affecting everyone, or maybe Idris read me like a book, because he shifted, pressing his face to my neck.

"I'm going to miss you." He shouted over the wind, but somehow, his words carried all the softness of a whisper, and the sharpness of a dagger, plunging into my stomach.

The tears streaked free and, safe in the circle of Idris' arms, I twisted. My fingers, miraculously free of the tangle of Saeth's mane, brushed the prince's temple. Even this high above the world, holding on to nothing but him, I couldn't find any fear. Not for the waiting fall at least. For the future? Maybe.

It was the easiest and most natural thing in the world to kiss his cheek.

Idris didn't flinch, didn't shy away. He held still, letting me be the one to break the contact of my lips against his skin. Easier said than done. I would miss him too, though there was no hope of the words breaking past the lump in my throat. I wanted to stay.

There it was. The cold, ugly truth. I *did* want to go home, to see my parents and my friends again, to let them know all was well, but did I want my life back? Did I really want to trade *this* for a mundane, ordinary life?

No, but I no longer had a choice. Anwir had seen to that. I turned my face forward again, clenching my jaw. Like it or not, this was my last day.

It was the right choice. The *only* choice.

One of Idris' hands loosened from Saeth's mane, snaking around my waist instead. My breath caught in my painfully tight throat, but he only held me, once more resting his chin on my shoulder. A cuddle.

I snorted, smiling and blinking away a fresh bout of tears at the same time. My hand folded on top of his, tucked against my belly. It stayed there as the sky darkened around us.

Night had fallen fully by the time we landed further along the mountain range, atop a broad, flat expanse of rock, over which a waterfall plunged. Further along, the river cut straight into the mountain face itself, disappearing into a dark cave.

"The Blood Gate is inside," Idris explained, patting Saeth's neck and vaulting from his back. "We'll walk the rest of the way."

I slithered to the ground with less grace and agility than my companion possessed in his little finger.

Home. Home was on the other side of this mountain. I gave Idris a tremulous smile before turning to the horse. "Bye, Saeth. Thanks for the flying lessons. I'll never forget them."

Saeth snorted, nudging me with a head the size of my torso. I staggered, laughing. "You're lovely. I should get a photo with you, shouldn't I?"

What he boasted in haughty elegance, Idris lacked in technical prowess. I set up the camera on my phone and steered the prince a suitable distance away. "Point the phone until you can see us on the screen, and make sure it's in focus and that you get his wings in it. Then press this little symbol on the screen." I hesitated, contemplating the likelihood of a successful first attempt. "Better press it a few times, to be safe."

He held the phone like it might take a bite out of his hand, but followed my instructions as I hurried back to Saeth's side, propped my arm on his withers, and smiled. The horse shifted a wing, tucking me to his side with the feathery joint. At least somebody understood the assignment.

"How do I know if a photo has happened?"

My smile stretched, squinting my eyes. "Did you press the symbol?"

"Eleven times so far," he said, continuing to jab the screen with his thumb, bringing to mind a memory of my dad the first time he'd got a smartphone for Christmas.

"That should do it then."

Idris sagged with relief, and I couldn't help but laugh as I rescued him from the horrors of technology. I flicked open the gallery and my screen filled with identical images of me and Saeth. They looked passable, much to my surprise. "I should have got a selfie of us flying," I grumbled. Now that I was out of time, it turned out there were lots of things I still wanted to do.

Idris' silence stretched for a few seconds, then he said, "You could stay for another day?"

"And risk Anwir catching up to us and dragging me to the altar in chains?"

"I wouldn't let him."

After his vicious reaction to Jacques, I had no trouble believing him.

Jacques. Another thing I'd have to leave behind. Not that I was feeling particularly fond of him at the moment, with a dull sting still throbbing in my neck, but I'd miss him eventually. I'd never know if he was okay.

My eyes flickered over Idris' numerous cuts. "Who came off worse in the fight? You or the vampire?"

The prince raised an eyebrow. "Do you really need to ask?"

My mouth went dry as I took in Idris' bulk. Jacques was barely taller than me, and severely malnourished, whereas Idris... well, I couldn't be sure, but I'd had his arms around me long enough to suspect that, beneath the clothes, he was something of a god. If only I'd paid attention when he was shirtless in the witch's ward. *That* would be a photo I could treasure. "Don't be smug."

He gave a velvety chuckle, but his expression quickly turned serious. "Can I ask you a question?"

"Only if you're prepared for the same evasive non-answers that you give me." I folded my arms, earning another small smirk.

His face darkened. "How did the vampire get in?"

Damn. My skin ignited, bypassing my ears completely. If only I hadn't asked about Jacques. "Through the window."

"All by itself?"

"*Himself*," I corrected without thinking. Idris raised his eyebrow again, and I conceded defeat with a sigh. It didn't matter what Idris knew; I'd soon be gone. "His name is Jacques, and he's alright. He's a friend. I met him on my first night in Neath. He's helped me."

Idris gave a sceptical snort, spreading his arms. I didn't need to see his wounds to know what he referred to. "I can't believe you let it in. It's a *vampire*. It would have killed you, Aliza. Friends don't do that."

As absurd as it was to argue against such a statement, he was wrong. It had been a moment of weakness after centuries of starvation. I wasn't about to admit to pushing Jacques though, to offering myself up as a snack, only for him to take a full banquet. "You didn't kill him, did you?"

"I tried. Unfortunately for me, it had just fed, and was too strong."

"Stop calling him *it*." I couldn't keep the bite of impatience from my words.

Idris matched me, equally waspish as he asked, "Why were you half naked?"

Why, oh *why* had I agreed to questions? Thank God for the dark, because my face burnt like a beacon. "I shouldn't have let him in," I admitted in an attempt to avoid the question and dampen rising tempers. "I'm sorry you got hurt. I never meant for that to happen. I trusted Jacques when I shouldn't have. Though, apparently, I'm a terrible judge of character, so that should come as no surprise."

His shoulders drooped slightly. "No need to apologise."

"Actually, there is. I was stupid. I put everyone in danger. Besides, this is the last chance I'll get. If I don't say sorry now, I'll spend the rest of my life plagued with guilt every time I think of your scars."

"Grief makes us reckless."

Grief. It was almost laughable. Anwir's betrayal barely registered, a blip on the radar compared to whatever unfathomable sorrow Idris suffered. The prince held my gaze as my lungs filled and deflated.

"I take it this is a no, then?"

I frowned. "No to what?"

"You refuse my generous offer to keep you alive for another day? One more flight?"

"Oh." The word turned into a smile as I allowed myself a brief fantasy about taking to the skies once more, with Idris' arms around me. As tempting as the offer was, I had a home to get back to. I conjured the image of Mum and Dad's faces when I walked through the door, alive and whole. Shock, disbelief... joy. I toyed with the golden letter A strung around my neck. I had a name to live up to. "No, thank you. I should go."

He gave a curt nod and turned to Saeth. "Stay here," Idris said with one final pat. "I'll be back soon."

Soon. I'd be home soon, and he'd be here. In different worlds.

Something swelled inside me, an emotion I couldn't quite place. All I knew was that it wasn't the excitement I'd anticipated. It was something... unpleasant. I kept it from my face, fighting it down inside as Idris and I set off, picking our way over the rock.

With every step I took along the slippery bank, war raged within me. A tornado of conflicting emotions, each fighting to be felt, to overwhelm me, but none succeeding. The effect left me half numb, half nauseous. I tried to remind myself why I was here, why I was leaving. I tried to imagine my return to Mum and Dad, how even Abby might cry when she heard I'd come home safe, but it evaded me. All I knew was that every step felt wrong.

But I didn't belong here. I had no home on this side of the rift, and only three true friends to my name. One of whom walked silently at my side, his eyes fixed firmly ahead. On the warren of caves leading to the rift, and then the human world. The place I'd always called home.

That all-engulfing sense of wrongness gripped me again. I lowered my eyes to the precarious path laid out before me and tried to remember why I'd worked myself half to death for a degree, and why I wanted to go back to that. I did want to go back. I *did*.

I heaved a sigh. I was going to miss this magical world. Or some of it, anyway. Maybe not the terrifying monsters, but I'd never go another Christmas without thinking of tiny little fairies humming over the flowers of Neath. Maybe when I was old and senile I'd tell my nurses about them, and they'd snigger and up my meds. The idea of carrying my adventure to the grave, of never sharing it, was like a vice around my ribs. I glanced at the prince from the corner of my eye. Nobody would ever know that he existed, that he'd become my friend. That he'd gifted me the sky, even if only for a moment. I could never tell a soul.

I'd never see him again.

Swallowing down the lump in my throat, I lowered my eyes.

There was no use dwelling on such things. By the time the sun rose, I'd be back in my own life, and it would be so full that I'd barely have a thought to spare for Idris and his weird but wonderful world.

Wrong. It was all wrong.

No, it wasn't. Coming here in the first place had been wrong. I was human. Mortal. I wasn't meant for this world, and everyone I loved was on the far side of the rift.

Everyone.

Idris paused at the entrance to the caves, looking down at me with eyes painted silver by the moon. As he had done the day we'd first flown, he held out his hand, palm up, waiting.

"It's dark in there," he said, his voice as soft as velvet. "I'll guide you."

Because who knew the darkness better than Idris?

Gulping, I nodded and placed my hand in his. My breath caught as his fingers closed, his cool skin engulfing mine. He dwarfed me in a way no human man ever had. Was this what it was like for short girls, to be surrounded by towering, powerful creatures, capable of breaking them? I could see how it could be frightening, but with Idris, I had nothing to fear. He'd kept me safe from the beginning, when we'd been lost in those pitch-dark tunnels. How fitting that we would end in much the same way.

I stepped close, pressing my shoulder to his arm, and looped my free hand around the crook of his elbow. Safe or not, I had no intention of being separated from him. Not yet, anyway.

"Ready?" Idris asked.

I spared one last lingering look at Neath. At the magnificent, starry sky. At the silver ribbon of the river, winding through the dark woods and the imposing mountains. Here and there, I spied tiny flecks of fairy light, vivid in a world of black and silver.

The prince squeezed my hand.

I would remember this moment forever, I decided. I wouldn't rely on photographs, which could never do it justice. I painted it into my memory, my last glimpse of Neath, and the feel of Idris' hand in mine.

"Ready," I rasped, and turned to face the gaping, impenetrable darkness of the Blood Gate.

37

What Can I Say? Emotions Ran High

I couldn't see a thing inside the cave. Darkness pressed against my straining eyeballs with a weight that made them ache. Blind as I was, my other senses sharpened. Every padding footstep was like a drum beat, marching us onward. Unyielding ridges of stone pressed through the soles of my boot. The damp mist of the rushing river, cool against my skin. Idris, warm and solid at my side. He smelt like the sky, cold and bright and fresh. I knew he could see, knew he wouldn't lead us straight over the edge of a gaping chasm, or into the river, but I couldn't help but imagine it. If the river claimed us, if we washed up in that shallow pool, maybe I'd just give up. I'd accept that Neath owned me now, and I'd stop trying to get away

But, of course, Idris made no such error. Sure footed and steady, he led me toward my home. It was a good thing he'd found me. I would never have found my way without his sharp fae eyes.

Idris stopped dead, tugging me tighter to his side. The air came alive, like thousands of tiny ants were marching over every inch of my skin, making every hair stand on end. I recognised the charge a moment before a flicker of blue-white light blazed against my retinas. Squinting, I hissed in displeasure, but my eyes adjusted. Idris' spare hand was once more wreathed in threads of electric light, only glaring because of the sheer density of the darkness.

To my immense horror, his bright hand rose up and over his shoulder, casting a glow over his hair, and closed around the hilt of one sword. Only one, because his other hand had tightened around mine. I couldn't have let go even if I'd wanted to. The blade rang faintly as he drew it, and by the time he'd brought it out in front of him, the metal was alive with electricity.

"What's wrong?" I demanded in a whisper.

His eyes gleamed like ghosts as they darted over the now faintly illuminated cave walls and ceilings, high above. Here and there, brighter spots and darker shadows stood out against the flickering light.

"Nothing. Just vampires."

"Vampires?" Fuck me, were those eyes glowing down on us? Were the creeps clinging to the ceiling like bats? I shuddered at the thought of them scurrying overhead.

"It's called the Blood Gate for a reason. There's a coven down here."

"Now you tell me?" My whisper rose to a squeak. I might have formed a foolhardy trust with Jacques, but he'd always had his motives to fight against his own instincts. This lot though? I was a banquet, dangled before the starving.

"Don't worry. They won't come near."

Easy for him to say. He wasn't natural prey, a veritable blood bank, ripe for drinking. He might be as much a predator as the monsters crawling the walls, but it didn't mean the vampires weren't desperate. Centuries of hunger might outweigh their fear of one fae prince. They might risk taking him down if it meant getting to me.

"Besides, I thought you liked vampires?" A hint of amusement danced in his voice.

"You are *not* funny, Idris."

"I happen to disagree." With his blade poised, the prince continued his resolute trek, dragging me with him.

I hunched my shoulders, trying not to catch the gleaming eyes of anything, but I could feel their hungry stares raking over me. I wanted to burrow under Idris' arm and squeeze my eyes shut, and stay like that until we came out the other side. Instead, with my heart thudding and my breath short, I took one step, and then another.

Idris gave my hand a reassuring squeeze. I tightened my own grip and didn't loosen it again.

Whose idea had it been to put a rift down here anyway? A more chilling thought occurred to me. Who had thought to locate their coven right beside a rift, and why? Easy pickings? As far as I could see, it wasn't the most desirable location. Before the rifts had closed, humans had come and gone all the time. I couldn't imagine many had made it through the warren of the Blood Gate unscathed. And worse, how many vampires had used the rift to cross to *my* world? Had they hunted there? The puncture wounds on my neck began to burn, but I resisted the urge to let go of Idris and rub my dressing.

It was a miracle I'd lived long enough to meet Jacques at all. Had I drifted down this river, unconscious, before emerging into the sunlight? I'd thought myself lucky not to have drowned, but I'd never before grasped the true extent of my good fortune.

"Aliza. You're cutting off my blood supply."

"Oh. Oh! Sorry." I hastily loosened my fingers, but only slightly. There was no chance in hell I was risking being dragged away by some fanged beast.

But Idris was right. Though I glimpsed movement and bright eyes, nothing approached as we picked our way through the caves. We were left unhindered as the ground began to rise.

Before long, I could barely hear my own thoughts over a relentless crashing roar of water, and I stopped to stare in wonder as Idris' light illuminated an underground waterfall, at least five times as tall as either of us. The path veered off around a wide pool, before twisting up the far wall at a steep incline, but Idris didn't follow it. He led me over rocks and boulders, waiting patiently as I scrambled up them, and holding my hand steady as I hopped down. By the time we reached the waterfall, I was flushed, and the icy spray came as a blessing.

It was too loud to speak, but Idris jerked his head, and together, we crept around the water's edge, pressing against the cliff face, and squeezed behind the curtain of black water, edged in blue-white light. A cave within a cave lurked behind the fall. The air was different here. Heavy. Hard to breathe. The sickly-sweet aroma of mold wafted up my nostrils, and I wrinkled my nose, wishing I actually *couldn't* breathe.

All at once, my feet slipped from under me. I lurched, grabbing onto Idris, but the world tilted anyway, spinning around me.

Then it stopped.

My feet were planted firmly on the ground, and everything was dark and damp and disgusting, just as it had been a moment ago, but I knew that everything had changed. Gone was the roar of the falls, and though darkness still pressed on me, Idris' light had sputtered out. I didn't need to see. Everything was bleakly familiar, right down to the stench.

"Is this..."

"We've crossed over," Idris answered my unspoken question. "You're home."

Well, not quite. "Can you still see?"

Idris huffed a laugh, but I couldn't bring myself to smile. "Of course I can."

"Good, because believe it or not, I don't live in a cave."

"Understood."

We began to walk again, and with every step, the cave lightened. My boot sloshed through a puddle, and I grimaced. Before long, I caught a glimpse of the Fairy Glen beyond the cave. It was...

"Daylight?" How long had we been wandering the Blood Gate? It couldn't be dawn already.

We emerged to a dismal, cloudy day. Typical English weather. Was it my imagination, or had all the colours faded while I'd been away, like a veil of translucent grey had been draped over the world? Or was it only that I'd never been exposed to the full spectrum until I'd arrived in Neath? Either way, the sight of the deserted glen didn't fill me with the same sense of joyous homecoming I'd anticipated. Even the birdsong seemed shrill, drilling into my head.

My stomach swooped at the sight of a decaying mound of bouquets, piled against the cave walls. I didn't need to read the cards to know they were for me. Faded pastel ribbons hung limp and dirty from the trunks of nearby trees.

"So, this is the human world?" Idris muttered, and I became aware for the first time since leaving the cave that he was still holding my hand.

I twisted to peer up at him. He surveyed the glen, giving no indication of his thoughts. "It's not much, I admit. And believe it or not, this is actually one of the nicer parts, not including the smell."

A faint smirk tugged at the corner of his mouth before he turned to face me. "Well, here we are."

"Yeah." I should let go of his hand. Instead, tears sprang to my eyes and my grip tightened. "I suppose this is goodbye. Just so you know, I hate goodbyes, and I'm definitely going to cry."

"I'm not too fond of them either."

"Idris..." This was it. Time to find something inspiring and profound to say, something that he'd carry with him for the rest of forever. A way for *me* to help *him* through the dark, even after I'd gone. I took a deep breath, opened my mouth, and promptly dissolved into tears.

Finally, I tugged my hand free, burying my face in my palms. Something huge and warm and smelling of a sky much brighter than this one wrapped around me. I sagged against Idris' chest, letting his strong arms take some of the weight from my legs.

"Well... that was quick," he murmured against my ear.

I tried to shove him, but the smug bastard's arms were clamped too tight for me to move. Still, through my tears, I managed a small smile. "I did w-warn you."

A broad hand swept over my hair, cradling the back of my head, holding me close. To think, barely weeks ago he'd seized me by the throat and berated me for being a liability, and now...

"Will you actually miss me?"

He snorted. "If you mean will I think of irritating mortals every time I'm trying to enjoy a moment of peace, then yes, probably."

"Good," I said, leaning back to scowl at him. "Because I'll think of you whenever I have to deal with someone who can't handle their alcohol."

"Listen, I drank *a lot* of wine that night, alright? It's strong stuff."

The smile his words coaxed out of me faded almost as soon as it bloomed. Just because I wasn't going to be there to help him, it didn't mean he couldn't save himself. "Maybe I shouldn't ask for this, but I want you to try to live, Idris." His expression froze, his eyes turning distant. He tensed beneath the hands I now noticed were pressed against his chest. I didn't dare pull away, not now that I'd started such a difficult conversation. "I want you to stay away from the wine, and to find things that make you feel happy and glad to be here. I know it won't be easy, but... try. Please. You're a good person, and I can't stand to imagine a world without you."

He didn't speak, only stared down at me, unmoving. Was he even breathing?

"Find-find someone, yeah? You're a prince. How hard can it be? Fall in love."

He shook his head fervently. What was he saying no to? Everything, or just the last part?

Finally, he swallowed. When he spoke, his voice was gruff. "Has anybody ever told you how incredibly annoying you are, meddling in things that don't concern you?"

"Idris—"

"*Fine*. I make no promises, but I... I'll try."

Relief washed through me. "Thank you, because I know it doesn't feel like it now, but you will be happy again. And... Thank you for everything you've done for me. I'll never forget it."

"It was nothing."

"I'd have died a hundred times over if it wasn't for you. And I'd definitely never have ridden a flying horse, or found my way home."

"It was the least I could do."

"No. The least you could do is smile for a photo."

He rolled his beautiful eyes, an incredibly human gesture from such a haughty beast. "You're infuriating."

"That makes two of us." I fished my phone out of my pocket, pivoting under his arm still wrapped around my shoulders. He didn't fight as I nestled beside him and held out the camera.

"Smile," I reminded him through my own bared teeth.

As I'd expected, he only glowered at the screen like a Goddamn runway model, but it was distraction enough. My free hand slipped around his neck, and before he could react, I hooked a finger into the corner of his mouth, pulling his lips back from his teeth.

I snapped away, howling with laughter as he jerked his head out of reach with a sound of sheer disgust. Tears rolled down my face, blurring my vision, but I kept on hitting the button, determined to catch at least a hint of emotion on his beautiful, miserable face.

"That was utterly revolting. When did you last wash your hands?"

My wheezing intensified. God, I was funny, and Idris was beyond help if he couldn't see it.

When I regained a shred of composure, I mopped my wet eyes and found the brooding prince standing with his arms crossed and an expression of deepest disapproval.

"Oh, come on, that was hilarious."

"You think so?"

I grinned at his glowering face as I slid my phone into my pocket. "I know so, and so do you."

Idris lunged.

Quicker than my brain could process, he was right in front of me. He seized my face, forcing my head back, and before I had time to suck in half a gasp, his lips collided with mine.

Every thought fled from my head, scattered by the surge of electricity that rushed through my body, rooting me in place. Idris ran his tongue over my lips, and without thinking, without even trying to resist, I parted them for him. He deepened the kiss, pressing closer until his body was flush against mine, warm and solid and delightfully large. Beside him, I was small and delicate, something I'd never felt in my life.

His tongue swept into my mouth, deep and insistent, claiming. The last of my defences melted away. I didn't care where I was, or who I was, or even that I'd been tempted to tangle with his twin. All that mattered was Idris' dizzying touch, and the rapidly pooling heat low in my belly. Everything he gave, I matched. My hands slid around him, clinging, as my tongue dragged over the tip of one fang, sharp enough to threaten pain. My needy little whimper sounded into his mouth at the sensation.

The prince blew a breath out of his nose and slid a hand around the back of my neck, burying his fingers in the base of my ponytail. With it, he steered my head, arching me further back until my body was crushed against his. Stars sputtered behind my eyelids, glimmers of popping light, mirrored by the cascade of tingles simmering over every inch of my skin.

Idris pulled away, leaving air where there should have been only his lips against mine. I might have leaned forward, seeking touch, if not for his hand still fisting my ponytail. My eyes fluttered open to find his face barely an inch from mine. Golden green scorched down to my soul. The green was a colour I'd never seen on any human. This close, I saw that the golden sheen came from threads and flecks of yellow, weaving into the green. Beautiful.

"See?" he breathed.

Oh, I could see alright. See the haze of desire in his eyes, telling me he'd enjoyed that unexpected moment as much as I had. Telling me he wanted more. My tongue darted over my bruised lips. Idris tracked the movement, his pupils flaring.

"It's impolite to stick things in people's mouths," he pressed, though he didn't sound convinced.

"Maybe you should teach me some manners." Maybe another kiss would do it. Maybe it would take more than that.

His hand tightened in my hair, but it wasn't my scalp that twinged in response.

"Maybe I'll have to stick something else in your mouth next time."

"Maybe I'll like that."

A sound, something between a snarl and a groan rumbled in Idris' throat, and a thrill of triumph raced up my spine. I'd done that to him. I'd dragged that noise from him. What other sounds could I coax forth? The heat between my thighs turned to a throbbing pulse at the thought of it, of watching him come undone at my touch.

I dragged my hands to his front, sliding one between our bodies, and down, down. Abs rippled beneath my palm, tensing as I went lower. My fingers snagged his belt, but I shifted my hips, making room, and continued my descent.

The prince sucked in a sharp breath as I palmed him through the fabric separating us, his eyes burning unflinchingly into mine. I was the one to blink in surprise, or maybe awe.

The *size* of him.

He was rock hard, straining against the trousers holding him at bay, and huge. Every man I'd ever known faded into insignificance as my heart galloped against my ribs. What would he feel like, buried in my body?

"Don't look at me like that." His voice was low and as ragged as his breath.

"Why not?"

"Because I'm this close to dragging you back through the rift and keeping you forever."

Forever.

Cold sweat beaded my neck as the blood drained from my head. I hastily withdrew my hand. Idris' face tightened in panic. He released his hold on my hair, allowing me to retreat, placing a few steps of safety between us. I wrapped my arms around my body, shielding myself from that piercing gaze.

What was wrong with me? What was I playing at? After weeks of longing, I was back in my own world. My old life was within my grasp. I shouldn't be fooling around with some supernatural creature, least of all Idris. I had no intentions of forever.

"I apologise." The prince's perfect face was stricken with dismay. "I should never have kissed—I didn't mean anything by it. It was a joke, a stupid joke. I'm sorry."

"It's fine!" My voice came out unnaturally cheery and bright. "I'm sorry too. I got carried away. I don't know what came over me." My ears were aflame. God, had I really touched him like that?

He gave a single bark of false laughter. "Nor me. Perhaps the lack of sleep—"

"Yes!" I seized the excuse. Anything to brush what had just happened under the carpet. "We're delirious, that's all it was."

Idris' shoulders sagged and a relieved smile spread over his face. He began to chuckle, and I was powerless to stop my own sheepish grin.

Thank God. How bad could things be if he was laughing? "Well, this isn't awkward at all."

"I agree," he said, his eyes dancing with amusement. "Thank the Mother I never have to see you again."

"Exactly what I was thinking." It was a lie. Forever and never were equally terrifying prospects. Both final. Both absolute. I didn't want either.

"Well, on that note..." Idris' face softened. My stomach dropped. This was it. He was going to say goodbye, for real. I wasn't ready.

"Have a happy life, Aliza."

I forced a small smile. "I'll do my best." Right now, it seemed an impossible task. I took a deep, wobbling breath. "Bye, Idris."

The prince stepped closer, and closer, until he was right in front of me again. My body hummed at the proximity, as though he was calling to every part of me. I half expected, and maybe hoped, that he would pick up where we'd left off, but he only cupped my face in one broad, cool hand, and pressed a kiss to my hair. "Goodbye, Aliza with an A."

I held my breath, determined to keep control of my sadness as he pulled away. His eyes were shining as he gave me one last half smile and turned to leave. He walked back the way we had come, past the pile of withered flowers. He didn't look back as the darkness of the cave swallowed him whole.

Gone.

My heart drifted down to my boots, where it lay heavy and aching. It was over. Everything. My whole unwilling adventure, which had seemed unsurvivable at times, had come to an end. There would be no fairies, or witches, or vampires. No more fae.

Brushing my fingers over my tender lips, I turned away from the cave, trundling through the damp grass. I wanted to feel relieved, happy, excited even. I was finally going home. My steps weren't supposed to be as heavy as my heart.

I should probably call my parents.

Sure enough, my phone had service. I smiled, unlocking the screen, only to find my camera still open. A little circle at the bottom of the screen showed a tiny photo of me and Idris. I tapped it.

A hand closed around my face, blanketing my mouth and nose, dragging me backward. My phone tumbled to the ground as I tried to scream. The sound died against the clamp of my captor. I grappled, trying to hook my fingers beneath the hand, but the air pressed in, heavy and black.

The Fairy Glen vanished.

38

Who Would Choose To Love A Mortal?

Idris

Wrong. Wrong. Wrong.

The word echoed through me with every step I took away from the rift, growing more insistent with every recitation. As though I didn't already know. I'd realised it the moment I found Aliza's room abandoned and decided there and then that I would help her find her way home.

Wrong for me, right for her.

I wanted her happy, whatever the cost to me. If delivering her home was the price I paid for that happiness, then I would spend the rest of my life without her.

Aliza. *Joy*.

With her, I remembered what joy felt like. Fleeting glimpses of light in a pit of darkness and pain. I hadn't seen it at first, too lost in grief and anger to pay attention, but she was nothing if not persistent. She'd driven me *mad*, and in my madness, I'd found the light.

Now the darkness stalked me, pressing ever closer with every step I took away from Fairy Glen. I didn't bother to light my path as I passed through the rift and into the Blood Gate caverns. Aliza was in a different world now. Did she match each of my steps with one of her own, back to her former life?

A life that had no room for me.

Everything had changed for me during that first flight, when she'd taken my hand, trusting me with that fleeting, precious life of hers. For the first time in centuries, I'd tasted joy. I'd felt alive. Some of it had been the thrill of flight, but there was no denying that it was more to do with the way she'd screamed and screamed, her arms clenched around me as we'd plunged over the cliff, only for that fear to turn to wonder. When she'd loosened her grip, reaching for the clouds, I'd given them to her. I'd give her anything she asked for, even when it went against every ancient instinct I had. Which was precisely why I'd let her go.

It was why I continued my resolute trek through the darkness, alone.

This was what she wanted.

Wrong. Wrong. Wrong.

She didn't want to live forever. Didn't want to be tied down by any bond but those she'd already forged in the mortal world. She would not accept the immortal life I'd tentatively offered her. And I... Whatever pain I felt at our parting was merely a taste of what would await me if she'd chosen to stay. If I'd allowed myself to give in to the call inside me. I couldn't keep her, even if she'd wanted me to. I couldn't allow myself to care for another human. My already broken heart would shatter to dust when, in a few short years, she left me.

It was better this way. Better to let her go now than to watch time destroy her. To watch as her body bowed and crumbled under the laws of mortality.

Wrong.

"I know!" I snapped, halting in my tracks in an attempt to silence the clanging chorus. My voice echoed around the cavernous space, and several filthy bloodsuckers scuttled higher up the walls. "*I know.*"

The day was young, and with any luck, she'd be long gone before the sun set and these vermin crept out of their hole to hunt.

I screwed my eyes shut. In the weeks since I'd been awoken from my slumber by the softest of kisses, I'd been unable to close my eyes again, plagued by the last moments of Taryn playing out in my mind. My nightly torture. But now, the image of Aliza, pale and limp, pinned beneath the monster drinking her dry, had burnt itself against the back of my eyelids alongside the other horrors. I'd thought I'd lost her too. I'd held her in my arms and begged her to stay with me. I'd meant it in every sense.

Stay with me. Don't die. Don't leave. Don't marry him. Stay with *me.*

And now I'd let her go.

My heart pounded a desperate beat, imploring me to heed its call. I *couldn't.* I couldn't take her away from the life she loved. I couldn't ask her to give up a single thing, not for me. Not when I had nothing to offer but hopelessness. Not when I was too broken to remember who I was without my shroud of agony. Not when I knew she didn't feel for me the way I did for her.

I'd be content to spend the next handful of decades knowing that, somewhere, she existed, and remembered me with some shred of fondness. After that... after that I didn't know if I could keep my word. How could I live knowing her life had blazed by, extinguished by the ruthlessness of time?

Wrong.

I let out a roar, raking my fingers through my hair. Letting her go was the right thing to do. It had to be. Because if I was wrong...

Who was I trying to fool? Despite my best efforts, she had broken through my walls of fractured rubble, and she had woken me up, literally and figuratively. Mortal or not, I already *cared* for her. More than that. It was too late to guard what remained of my heart.

I turned back the way I'd come, stumbling over slick rock in my haste. I had to be certain. I had to tell her, and if I was wrong, as I was almost certain I was, then I had to hear it from her own lips. If I didn't, I'd never know another moment's peace.

I was almost at the rift before I realised that the warning toll in my head had silenced the moment I'd changed my mind. The right direction at last.

Something was wrong.

How I knew, I couldn't say, but I felt it as soon as I set foot in Fairy Glen.

Aliza was nowhere to be seen, and while that made perfect sense, considering the time I'd wasted, it didn't explain the quickening of my pulse, or the needling of electricity beneath my skin. It didn't explain why every nerve in my body refocused, searching for a sign.

The birds had ceased their ear-splitting racket. What had silenced them? They certainly hadn't been diverted by my earlier arrival with Aliza.

Taking a cautious step away from the shadows of the rock, I peered around, searching for anything out of place. I didn't know the mortal world, but hunting was the same in any terrain, and my instincts told me there was something here for me to see.

The muggy breeze shifted direction, stirring the lock of rogue hair that perpetually fell into my eyes, and I *felt* it. Magic on the air, dissipating rapidly, but still fresh.

Another sweep of my eyes failed to find another living soul. I ventured further into the open, my body tense, my senses straining. A wink of light caught my attention, drawing me to a patch of grass not far from where I'd kissed Aliza goodbye.

The blades were trampled flat, torn in places, and though that was enough to chill my blood, it was the sight of her phone, abandoned, that sent a rush of ice over my skin. The device was alight, an image of Aliza and I staring up at the grey sky above me. Tentatively, I picked up the phone. There she was, with her head thrown back, her face glowing with laughter. And that was me, staring down at her with a smile I couldn't remember giving, my eyes soft with adoration. My heart stilled. It was right there, as plain as day in the way I gazed at her. She knew. If she'd seen this, there was no way she couldn't know.

It didn't matter.

Slowly, I rose from my crouch, surveying the surrounding area. A slightly trampled trail through the dense grass led to the spot I'd discovered, and stopped. As though she'd disappeared into thin air. Which, I knew with a sinking sense of dread, was exactly what she'd done. The hint of magic on the air, the lack of tracks, the struggle. The dropped phone. Aliza had carried that little rectangle everywhere.

She'd almost killed us both to save it. There was no way she'd leave it behind, unless she hadn't been given a choice. Unless she'd been taken.

I could think of only one person who'd do such a thing.

Stowing the phone in the inside pocket of my cloak, I fought down the storm of questions warring in my mind and conjured an image of the waterside entrance to the Blood Gate, where Saeth awaited my return. The air pressed in, crushing against me as I slipped between worlds.

39

I Won't Be Doing Any Of That

Aliza

T*his isn't Idris.*

Darkness pressed in, forcing the air from my lungs, and all I could think was that it wasn't Idris dragging me through empty space. It wasn't Idris' hand crushed against my face, hard enough that I thought my nose might break. It wasn't Idris' body pressed against my back, or his arm like a vice around my middle.

The air lightened, making my body seem as weightless as a bubble, but the darkness remained. Most of it, anyway. My knees buckled, trying to throw me, retching, to the ground, but my captor had no intention of releasing me. They hauled me along, seemingly unaffected by the teleportation, heedless of my useless legs. The toes of my hiking boots dragged along the ground.

Fight.

I couldn't. I wanted to, but teleporting robbed me of my faculties at the best of times. I was as useless as a newborn calf, stolen from its mother and headed to slaughter. I tried to suck in a breath, but the hand clamped over my face blocked my airways with unyielding strength. The ache in my chest grew. It wasn't from teleporting at all. I was suffocating.

As though that knowledge was the code to rebooting my body, I twisted, grappling at the stranger's hand. I raked my nails over skin, earning myself a hiss against my ear. I kicked with all my strength, driving my heel back, hoping to find a kneecap. I made contact, for all the good it did me.

My eyes began to adjust to the darkness, even as the edges of my vision clouded. A thin, arching line of light appeared ahead. The pearly gates? The end of the tunnel? Should I stay away from the light, or rush toward it? I had no choice in the matter.

My captor twisted, throwing their weight against the dark in the middle of the arch. Blinding light erupted all around me as I was dragged into its centre.

"You found her!"

I didn't know that delighted voice, nor could I see its owner, blinded as I was.

"It was only a matter of time before the stupid bitch showed up." I didn't know the male's voice that sounded in my ear, either.

"Maelgwyn won't be happy if you kill her." The female drawled, completely unperturbed.

"I haven't harmed a hair on her head."

"No, but she's suffocating."

With a shove, I crashed to the floor. Air, warm, blessed air filled my lungs, seeping into the swirling desperation of my mind. I gave myself over to a fit of coughing, sucking down rasping breaths in between. Breath by breath, my senses sharpened.

My hands braced against a cracked, marble floor. Light gleamed off the shiny surface. My skin was sticky with sweat. Heat or fear?

Maelgwyn had been mentioned. Was I in Tir o Haf?

I lifted my eyes.

The room I'd landed in wasn't large by castle standards, but my entire human house could have fit snuggly inside it. One long wall was lined with enormous windows, but the others bore doorways, firmly closed. Which one had I come through? Which one would lead me out? A gallery overlooked the room, and a fireplace stood empty below it. And before the hearth was an enormous, sturdy table carved of dark stone. It was there that a fae female lounged in her seat, her booted feet propped on the table amongst a mess of plates and cups. She grinned when she caught me staring.

"Welcome, Human Queen. We've been expecting you." There was nothing welcoming about her tone, if my method of arrival hadn't been indication enough. My already flushed skin prickled with unease.

"Where am I?" I demanded, sounding braver than I felt. I pushed myself to my feet, swaying on my hollow legs. Nausea coated my tongue. "What do you want?"

"Me?" She pointed at her own chest, mock surprise lighting up her flawless face. "Oh, honey, I just want to get paid."

"Hey, I found her!" the second voice, belonging to my captor, barked out behind me. I jumped. I'd almost forgotten he was there. I edged sideways, bringing him into my peripheral vision, where I could keep an eye on him. The world swayed alarmingly with that tiny movement. "I'm the one who's been waiting in that shithole for weeks. It's *my* reward!"

"Relax, Hari," the female drawled. "We'll all get paid for *this* prize." She rose gracefully to her feet. She was short by fae standards, probably an exact match in height to me. Not that I laboured under any illusions of taking her in a fight.

"Where did you find her?" she shot the question at my captor.

"The other side of the Blood Gate," he grunted. "I had to wait on her side. The vermin have been getting bold lately."

"I was going home." The words spilled out in a rush. "I wasn't going to help the princes or try to steal the throne or anything. I just wanted to go back to my world."

"But you *did* help the princes," the female crooned. "You woke them from the curse. King Maelgwyn isn't pleased with you."

My insides turned to ice cold liquid.

"In fact," she continued. "Somebody should let him know of your arrival."

"I'll do it," Hari snarled. "I found her. I'll be the one to tell him."

"Oh, I thought you'd want to deliver her to the dungeons."

Dungeons? I couldn't go to any dungeons. My eyes darted to the doors. There was no telling where they led, but anything had to be better than whatever Maelgwyn had in store for me.

"I'll do both!"

Was I faster than a fae? Probably not. Would Maelgwyn care if a blade or arrow lodged itself into my fleeing back? He'd probably be irritated, but not as pissed off as he'd be if I escaped. I was dead either way. My heart hammered in my ears. I had to try. I'd come so close to freedom. I couldn't simply accept this twist of fate.

"He won't appreciate the delay."

I ran.

A shout echoed around the room as I hurtled toward the nearest door. My feet pounded the marble, the impact jarring up my shins, but my footsteps weren't the only ones. I barely slowed my pace as I reached for the latch, throwing my momentum against the door.

It didn't budge.

No.

I shoved, jangling the latch, but the door remained unmoving. The thundering footsteps closed in, and I shrank, sliding my back against the door. Both fae approached, glowering. The male held a sword. It was useless. There was no way out.

"Nice try," the male growled.

He swung his arm. The metal hilt of his sword collided with my temple.

Darkness swallowed me up again.

Boom. Boom. Boom.

A dull, throbbing beat of pain filled my skull, pulsing from one side to the other with growing insistence. I stirred, trying to get comfortable, but when I rolled, I didn't find a soft spot of pillow, or a squishy bit of mattress. Just cold, hard stone.

My eyes snapped open.

Memories came rushing back. The Fairy Glen. Idris leaving. My kidnapper. Talk of a dungeon. My attempted escape.

Gripping my pounding head, I struggled up from the floor. Gone was the cool, smooth marble, replaced by dark, dusty slabs of rock. This was no grand room. A hint of light leaked through thick metal barring a tiny slit of a window, set high in one wall. A bigger set of bars loomed opposite, and through them, eyes stared back at me.

I scrambled back against the wall. I didn't know if the pale monster I'd glimpsed could break through metal, but I wasn't about to take any chances.

"I see you have returned to the land of the living." The voice that drifted to me was hoarse and scratchy, but otherwise... normal. It didn't sound like a monster, but I'd long since learnt that monsters could speak pretty words and hide behind beautiful shells.

I peered through the gloom, trying to make out my companion beyond a pale shape and bright eyes. There was nothing beautiful about this particular shell. The creature was taller than I was, but hunched, like an old man. Maybe it was an old man, and I'd simply grown so accustomed to everyone being eternally young and beautiful that the sight of sagging, waxy skin and gnarled hands took me by surprise. A few wisps of shoulder length, white hair clung to a papery scalp, catching the faint light like a halo.

"Who are you?" I called, my voice high and quivering.

"Where are my manners? Allow me to introduce myself. I am Maelgwyn, king of the fae courts. And you, I take it, believe yourself to be the long-awaited Human Queen?"

Oh God. This was bad. Things couldn't get much worse.

Despite the tremor of fear that crept down my spine, I blinked in surprise. After all I'd heard about the dreaded King Maelgwyn, wielder of forbidden magical power, and unchallenged conqueror, to be faced with such a shrivelled old man was rather anticlimactic. Still, I would be a fool to be deceived by such harmless appearances. I knew what he had done to his nephews. I'd seen the beasts he'd created and sent after me. It was a wonder I was alive at all.

Which begged the question, *why* was I alive?

"I'm not a queen," I answered, trying to inject some confidence into my voice. "I don't want any trouble. I just want to go home."

Maelgwyn shuffled closer to the bars, his bright, watery eyes roving over me. I forced myself not to shy away.

"Undoubtedly. And yet, you have, inadvertently I'm sure, created trouble for me. You broke my curse, did you not?"

Even now, locked in a cell at the mercy of an evil sorcerer, I couldn't bring myself to regret my actions. Idris deserved to be free. He deserved a chance to be happy. I didn't much care about Anwir's happiness, but even he didn't deserve to be cursed. Well, maybe just a *small* curse...

"I didn't have a choice," I admitted, deciding honesty might be the best policy. "I was told it was the only way to open the rifts. All I ever wanted was to leave this place."

"My dear woman, you were deceived."

I knew that now. I'd been deceived at every turn.

"By breaking my curse, you forever removed the option of leaving."

Oh. That didn't sound good. My pulse quickened, and with it, so did the beat of pain in my head.

"You see," Maelgwyn continued, wrapping his skeletal fingers around the bars, "the prophecy of your coming was only ever a story. A possibility. It could have applied to any unwitting human to walk through the rifts, or none at all. By waking my dear nephews, you set its predictions into action. You cannot stop it now. It is an avalanche. It will gain momentum, gathering speed until it is fulfilled. She was destined to rid evil from my bloodline. You might have opened those tombs, looked upon the princes, and walked away, unscathed. But by waking them, by casting the first stone, you *made* yourself the Human Queen. There can be nobody else. And now, as long as you live, the throne belongs to you. It will answer to no other, waiting for you to rid the world of... well, *me*. I think it's safe to assume that our dear Queen Claudia foresaw my coming, as well as yours. I'm sure you see what a tricky situation you have created."

I gulped. *As long as I live?* I didn't like where this little chat was headed.

"You have two options, my dear. The first is rather unsavoury, but should your life be snuffed out, the throne will be mine again. I'm sure you can see why that might appeal to me, though I imagine you are less than thrilled at the prospect. Your second option is marriage."

Marriage, or death. I wasn't sure which was worse, especially as I was certain he didn't want me to go ahead with my impending nuptials to Anwir.

"Marriage?" I whispered.

"As my wife, you and I could rule together." His fingers tightened on the bars. "Through you, the throne would accept me. Nobody could stand against me, not even my nephews. Through me, you would be allowed to live."

God, what a match. What an offer. I took in his face. The sagging brow, the waxy, translucent skin, almost like baking paper. The watery, drooping eyes. The bald pate. The sad wilt of the pointed tips of his ears, collapsing in on themselves like floppy little pizza slices. I'd never seen an elderly fae, but it wasn't age that had ravaged his body. It was magic. He had pushed the limits. Delved into darkness. He had done this to himself. But it wasn't any of that which had me recoiling. It was the soul hiding within. Maelgwyn had ordered the death of Idris' son. He had forced Idris to watch. He was the reason that my friend was hollow and broken. He was the cause of the agony that had flowed straight into my heart on the night of the ball, raw and consuming.

"I would rather die," I hissed.

I meant it, but that didn't mean I was brave. My heart thundered sickeningly as I spoke the words, coating my skin in cold sweat. Maelgwyn didn't care; he had no qualms. He'd said it himself, my death appealed to him. Well, let him have it. I would never marry him. I would not share a throne, however unwanted, with such a beast.

Maelgwyn straightened, his hands falling to his side. "Very well. I shall order the arrangements. But know this, human. This chance will not be given again. When I walk away, I take my offer with me."

"Don't let the door hit you on your way out."

I almost groaned at my cliché comeback, but given the circumstances, I couldn't be expected to be at my wittiest.

Maelgwyn glowered, leaving without another word. I rushed to my bars, pressing my face against the rough metal to watch the king's progress. For all his sagging skin, he walked with the grace of a man in his prime, with not even a hint of doddering. There was something unnerving about the clash of his appearance against whatever strength lurked beneath. Before long, the gloomy corridor swallowed him up, leaving me alone.

I sagged against the bars.

I'd chosen death, but I wasn't actually going to die, was I? The very idea of it was ridiculous. I was a young woman, in her prime, fit and healthy and strong. Okay, so I preferred pasta to salad, and the gym and I did not get along, but I had years, *decades*, before that became a problem. I couldn't die.

Somebody would come for me.

Somehow, someone would realise I'd been taken, and they'd rescue me. They all owed me a favour, except maybe Idris or Pansy. I didn't care who came. The witches, Jacques, even Anwir. Somebody. Anybody.

They were coming for me.

Nobody was coming for me.

Down in the dark, I had no idea how many days had passed since Maelgwyn's proposal, but I knew I was starving. The last meal I'd eaten had been the one Idris and I had shared in the mountainside cave. Since then, my stomach seemed to have caved in on itself. My entire midsection ached, as did my head. There'd been no water either, but I'd found a drip in the corner of my cell. At first, I'd refused to touch it, afraid of what it might be and where it might have come from. I'd seen enough bodily fluids to have a healthy respect for unknown liquids. But before long, desperation had driven me to hold out my tongue, waiting for droplets to fall.

Maybe Maelgwyn was planning to leave me to die of dehydration. I could see no reason why the fae rules about killing blood relatives should extend to me, especially when Idris had said it only applied to his family, but maybe it applied to the rightful ruler too. Maybe he was simply being careful. It was strange to think that somewhere a throne awaited me, refusing to accept any arse but mine. I was a queen, and yet I'd never felt less like royalty than I did huddled in my cell, waiting to die.

Because nobody was coming for me.

I was alone.

40

This Girl Is On Fire

Aliza

I couldn't feel my feet.

That was all I could think about as my wrists were bound behind my back and I was frog marched from my cell. I couldn't feel my bare feet touching the cool stone, and I was going to fall and humiliate myself. I'd heard crowds assembling through the bars of my cell for the past hour. I'd gathered what remained of my strength and balanced on my tiptoes to glimpse them, but I'd seen more than I bargained for. A wooden structure had been erected, with a tall, sturdy post in the middle. I'd seen enough TV to know a stake when I saw one.

Fae had come in droves to watch the Human Queen burn, and they were going to laugh when I inevitably fell over. I wanted to scream. I wanted to lift my feet off the floor, letting my guards take my weight, and scream at the sky. It wasn't fair. If I had to die before an audience, why couldn't it be with some shred of dignity? I had given everything to these people, these fae. I had done everything within my power to free them from a tyrant.

Not everything

I'd tried to leave. I'd had my pride dented by Anwir's lies, and I'd thrown in the towel. I could have, *should have* done more, but now it was too late.

Nobody had come for me. Not Idris, the male I'd come to consider a real friend, and maybe something more. He'd asked me to stay another night. Maybe I should have. Maybe none of this would have happened, and maybe one night would have turned into two. A week. A month. Forever. I could even now be repeating the kiss we'd shared. But I'd left, and Idris hadn't come.

Neither had Anwir, who had taken my trust and shattered it. Nor Jacques, the vampire I'd pushed too far. Not even the witches, who had lied to me from the moment I found Sage's cottage. They'd all abandoned me, after using me and lying to me and tricking me. I'd given them as much of me as I could, and for what?

To get home.

My heart sank to the soles of my hollow feet. I'd been selfish without a doubt, but death seemed a harsh punishment for wanting to return to my own life. As did being abandoned by my allies in the final hour, but it was my own fault. If I'd stayed, if I'd put the cause of Neath before my own selfish desires, if I hadn't run away, none of this would be happening.

My fault.

My guards led me through grim, twisting halls. Through the haze of disbelief coating my eyes, I glimpsed bare walls. No tapestries. No art. Not a single carpet, or even a chair in which a weary wanderer might rest for a minute.

"Who lives here?"

Was that thin, trembling voice mine? I resolved not to say another word, which was just as well, because my guards acted as though I was already a ghost and hadn't spoken at all.

This couldn't be the palace of Tir o Haf. I couldn't imagine a king, not even Maelgwyn, living anything less than lavishly. Which meant I was somewhere else, somewhere less obvious. Maybe somebody had tried to find me after all, but had gone to the wrong place. It was a clever trick, even if the thought of it flooded my eyes with tears. With my hands trapped at the small of my back, I couldn't wipe them away. They spilled silently over my cheeks, dripping down my front, and it was only then I realised that I'd still nursed the tiniest shred of hope within my heart. That previously unnoticed ember sputtered out, its glow growing cold and dark. Nobody was coming. This was the end.

Ahead of me loomed an open doorway, and beyond, the milling crowd, come to see me burn. The sight brought feeling rushing back to my feet, and I planted them against the floor, unable to take another step.

I couldn't walk. I couldn't die. This couldn't be real. Burning had happened to so-called witches, hundreds of years ago. Not to me. It couldn't happen to me.

My guards hoisted me forwards, their hands tucked under my armpits, and I scrabbled for purchase. I was no match for them. The stone snagged my toes and scuffed my soles, but I gained nothing in the way of a delay as they hauled me into the courtyard.

Daylight bored into my eyes, which had grown accustomed to the gloom of the castle, all but blinding me. The courtyard was eerily silent. If I couldn't feel hundreds of eyes crawling over my skin, I might have thought the crowd had vanished. I'd expected jeers, a hurl of insults, maybe a barrage of rotten fruit, but this was much worse.

Silence.

My panting breath, my grunts of struggle were plain for all to hear. They'd hear me scream too, when the flames devoured me.

A sob burst through my clenched teeth. It was a wonder I was still conscious. My heart pounded at a violent speed, more of a rapid hum than a beat. Maybe I'd faint. It would be better that way. At least I wouldn't feel any pain. Or maybe I wouldn't faint at all.

It was going to *hurt*.

Twisting, I writhed against the vice of my captors' grip, but they hoisted me clean off my feet, suspended between them. My legs kicked in a frenzy, but through my tears, I glimpsed the dark, hulking pyre, coming ever closer.

No, no, no.

"No!" I sobbed.

No. This couldn't be real. It *couldn't* be. It couldn't happen to me. I was nobody. Just an ordinary woman, with an ordinary life. I was supposed to die in an ordinary way. People didn't just burn to death. I *couldn't*.

My thrashing foot whacked against the wooden platform and pain shot up my leg, turning my sobs to screams. The guards hauled me up, shoving me back against the unyielding stake. A fucking stake. How was this happening to me? I fought, twisting and shoving uselessly against their brute strength, but even if my hands had been free, it would have been hopeless.

A rope tightened around my waist, wrapping and wrapping, cutting into the soft flesh of my belly, trapping me. The guards stepped away, down to safety, and began tossing bundles of brittle sticks around my feet. I blinked my tears free, staring down at the wood that would catch and burn, taking me with it.

This was it. This was the end.

Nobody was coming for me.

The crowd wouldn't intervene. My breath came in shallow bursts as I took in the grim faces of my audience, meeting their eyes. One or two gave small smiles of reassurance, as though that was enough. As though that would make me feel any less terrified or alone. I might have preferred jeers. At least my anger would have carried me when everything else had fled.

Movement caught my attention, and my guts turned to jelly as I whipped my head to look. Was it my executioner, come with a flaming torch to set me alight?

King Maelgwyn strolled toward me, a pleasant smile pasted over his waxy face, and three lion-sized hounds trotting at his sides. The dogs resembled blunt faced bears more than anything, but for once in my life, I had no interest in them. Maelgwyn was here. He'd stayed to see his orders fulfilled, had he? He halted before my platform.

"A beautiful day for a burning, wouldn't you agree, human?" His tone was light, just an old man remarking upon the weather, nothing more.

I couldn't find any words for him. Nothing clever. Certainly no begging or pleading. I gave him my silence instead, my gaze drifting to the almost empty sky. Dark clouds loomed on the horizon. If it rained, would that be better, or worse? Would it put out the flames and delay my death, giving my allies another day to find me? Or would it simply make the fire burn slower, dragging out my suffering?

"Unless, of course, you've reconsidered?"

My eyes snapped back to the king, and at last, anger ignited in my chest. It burnt as violently as I soon would. Maybe it was stupid of me, maybe I should have lied, but I spat, "Light me up, bitch."

Maelgwyn raised a bald eyebrow. "Very well, but know this. I will enjoy hearing you scream. And when your ashes have been swept away, I will hunt down your prince. There will be no mercy this time. I will make him scream too."

He meant Anwir, but my mind went straight to Idris, and my heart stalled at the thought of him in danger. I couldn't even pretend to believe that he would fight back. That pain that had flowed between us... he'd already given up. He would let them take him. Maybe it would have been better for everyone if I'd left the princes sleeping.

"Is this the only way you can make a woman scream, you ugly old cunt?"

Mum would have had my head if she heard such filth coming from my lips, but given the circumstances, she would understand. At the thought of her, a new wave of tears poured down my cheeks, but I held my glare level. My letter had never been sent. She thought her daughter was dead at the bottom of some underground canyon. She would never know the truth. This truth. It was a mercy. I couldn't stand for her to know *this*.

Maelgwyn's pallid face paled at my words, the last hint of colour draining from his thin lips. I expected a retort, but none came. The king turned his back on me, strolling away from me as though he was enjoying a walk in the park.

My heart racketed around my chest. I couldn't breathe. I was going to vomit. If the rope around my middle hadn't been tied so tight, my legs wouldn't have held my weight.

A glimmer of orange caught my eye.

Fire.

A flaming torch, approaching, held aloft by a guard.

No.

This was it. It was actually happening. I clenched my teeth together, determined not to give that bastard king the satisfaction of hearing the screams he coveted. A fool's hope, but I ground my teeth together all the same.

As the guard drew near, my body succumbed to violent shaking. The rope cut into my belly as my knees buckled from under me. I fixed my eyes on the sky, but the rapidly approaching steel grey clouds weren't enough to distract me from the glimmer of firelight in my peripheral vision.

A whimpering sob hummed against the back of my clenched teeth, my quivering lips. Once the wobbling sound started, I was powerless to stop it.

With a hideous crackle, the flames caught my pyre. The glow flared brighter. Heat blared against my bare legs, and a moment later, the stench of smoke sucked into my panting lungs.

God, let it be quick. Please let it be quick.

The sky. I had to look at the sky. It was half blue, half grey, nothing like the orange dancing closer to my feet. The sky was beautiful. I'd take a picture, if I could.

Smoke billowed, all but obliterating my view. The crackle grew to a roar. The scorching heat intensified. I tried to draw my legs away, but the flames closed in on all sides. I clenched my teeth hard enough to crack them as my skin began to bubble and split.

Despite my hopeless determination, my whimpers turned to a scream.

Heat. Terror. Agony. Scorching, unimaginable agony.

Smoke clogged my lungs.

I screamed.

41

No, No, No

Idris

The thunderclouds followed me, raging like the storm inside me.

Most of my life, I'd kept my power hidden, but at the sight of the crowded courtyard, at the smoke billowing skyward, I couldn't remember why it had ever seemed important. Electricity surged beneath my skin, burning through my veins in pulses, lighting them beneath my skin in a blue-white glare. Not exactly subtle, but I didn't care who saw. Didn't bother to suppress it.

I vaulted to my feet atop Saeth's back, crouching low to avoid the riptide of wind.

"Bank!"

The horse veered sideways as I leapt into the sky. With an ear-shattering crack, lightning erupted from me, lighting up the dark clouds.

I began to fall, plummeting towards the courtyard far below. I twisted through space, reappearing a moment later, barely a leg-length from the floor. Upon my landing, a second whip of lightning shattered over the ground. Several armoured guards blasted off their feet and lay in lifeless heaps.

Screaming.

At my appearance, the crowd began screaming, shoving and surging towards the exit, but one drawn-out, high-pitched wail cut through them all, right into my soul.

Aliza.

I reached over my shoulders, drawing both swords as I rose from my crouch and turned to face the coming onslaught of guards. I sent my power surging down the blades, lighting them with a skittering, blue-white gleam.

"The king!" somebody cried. "The king has come!"

Unimportant.

Crackling blades poised, I charged.

I pivoted as I drew level, swinging one arm out wide. The sword cut through flesh and bone and sinew. Several heads, I didn't stop to count how many, rolled. Onwards. A fool met my blade with his own. The swords connected, and lightning plunged into his body with a crack, launching him off his feet.

Beyond him, revealed by his fallen body, stood my uncle. Our eyes met over the corpse-strewn courtyard. Hatred and magic rushed through me, swirling together in a potent storm. The light beneath my skin surged. The snarls of his monstrous hounds turned to yelps as they turned tail, cowering behind their master.

Aliza's screams fell silent.

No.

A roar shattered from my throat, and power burst from me in every direction, a blinding light cutting through the charged air. Maelgwyn and his dogs vanished a moment before my power reached them.

I sprinted the few remaining steps to the pyre.

For half a heartbeat, I hesitated, my breath trapped in my throat. Roaring flames, crackling, spitting. Hot. They towered over me, engulfing any signs of the woman I had failed.

Aliza was in there.

Smoke scorched my eyes, but I forced them to remain open. Sheathing one sword, I tightened my grip on the other, took one last breath, and stepped into the flames.

My scream curdled against my clenched jaw as I fumbled through the searing agony, reaching blindly. Searching. Every nerve in my body, every instinct, shrieked at me to recoil, to back away, but I had come too far. I would not be overcome. Not now, not if there was still a chance...

I couldn't see, or hear, or think. Only feel. Feel my skin blistering and peeling and charring as I fought against every reflex I had, and kept my hand outstretched.

The ropes binding her were still intact, barely, but my sword made short work of them. Her scorched body crumpled, and I pulled her to my chest, even as she burnt through my leather, the stench of her cooked flesh finding its way inside me, choking me, even as I held my breath.

Together, we tumbled from the pyre. I wrapped myself around her, fighting the desperate urge to pull my skin away. To save myself. I would heal, but her...

Staggering to my feet, I hauled her out of reach of the flames, and only when the air was cool and clean again did I allow myself to let her go, laying her down on the blood soaked ground. What was left of her, at least.

"Aliza..." My voice scratched, hissing from my throat.

She was a ruin. Her features had melted away. There was nothing left, nothing to mark her as that bright, shining human girl who had mercilessly bullied me into being her friend. Even that rainbow of hair had turned to ash. Her skin was a monstrosity of split, red flesh. And her legs, her poor legs...

Tears streamed unchecked down my face as I took in her charred, bare bones. I was too late. I had not made it in time. I had failed her at the final test. I was always too fucking late.

My chest splintered.

Not again. Not again. I could not stand it. I would not allow it to end like this. I could not stand to lose another person I...

"Aliza," I rasped, pleading, laying my shaking hands on her raw chest. My already healing skin sizzled, but I bit back my pain and focused on her. Only her. "Don't go."

I didn't know how to use it, this fabled magic. Rhodd Anfarwol. I had not the faintest idea of how it was supposed to work, or if it was even real. In all my years before the curse, I'd never met anyone who'd used it. For all I knew it was just another piece of propaganda, designed to lure our human victims into our clutches. I'd trusted the stories, laid all my faith in them, but now the moment was upon me, doubt set it. But it was my last hope. *Her* last hope, however little she wanted it. Fuck the consequences. It was a small price to pay. I could live with her anger, but losing her? No, I could not live with that.

I screwed up my streaming eyes, and I *wished*. I wished with every piece of my ravaged heart, with every fibre of my shredded soul, with every breath I had ever taken, with all those I was yet to take. I begged. I pleaded. I bargained. I promised that, if only it worked, I would not give in to my darkness. I would not take the easy way out. I would live, for as long as fate would have me. I would do *anything*. If only it worked. If only.

Rain began to fall.

The first cooling drop landed on the back of my splayed hand, and my thoughts were only of her. Of how she would need this when she woke, to drive away any lingering heat. Because she *would* wake. I was going to fix her, and she would wake, and at least one thing in this wretched, fucked up world would be alright again.

Something new flowed through me. Not electricity, not pain. Something gentle. Something warm and bright and hopeful. Was that it? Was that the magic we'd all heard of in bedtime stories as children, in those tales of great love between our kind and theirs?

"Please," I whispered, more to myself than anyone. "*Please.*"

I opened my eyes.

She was my Aliza again.

Somehow, against all odds, it had worked. Her skin was smooth and cool and as pristine as freshly polished marble. And the hair; I was in big trouble, but if she wanted to fight about it, I would do so gladly. Gone were the pastels, but so too was the scorched, twisted, hairless scalp. Beautiful, shining locks the colour of fudge spilled out behind her. And her face...

My breath hitched.

She was so still in her perfection. Too still. My hand, flat against her chest, felt nothing. No reassuring beat. No rise and fall. I dragged her into my arms, cradling her in my lap. She would open her eyes at any moment, she would smile, then tell me off.

Her head only lolled against my arm.

"Aliza." I tapped her face. "Aliza, come on."

There was no answer. No flicker beneath her eyelids.

"Please." The word burst out of me in a sob.

Nothing.

It hadn't worked. I was too late.

Only, it couldn't be. I couldn't accept it. She couldn't be dead. I couldn't give up.

As though she was made of cracked glass, held together only by the intricate angles of the fissures, still slotted into place, I laid her down on the ground.

I was cracking too, the already fractured pieces of myself crumbling at the sight of Aliza, still and perfect and dead.

There was no magic among fae or witches or elves capable of bringing back the dead, but the humans had a way. I'd knelt beside Aliza as she'd demonstrated. It hadn't worked for the witch, but it would work for Aliza. I would make certain of it.

Kneeling, I laced my fingers and pressed the heel of my hand to her chest. I'd watched her long enough. I knew what to do.

The first time I threw my weight down my arms, against her chest, I grimaced. As senseless as it was, as far from pain as I knew her to be, I cringed at the thought of hurting her in any way. I had to do this. There was no other option.

Again and again, I pushed down on her chest, willing her heart to beat. Begging, praying to gods I had no respect for, wishing. But as with Hyacinth, there was no answering flicker of life.

I'd lost count. Not that I knew the details of how this magic worked. As I'd seen Aliza do, I lowered my lips to hers, pinched her nose, and blew my own breath into her lungs.

Live. Come back to me.

When I lifted my head, she was still dead.

I almost gave up then, almost let the familiar black wave drag me down to the crushing depths, but she needed me. I needed her.

Resuming my efforts, I racked my brain for every word she'd ever said, playing over her enthusiastic explanations, searching for a clue. A sign as to what came next.

A defibrillator sends an electric shock to the heart. It can restore the rhythm.

Electric shock. I could do that.

All around me, the bodies of the guards I'd slain littered the ground. My power had stopped their hearts, but humans... Aliza said it could help them live.

If only I'd asked more questions. If only I had the faintest idea of how this was supposed to work. I should have listened. I should have asked. Thanks to my own determination to keep her at arm's length, I was blind. But I had to try. I couldn't inflict any more harm than I already had.

Ceasing my crushing jabs, I spread my palm over her chest once more, as I'd done to transform her body. With a glow and a crackle, I sent a pulse of lightning from my flesh to hers. Not enough to injure. The same tiny flicker of power I'd used to revive her phone.

Nothing.

Fine. Not enough. I could do more.

The second bolt was stronger, but as unsuccessful as the first.

"Come on, Aliza." The third bolt had her arching away from the ground, and my heart leapt, brimming with hope, but when the current died, she lay limp and lifeless once more.

Rain pattered the ground, the drops on her skin shining like tears.

A nearby clatter had me reaching for one of my swords, but it was only Saeth landing. He shook the rain from his mane and approached, his head held low. With all the tenderness of a mother, he nudged Aliza's cheek. Her head lolled away.

The black wave inside me rose, filling me, obliterating everything but the pain. The all-consuming agony I had grown to know as well as I knew myself. The sky darkened too. Rain splattered my face as I stared at the clouds.

I had come too late. I had tried, raced against the clock, but come too late. A minute earlier, maybe two, and Aliza would still be alive. If I hadn't fought against the compulsion to turn around, to go back to the human world... If I had known where they were keeping her... If I had leapt from Saeth's back earlier...

Saeth's back.

I scrambled to my feet, scooping Aliza into my arms, trying to ignore the way her limbs flopped. Without stopping to think, I threw her over Saeth's withers and vaulted up behind her. I gathered her, holding her tight to my chest, and buried my free hand in Saeth's mane. As though reading my thoughts, the horse's wings spread, thrusting us into the sky without hesitation.

Rain streaked past, a freezing, blinding barrage, but I fixed my squinting eyes on the clouds. Up there, in the charged sky, my magic would be at full strength. Up there, I would try one last time.

My fist tightened on Saeth's mane as he tilted, almost vertical. The soaking wings pounded relentlessly, with great booming beats. Up and up we surged, riding the wind, and I clutched Aliza to me as the ground fell away. I'd never teleported from the sky with a passenger before, but I would do it today. In the grand scheme of things, the sky and the ground weren't that far apart.

The clouds loomed, closer and closer, and then all at once, we were plunged into swirling grey mist. It soaked through my clothes, freezing me to the core. I couldn't see. My lungs filled with watery air.

All at once, we burst out of the clouds, into a breathtaking skyscape of sun gilded, fluffy clouds, and clear blue sky. Gone was the driving rain, the gloom. Aliza would have loved this.

My heart buckled in on itself, and as Saeth levelled out, his wings held wide, I gripped her tighter. Her freezing skin was slick beneath my hand. Her newly grown hair hung in wet tendrils, clinging to her pale face. I was running out of time.

"Same again, boy," I muttered, easing my stiff limbs into position.

I wedged a foot on the wing joint and detangled my hand from the sodden mane. I could do this. I had to. I could not fail. With one last glimpse of the deceptively serene view, I threw myself into the air, taking Aliza with me.

Saeth wheeled away, and together, Aliza and I plummeted.

Before I could even take a breath, the clouds engulfed us. As we sped through the freezing dark, I eased my hand between our chests, crushed together by the strength of my single-armed grip. I settled my palm between her breasts.

Live.

Lightning bolted between us with a crackling boom. Aliza stiffened, jerking away from me. I tightened my grip, holding her as the magic dissipated and we plunged out of the clouds.

The ground sped towards us, faster than I could have imagined. I screwed my eyes shut, thinking of the cave I'd found her in when she'd stolen my horse. Secret. Warded. Safe.

Darkness swept in, claiming us both.

42

Wait, What?

Aliza

I hated the sound of rain first thing in the morning. There was nothing worse than leaving the warmth of my bed and having to brave the dismal, English weather. How long until my alarm went off? Hopefully, the rain would stop before then...

With a grumble, I tried to curl deeper into the comfort of my bed, only... my body refused to move, and my bed wasn't comfy at all.

I opened my eyes.

That wasn't my bedroom ceiling. An expanse of grey rock stretched above me, and my breath hitched, my eyes widening. It wasn't *just* grey. Grey was dull and drab, the colour of a city in the depths of winter. Grey skies, grey buildings, grey pavements, walked by grey-faced people on their way to dreary, grey jobs. This was different. This was *beautiful.*

I'd never seen so many shades of one colour, all marbled together in such a magnificent ripple. There were hues I'd never seen before. I'd never known such a spectrum existed. My phone would never be able to capture such detail.

Wait, my phone. Where was it? Where was *I?*

I shifted, propping myself on my elbows. A warm, green cloak fell away from my shoulders, but the bottom half wrapped around my legs like a burrito. Beneath the cloak, I was wearing *black*.

Gross.

The soft, oversized shirt was definitely not mine.

My head was too heavy for my neck, but I turned it, examining my surroundings. At least I wasn't in some stranger's bedroom, facing the walk of shame, but I *was* in a cave, which was arguably a worse hook up location than a sparsely furnished bachelor pad.

Sitting with his back to me, a shirtless man stared out over the dismal, grey clouds beyond the cave mouth. The tips of his pointed ears peeked out from beneath his inky black hair. Not a man. A male.

A friend.

"Idris?"

The muscles in his broad back bunched at the sound of my voice, and his despondent shoulders lifted slightly, but he didn't look around. My gaze dropped to his lower back, where four deep but healing gashes slashed through his flesh. What had happened to him?

My brow bunched as I slogged through my sludgy brain, sifting for memories. I should remember this. I should remember how he'd been hurt, and why it made my guts tighten with shame.

My arms wobbled dangerously under my weight as I pushed myself to sitting. The cloak settled in my lap, and the black shirt–Idris' shirt–gaped low over my chest. A strange, red mark unfurled between my breasts, an oddly beautiful, fern-like pattern, etched into my skin.

It was like nothing I'd ever seen before. Was it a tattoo? I probed it with a tentative finger. The slightly raised mark was tender, but not painful.

Weird. I couldn't remember why, but I felt certain I should be in pain. Its absence only stirred the confusion already clouding my mind.

Dropping my hand, I peeled the cloak away from my lap. The faint scent of smoke wafted up my nose as I exposed my long, bare legs, and fell still. Those weren't *my* legs. My legs had annoying little dimples peppering my thighs, not to mention an ugly scar on the inside of one ankle, courtesy of the surgeon who'd pinned my broken bones back together. These legs had neither. The skin was smooth and flawless, glowing with a dewy sheen, and the perfect toenails lacked the hot pink varnish I seemed to remember applying at some point.

No, they couldn't belong to me. So why were they attached to my body?

"Idris?" I said again, a faint note of panic sneaking into my voice.

I didn't give him a chance to reply before kicking free of his cloak and scrambling to my feet. I barely made it halfway to my full height before those stranger's legs buckled, sending me crashing to the floor.

The impact jarred through me, but the crack of rock against flesh and bone was oddly painless. I'd barely hit the ground before Idris appeared before me, on his knees, his hands hovering over me but not touching. Since when had he been afraid to touch me?

"Are you hurt?" he asked, worry evident in his low tone.

I wasn't, but that seemed like a tiny, irrelevant detail compared to the leg situation. I lifted my eyes to his, and though my heart stilled for a moment at the sight of that beautiful shade of yellowish-green, I asked, "What happened to me?"

A smooth mask erased the concern from his face, leaving it blank and impassive. I knew that face. Knew it was nothing but armour.

Slowly, as though I was a dog primed to snap, Idris lowered his hands. I followed the motion.

The slashes across his back weren't his only injuries. The red-raw skin covering his hands was twisted and pitted. Burnt.

Flames. Maelgwyn. Flames and brutal, flesh-melting agony.

With a tremulous breath, I dissolved into violent shivering. I remembered. The memory unfolded, replaying within me, every torturous second of it. I'd screamed before the end. I'd screamed, and nobody had come. Except...

Idris lifted his burnt hands again, gathering me to his chest and folding me in his steady, reassuring strength. I'd been alone. There'd been crowds and guards and even the human-hating king himself, all there with me, but I'd thought I was alone.

I'd been wrong. Someone *had* come for me. Someone had cared.

I wrapped my arms around the prince, clinging to him as though his uncle would appear and attempt to pry me away at any moment. Idris cradled the back of my head, his injured fingers sliding into my hair.

"I'm so sorry, Aliza," he whispered. "Forgive me."

Sorry for what? For saving my life? My weak, trembling limbs should be covered in third degree burns. I shouldn't be here at all. I should be dead. The fact that I wasn't, the fact that my skin was flawless and new, my scars erased...

I unhooked a trembling arm and lifted my hand to my ear. My fingers jittered as I brushed them over the new, pointed shell. Fae ears. My breath sawed in and out of clear, strong lungs. I was alive. I was fae. I was immortal.

I was never going home.

My face and heart crumpled in unison as unbidden tears spilled down my cheeks, but I ground my teeth together, fighting against the black wave of loss rising inside me.

"There was no other way," Idris said, desperation leaking into his voice, as though he was trying to convince himself as much as anyone.

He didn't need to tell me. I'd suffered it. I knew better than anyone how beyond help I'd been.

I straightened, shifting away from him. He released me at once, and when I looked into his beautiful, stricken face, I forced my lips to twitch into a brief smile. "You came for me."

Idris dropped his gaze to my wet cheeks. When he swept away my tears with gentle, sure sweeps of his thumbs, my eyes fluttered. He didn't drop his hands, but cupped my face, holding our gazes steady.

"Where else would I be, if not with you?"

My breath died in my lungs at his words, as he leaned in close. My lips parted, anticipating another moment like the one we'd shared in the Fairy Glen, but he pressed his kiss to my forehead instead. The soft, tender touch lingered, and my eyes finally slipped shut as my flare of panic and grief faded into a sense of surety. A tranquil understanding. An acceptance.

I'd never go home, but this, here, this was right.

I wrapped my fingers gently around Idris' wrist, leaning into his touch. When he straightened, when his hands fell away from my face, his fingers wound through mine. Our entwined hands rested between us.

"You need a hospital," I observed. His burns, raw and shiny, were healing, but there was always the risk of infection. He should be in dressings, at the very least, though the formation of new skin suggested he'd narrowly avoided a skin graft, at least. This cave was probably riddled with bacteria, and I couldn't remember the last time I'd washed my hands.

I tried to extract my fingers from his, but he tightened his grip, refusing to allow it. "I'm fine," he insisted gently. "I'll be as good as new by morning."

Morning? Impossible. I opened my mouth to argue, but he added, "I'm fae, remember? Most of my burns have already healed. My hands are taking longer because they got the worst of it, but I'm alright. I promise."

My eyes flickered over the flawless skin of his face, and lower to his torso. I tried not to let my gaze linger on those scandalous muscles, choosing instead to focus on the cuts and slices peppering his body. They were undoubtedly healing, but if his burns had already given way to beautiful, fair skin, why had the cuts remained? "What about those?"

"Vampire venom," he gave me a wry smirk, "hinders the process."

My free hand shot to my neck as another memory slotted into place. My fingers found no evidence of the stinging puncture wounds.

"You have an advantage," Idris said, but his tone suggested condolences rather than congratulations. He dropped his eyes to my chest, to the new mark that hadn't been eradicated by budding immortality. "Does it hurt?"

I glanced down at the oddly beautiful mark. "No. What is it?"

His throat bobbed before he answered. "It's a lightning scar."

"A–what?"

"I was too late," he murmured, his eyes never leaving the fern-like mark. "I used Rhodd Anfarwol, and you changed, you healed perfectly, but you were still…" Another gulp. "I had to strike you to bring you back."

Did he mean a *lightning* strike? Had my heart stopped? I didn't know much about lightning, but I did know that those little fronds of light that had charged my phone couldn't possibly carry enough voltage to restart a human heart.

Not human anymore…

I shoved the thought away. What did it matter what I was, as long as I was alive?

But how? It wasn't possible. Only Anwir could summon that sort of lightning power. It was why the witches had fought so hard to break the curse. Only he could fight the shades. Only the eldest prince…

A glittering rain of realisation settled over my skin, like stardust drifting from the sky as I stared at *my* prince.

When he'd charged my phone, Idris asked me not to tell anyone. To protect his image as the brooding prince, or to protect his image as the *youngest* prince? Now, he continued to study my scar, avoiding my gaze.

My fingers tightened around his. Hardly daring to voice my suspicions, I whispered, "You. You're the king, aren't you?"

Idris looked up at last. The confirmation was written in his wide, wary eyes even as he said, "No."

"But…" I racked my brain, sifting through my early lessons. "But the witches said it was the eldest twin who had lightning magic." Anwir had said he never used it, that it was too dangerous. He'd never shown me any evidence, but I'd accepted his story, because why wouldn't I? I knew better now. I knew him to be a liar. I knew

Idris could charge my phone and light up the dark with shimmering, electric light. What else could he do?

I touched a hand to the mark on my chest. My heart thudded beneath my fingertips, true and strong. Idris had struck me to save my life. Idris had the lightning. Idris was the king.

"Ever since I crossed the rift, I've been kept in the dark. I've been used and manipulated and lied to. You're not like the others, Idris." My bad-mannered, stand-offish prince had become one of the few people I trusted. The only person who'd helped me simply because he could. "Please, don't lie to me."

"I'm not the king," he said, and my heart fell at his bare-faced lie. I knew. I knew I was right about this. The evidence was stacked in favour of my conclusion, and none of the alternatives made the slightest sense. "You're correct, though. I am the eldest."

I opened my mouth, primed to present my argument the moment it occurred to me, but Idris smiled sadly. "I abdicated, many years ago. Not formally, of course, because my father was still alive, but..."

"You swapped places with Anwir," I supplied, and Idris nodded. "Why?"

His voice was bitter as he replied, "Because I watched my brother, younger by minutes, enjoy the freedom that I would never have. From the moment of my birth, I was a servant of the throne. I never asked for it, never wanted it. Did you know that an heir apparent cannot join a drift? It's considered too dangerous, but I wanted to *fly*. I wanted the freedom to sleep under the stars and marry whomever I chose, rather than some prim young female with excellent bloodlines chosen for me."

Something twisted into an ugly knot inside my chest at the thought of Idris choosing Jane, of him marrying her for love, but I willed my face to remain neutral as he continued his story.

"Anwir, on the other hand, loved life at court. He was as jealous of me as I was of him. We were barely twenty years old when we traded places. He cut his hair short like mine so nobody, not even our mother, could tell us apart, and kept it that way for decades. We made a deal never to use our magic, the last tell. I've broken the terms of that deal twice now. First, when I charged your phone, and then this morning."

His eyes dropped to the scar again, his face paling. "They all saw me. They witnessed my power."

He lapsed into silence, which stretched between us. Beyond the cave mouth, rain pounded against the rock. It was grim and dark out there. Not nighttime dark, but the blanket of thick grey clouds robbed the world of light. Where had this rain been when Maelgwyn had ordered the flames lit?

"You still don't want to be king?" I asked at length.

He shook his head fervently, setting his hair swaying across his forehead. My spirits sapped slightly. Idris, quiet, kind, thoughtful Idris would make a better king than Anwir ever would. Not that it was any of my business. Or was it? Maelgwyn believed the throne had passed to me the moment I broke the curse. Could I abdicate, as Idris had, and if I did, who was next in line?

What did any of it mean for me? For... us?

Was it even true?

Maelgwyn wouldn't have thrown me the lifeline of marriage if it wasn't. My stomach churned. I would think about it later, when I had time to stew over every possible outcome. If there was one thing I had in abundance now, it was time.

"And did you announce your name when you swept in to save the day?"

"I... no?"

I smiled. "Then nobody saw you. They saw a prince, yes, but they think they saw Anwir. Maybe he'll just have to cut his hair short again. He's been lying for most of his life, I'm sure he can manage a few more. He can pretend *he* made me... immortal."

Idris' stared and stared. "How can you stand it?"

"Stand what?" My brow furrowed.

"You didn't want this. You told me so yourself. You didn't want to be immortal, or to be bound to me. You wanted to go home. I did this to you, so how can you sit here and think of ways to protect me?"

"You didn't do this to me, Idris. Maelgwyn did. You saved my life. It seems to be becoming a habit."

Finally, he smiled. A small, sad smile, but it was an improvement. Something purred to life in my chest, something glowing and warm, only to be extinguished a moment later. Was it any wonder he didn't want to smile at me? I was a burden, always ending up in situations that forced him to risk his life for me. Now I'd gone one step further and gotten myself killed. He'd had no choice but to waste his precious, one-time gift of immortality on me, when it should have been treasured and saved, waiting for someone he could love. He hadn't been able to use it on Jane or Taryn, but there would eventually be someone else worthy of his affection. I was under no illusions that one kiss was enough to secure that position for me. I'd cost him the chance to spend eternity with someone who made him happy. Now he was bound to me forever. I didn't understand exactly what that meant, but I knew it couldn't be a good thing. Tears burnt in my eyes again. I'd ruined everything.

"Idris." I didn't care that my voice wavered, only that he must despise the sound of it. "I didn't want—"

"I know. I know, Aliza. I know you wanted to go home, but I couldn't let you die like that. I couldn't let this be the end. I don't want it to be the end." His gaze was pleading, begging me to understand. He'd mistaken my meaning, but his was clear. He blamed himself for this mess as much as I blamed myself. He didn't hate me.

What would happen when he discovered the throne, which had been in his family for thousands of years, had abandoned his bloodline in favour of me? Would *that* be the end? Would he hate me then?

"It's not," I insisted, mostly for my own benefit. If I said it firmly enough, I might start believing it. "After they caught me, it was game over. I wasn't seeing my parents or my friends again whatever happened. I am *glad* you gave me another chance at life. Obviously, I wish I could've gone home, even just one last time, but..." The tears that had threatened to resurface since I'd stemmed them finally spilled over, trailing down my cheeks as the truth walloped me straight in the chest. I would never see Mum and Dad again. I was dead to them. They would never have answers. They were forever out of my reach. "I wanted you to come. Even when they tied me to that pyre, I didn't give up hope. When the flames started, I thought-I thought it was too late. I thought I was going to die. Compared to that, being young and beautiful forever isn't so bad."

"You forgive me, then? You don't hate me?"

"Not even a little bit. There's nothing to forgive, Idris."

His shoulders sagged in evident relief. "We'll find a way to make this work, I swear. I know you didn't want to stay, but I'll find you a home, if you don't want to stay at Nairsgarth. I'll get you anything you need. We'll figure this out. And, Aliza..." He lowered his eyes, frowning at our entwined hands. "I know you didn't want to be bound to anyone, but please, don't worry. This bond, it doesn't mean anything. We can ignore it."

After all that had happened, this blossoming friendship, that kiss, dying and being reborn, losing my parents... the cold, sharp knife twisting in my gut cut deepest. Of course it didn't mean anything. As if I'd think otherwise.

"Nothing at all," I whispered, glad that he refused to look me in the eye. Glad that he wouldn't see the new wave of unexpected tears welling there. "Everything's going to be fine."

His expression, though pained, softened slightly as he finally looked up. "You are the most relentlessly positive person I have ever met, do you know that? You deserved better than what happened to you."

"Everybody deserves better than that," I said, my skin icing over at the reminder. "Except maybe your uncle."

That momentary softness faded into darkness. Pure fury rolled off Idris in palpable waves. "I swear to you, he will suffer worse. For everything he has done to you and Taryn, he will pay tenfold."

I will hunt down your prince. There will be no mercy this time.

I couldn't let this happen. I couldn't have Idris anywhere near Maelgwyn, not when the laws preventing blood relatives from seizing the throne through violence no longer applied. Idris had abdicated, and the throne had chosen me. Maelgwyn knew it. Knew he was free to slaughter his nephews without the repercussions of some ancient law. But if the princes didn't put a stop to him, who would? How many innocent people would suffer a fate worse than mine? I couldn't allow that, either.

There could be only one possible outcome to this mess. Maelgwyn had to die.

My fingers tightened around Idris', and despite myself, I reached for his other hand, too. He allowed me to take it without question or hesitation.

"Is this it, then?" I breathed, hardly daring to voice the words aloud. "Are we at war?"

Playing Anwir's game had been easier when I had a home to go to afterwards. Now, whether I liked it or not, I was a resident of Neath. I was no longer a smiling, simpering mascot; I was the heir to an ancient, powerful throne that I didn't want, but had little choice but to fight for. A throne guarded by a bloodthirsty monster.

This wasn't supposed to be my life.

"You need not have any part in it. I can take you back to Nairsgarth. You'll be safe there."

Nowhere was safe, not anymore. It never had been; it had only ever been an illusion. I shook my head. "I'm the Human Queen, remember? You all need me."

Idris' eyes flickered over my face, his lips parting as he squeezed my hands. Was it my imagination, or did he lean in closer? He drew in a breath, as though he was about to say something.

I waited, the air trapped in my lungs, but instead of speaking, he rose to his feet, steadying me as he guided me to mine. My legs shook but took my weight. Idris' shirt skimmed my thighs, covering everything, but leaving very little to the imagination. Not that he hadn't seen it all before as I'd paraded around Nairsgarth in my little shorts.

"We do need you," he agreed at last, "but you won't be forced into anything. Your life is still your own, Aliza. You don't owe any of us anything."

"I want to help," I insisted. I wanted to put a stop to Maelgwyn's atrocities. I couldn't let anyone else get hurt, or worse. There was even a tiny, foreign part of me that bayed for Maelgwyn's blood. I wanted him to pay for what he'd done to me, to everyone else. That new part of me wanted cold, brutal revenge.

I didn't voice that part. Idris wouldn't judge me, but I did. It wasn't me. It wasn't who I wanted to be. If Maelgwyn died, it would be for the greater good, not for my own savage satisfaction.

As for the part of me that recoiled at the thought of staying behind while Idris went off to war, I didn't voice that either. Didn't dare let myself dwell on it, or what it might mean. I wanted to be wherever he was, whether it was a battlefield, or the sky, or even right here in this cave, high above the world. I wouldn't even mind if he kissed me again. Not the chaste little forehead kiss, but the one that had turned my blood to bubbling, heady fairy wine and my brain to slush.

No, I wouldn't dwell on that.

"Whatever you want, you'll have it," he said, his voice soft and earnest. "Name it, and it will be done. But might I make a suggestion?"

His sombre tone, his earnest expression, had my eyes widening in mild panic. "I'm listening."

"As enticing as that outfit is..." He cleared his throat, his eyes straying south. My ears, my new, pointy ears, began to heat. How typical that such an annoying trait had transferred into my new body.

"Perhaps you should go home and collect some underwear, at the very least."

My brain short circuited, snagging on the two entirely separate but equally shocking suggestions he'd crammed into such a short sentence. Underwear? Home?

"I–what did you say?"

The bastard smirked at me, his eyes creasing, utterly delighted with himself. "I said you need some underwear. Your clothes were destroyed in the fire, and though my shirt has never looked better, I didn't have any suitable undergarments to lend you."

"No, no, no. The other bit. Did you say–"

"Home." His smirk softened into a smile. "I told you, I'll give you anything you ask for. You're fae now, and the human world is poison to us, so you can't stay forever; a few days at most, but you told me you wanted to go home, and that is where you'll go."

So, Anwir had lied. No surprises there. Idris had taken me as far as the Fairy Glen, and I'd just assumed he could go no further, because his twin was a lying piece of shit. The sting of yet another deception faded into insignificance in the face of all the other emotions surging inside me.

I looked into his expectant eyes, slightly upturned, just like his twin's, but somehow rarely smiling. I trusted *him*. Maybe it was the bond that meant nothing, fooling me. Maybe it was because he'd been the only one who'd tried to help me. Maybe it was because he'd given a piece of himself to save me, but I trusted him.

I was going home at last. After all these weeks, all this danger, I was going *home*.

I launched myself at Idris with a strangled sob, jumping to wrap my arms around his neck. He laughed, catching me around the waist without hesitation. Whenever I'd hugged him, there had always been a moment of resistance before he gave in and returned the gesture, but not this time. This time he held me tight, my feet dangling as he twirled me around. The cold, crisp scent of him filled my nose. A winter's morning. A clear sky. Something deep within me calmed, soothed by Idris' proximity. The bond? Did he feel the same? Would it demand he remain close to me until the end of time? The idea didn't paralyse me with fear as it should have done. A small but growing selfish part of me wanted it to be the truth, even if the bond meant nothing. Even if it muddled my emotions. Bonded or not, he'd first and foremost been my friend.

"Thank you," I sobbed breathlessly. "Thank you."

There were no words in any language that could convey the enormity of everything he'd done for me. Thank you wasn't enough. Nothing would ever be enough.

Idris set me gently back on my feet. Though we broke apart, we didn't let go. His hands remained on my waist, mine on his shoulders, as though the thought of parting was intolerable for either of us.

The prince gazed down at me with soft, shining eyes. "I'm glad you didn't die, Aliza."

Me too.

I smiled, not caring that my cheeks were stained with tears again. At least they were happy ones, for once. Maybe that happiness wouldn't outlast the coming war. Maybe this new chance at life wouldn't last, but for now, it existed. I existed, and so did Idris, and I couldn't be anything but happy.

My chest rose as I drew in a deep breath. As it did, something caught my eye.

In the disarray of the hug, hair had spilled over my shoulder. Not pink, or lilac, or green, or blue.

Dark blonde.

I snatched a handful of it in my fist. A tug confirmed the dull locks were indeed attached to my own scalp. I lifted my eyes to Idris'.

"What *the fuck* did you do to my hair?"

Acknowledgments

As always, I want to say a massive thank you to my girls at Poison Quills. bv Sloan, Chelsey Fay, HM Brandon and Moa Eriksson, without you, this book wouldn't be what it is today. Your love, support, critique and brainstorming is invaluable to me, as is the opportunity to work on all of your incredible stories.

Brianne at Feather Pen Editing, you've once again whipped both me and my book into shape. It stings a bit sometimes, especially when you make me add entire chapters, but the end result is always worth it.

Here's a little story for you all. For the longest time, our family pets have been cared for by the same family of veterinarians. Andrew has been my vet for as long as I can remember, and before that, his father took care of my grandparents' pets. A few years ago, in a completely unrelated environment, I met a woman called Victoria, who insantly became one of my favourite people in the whole world. After a few months of excitable, fast-paced chatter, we realised that her partner was none other than my vet! Small world. Unfortunately for Andrew, his subsequent marriage to Victoria came with a promotion to chief medical advisor to a fantasy romance author, something I'm not sure he'd bargained for when he bought that diamond.

Thank you to the long-suffering Andrew McVey for all the patience and medical knowledge that went into creating Aliza and shaping her decisions and thought processes, and of course, thank you for all the care you have provided to my pets over the years.
And of course, thank you to my beautiful friend, Victoria, for handling all my questions while your husband was busy saving furry lives.

Finally, a huge thank you my wonderful readers. Your messages, comments and support mean the world to me, and make this whole process fun and worthwhile. I'm excited to share more stories with you in the future!

About The Author

Hailing from Liverpool, England, Aimee spent the majority of her childhood in the saddle, or wandering the country parks, pretending to be the lady of the manor. Sadly, as she got older, she realised that an immortal prince was never going to sweep her away on a magical adventure, and she took matters into her own hands. These days, she spends her time writing about all things swoony and magical. When she's not writing, she enjoys indulging in a spot of art (visit her socials to see some of her work, including character art), trying to stay aboard feisty horses, and catering to the whims of her pet hamsters.

Aimee lives in the UK with her husband, children and a menagerie of pampered pets.

Printed in Great Britain
by Amazon

47204589R00290